About the Author

Paul Clark has served in the Royal Marines for more than forty-five years and lives in wonderful Dorset. He first wrote short stories and sent them on an Armed Forces Operational bluey to make that most personal engagement with his wife and sons from around the world. This is his first novel.

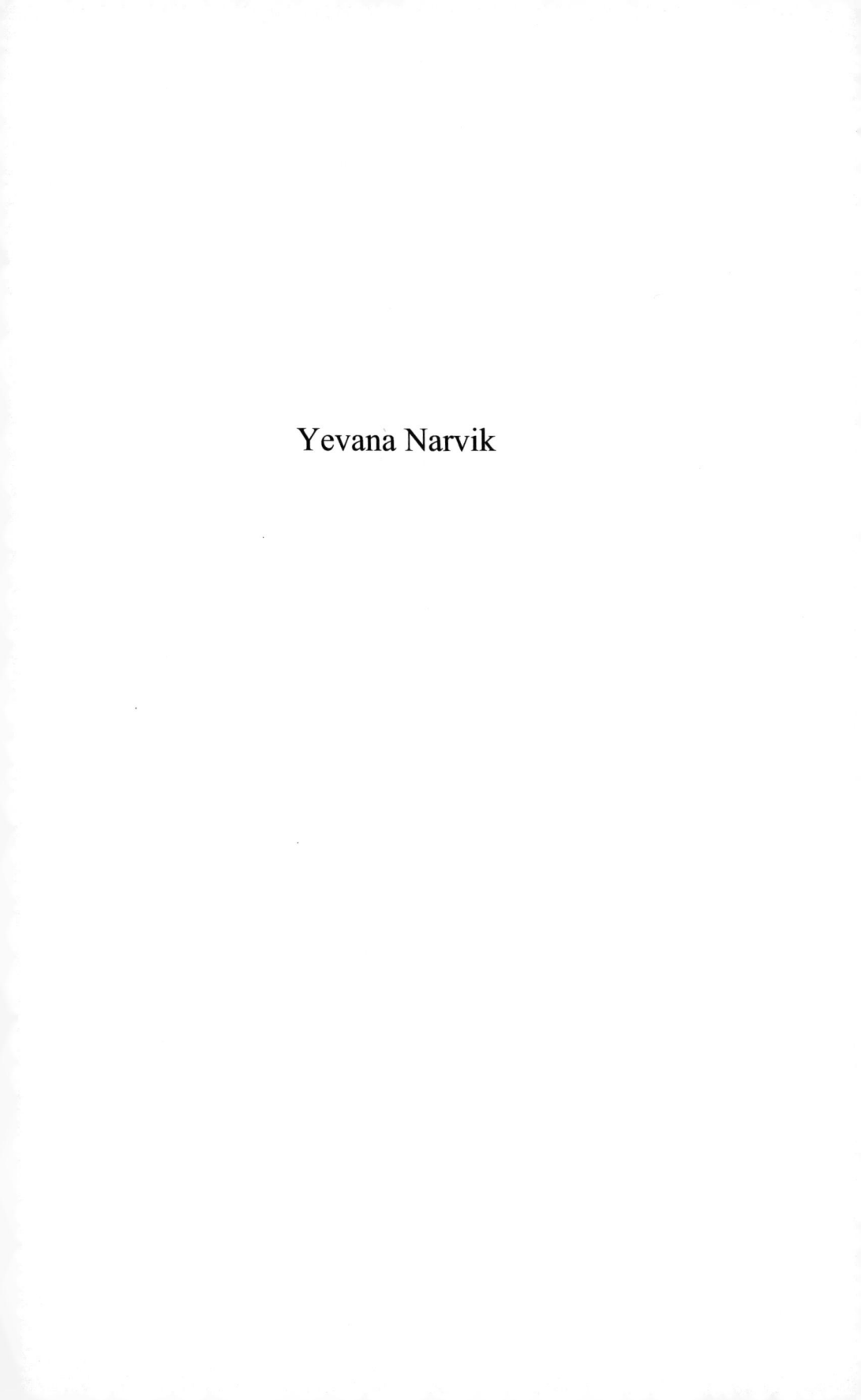

Yevana Narvik

Paul Clark

Yevana Narvik

Vanguard Press

VANGUARD PAPERBACK

© Copyright 2024
Paul Clark

The right of Paul Clark to be identified as author of
this work has been asserted by them in accordance with the
Copyright, Designs and Patents Act 1988.

All Rights Reserved

No reproduction, copy or transmission of this publication
may be made without written permission.
No paragraph of this publication may be reproduced,
copied or transmitted save with the written permission of the publisher, or
in accordance with the provisions
of the Copyright Act 1956 (as amended).

Any person who commits any unauthorised act in relation to
this publication may be liable to criminal
prosecution and civil claims for damages.

A CIP catalogue record for this title is
available from the British Library.

ISBN 978 1 80016 982 1

This is a work of fiction. Names, characters, businesses, places, events and incidents are either the product of the author's imagination or used in a fictitious manner. Any resemblance to actual persons, living or dead, or actual events is purely coincidental

Vanguard Press is an imprint of
Pegasus Elliot Mackenzie Publishers Ltd.
www.pegasuspublishers.com

First Published in 2024

Vanguard Press
Sheraton House Castle Park
Cambridge England

Printed & Bound in Great Britain

To Jane: The most caring, intelligent and beautiful wife, mum and grandma. Tom and Jack: You inspired me to be a writer. Mum: Always there - Thank you.

A New deal

The deal was done, the meeting finished and the conference room doors closed behind the other attendees as they left. The adrenalin in the room was electric; you could almost touch it. Outside, the sun was pouring through the floor to ceiling windows of this 101st floor conference facility. Their secretary called in on the suite telephone and asked if she could come in and clear the room. The offer was declined; it would wait. A $300m property deal to seal the bid for an entertainment complex was a special moment, their special moment. Toby looked at Yevana, his business partner and equal, pulled her onto the table – where the Rothschild Bank senior representative had been sat to agree the deal – pushed her face down and threw her arms forward so she was unable to grip the table ends. He quickly unbuckled his trousers and freed himself before lifting her skirt and in the absence of knickers, penetrated her soft flesh. This was the final act of the deal. At the moment of culmination, the intercom broke the silence and the secretary informed Yevana that her boyfriend was waiting in his car outside the main entrance; the intercom crackled off.

Yevana

Yevana Narvik was the straight 'A' student that seemed not to try too hard but excelled at most things. She did not struggle at anything and was particularly brilliant at maths. All secondary school exams were passed a year early as were her A-levels; all taken at state schools in East London. It didn't stop there though as she had a tall, athletic body that was suited to most sports, again she excelled especially at athletics and the 800m in particular, where she was GB Standard although she would not attend the training and races required to advance further whilst in education. The point is if she wanted to do something she was unbeatable. She was far from ordinary but at an early age nobody quite knew why that was or what that meant as she was neither tomboy nor girly. She liked her friends both male and female but it was all fairly routine in her younger years. Her character though centred on getting what she wanted and not shying away from making difficult decisions. It was obvious when Yevana was taking control and you sensed that there was an element of satisfaction in the act.

Yevana was born of East German parents who left the fatherland to make a new life in England at the end of the Cold War, just as the Berlin wall came crashing down. The father was an intelligent man who eventually rose to a management position on the London Underground organisation where he worked as many hours as he was allowed in order to give his family the best life he could. Her mother worked part time in a local supermarket but was at home mostly bringing up their four children. It was a basic life but one full of hope in this emerging new world after the Second World War. Her two brothers and a sister were all bright kids but not on the same level as Yevana who was widely acknowledged as gifted. This family was very close though and they stuck together in all respects especially as they were very much outsiders in the hard knocks London East End community they had settled in. Yevana was only a one-year-old when the family moved to Britain so grew up with a slight German accent from living with her family although it was enough in the very patriotic capital, to be given a difficult time in school playground. This coupled with the reaction from other kids at school who were jealous of her talents, meant the presence of her stronger older brothers and sister was initially built in family protection. As she grew up issues were swiftly sorted out with many of her detractors being girls who she was happy to address no matter what their ages; she was ruthless and unforgiving. If not her, then big sis was on hand to deliver the bad news!

One of the school bullies thought she would bring down 'little Miss Narvik' a peg or two on one particular occasion of note. Yevana had been using an ink pen and on passing her desk the bully nudged the open black ink bottle so it spilt over Yevana's grey school uniform and on her bare legs. Everybody who saw it, except Yevana's friends, started laughing at the ruined dress and her stained legs, which took forever to clean over several days. Swift meticulous retribution was sought and with some glee. Yevana waited for a netball class and for this particular class feigned illness, waiting in the changing rooms for the class to finish out in the playing fields and return for their shower. This planned exercise ensured that she was able to deliver her retribution and this was dealt with by breaking both high heels on the girl's shoes. They would fracture properly once they were stressed hopefully when the girl was walking down some steps or staircase. Yevana didn't have to wait long because as the bully was walking from the games complex and happily chatting away to other girls, she approached the first set of steps placing a foot on the first concrete step then moving forward with all her weight onto her other foot which collapsed sending her and all her bags flying in the air and down a fairly long flight, breaking both ankles and an arm; Justice! Yevana stood at the top of the stairs and was the first person the school bully saw through the haze of her pain. She may have just noticed a smile too! Nobody ever found out what caused such a horrific fall. The school blamed the poor quality of the excessively high heels that the girl had already been warned about.

Brains were one thing and beauty was definitely another major asset in the Yevana armoury. The fact is that the boys fancied Yevana and she could have her pick if she wanted to. However, annoyingly to most of them, she showed little interest in love even by the time she was well into her secondary school as she was too focused on her studies and sporting activities. On entering college to undertake A-level studies she started to have more emotional feelings but was surprised how they were emerging, as she found one person she admired more than any was a lady called Mrs Jean Strawley. Unusually for her subject matter expertise, she was a very modern individual in terms of the clothes she wore, the music she listened to and the company she kept. She was a twenty-four-year old history lecturer newly married and very attractive. Jean had very short boyish like blonde hair, a slim physique and long dainty fingers and her nails were always multi coloured. Although very feminine and attractive to most of the college boys, there was something male-like about her bearing. It wasn't long before people in the college started to talk, wondering about their friendship as they had been seen together in Jean Strawley's car and in local coffee shops in town at weekends. Nobody ever discovered anything romantic or untoward about them, although the college principal did ask Jean a question that she thought may have alluded to her relationship with Yevana one afternoon in the staff room.

'Jean, I haven't seen your husband recently. I trust he is well?'

'Yes, sir' she replied, 'very well, thank you.'

Eventually the rumours petered out as they made a concerted effort to be seen less in public. Point to note: At the end of her A-level studies and after Yevana moved on to university, Jean Strawley was seen to became slightly shabby in appearance paying much less care of her appearance, growing her hair long, losing her spark and drinking to excess on a regular basis. This lasted for several months before she was forced to take a break from the college for two months in order to regain her appetite for teaching and concentrate on her embryonic marriage. It didn't work and she split from her husband shortly after spending four weeks in a drying-out clinic. Apparently, she was never the same person again, losing her enthusiasm and moving away to begin a new life living alone. To her friends and colleagues, it was very strange and unexplained for a woman who had been so lively, bubbly and inspiring in her whole outlook to life. She wouldn't listen to advice and take help, even from her close family who she had upset badly with her behaviour.

This was the effect that Yevana had on people. She had become tall and slim with long, wavy dark hair that shone even on a dull day. Naturally striking, she wore little makeup but her high cheek bones highlighted a natural beauty. Her legs never seemed to end and in proportion, she had breasts most women would 'die for.' Her eyes were slightly narrow oriental like and focused; determined. Yevana's wardrobe in the main consisted of shorts, short skirts and the shortest tops, which showed off her lean, muscled stomach and stunning set of thighs that many of the boys would have been proud of. However, when in more formal evening wear and makeup she was simply stunning. A local agency capitalised on her good fortune and took her on to their books for some part time modelling work that earned her decent pocket money. She really enjoyed it but did not take it too seriously.

After college she took a gap year break and headed for Cuba. Why Cuba people asked? She told her family she wanted to go off the normal circuit and live in a different culture for a year. She informed them she would write once every three months to let them know she was okay, but otherwise she wanted to be alone and discover her inner self ready for her studies at university; this she did without regret. Only those who were there know what she did in Cuba. Nobody is allowed to ask and certainly it is her secret and she treasures that very private memory. Much to her mother's consternation, she left the UK with only what she was wearing on that day and left behind essential belongings most people would not want to go without, even taking shipping to get there rather than travelling by air. The St Christopher her parents gave her especially for the trip was discarded over the side of the ship; this was a self-help journey; no external assistance was required.

From her time in Cuba, she does wear a small antique gold ring on her right little finger that she will not be parted from, which she says is from a special memory on that gap year. She went to Cuba a teenager and came back a young woman with fire in her belly because in her view she had stripped back to the soul of who she was, and developed further deeply rooted survival instincts which would bear fruit for the challenges that lay ahead. She was even known to smoke the odd cigar since this trip! Yevana knew one thing was certain in life and that was she was preparing herself to be successful. She was so convinced she had told family and friends that nothing would get in the way. Yevana Narvik would run an empire; a big one!

University was going to change her life forever as she was to meet somebody who would play a huge part in it and help shape her future. She chose Durham University in northern England where she would study business management and use all elements of university life to get the experience she yearned to initiate her future career. In her natural style she put everything into both her studies and sport, earning sports colours in athletics and rowing. In fact, she stayed unbeaten in both in all four years there, which included her time in the master's programme. British Athletics begged her to join the elite squad for 800 metres; however, Yevana had other ideas as her studies could not be compromised for anything. Sport was fun, studies were the future. During her time in Durham, she did socialise quite hard and had brief sexual friendships with a couple of men but they were never close enough to be called boyfriends; there wasn't time in her programme! In her second year at university, she even modelled some clothing for a third-year textile student in an Autumn show in London, an event that was often attended by agents across the country looking for new talent in the modelling world. During that show and the following show, a month later Yevana had nine offers of work, mainly in London and Paris. Unbelievably for some reason, she declined them all.

It was in her third year that she met somebody, that somebody with ambition to match hers – Toby Dalrup – another third-year student reading business studies. They met by chance one day in the student union, where he was with a group of friends celebrating a birthday. During the evening their eyes met late on and eventually, neither could remember how, they started talking. Business was a strong topic of conversation, but the physical attraction was there to be seen and felt strongly by both of them. This level of attraction that gave her goose bumps had not happened to Yevana in this way before; she didn't know how to handle it, it was strange. It would be another six months and into the master's programme that they had both stayed on to complete, before they would meet again, socially.

By this time Toby had a girlfriend relationship that was partly serious and Yevana had developed a very strong bond with a business consultant in the local area called Caren Lords. They had met through mutual friends at a party in the city in this fourth year at university. Caren was a good person to learn from in the business world and she was gorgeous so far as Yevana was concerned. Small, very fit and glamorous, Yevana really enjoyed her company and often stayed over at Caren's house in the city centre where female lovemaking reached fever pitch. Caren eventually moved from a long-time boyfriend to spend more of her spare time with Yevana, who could be very demanding. They soon became very good friends and spent a lot of time socialising with various groups, especially at weekends. The more hedonistic groups they engaged with broadened Caren's former idea of a relationship and given the gentle guidance of Yevana who clearly had some experience in this area, she grew to look forward to these encounters. Yevana once told Caren about an older couple she knew in Cuba who had introduced her to this type of experience, but that was all she would say on the matter.

The next time Toby and Yevana were to meet the fireworks would fly and sparkle. After a long night on the town, they had ended up at the same student party somewhere in the city and once again they got chatting. Yevana was with Caren and Toby with a current girlfriend of two months he had become quite attached to. Toby couldn't keep his eyes off the scantily clad Yevana though and at one stage his girlfriend asked with a hint of jealous if he had known Yevana long.

'She seems to want to discuss many things with you which is quite off-putting, really. Are you sure she has a partner at the moment?' Cassy enquired.

'Of course, don't be stupid, Cassy,' replied Toby, 'that is her partner with the short blonde hair; a female!' You see all is not what it seems,' he sighed.

Cassy sighed also, feeling silly and looked at both women across the room. Having had a few more drinks most people moved on in a large group to another party at one p.m. and they continued chatting in several different conversations until around three a.m. Yevana leant over to Toby who had his back to Cassy in this lounge type room with lots of old student furniture and in a late-night throaty voice and businesslike tone, Yevana said, 'Get rid of the chick, I am going to love you forever.'

This was an order, not an invitation. Toby stared at her, looked round keen to see that Cassy didn't hear a word of this preposterous statement. He soon walked out of the room having said nothing, blanking it out completely on his way to the toilet where there was a very inconvenient queue and pondered on what was going through his alcohol and testosterone-driven mind. He was sobering up pretty quickly and was stunned, no shocked, on realising that he was already considering doing what this Yevana Narvik had ordered. He liked her and was impressed with her work ethic on campus and her ambition for the future, which he found stimulating on several levels. He walked back into the room and rejoined the group.

Yevana leaned over again and said in the most sarcastic tone, 'Well, are you capable of making a decision?' Toby looked a little red faced and felt a little flustered which was really annoying him. Hang on, why, he thought; this is stupid. His brain was racing and he then leaned back towards Yevana and quietly blurted out, 'I will have to escort my girlfriend home first, should I choose to.' Yevana laughed. 'Tell her it's over, get her a taxi and come back here before we leave!' Yevana loved this man, she had not chased him – it would wait – but the first time she saw him she knew, they would play a part in each other's lives and it was time to act.

Toby

Toby Dalrup was a slow starter in life. He was one of those boys that got picked on as a young kid and wasn't particularly good at sports. This had frustrated his father who was a sportsman and a talented officer in the Life Guards. Having to move schools regularly didn't help either as every time he made a new friend they seemed to be moving house, from one military married quarters estate to another. His parents eventually came to a decision when he was ten to send him to private school. Basically, his parents did not have enough time for their son and his two sisters amongst his father's duties in the military and their Regiment social calendar. His two elder sisters had already gone off to school and he followed them.

Life at school in Surrey was difficult to begin with as he took time to learn the rules of the establishment and got used to the pranks and tricks of the other boys in this all-male environment. The stand-out good bit at the school was the fabulous Miss Rilesby, a twenty-eight-year-old maths teacher who was the epicentre of this male dominated world. Tall, elegant and single she filled every male teacher and student fantasy; bar none!

Toby was intelligent and had a mind for figures. He was getting good early results and was top of the class in Maths and English. He eventually started to excel in some sports as he grew into his teens. He was a house centre in the all-conquering rugby team and was the leading goal scorer in the hockey team. Without doubt he was now a 'player' in the school and his confidence had grown as had his appearance. Even one of the gay students in the sixth form had sent him an amorous card on Valentine's Day when he was sixteen. Toby tore it up immediately and was very embarrassed, making every effort to avoid the individual concerned. His best friend knew of this and couldn't stop laughing. It was very innocent, adolescent love! His academic grades were now in the fantastic region and his parents even found time to attend the GCSE awards ceremony in which he received a series of awards for his examination results and sporting success alike. Toby was extremely happy and this day capped it for him, knowing his father was there looking magnificent in his No 1 uniform and medals and that he was now one of the most popular boys in school. How things had changed since those early school days.

His time spent during A level studies followed the same pattern although he had a small distraction in that he had a girlfriend from the girls college in Cheltenham whom he had met at a joint schools outward bound weekend in the Welsh Brecon Beacons. They were a good match and enjoyed each other's company tremendously. He had a problem though and that was that he had two girlfriends – the other was Miss Rilesby.

There was a charity ball in the school coincidentally on his eighteenth birthday and the theme was doctors and nurses. Invites went out to all and sundry which turned into a great spectacle on the night. The views on display were stunning generally, for both male and female eyes! He wore a doctor's coat and shoes only, as did many other young men of derring-do. Toby had only just started his relationship with his girlfriend from Cheltenham Girls College when on this particular evening he was getting the eye, from of all people, Miss Rilesby. He ignored it to begin with but later noticed that it was sustained and although he started to feel uncomfortable the excitement was beginning to build, especially when at one point she beamed a great big smile of intent in his direction. It turned out that she had had a fair amount of champagne and even had the confidence to come across to Toby and his girlfriend and ask him for an overdue dance of which he gladly accepted. The girlfriend wasn't particularly bothered as they were with a whole group of people who were dancing together and with each other whatever the relationships. In the event it didn't seem to matter in any case as morale was high, the drink was flowing and during the rest of the evening Miss Rilesby had been all over a married male teacher which seemed nothing untoward to anybody. In any case a bit of harmless flirting didn't matter; did it? Toby thought to himself. Miss Rilesby pulled him into the middle of the packed dance floor and was so close he thought she was trying to get into his coat. What became obvious very quickly was that Miss Rilesby was as horny as hell. Stockings, short nurse's dress, open cleavage etc... normal fancy dress nurse's attire. They danced to three tunes then when the third track finished he went to thank her in order to go back to his girlfriend, when she leant over to his left ear and whispered in a low gravelly and most sexy breath, 'Meet me by the building rear entrance fire escape at two a.m.' and proceeded to walk off without even a glance backwards to see his astonished reaction. She must be damned mad, he thought; my goodness what is she thinking, we are teacher and student! He had to admit there had been rumours for a while about what she did in her private life and Toby was now beginning to think they had a strong possibility of being true. Slightly bewildered by this he thought about saying goodnight to his girlfriend and going straight to bed as he had had quite a bit of alcohol. It was past midnight and he had important rugby training at lunch time the following day. Self-doubt was running rife throughout his veins and surely it was a brilliant prank his mates had set up, he pondered. He could imagine they were secretively watching him fall for the bait from which they would crucify him 'forever and a day.' What am I doing even contemplating it? he thought angrily. He wandered back to the group for at least the next hour then shortly after one a.m. he made his excuses and said goodbye to his girlfriend. She wondered why he seemed so eager to get to bed, as sometimes they would slip out onto the playing fields and make love when she met him there, sometimes even inside in a corridor if they were really playful before the end of an evening. Subsequently and very disappointed, she got on the coach back to Cheltenham.

Once the coach had left Toby went back into the hall for a last left-over drink with a friend then shortly before two a.m. he headed for the fire escape; he thought it was just too good an opportunity to miss if it were true and it was worth the risk! He quietly tiptoed along the corridor with the lights turned off which made him feel slightly more secure in what he was doing. What he saw when he got there confirmed all of the rumours about Miss Rilesby. It was dark but there was enough light shining from security outdoor lights to see she had cuffed one hand to the fire door handle, had a full head mask on with only eye, nose and mouth openings and was bent over looking out of the glass door. Toby didn't need telling twice, so he positioned himself behind her and without a thought, lifted her white nurse's skirt held onto her suspender belt and gave it all he had; and more! During the act she told him she wanted more and he was to be at her flat on Saturday to stay the night and didn't expect to be disappointed. He laughed and left her tied to the fire escape. As he got to his bedroom dormitory he heard the fire alarm go off and literally dived into bed having wild imaginary thoughts about what was happening at the fire escape and whether his part might get played out in full! He needn't have worried as the efficient and daring Miss Rilesby had set it off on purpose and then reported it and closed the incident as all good teachers would do, she told Toby. 'I trust I didn't frighten you though, a big strong man such as yourself.' She smiled the assassin's smile. Toby look aghast realising she did it on purpose. 'Don't look so shocked I enjoyed it,' she finished. Stood outside the teachers' staff room, she grasped his hand, slid the key into his palm and closed it. He arrived on time. The relationship lasted for the rest of his time at his school until he passed his A levels once again with distinction. The girlfriend was of little use to him now and although they were good friends he only met her infrequently and soon the relationship petered out. Miss Rilesby was complicated but taught Toby many lessons about adult life that would see him well for the future. They parted good friends and it was with a smile that on hearing she had selected his replacement shortly after he had left he knew that that person was in the hands of a great 'teacher.'

Off to Durham University he went to enjoy being a full-time undergraduate reading business studies. He got straight into university life and played as a centre in the rugby fifteen, quickly gaining recognition as one of the best they had had for some years. Hockey he played a little, but it was rugby that took his time outside of studies. Halls were good fun and he was well known on the party circuit where a string of girls succumbed to his charm and good looks. The second year was pretty much the same but living with five others in a town house out of campus was a riot, albeit course work was already getting serious if you wanted good grades, and he did. He fully intended to complete his masters which after completing his degree with honours he duly completed this too. During the previous few months, he had begun a relationship and acquired a steady girlfriend called Cassy, someone in the year below studying history of art. She was the most beautiful person and they couldn't keep their hands off one another. Her long blonde hair and large bright white teeth had her standing out above her equals. They were a good match and got on well; Toby was very keen and happy.

It was during the third year of his degree that he was to meet somebody who would play a significant part in his life going forward. They met firstly in the students union one night, chatted and did not follow it up, until six months later once into his master's programme, where he saw her again at a party in the City. She looked stunning. He saw long dark hair, slim, pretty, slightly narrow almost oriental type eyes, beautiful features, lovely breasts and long, long legs complemented by her clothing which left very little to the imagination. Their eyes met and it was hard to ignore although Toby was more concerned that his girlfriend would notice. The evening went on nicely and they eventually started chatting in the group that had got together through mutual friends. There were no signs of what was to come as they moved on at one a.m. to another house party in the city belonging to more students. As the party was nearing three a.m. he had a conversation with Yevana that left him almost speechless; what's more her close friend heard it all but luckily not his girlfriend. The way she spoke to him would normally have earned a swift rebuke and a no thank you – 'I am okay as I am thanks'. However, this was special, just the way they talked together, interests, focus, chemistry; it clicked. Toby collected his thoughts and let the evening naturally end as the party started to get down to smaller groups in various states, lingering into the depths of the night. He ordered a taxi and walked out taking his girlfriend with him. She wanted to stay on and find a corner or go back to her flat and stay over as they often did in each other's flats but he ignored this and seemed distracted. As they travelled under the neon light of the streets Toby's mind raced in unison whilst he contemplated the unthinkable; he was going back! They pulled up outside Jenny's flat and as she tried to pull him out with her on the pavement side she felt him hang back. 'What are you doing? Come on!' she teased. He jumped out, gave her a hug and said goodnight explaining, 'I can't stay over as I have a very important rugby match tomorrow and as captain I want to be recovered and to set an example, Sorry.' 'All of a sudden Cassy looked forlorn and tired. 'Okay, buster, if rugby is more important than me, so be it.' With a long kiss and a swift swirl of her blonde locks she turned and disappeared across the pavement and into her flat complex. He felt a heavy heart but his adrenaline was running on max and intrigue was pinching him hard even though he wasn't sure what he was going to do next. As originally requested the taxi driver was taking him to his rented accommodation but just as he entered the road he lived in he told the taxi driver to change direction and asked him to take him back to the pickup location at the party. The driver looked in his rear-view mirror and smiled saying nothing; he didn't need too. On reaching the destination Toby paid the driver who leaned back with some change and said, 'It's going to be a long night, sir.' It was now three-thirty a.m.

Toby expected Yevana to have disappeared as he had given no indication that he might even consider ditching his girlfriend or returning here without her, as who the hell did she think she was anyway? It did quickly dawn on him though, that he was there! The party was no longer in full swing, people were sparsely scattered around the house high on an array of recreational drugs and alcohol, of course. The doors to various rooms and bedrooms were full of student bodies in many states of undress, motionless or fornicating in twos and threes! This was a house of poor multi-coloured decoration typical of student lets everywhere, with walls covered in posters of peace symbols, music groups and anything else that had been lifted from somewhere dubious. It smelled of many things but mainly fried food that had seeped into the woodwork. Toby walked on through into the lounge which had emptied out from the throng of pumping music three hours earlier. But now there was a Sad Cafe song playing more sedately in the background which seemed ironic, perhaps. 'Nothing left Toulouse' Toby loved it. He couldn't see Yevana anywhere so he carried on walking straight through to the kitchen and collected a can of lager from a fridge and walked back into the lounge. Suddenly he realised Yevana was lying on the floor near the far corner in the partial darkness, next to an armchair with her head on her friend's stomach, who was also lying down at ninety degrees to her in a figure T. Her friend was stroking Yevana's hair and they were completely unaware that Toby was stood staring at them drinking from his can. Sensing something had changed, Yevana looked up at Toby and having looked around to see the lounge was empty, and without hesitation or considering whether anybody else was in the room, she said, 'Go down on me lover and taste your future.' They stared at one another and almost by hypnosis, as if he had lost control, he dropped to his knees, lifted her skirt onto her bare lower belly and pulled her panties to her knees doing as she asked. Her friend kept her eyes closed but the electricity was palpable. Yevana's fingers dug into the skin on her friend's leg and shoulder in the crucifix position they were in, so much so she drew a little blood from her leg. Within a few minutes Yevana came, holding on to his head, just as somebody came into the room. The guy was as high 'as a kite' and stumbled past them not realising they were there. Regardless, it wouldn't have mattered to Yevana or her friend. Toby slumped back against another chair in the room and carried on drinking from his can in a very matter of fact way. He considered that this must be how drugs feel, and he didn't do drugs, because somehow it felt surreal in the moment. He considered perhaps it was a dream. There was definitely a pause for reflection in the lounge and it was about an hour later that they eventually all went back to Yevana's friend's house by taxi. If he thought what had passed previously had seemed a trifle strange it was about to get stranger! They walked into a very smart and modern home owned by this friend, Caren Lords. It was sparsely populated with mainly white furniture and futuristic portraits of beautiful men and women in the brightest colours of the rainbow on the walls. Sculptures positioned in the lounge were of nude females in the form of Greek goddesses.

Caren went straight to bed without saying anything. But Yevana insisted that she and Toby make love on the floor in Caren's bedroom. She held his hand and directed him to a space beside Caren's bed. 'Hang on,' Toby insisted. 'What about your friend' 'Don't be silly let's make love; we are wasting time!' she mocked. He looked bewildered but it didn't last long and what followed was over two hours of noisy lovemaking and at times very noisy lovemaking; so much for his rugby match and his example! He didn't know if Caren had been awake for the whole episode but guessed she had not missed or wanted to miss much of it! Eventually Yevana got up and slid in beside Caren without a word to Toby. He got up and stared at them and noticed Caren put her arms around Yevana's midriff. He walked out.

Relationship

Toby and Yevana started dating and perhaps unsurprisingly their first outing was to the City Arts centre to see an exhibition by the new erotic artist Renolda Newwing. This was a quirky modern look at the sexual art form. Several other outings followed mainly in secret and platonic due to student commitments, sport and girlfriend issues. It was not all about sexual attraction, although this was the foundation of their relationship entwined with respect and the fact that they actually liked each other. Toby had a girlfriend of course but unlike his time at school he could not find the time to accommodate two girlfriends. In any case, Yevana was getting irritated and most seriously, telling him, 'Sort it out or move on, I don't have the patience and I don't like her.' Toby thought that was rich but even though she was still seeing Caren, he couldn't give her up and so he was left with no choice but to ditch Cassy. He was gutted for his girlfriend because they too were well suited but Yevana had hooked him, in many ways because her business ambitions matched his and this is what he wanted the next decade to be about. Time for all-out love and families would be limited, very limited. When the moment came it was nasty as Cassy had heard rumours of an affair and eventually he admitted as much as he did not feel the need to lie. Cassy, the most unaggressive person you could imagine, started punching his chest, which he took full on until she fell back and walked slowly away from his life, desperately numb with disappointment. She honestly thought they might be an item for good as she loved him dearly and would miss him so much. Toby was soon missing Cassy and found it painful when they saw each other across the campus, but there was nothing he could do. It would pass and it did.

The relationship between Yevana and Toby on the other hand now took off in their new position of freedom and openness; the complication was Caren. This beautiful and very successful woman was an inspiration to Yevana and they had built a strong relationship and enjoyed their time together as both friends and very active lovers. Caren was bi-sexual but only had Yevana as a serious relationship at this time and was heavily in love. Yevana felt the same way and was equally smitten with Caren. They both had the same sexual needs which helped although both had similar interests more generally and Caren knew she had found the love of her life. Whilst she hated anybody else touching her girlfriend she could put up with Yevana's dalliances, as long as she knew about them and there was no deceit.

Yevana and Toby came to the end of their master's degrees and everything was taking shape. They were both on course for top marks and life beyond that looked rosy. However, near the end of the summer term just after their last pieces of work were submitted, there was some trouble which came 'out of the blue'. Toby had been chatting to another woman, a PhD lecturer, on a regular basis in and around the university. It was nothing more than this and it was conducted in open spaces on campus, mainly subject-based but in a low-key way, getting advice whilst finishing his last dissertation. One evening the lecturer in question, a lovely, single and gentle woman in her early thirties was attacked walking home, had her clothes excessively ripped off. She was punched in the face several times and her nose was badly broken. Before the assailant ran off – it was definitely a woman – she told her to 'leave other people's friends alone or there will be more of this.' The lecturer was off site for three months before she could work again. As well as her injuries she had also suffered psychological problems. Toby was questioned by the police but told them he had no idea and was flabbergasted to say the least. He sent her flowers and a card explaining how terrible he felt about what had happened to her. It had been a complete mystery.

A few nights after that attack he arranged to meet Yevana at her digs and on his arrival he noticed Caren was there having just popped in from work. They chatted away and it was only just as she was leaving to go home, that Toby noticed Caren's knuckles as she went to pick up her briefcase. She had bruising and scratch marks across her left hand – apparently the assailant appeared to be left-handed – and to say Toby was shocked was an understatement. My God, he thought, could Yevana really have been jealous? Had she been following him around the campus? Did she arrange this beating? Did he really know Yevana Narvik? Was she dangerous? The other more worrying issue was that the attacker had wrestled the victim to the ground and stabbed the lecturer in the rear with her stilettos and Caren often wore very pointed stilettos! Yevana, when asked what she thought about the incident, would only say 'somebody obviously had their reasons to want to warn this woman'. Toby looked on in amazement – she damned well had done this; he knew it.

Nothing came of it, although Yevana was questioned by the police because she was Toby's girlfriend. She told them she was 'horrified' and thought that she must be careful if a jealous person was out there, especially as she was his current girlfriend. He was not sure they believed her as there was no evidence whatsoever. The time came to leave Durham and head out into the world of business, but where? They had both had job offers in London and for different reasons turned them down as the circumstances did not appeal and they were both looking for 'the challenge' not mundanesville!

Manchester here we come

Yevana and Toby had decided that they were committed to going into business together and they had centred on one idea and that was the top end of entertainment and leisure and being their own boss. They weren't interested in working for anybody else; it just didn't do it for them as their ambition was to be recognised as a serious institution whilst having some fun on the way. Their ultimate aim was to build a hotel chain that comprised five-star luxury with sumptuous bedroom suites, bars, cafes, leisure facilities, gambling, fine dining, cinema, helicopter pad and an exclusive private members club in all major cities, firstly in the UK and it would all start in Manchester. Between them they already had friends in Manchester within the banking sector and could get property there cheaper than in London, which would be an obvious target audience when the project took off.

First of all, they needed a base to start their business including some accommodation and finance. Friends were one thing but the finance was still going to be difficult. The business loan was secured on pretty dubious rates; however, the options were very limited and they would do anything to get started at this point. It was not long before they found a base in the Ranstone area north of the city; it was an old shop with a flat above it. A fairly cheap rental rate was secured which they could afford to be able to concentrate on the main effort and build the business from there. Over the following weekend they received the keys and immediately started redecorating, stripping the decor back to basics and painting anything and everything to give the place a much-needed lift.

Yevana had decided to make a clean break back in Durham and get rid of Caren; she had fulfilled her purpose and although she loved the sheer decadence she had with her she had to move on as all the focus and energy had to be business now. In the short-term Toby would take up the love interest. It was not going to be easy as Caren was besotted with Yevana and so it was going to really hurt when she broke the news. She informed Toby saying, 'I need to go back to Durham tonight.' 'Why?' he replied matter of factly whilst painting a wall 'Darling, I have not got time for the business, Caren and you,' she stated without turning around to look at him, 'and I am going to deal with this situation once and for all tonight, with or without you.' 'okay, that's fine, arrange it and I will drive,' Toby replied. 'Thank you' was all she added.

Later on, that night she decided how she would do it. It was apparent that she was feeling particularly horny and ruthless, so on making the call, they arranged to meet in a bar as they did quite often, with Yevana telling Caren to dress in a long pencil skirt and heels. This was good news for Caren who had not seen Yevana for a couple of weeks which was making her nervous.

After a few hours drinking, dancing and chatting they disappeared back to Caren's in a taxi. As a leaving gift Yevana carried out Caren's favourite sexual act, which was to tie one hand to the headboard and tie her hair into a ponytail whilst getting her on all fours. She then left her on her own for a few minutes whilst Yevana put some classical music on the in-room system pulled on their favourite strapon and then pulled down her pencil skirt and mounted her. Feeling ruthless, when all was done Yevana pulled her ponytail back towards her then whispered in her ear that it was over and that she was moving away, tonight, and under no circumstances was Caren to follow. Subsequently she pulled out and walked out. Toby sat in the car outside having received the 'be ready as planned' text. He could hear the screams out in the car as the door to the house opened and out ran Yevana without looking back. She jumped in and they sped off. Caren was raging and trying to get out of the tie but couldn't of course for some time. Yevana had decided on this act on purpose as she felt in her mind it was the logical way to end such a complex relationship; it felt natural. Toby wasn't sure that this would be the last they would hear from Caren as he always had an instinctive feeling that she was different and the way she dealt with the university lecturer backed that up in his eyes. He glanced at Yevana and she was looking in the front seat mirror, applying some lipstick to freshen up. Toby raised his eyebrows in recognition that if she was as ruthless in business they were in for a successful but bumpy ride. Mobile phones were changed and life moved on; nothing would get in their way now.

The flat scrubbed up very quickly and they moved in with just the basics intending to keep a minimalist space to live and 'live' in. The office was modern with all the essential office furniture which enabled them to get up and running. More meetings were quickly arranged with bank managers and friends, initially, to generate more detailed funding in order to be ready to start their first entertainment complex. They found a three-star hotel just on the outskirts of the city centre that needed a lot of work but it was of a good size that would require some restructuring in terms of building work but not so much that their budget wouldn't be able to cope. The manager at the Allied Manchester Bank Corporation gave them a substantial business loan to do the work to the tune of over four hundred thousand pounds. A loyal friend of Toby's called Bob Ray had chipped in one hundred thousand pounds more as he had already earned a five hundred thousand bonus that year working with hedge funds in Switzerland and London. They had met at school and had remained friends and had skied most years since. Bob, he knew, would be a loyal friend for life and being a couple of years older he was already a hand of experience. They played centre together in their all-conquering school rugby team and although they went to different universities they kept in touch and enjoyed their old school reunions. Bob was a stud. He had never had a relationship that lasted past the next party he attended, as he was always tempted by the next conquest. He fancied Yevana, as most people did, but knew she was off limits and she made it plainly obvious that she was not interested in any case, which amused Toby and Bob. They got on though, which was proving helpful all round.

From their office they co-ordinated and project managed the rebuild which had a six-month completion in service date. The first real disappointment and difference of opinion between Yevana and Toby had been about how much cash would be required to get the project up and running to the exacting standard they could expect for this inaugural project. Yevana was thinking big but Toby was more conservative which frustrated her a little but nevertheless they pushed on. The build construct was a much-simplified version of their ultimate design but they had to start in a realistic way in line with their budget. There would be a cafe, sixty rooms of premier standard, a bar, a fine dining restaurant and a swimming pool with a gym. Also, there was a small club in the basement, which was for members only, a small casino area, bar, DJ, dance floor and a secluded private area with waitress service. The lounge area just off the main entrance was quite Dickensian but with a modern twist.

Their love life was great and living together was stimulating their desires as a couple. No matter how tough the workload, they were enjoying Manchester and making some interesting friends around the city. They trawled all the clubs and casinos, bars and hotels to learn how to be competitive and make their new establishment not only work but be the place to go or stay for an evening. Some of the people they met were from the side of the community that played on the tightrope of common law; quite often falling off but always bouncing back. This was violence and accountancy; there seemed to be a game to play and if you didn't get the right advice, use your savvy and take some risk, your business would fail or be a mediocre low profit-making establishment, as the old three-star hotel they had taken over had been until it was forced to close having failed miserably. Yevana and Toby intended theirs to be neither and so learning the lessons and quick, was especially important. Their accountant, Bernard Tomas was astute and he played a tight game helping them push the boundaries, but he came with a strong reputation and was paid very well; good advice cost money and he was a safe pair of hands who knew the form and essentially had expertise in this area of business.

One evening they went to one of their competitors at the high end of the market in Manchester, took a few drinks at the bar, had a delicious meal then played some poker. At two p.m. they joined the select club for one hundred pounds each and sat on one of the sofas and relaxed to some Barry White type smooth music and admired the beautiful waiters and waitresses. After about an hour a tall, dark Polish waitress came over and Yevana started talking to her before replacing her drink. It wasn't long before Yevana pulled the waitress into her lap and slowly tucked fifty pounds into her skirt belt. The waitress sat on Yevana's lap for a few minutes, where Yevana took in her manner, smell and erotic beauty, all which she considered important ingredients of a successful staff in this environment. This was the difference between empty and full in this type of establishment if you wanted to survive in a tough competitive market place! Toby knew what Yevana was up to and watched with amusement. Yevana being who she was managed to arrange to meet the Polish waitress in the toilets and swap knickers for another fifty pounds. Back at the flat she stuffed them in Toby's mouth and told him the tale as she drank him dry; it didn't take long! The education garnered was valuable from their countless days and nights out using their spare time and soon enough, slightly over time and budget, the new venture, their first, was ready. Had they done enough preparation? Was it the right building project? Would they be able to recruit the right staff and clients? They agreed. Yes, bring it on.

Y&T Entertainment.Inc

The building, fixtures and furnishings were actually completed one month behind schedule, which in the grand scheme of things was good for a fairly large project such as this. They had recruited most staff and at the rates they were paying, were reasonably happy. They closed down the office but continued to live away from the complex as they called it, in their flat, their escape for now. The general ideology adopted across the complex was that men and women were required to look good and sound intelligent no matter what the accent. First, they vetted application forms which included full length and head and shoulder photographs which excluded sixty percent immediately, and then they were interviewed by Toby for general work ethic and ability to communicate. This was everybody, bar staff, DJs, security staff, waiters, although this rigorous process was somewhat relaxed for cleaners and behind the scenes staff where focus was removed from the general meet and greet. Final interviews for staff in the complex basement club called 'Luxury' were dealt with exclusively by Yevana; she had that ruthless but sensual instinct that understood the human requirement for night time entertainment. It needed to be classy, approachable but just frustratingly untouchable for it to be the class establishment that they were aiming for. The episode in the toilets with the Polish waitress at the top end competition was not what was wanted in their clubs and why she tested that particular establishment which was generally seen as top end in the area. Last of all Yevana talked with the waiters and waitresses one by one where she would ensure they had what it took to entice and encourage the return of new customers. They were each given a task to test their sensitivities. They were asked to walk into the private lounge, approach Yevana and ask what drink she required, deliver it, then as Yevana stood up they were to lean forward smell her exquisite perfume around the neck line, without touching her, then drop to their knees and gently remove a drop of red wine from her bare stomach – she was wearing a tight lamb's wool jumper crop top that nestled tight but perfect on her shoulders and breasts – without touching her in any other way. Bizarre, perhaps, but it was about 'almost but not quite'. They had to make the customer feel like they could be bought although the reality was they couldn't, but they would come back to try again. It was equally important that this was both male and female. At the end of the final interviews day, Yevana was crazy. She had set up a day of interviews with some of the most enchanting and gorgeous people who, either recruited or rejected, had driven her senses wild. That night she walked back to the flat which was only a mile away and in the pouring rain to allow her nerves to settle or she would have driven herself stark raving mad. What she did know was that she had recruited some amazing staff from far and wide. There were men and women from as far afield as New York, Argentina, Russia and Germany. The UK was pretty much represented in its entirety which overall gave the very first Y&T Entertainment.Inc complex a very cosmopolitan ingredient. It was youthful but had a good mix of more senior folk who also fitted the bill and give it that sense of authority on all floors in support of the owners who couldn't be everywhere all the time.

Yevana was soaking wet in both senses on her return home but any sensual frustration would have to wait for later. They discussed the outcome of the day's activities back in the flat on Toby's return as he had stayed away from the final interviews for club staff; although he was intrigued to know what Yevana could be like with her very exacting manner. It turned out that one black girl called Mobola Yemba had driven her wild. 'I must admit Toby I have found an absolute gem in this girl Mobola who you initially interviewed and recommended for the club interviews and you were spot on darling. She is so tall, beautiful, athletic, long limbed with perfect breasts and a soft sensual manner that made a significant impression on me.' Yevana sighed.

'If you feel slightly frustrated or shall we say, under done,' Toby laughed, 'then you only have yourself to blame. It serves you right, you set this final interview technique up after all,' he chortled as he watched Yevana twitch sipping her G&T.

That night Toby had to pass the same test! The difference was he tied her up, set his alarm and went to bed, made her wait another two hours then got up and satisfied her with some brutal sex. The love bite on her stomach was the start point that was another slight difference with the test!

Everything was in place. Grand opening day came on the sixth of November, which gave them enough time to test and settle into routines in the complex before the Christmas period when they hoped to maximise the potential this type of establishment could expect. The flyers and internet sites had been set up in advance and early indications were good as bookings were already high. The atmosphere was electric from as early as five a.m. when Yevana, Toby and others arrived and added the final touches to the complex. In fact, the last touches of paint to be applied were only just drying but luckily these were not in prominent places. The doors would open to customers with an official opening due at one p.m. This allowed for some atmosphere in the building and set the tone for business as usual and open all hours. At midday Toby grabbed Yevana by the hand and in that less formal mode they had a walk round the whole site. The car park on the roadside level was not large but would hold enough cars to satisfy their needs they believed. They walked around the front and up a flight of stone steps and in through the racing green wooden doors at the entrance porch which had that Victorian feel especially with its grand glass panels and solid brass furniture.

'Do you know Toby,' Yevana commented, 'every place we ever own will be bigger and better than this, I want more dramatic copies of this entrance as it is magnificent by scale; I love it.' Toby looked her in the eye, smiling and saluted.

'Yes, sir,' he replied.

She smiled too and tugged at his arm as they moved into the foyer. They were met by the reception manager who gave them a brief to confirm that she was happy and that all staff were briefed and content with the mission. The reception area was modestly sized but no expense, relatively speaking, had been spared on the design and décor on view. It had a classy but classical feel and was light and airy with plenty of lounge suites for customers if they wanted to wait there for any reason. The paintings were by local artists making their name and depicted humans in a variety of artistic forms, some of which needed imagination. For good measure, there were also landscapes of the west coast of Scotland which was a favourite weekend destination for Toby and friends from time to time. The mountainous features, weather and life were a potent backdrop to adventure for him. Yevana didn't quite get it but understood his animalistic need that could not totally be exhausted in the bedroom, no matter how hard she would try she thought to herself with a deep and sadistic smile. The general feeling though was one of opulence and style on entering this now fine establishment and one where it was supposed to encourage you to linger and definitely return again and again. They carried on into the restaurant where they were met by a very enthusiastic French chef of middle age who believed he was god's gift to woman kind. Yevana had plans for him one day but that would wait.

'Jean how are things in the kitchen?' she asked him.

'Very fine, Madame Yevana, you know you must not ask that' he laughed albeit nervously.

'I will and you must know that Jean as you also know that I will not accept second class service and so I want you to have the best and deliver the best. Do we understand each other?'

'Mais Oui' he replied. Toby had moved on because everything looked fine and he didn't see the point in pushing it as Yevana did. However, she was making the point that they were paying well and she wanted every ounce. From there they walked down a short set of steps into the gym and pool area which were immaculate as were the staff. The chief fitness instructor was a six foot six-inch-tall athlete and had all the things in all the right places which even the most red-blooded male could not miss and the women certainly didn't. Tim was going to keep a lot of very frustrated housewives on the end of their nerves as he worked his magic. They had also managed to build in a small but adequate beauty salon which complemented the other facilities well and was essential in this type of complex. The young women working here were the right type to listen and care for their fee-paying customers.

Lastly, they headed for the exclusive and relatively expensive to join Luxury Cub, where everything was in order for its first run out for people to view and dine that afternoon but mainly in preparation for the full on-night activity later. There had already been keen advanced membership interest which showed their advertising campaign had worked. The club had a lot of natural light from large roof windows at a side angle in this lower area for daytime use, where the red decor gave the place a really warm feel. The private suites were extremely comfortable and there were plenty scattered around the club with dynamic modern artistic décor complemented with small sofas, soft chairs, stools and tables. Very explicate artwork hung on the walls and from the ceiling designed to encourage the hedonistic theme which Yevana and Toby hoped would move customers to pay good money for the private privileges they would enjoy. This area had a bar, dance area with pole and several booths open to all fee-paying members of this club. The staff here were dressed in the appropriate minimalist fashion, girls in emerald short skirts and crop tops and boys in same-coloured shorts and tennis style shirts. Toby looked around and knew that Yevana had hit the spot here as they all looked magnificent. Keeping the hand of the male and female customer off their staff would be a challenge. The exclusive VIP club area was also ready and staff talked the owners through the preparation and routines, all too good effect. Mobola, the young black girl, was there looking magnificent, in the complex VIP area red hot pants and black high heels outfit, but Yevana avoided today; it would be inevitable she thought, but it would wait. Toby gave the staff the thumbs up then turned around and led the way back upstairs; they were ready.

The first customers came in that day in a fairly brisk fashion proving that their early canvassing and media work had gone well. Toby managed to get a local footballer from Manchester called Ted Daxter to open the Luxury Club even though there was risk attached as he had a reputation for being late. Toby knew he also had a reputation for the high life and always had gorgeous chicks on his arm so he got him on board as the ideal man to set the scene and so took that risk. The local press turned up for the opening ceremony and ribbon cutting, taking a tour of the complex. One ventured to ask Yevana, 'Why do you think this will survive when other five-star establishments have failed?'

'Because they didn't have me on the staff, darling and you will find out why, when and if you use the facilities. Next question?' she dismissively carried on. Toby looked across at the journo and couldn't make out whether he was angry at his putdown or that he was worried that Yevana had him down on a black list already. Yevana was dynamite and they were finding out why.

Business was brisk, the bar and restaurant were busy at reduced rates for opening day and all staff seemed to be working well and very hard. Some of their new acquaintances were there including Bernard, their accountant, bank manager Ferry Barnes, along with Jonas Ramand, who was a local security company owner who had his ear to the ground; useful! If anybody wanted to know anything about security in Manchester Jonas was tied up in it somehow, except Strangeways Prison of course, although many of his employees had passed through their gates! Also, there were a few C and D list celebrities that always turned up at these events, strutting their stuff in various stages of undress. Their friend and investor Bob Ray arrived to look at his investment and was impressed to say the least. 'Hi guys, you have entered a tough, tough market but if anybody could crack it you two can,' he declared.

'Correct,' Toby replied, 'but hold your breath Bob old boy, this is just the beginning and we will be back for more.'

Bob coughed into his drink, looked up, smiled and said, 'Let's get started first shall we before we get ahead of ourselves Toby...old boy.' They both burst out laughing.

Yevana was dressed in a stunning yellow suit by the Spanish fashion house Volta, whose designer was the owner Emelsa Volta, her favourite designer. It was a tight-fitting top without a blouse and a twelve-inch skirt (pleated) and stacked black heels to dazzle. Some black sheer tights complemented the devastating look. Toby was proud of her and what they had achieved in such a short period especially considering their start point was from nothing. He looked on with pride as she swept through the rooms of guests and VIPs making them all feel welcome and important. He did find the very obvious personal attention she was receiving from some male guests hilarious as some did not get the message easily, that she wasn't personally interested, just professionally!

The evening was a roaring success with taxis arriving and departing throughout from which they counted over one thousand attendees throughout the day. Entry to the Luxury Club lounge cost one hundred pounds and a couple of exclusive parties retreated into that area during the evening. Toby spent some time in there initially and thought they had generated the right atmosphere from the reactions he was getting and the money that was being spent. The customers loved the standard of service from the waiters and waitresses and there were no problems for the security staff throughout the day. Yevana did spend some time during the evening in the VIP club where she spent quite a lot of time with Mobola and a couple of the other waitresses to gain some hands-on experience the customers were enjoying. Yevana had recently confided in Toby that as much as she loved him she was missing her relationship with Caren, particularly some parts of it, so she knew if she needed this then pastures new were required. That night Yevana slipped Mobola her business card, put a line through the details and wrote her private mobile number on it. 'Darling, give me a call when you are off duty and we will take a coffee together if you have some spare time; it would be good to get to know each other' Yevana ventured.

'Yes' said Mobola, 'I would love to spend some time with you Ms Narvik, I know you were a good athlete so we have much to discuss.' The blossoming sportswoman turned away in an almost dismissive manner to carry on working. Yevana looked at her walk away and her excitement grew!

Toby knew that Yevana had needs, which was cool with him as their love was strong and business was the vital part of what they were about too, but they were both sexually experimental; they played life in the fast lane and nothing was in or out. Simple. However, there was a rule: no secrets. This had been an early discussion to stop the intrusion of deceit and anger that would seep into their plan for sure if they allowed it to. They argued, sometimes badly with Toby finding himself as the peacemaker most often; it was easier as he didn't like the silences or need the hassle.

Later on, in this particular evening with excitement running especially high as one would expect on such an occasion, Yevana stayed on until closing hosting anyone and everyone who wanted her time and there were many as they wanted to meet this woman who was dressed to kill and please. So, when the club closed at five a.m. the staff cleared up in the entertainment areas and left and then Toby disappeared to a vacant room for a sleep once reception was happy that everybody had left who hadn't booked a bedroom. Yevana eventually ventured down to the VIP club to catch Mobola before she went home and luckily she caught her leaving with a friend. They were immersed in conversation and Yevana had second thoughts, so she was really impressed when Mobola immediately decided to stay behind.

'Hi, Mobola, I thought we might just have that chat now if you like? she asked. Mobola looked at Katie her colleague and said, 'Kate, sorry but I will just hang on here for a while. I will meet you as planned tomorrow lunchtime for a bite to eat before we come back to work.' 'Okay, Moby, I'll see you then, bye.' Katie waved and swaggered out of the rear exit of the complex.

'Where did we finish off earlier?' Yevana ventured before taking a seat at the VIP bar. 'I can't remember,' Mobola said, 'it's been the most fantastically busy evening but if I remember rightly you mentioned getting a coffee sometime.' 'Well,' replied Yevana, 'I would like a G&T now instead if you don't mind.'

'Of course,' Mobola came back, 'it's your show isn't it?' Mobola walked slowly over to the bar and poured them both a drink. 'Okay if I have one?'

'Of course, darling. Please help yourself, we are closed,' Yevana smirked mischievously.

Mobola replied, 'Thank you, I will, that is kind of you.'

Yevana got up and walked over to the music station and selected a seductive Barry White track then went over into a dark corner of the still dimmed lounge area and waited for Mobola to look up, notice her movement then start to walk over to her. Mobola walked like a world class model on a catwalk as she balanced the two drinks in her hands and rejoined Yevana on a sofa. First of all, though she bent forward and placed the drinks in front of her new boss. Yevana thought Mobola smelled of a slightly strange but intoxicating fragrance as she motioned for her to join her on the sofa. 'What is that perfume you're wearing tonight Mobola?'

'It is a fragrance my mother sends me which she gets from a relative in the Caribbean and one that I feel very comfortable with. Do you want a drop?' she asked.

'Yes, of course.'

Mobola went back to her handbag and brought the little tube back with her. She gently took off the screw top of a small homemade jar and let a small drop fall onto her index finger. She said, 'Drop your head to one side,' and then very gently rubbed the small drop onto the side of Yevana's neck and massaged it in before moving on to her nose and very gently rubbing a little extra onto the outside edge of her nostrils. 'There, what do you think? Strong isn't it?' Mobola asked.

Yevana sniffed the aroma and rolled her eyes into the top of her head enjoying the moment and wanting more. Sensing this enjoyment Mobola passed the bottle under Yevana's nose and then replaced the cap.

Yevana stood up and took off her yellow jacket leaving just her bra showing. Looking down at Mobola on the sofa, she ordered her to kiss her stomach. 'Get on your knees and kiss me, darling.'

Mobola looked into her eyes and slowly stood keeping the gaze fixed, then placed her lands on each of Yevana's shoulders and gently slid them down her arms as she lowered herself until her knees were on the ground and her mouth was just above Yevana's waistline. She breathed heavily onto Yevana's skin and licked her belly once, planted a red lipstick kiss mark then stood up and gave Yevana her card and said, 'If you want more of that call me.' Her mobile number and a lipstick kiss were all that was on it. Mobola turned, picked up her bag and didn't look back. Yevana's knees buckled momentarily as the shock of immediate withdrawal was not anticipated; however, she soon composed herself and watched this gorgeous creature walk out in her striking heels and hot pants.

Yevana quickly got herself together and went to find Toby who was already asleep upstairs in a VIP suite that was vacant that first night. She woke him up and explained what had happened and he looked at her and said, 'Tough, it's late we have a big day again tomorrow and I want to be fresh. Also, you should leave the staff alone, it's not good to start playing with fire like that. Anyway, I'm going back to sleep, it's been a famous day for us. Good night.' He stretched up and gave her a kiss and slipped straight off to sleep.

Yevana was desperate though, her mind was racing and she could smell nothing but the fragrance under her nose or think about nothing except her rejection by Mobola, all of which was driving her insane. What could she do? This wasn't like her but little did she know this twenty-three-year old black girl was made of steel and was happy with her bi-sexuality and had numerous suitors. It might be five p.m. by now but Yevana was in one of those moods where the adrenaline wouldn't subside, and especially after the first night success. She grabbed her phone and the card and soon Mobola had picked up her phone 'Yes?' Mobola answered.

'I am desperate' Yevana said but at the same time she told herself that this really wasn't Yevana speaking.

'Where are you?' Mobola replied thinking on her feet for a moment. Did she want this? She was a top athlete just earning some extra cash and this woman was her boss and what about "don't mix business with pleasure." What the hell, she was an extremely highly sexed female and she fancied her boss something rotten!

'I am at the complex,' replied Yevana.

'Okay,' said Mobola in a husky very late at night tone, 'I am at my flat across the city, get a taxi! I'll see you when you get here.' Yevana put the phone down then ordered the taxi before applying some lipstick. She bent over and kissed Toby then departed. Toby half listened and fell asleep; he was knackered and tomorrow would be sorting problems and kickstarting the business which hopefully was the start of something enduring and big. In any case he didn't have the nocturnal endurance of Yevana; once more, he was glad!

Mobola had a basic flat in a loft at the top of an old canal wharf. It was ordered and sparsely populated with furniture and possessions all acquired from second hand shops but showed an artistic hand on first viewing. The most striking item on show was actually above the mantelpiece where a bright pink bikini was framed. It turns out it was once owned by a Russian Olympic pole vault champion she had encountered, who had subsequently signed them with a message 'Mobola, darling.' Nobody needed to know more as far as Mobola was concerned.

Yevana sat in the taxi on a perfectly clear night thinking about their day, their future and then what coming over at five a.m. to meet a virtual stranger and worse still, an employee, outside of her relationship with Toby, really meant to her. She didn't know of course as it was all a matter of instinct for Yevana that should not be disrupted by anything; it was who she was, for better or for worse. The street lights shone through the car window onto her lap almost highlighting the fact she was there, a figure travelling in a mysterious world of unknown excitement and mystery, which was starting to have its effect even before she set eyes on the glorious Mobola. There were still revellers of the night bouncing off the city infrastructure finding their way home in that delirious world of social drugs. The taxi came to a halt outside the wharf and she placed the fare in the tray between her and the driver who commented, 'it must have been a long night, lady.'

'It hasn't finished yet but I am looking forward to the last bit,' she replied smiling as she stepped out.

'Enjoy' he shouted back. Yevana slammed the door a little hard and walked across the pavement past a drunk lying comatose against a wall, with his belongings and a brown bag with the contents of a bottle of something alcoholic and strong having leaked out. She looked down and thought to herself 'What could I do to change this guy's life?' The answer was probably very little, and on second glance she saw the delicate hands of a woman. 'My god' she sounded under breath, 'what must your life have been like to get to this?'

Yevana walked to the door, pressed a buzzer for flat ten and on reply pulled a double door open and started up a draughty set of stairs, typical of this sort of basic restructured wharf. The stairs were metal and quite noisy and one could see up the four-floor stairwell. She pulled herself up by the railings until she reached the fourth-floor landing. In front of her was flat ten. Outside was a nameplate with Ms M Yemba neatly written for visitors. Yevana stood in front of the door and got her breath back from the walk up the steep staircase and thought for a moment. 'Do I want this? Can I walk now and what's the point?' She pressed the doorbell without thinking any more, as time for thinking had elapsed; she was here and wanted to be.

Yevana was stood in absolute silence for over a minute, which seemed like forever, when the door opened wide and there stood in the doorway was an absolute goddess of true human perfection as Mobola ushered her in.

They were roughly the same size so Mobola had quickly busied herself and had everything planned to suit the occasion. She left her short waitress uniform on and had refreshed herself with fragrances and lipstick but replacing hot pants with a very short skirt.

Mobola had heard the bell and had looked through the peephole taking her time, keeping her guest waiting in anticipation whilst noticing that like her she had not changed since they were in the complex together and had not brought a coat. She slid the catch and let Yevana in not saying anything but let her take in the room fragrances, aromatic candles and the S&M video on the TV running in the background. All of this had an immediate effect on the senses and Yevana walked into the centre of the room and stood watching the muscled black female penetrating the bound, beautiful white more fragile looking female on all fours. Mobola spoke first. 'I thought you wouldn't come'.

Yevana replied, 'I thought about it but I wanted to, in fact I won't lie, I needed to!' 'Okay, take your clothes off Ms Narvik and lay them on the table in front of the TV.' At the same time Mobola took all her clothes off including her two-inch looped silver earrings. 'Take your earrings off also Ms Narvik.' Once this was done Mobola told Yevana to dress in her clothes and simultaneously she did the same getting into Yevana's, including her earrings. Yevana looked stunning in her red waitress outfit. Before Yevana had arrived she had purposely replaced her tights with stockings and suspenders for easier access later. Mobola also looked a million dollars in Yevana's yellow Volta suit which she had designs on now herself; it looked too good to give back, she thought! Yevana was falling in lust in a massive way with this woman. This was different from Caren though as that was a meeting of minds and she had been totally in control, whereas this was not related to business minds but certainly sexual minds and she did not feel totally in control which she found both worrying and exciting, mainly the latter.

'Your clothes are fantastic, Ms Narvik. I will tell you what is going to happen. I am going to keep this suit as it fits so well and you are going to leave in my work clothes but as I require them tonight you will replace them in my staff locker before I turn up for work; cleaned. Do you understand?'

'Yes,' Yevana stuttered.

'I am going to tie you up and pleasure you, then you will leave in my clothes and heels and return to the complex by taxi, which you will pay for.'

Mobola walked over to Yevana and carefully placed her over one end of the coffee table in front of the TV then freed her breasts from the red top which allowed them to hang down like ripe pears over the edge then subsequently her hands and ankles were tied by rope across the room; she was fixed. Yevana looked up at the TV and then the bikini wandering what the relationship might be between them. She certainly couldn't move and felt quite uncomfortable. Listening above the noise of the general grunting on the TV she could make out Mobola making some noises in the kitchen for a while before reappearing with a small instrument which she placed on the floor in front of her. She then took her knickers, now being worn by Yevana and stuffed them in Yevana's mouth before applying an iced spray onto Yevana's nipples one at a time and then piercing them and placing Mobola's two-inch loop earrings into the new holes. Yevana couldn't believe this was happening as she was tied and spreadeagled in a room she had never been in before with somebody she really didn't know and she couldn't stop what was happening now even if she tried; but she loved it! Mobola then walked around behind Yevana and said, 'Ms Narvik that makes you my bitch, if I tell you to wear these earrings at any time, do so. Do you understand?' Ms Narvik nodded. Without further ado, Yevana was then mounted, pleasured whilst watching the S&M video that Mobola seemed to be fixed on and eventually released. There was a large mirror opposite that was set up by Mobola so that Ms Narvik could also watch herself being pleasured by her waitress, in her own smart suit that had now been confiscated with two loop earrings dangling from her breasts: horny indeed. Eventually, Yevana was allowed to dress in the black heels, red top and skirt but nothing else. Mobola picked up their underwear and walked off into her bedroom with it. Yevana looked back then opened the door and quietly closed it again walking down the echoing four flight stairwell and out to the kerbside where she called a taxi whilst feeling well and truly abused but satisfied. Yevana had not touched Mobola once! At the complex she dressed but did not shower as she wanted to smell her mistress all day, then walked straight into work; it was daytime, time to work again.

Problem – Recession

The hotel was running well and business was good. The luxury VIP club was doing very well and was popular with A, B and C list celebrities. The point was that if you could afford it, adhere to the dress code and behave in an acceptable manner you were invited to remain a member. Many fell by the wayside for a variety of reasons and as it became increasingly popular some begged to have their membership reinstated or be invited in on special invitation-only events. Toby and Yevana were careful to play a balancing act to keep expectation of attendance for most achievable. They could be cruel though and were known to invite certain individuals without their high profile partners if they felt like they had been let down. There were rates for periodical membership or more expensive rates for daily entry that applied across all areas of the complex. Toby and Yevana were only frustrated by the general lack of opulence that they were able to bring compared with their ambitions. It wasn't that the complex wasn't nice, it was but they wanted better. In the future they wanted to increase capacity and grandeur in all areas, but not yet. They had to walk before running but their ambition was top end and sloppy seconds were not on the agenda. Bernard Tomas kept them on a very sure footing regarding tax and the ever-increasing profit which was quickly utilised for improvements where it would make a significant difference. Toby was also instructing architects to draw up the requirements of their next city complex. Although this was a little way down the line, the initial success here allowed them to at least make plans for the future which could be adapted for any suitable projects in other locations.

Competitors in Manchester had made a few noises and there had been word that a local player in the adult entertainment market was watching closely in case they trod on his toes in terms of what was being delivered in the private areas of the complex. Toby took that as a warning from the sex trade, of which he and Yevana had no intention of being seduced into. This was a high-end quality adult entertainment complex that should heighten the senses for what happened outside of this establishment. Anyone who even thought of plying the sex trade was removed by security immediately without question. There was a level of customer confidence which people became comfortable with and they got this at Y&T.

The staff stayed particularly loyal as they were paid at relatively good local rates and there was strong and consistent leadership throughout, which was important to both Yevana and Toby. He was very popular in all areas especially in the club areas, where he was regularly hit on by the female population who offered him the world on a regular basis. He enjoyed this but never allowed this to drop his focus on the delivery and they got to understand this albeit reluctantly. It didn't stop them trying though which was why he often found knickers with messages on them in his jacket pockets planted there by very devious women often staying overnight with their girlfriends on well organised hen style parties. He and Yevana used to laugh at these ploys to get him in the sack, and then use them! In the same vein Yevana obviously had to be as accessible as the business would allow with both men and women who all found her extremely attractive, but too often found that those who had had enough alcoholic drinks would try it on with her, some becoming quite aggressive. After about a month they had both had proposals of marriage from both sexes, all denied of course. Yevana was always polite but dismissive and had the worse for wear ushered out of the complex at the earliest opportunity. Over time this became common knowledge to regulars and people were warned off if they aspired to have access in the future. Of great importance to them, Toby and Yevana never acted as a couple in Y&T; it was their business policy and it worked.

Mobola continued to work in the Luxury Club VIP area but you would never have known if there had been or was a relationship with Yevana. After the first episode in her wharf flat they didn't see each other out of work for three months and that was at another bar in town on a night off from the complex. Mobola was with a bunch of girls from her athletics club and to Yevana's amazement was wearing her yellow Volta suit. She looked unbelievable in six-inch bright blue heels and a new cropped haircut. Their eyes met and they ignored each other by turning away as if in denial. Yevana had waited for a call but had not received one, which infuriated her as she couldn't believe that this woman was being allowed to frustrate her. Surely it should be the opposite as she was the boss. This was frustrating but she understood there was a very strict game being played here. The next occasion she saw her out of work she was being collected from outside the Manchester complex by a girlfriend and that was a real test with which Yevana struggled. This was made more acute as the friend was at least ten years older than Mobola and seemed wealthy if her clothes and the Bentley car she was being chauffeured in were anything to go by. Mobola was now also the top female 400m track athlete in the British Isles, so her work in the complex was strictly part time which had been expected by the management. Her profile increased with her success and she was out of the United Kingdom for long periods racing and training with the British team. On this occasion Mobola and her friend smiled and departed which made Yevana jealous and she refused to sleep with Toby that night which she couldn't explain. Instead, she slept on a sofa.

Toby had other things on his mind as the drawings had been delivered from the architects as planned for their next property purchase, hopefully in London. Opulence would be the word and five-star was the grade. The cost would be hundreds of thousands, maybe millions of pounds more than Manchester to refurbish the building once found. Their business case was going to need to be strong and backers' wealthy if this dream was to become reality. One spring morning they were sat in the club drinking americanos before opening, with the plans laid out on a coffee table discussing the detail and the viability.

'Darling, it looks magnificent, doesn't it? We are going to do this I know it. It is not even a doubt in my mind because everything we have planned and worked for here has happened and in some style' Yevana commented.

'I know,' replied Toby 'and some, but it is absolutely essential that we continue to get it right in Manchester and prove that we are not an overnight success but a sustainable one that people feel is a safe investment.'

'We will,' said Yevana, picking up her cup of black coffee and walking off.

It wasn't long before they had the loft converted in the complex to allow them to live on site and let the original rental go. It had been really useful but had fulfilled its purpose and was no longer needed as their love pad.

After nearly a year they had had some various bits of luck, good and bad but mainly bad. First, the dining room and entrance hall were gutted by an electrical fire after closing one morning, which turned out well, eventually, as nobody was hurt and the refurbishment allowed for a significant upgrade, with full compensation for loss of revenue, although they kept as much of the complex open as they could during this period. If that turned out to be good luck then what followed was certainly another dose of bad luck as a global recession hit and it hit Manchester and the whole of Britain hard. People weren't travelling, businesses were going bust and suppliers couldn't take credit. Toby and Yevana were struggling. As things got tighter, staff were laid off and profit crashed. These guys were fighters though and did shifts of various jobs to fill gaps during absences for illness or even maternity leave. Their relationship was struggling, too. They were living on top of one another; and not socialising and thinking their dreams were about to dissolve around them, made it all seem much worse. Hotels and similar complexes to theirs were suffering equally and many had succumbed to a financial meltdown. What they didn't want to do was ask for more money; they wouldn't get it from a bank under these circumstances that was for sure. So, for now they would march on and ride it out.

Worse still for Yevana, she was missing a female relationship which she had not come across since moving to Manchester. She hadn't met anybody that flicked her switch other than Mobola and that flickered very dimly. Then one night out of the blue her mobile rang and it was Mobola saying she was at a loose end as her girlfriend was away on business and she didn't have a boyfriend at the moment and without drawing breath she told Yevana, 'Seven-thirty at Rubens and be in a skirt, heels and tight-fitting top wearing the earrings.'

Mobola smiled to herself then called off and put the phone down after which she called her lover who was on business in Switzerland with her husband then another call to a boyfriend and passed on a request. How complicated she thought, but on the other hand, how exciting. Mobola dressed and walked out of her flat and into the next available taxi. When she arrived outside the pre-arranged restaurant she stood looking in through the glass windows and soon spotted Yevana who had arrived earlier as planned. Mobola sighed as she set her eyes on this 'beautiful creature' and then out loud whispered, 'I am coming for you, darling.' She walked in and looking around to see who was watching, which was everybody, she approached Yevana from the rear and bent down and lifted Yevana's hair and kissed her right ear before sitting on the stool next to her. You could sense the atmospherics fizz in the air. They had a good evening eating and drinking whilst chatting about anything and everything; Yevana loved it. She had felt run down lately with everything that was happening and her relationship with Toby had felt strained especially since the move from the rented flat, which they both acknowledged had been a mistake. She also had a suspicion that Toby was getting close to one of the architects who had been working on their projects, called Christina Maxtor. This was all rather upsetting but she hoped they would be able to sort it out. After midnight Mobola ordered a taxi and took them back to her flat where, to Yevana's surprise, a friend of Mobola's, another African male, well built, with a huge meaningful smile on his face, awaited. Mobola unlocked her door at the wharf, led Yevana inside then shut, locked and bolted the door. Yevana thought this was crossing boundaries as she was just so hoping for a night with Mobola, but she was the bitch and did as she was told for over seven hours. It was degrading, powerful, liberating and the earrings remained in place throughout. When they were finished with her she was ushered out through the door of the flat and pushed out with her clothes following, thrown out after her. They were not in good order and she looked a mess. She quickly changed, ran outside for a taxi, drove to the complex then ran upstairs, showered and went to bed as it was still five a.m. on her day off. Ridiculous, but she would want more and that was the point; she needed more. She would not be able to wait that long again and the intensity was what she enjoyed. When she looked in the mirror on her back was written 'I love you (M)' written in red lipstick – it was quite hard to remove and even harder to explain, or was it?

Toby wasn't in as he had been out celebrating a birthday of a good friend and at that party was Christina Maxtor. They had good reason over a number of months to meet because of work but just lately there had been more and more social gatherings with mutual friends. This particular night they had eaten five-star, then went to a notorious club in town aptly named the 'Riot'. It was a place that had been raided by the police from the vice squad on several occasions and usually people were arrested for handling drugs, being under age or plying the sex trade. This was a dark and dingy establishment but of an evening it felt good and people from all walks of life liked it. Christina was a fun-loving woman in her late twenties currently single having finished with a boyfriend of three years. She and Toby hit it off from the start and he admired her intelligence and mild-mannered feminine attitude. Christine had blonde hair and was strikingly tall and lean; how Toby liked his women to have slender hips, decent breasts and a pert bum. Delicious, as he called her often. He was tempted. They both knew he was spoken for and it was not her style to encroach and she was also put off by what she saw as a potential viper in Yevana; it was a woman's intuition. Toby had sensed this, so he was planning to take his opportunity on this particular evening because although he loved Yevana he was feeling something for Christina and he felt his relationship needed some 'fresh air' as he put it to Christina. However, he noted that he needed to be careful remembering what happened to the university lecturer back in Durham. Riot was in normal Friday mode with the glorious array of characters bouncing off the walls. They had had quite a few drinks and towards two a.m. Toby pulled Christina away into one dark corner of the Riot's deepest recesses. He thought to himself. This is either going to make it or break it, he wasn't sure, but what the heck, why not? He could hardly see Christina as he pressed her against a wall before leaning into her neck and whispering in her ear 'satisfy me'. He could hear a sharp intake of breath, a momentary pause, and then suddenly she dropped down, unzipped him and in that dark secluded spot, did so. She stood up, wiped her lips and he leaned back in. He clutched her waist and gave her a love bite that nobody could miss, then turned and went back to their friends completing the perfect end to a perfect evening. When he arrived back at the Y & T complex he crashed into bed and looked at Yevana who was half out of the quilt and read on her back, 'I love you (M)'. He fell asleep.

Caren Lords

Caren had really struggled after the shocking exit of her beloved Yevana. She had honestly thought that they had a future together. The nature of the breakup was hard to take, as Caren never understood why it had to be so sexual and callous. That night she had chased the car, naked, down the road in the pouring rain until it was out of sight. Slumped in the road soaking wet she eventually gathered her strength and walked back past twitching curtains to her modest home and didn't leave it for seven days where she was constantly trying to get in touch with Yevana, message after message. None were ever returned and soon the number was showing 'no longer recognised.' Having gone around to her home several times to no avail, she found Yevana had left her current flat and seemed to have vanished. As the months passed by Caren didn't just get rid of Yevana's possessions, she destroyed them with some venom, that was, except a blanket they used to throw over themselves after making out downstairs in the lounge. This was bought on holiday in Tangier and was a memory Caren would not be parted from; she just couldn't as much as it hurt her too keep it. Photos, clothes, sex aids – all gone!

    Caren started to move on and she dabbled with both men and women. Although feeling very confused and emotional, getting out meeting people and conversing fully once again inspired here to regain the passion she felt she had lost. She was in demand and that felt good. Her first relationship was with Steven, a local hotel manager in his mid-twenties. Steven was a friendly, good-looking man who ticked a lot of boxes for Caren. He was fit with a dark complexion, very romantic and safe but ultimately quite ordinary although he wouldn't have recognised that description, she thought. Indeed, he was almost too good to be true. In Caren's eyes he lacked the edge that Yevana had: the unknown. Caren thought to herself 'but surely I hate the unknown after what happened with Yevana.' The truth was she didn't, in fact she was energised by risk and the ability to be shocked. She had always known Yevana was going to move on but she refused to believe it would happen. It had ruined her life for a while but the past was the past and she knew she had to look forward.

Being with Steven and firmly in control of the relationship started to irritate her and as much as she hated feeling this way it nagged at her. Steven knew of Yevana from their early days together but knew never to mention her name. Caren's obsession continued. She would invariably ride Steven even though he tried otherwise but he would never dare argue particularly after they had an argument in the first few weeks of the relationship. Frustrated by his lack of progress to dominate more of their sexual liaisons he tried to throw Caren onto her back in the back of his car one Saturday evening. Caren had fought him off and punched him in the face before riding him in an aggressive and violent protest. Steven shouted out 'sorry, darling' as she charged out of the car, but all Caren replied was 'don't do that again without my permission.' That was it, he felt humiliated and had a black eye but felt powerless to do anything under the circumstances. She would only think of Yevana when she was having sex. On another occasion he had protested and Caren had walked out and broken contact as a punishment. The next time he saw Caren she was at a bar in the city with another guy; he was devastated. The guy had his hands all over her but they did leave separately. He tried all ways to get her attention again but she did not return any calls and on this particular night she would not acknowledge his existence and so he knew he dare not approach her.

Worse was to come as two days later Steven was out with friends in a top restaurant when in walked Caren with a young blonde and he knew better than to ask what she was doing or even acknowledge her. Once again he knew Caren well enough not to even think of making an approach and surely the girl must be a work colleague. He didn't recognise her though and he had met most of her friends, which he did find a bit strange particularly as Caren seemed to be very attentive with the blonde. The situation was disturbing especially as his friends looked straight over to them, even the girls, and John, his best mate, said, 'That looks very much like that girl I saw you with a few weeks back.' 'No mate, you are mistaken,' replied Steven, the colour of his cheeks turning bright red. The young blonde was dressed in very little and seemed awestruck by her companion. Caren looked like dynamite as she had planned when she arranged to eat locally in a favourite restaurant, where she guessed Steven would be with his friends. Boots, dress and earrings, and oh yes, bright lipstick, that was it; no more no less. More worrying for Steven as he filled with jealousy, was the killer glint in her eyes. She was on it! He knew it!

About two weeks later Caren answered one of Steven's text messages and invited him for dinner. She was in an evil mood and needed to send the permanent 'end message.' This was the beginning of the end of this relationship. She didn't need to go down this road but something inside her wanted to grab the opportunity and get a kick out of it. Was she as bad as Yevana or did she want to be like her? She couldn't answer that which was more worrying, she thought. Caren humiliated him again that night as she called out Yevana's name in the bedroom whilst they made love and thought only of the twenty-year-old straight, blonde girl she had seduced in the night club after leaving the restaurant two weeks previously! Steven was just happy to be back and could put up with anything from Caren as long as they were together. He had never taken her to see his parents though; he didn't trust her, and although he wasn't sure what that meant he just wouldn't do it and he knew she wouldn't have gone with him in any case; she wasn't doing the visit mums and dads thing!

In fact, Caren had already embarked on a new relationship of blonde delirium. Rosie was delicious, carefree and besotted with Caren. She attended the local college studying art and design and was enjoying her first relationship with a woman which she found exhilarating. She was beautiful with bright sparkling wide eyes and delicious full lips and had been curious about her sexuality for some time. She wore casual clothing most of the time in line with general college day wear but had the knack of looking drop dead gorgeous whatever she wore at night. All the boys and men including lecturers fancied the pants off her but she was a class act and studied hard.

On one particular evening in town Caren was enjoying time with Rosie and as they sat down in a popular local pub and regular haunt of Steven's, she pointed him out.

'That's my ex, baby. Unfortunately for him he doesn't know it yet. Nice boy but no balls.'

Rosie took this as a sign of better things ahead and looked into her eyes and all Caren could see was love and hence Rosie just commented, 'God, I love you, Caren.' That night Caren treated Rosie to her first night of gentle bondage in her student digs. It wasn't wild; it was meant to put Rosie under her control, which it did.

Soon Steven twigged that there was somebody else on the scene and when he found out it was Rosie he was devastated. Although he knew them to be good friends who went to the gym, eat out, sometimes with others, and shopped together as all good friends do, he was becoming suspicious about the number of times she cancelled a date with him only to find out Caren was going out with Rosie; it just didn't seem right. If he complained then he was given the silent treatment until he sent several messages of apologies. It was degrading but he was hooked. He said nothing about Rosie as that would be 'curtains' and just hoped it would end naturally; it didn't, it was more dramatic than that. The end came when Caren took Steven out for a meal to a pretty swish restaurant with all the trimmings. Caren seemed so happy and he on top of the world got brave and even suggested that they should consider moving in together, perhaps.

'Steven, if we did live together I don't know if I could live in a conventional way. I need my space and I would want to give you yours too,' she indicated.

'I would want to give you your space, Caren, of course I would. I think we would make a great team,' he replied

However, it left more questions than answers for Steven as he was unsure of what 'space and unconventional' meant in Caren's mind which at the best of times was unconventional. This worried him somewhat. Unfortunately, Steven didn't have to wait long. They walked the mile back to Caren's arriving in darkness. There was just a side lamp on in the lounge and the sound of a radio playing dance music in the background. Steven thought he heard somebody move in the lounge and as he led the way he saw some perfumed candles and a figure lit by the side lamp and on all fours on the large orange comfortable sofa. To his horror it was a female wearing only a very pink seductive baby doll. She didn't move or show any form of surprise even when Steven said, 'What the hell is this?'

Caren replied, 'It's your birthday present from me and in the spirit of our unconventional relationship this is Rosie I don't believe you have met, but never mind, she and I share a certain bond and I would like you to get to know her.'

'Rosie, baby, lift your head up and do not look back.'

She looked at Steven and said, 'mount the bitch.' He was aghast as there was no way he was doing this. It was madness, absolute madness. There was more to come as he tracked Caren's movement across to one corner of the room where there stood a video camera on a tripod.

'Unbelievable,' he shouted. 'Not me, no way, you are crazy' he said. 'You must take me as a complete idiot and our relationship must mean nothing to you; I am not sharing you with anyone and I am definitely not being filmed doing it! That crazy woman you always refer to has curdled your brain.'

This was the last straw for Steven, 'I loved you, Caren but you are a user and you do not understand love; we are damned well finished.' He had to get out of her life and the town to another life. He was devastated; he loved Caren and could not bear to see her with another man never mind a woman; 'crazy, flippin crazy!' He stormed out of the house and started running down the road, shaking and breathing heavily trying to come to terms with what he had just witnessed. Was it a dream or some sort of nightmare? Caren watched Steven burst out of her life and showed no emotion; it was inevitable. She was not moved, she just shrugged and looked over at her latest muse, this detectibly ravishing younger version of Yevana. Rosie had the same legs; muscled shapely thighs and calves. She was beautiful. Where would she start? Still looking adoringly at Rosie, she flicked the on switch of the video recorder and the red light glowed on. She walked across to the side light and turned it off leaving just the candles. 'Rosie, it is time to have some fun so smile into the camera please' after which Caren then proceeded to tie Rosie's hands and ankles together and gave her a Yevana-induced night to remember or forget! Rosie did not leave Caren's for a couple of days until the bruises went down. It didn't seem to matter to Rosie as she was hopelessly in love; she would have had sex with Steven!

As the months went by Rosie spent more time at Caren's, practically moving in. Rosie continued to do well at college and Caren's schedule was hectic which kept them both very busy indeed. They were definitely a hot couple and in certain circles it was well known that they were an item, although anybody that knew them knew to stay well clear of either individual as Caren could become quite unpleasant. With their striking good looks and flair for wearing very little but giving nothing away made them attractive to both sexes. From time to time, they did bring in other members of the art college for hedonistic nights under candlelight. This relationship was definitely unconventional and probably doomed from the start. Things began to get out of hand and on one occasion Rosie was hospitalised when one 'enthusiastic' sexual encounter with Caren and friends went too far. After over a year together and realising her interest had started to wane she unceremoniously dumped Rosie for good. She dealt with it simply by explaining to Rosie that she did not want a long-term relationship and she had reasons to move on.

'Go upstairs, get your bags and get out, now!' Rosie didn't mess about as she knew when Caren was in business mode.

Caren had planted a seed though as she heard later that Rosie had moved in with a female college lecturer in her thirties from another local university, who was soon besotted with Rosie. Rosie texted her now and again and let her know how things were going, although Caren never replied. On one occasion she let slip that she had turned out to be the leader in this new relationship even though she was much younger, and on one occasion after an argument had ended the relationship. Over the following two weeks the lecturer begged Rosie to take her back and after a series of events they had become engaged to the horror of Rosie's parents. They had witnessed their daughter turn from a girl regularly dating men to being engaged to a woman. They were devastated and Caren knew she was responsible.

Whilst her social life could be likened to a volcano Caren's business practice was doing remarkably well and increasingly taking so much of her time, that this actually allowed her to put relationships on hold and she was therefore feeling much more relaxed. When she did venture out with others she was disturbed by the way she took out her passion and love for Yevana in different ways on her lovers without wanting too. They always seemed to become besotted with Caren which puzzled her as she never reciprocated and couldn't, wouldn't.

The next live-in lover who was of a similar age to Caren and another businesswoman, initially enjoyed a very loving, romantic and passionate relationship until one particular evening, when Yevana came into their lives. Julie, a tall athletic beauty, came from an upper-class background and was mainly conventional albeit she preferred women to men. In terms of intelligence and lifestyle they were very similar. During the evening in question whilst cuddled on the sofa they were watching the highlights of a film premiere from London on TV. To Caren's great shock and sensual arousal Yevana was shown walking along the red-carpet hand in hand with Britain's world record holding athlete, Mobola Yemba. Caren was in shock; the star athlete and her friend were a drop-dead gorgeous couple. The programme was shown again later which Caren recorded. The shock was all the greater as Caren could see why Yevana was escorting this tall, most delicious black beauty. The jealousy was burning fiercely.

Having thought she had perhaps started to finally confront her demons this episode threw Caren back to the instability of the past, in fact it was driving her crazy and there was trouble ahead. The following visits disturbed Julie as Caren had changed and very noticeably. Impatiently, she insisted on watching the video over and over whilst her girlfriend laid under her trying to draw breath as Caren rubbed back and forth having orgasms until practically exhausted. This continued for many weeks until Julie confronted Caren and told her enough was enough. She could take no more.

'Caren, you are being ridiculous, this is not a relationship, this is nothing.'

Having been head over heels in love with Caren, this form of humiliation and rejection was too much to bear.

'You need to grow up, you are making my life a misery. I can't concentrate at work and I feel humiliated. What do you want, what are you looking for?'

'Well, Julie, darling that just the way it is,' Caren replied, 'take it or leave it, I made no promises.'

'Goodbye, Caren, I hope you get what you are looking for.' Julie dressed and left for good.

'No problem, darling, so do I.' Caren sighed a 'ha' and went to the kitchen.

Caren received a call from a friend of Julie's months later saying, 'I hope you are proud of yourself Caren as Julie loved you but you discarded her like a bad dinner. She has killed herself and everybody who knew her is distraught.'

Caren regretted the death of her previous lover but the feeling of love had always been very shallow on her part and so there were no deep feelings of loss. She knew she had emotional problems that were deep seated but she did not intend to pursue this matter, ever. On this occasion she pressed end on the call without further ado and rejoined Andre Correnti, her latest bodybuilding muse who remounted her whilst watching the film premiere re-run. He was also a drop dead gorgeous intelligent and athletic stud who was a master of IT and all things electronic. It started on holiday in his home city of Madrid where Caren was enjoying a peaceful week with her then boyfriend. Ten years younger he may have been but he was in tune with Caren's needs. They met eyes across the tables of a lavish restaurant and fell in love or lust, there and then. This was a stellar moment for the hard-faced businesswoman. They were in his bedroom within an hour and bizarrely, Caren had the boyfriend watch her getting 'skewered' to the headboard and on finishing got rid of Andre to the bathroom and had the older aged boyfriend clean her out after which she gave him five minutes to vacate the room; permanently! It was over before it had begun.

Andre was a revelation and helped lift the drama, fatigue and psychological pressure of the previous protracted period off her shoulders and out of her life; for now. This guy would be useful in many ways and she had plans! Because although time was a healer it could only help so far!

Over the coming months they flitted between Madrid and Durham both being fully focused on work meaning that they had to build a friendship from afar. So far as Caren was concerned it was well worth pursuing for a number of reasons, including he was fit and useful. One of the useful reasons was that he had very wealthy and influential parents and it wasn't long before Caren engineered a chance to meet them. The family had wealthy friends in all parts of Spanish and European society and in particular his father was a serious player in the banking industry. Their home which sat on the outskirts of Madrid was a sixteenth century palace with a large staff to maintain both house and gardens. As you approached there were magnificent gates which were the only gap in a continuous eight feet high stone wall around the estate. On proceeding through the gates via permission from security staff, there followed a long drive of over quarter of a mile after which you reached a classically elegant monumental fountain in front of the house that would not be out of place in the king's palace. Water cascaded out into a large pool from which it recycled; beautiful. Caren was very happy and was intrigued to meet the owners of this most dramatic and manicured estate. A group of staff attentively met the car as it stopped at the steps leading up to the house and were soon disappearing with all of the bags belonging to Caren and Andre without a word of command or the chance for Caren to collect any items from her bags. A butler led them to the greeting room and asked them to wait for a few minutes until Andre's mother was available and then she would be down to greet them. Caren thought to herself, 'She is pampering herself having seen me get out of the car in a short skirt, high heels and looking distinctly slinky. I just know it.'

Andre muttered, 'She always keeps visitors waiting, it's just her way of wanting to be important.' In the meantime, a delicious plate of scones and Sri Lankan tea was brought to them in delicate porcelain. Whilst waiting Caren walked around this spacious room of antique furniture and studied the coffee table where books were scattered on the surface. Of note, there were several artistic covers of a teasingly fashionistic sexual nature, which was hot enough to stir Caren somewhat even though it was definitely not pornography. She considered who was the family member who placed these.

'Andre, darling. Yours?'

'No, actually my mother loves those books/pictures and often views such images at the galleries. She loves her clothes and can be quite a provocative dresser, which sometimes I find embarrassing.' He laughed a little and watched Caren study a black athletic-looking model of some stature.

His mother entered the room and it was quite a shock as she immediately had a strong presence and looked stunning with long dark hair running down each side of her face falling in curls on her breasts but with the majority falling halfway down her back. Her clothes were classic three-quarter length black pencil skirt, stiletto shoes and a tight-fitting red blouse, open to her cleavage where there was a glimpse of a white bra. She had an aristocratic slender figure but filled her clothes in all the right places Caren noticed as she rather unceremoniously 'ran the rule.' As she approached Andre, Caren noticed that her makeup and clothing had been freshly applied in a quick change to suit the circumstances. His mother introduced herself as Rydeesa Correnti, a most beautiful woman but with an air of authority and strength, now in her mid-fifties.

'It is very good to meet you Caren,' she continued in immaculate English and went on, 'I have been so looking forward to meeting you and have heard so much about you, in fact, more so than most of Andre's girlfriends and he has a lot of friends you know.' Ouch, thought Caren that was a quick putdown indicating 'don't get comfortable, we don't want gold diggers here.' When kissing Caren on both cheeks she noticed that her complexion was of an eighteen-year-old and her perfume was to die for and most definitely the new fragrance from the House of Volta. Breathing it in made her feel 'heady.' Over a cup of tea Rydeesa gave a short history of the house and explained that Caren's bags had been taken to Andre's room.

'If you are interested I would be pleased to give you a short tour of the house and point out some of the history.'

'I would like that very much,' Caren returned. The library and dining room with all their paintings and books were spectacular and historic as you would imagine them to be. A more puzzling room was Rydeesa's quiet room where the walls were adorned with portraits of men and women in the most striking costumes and various stages of undress, some not leaving much to the imagination. 'I love this room; it is most beautiful' is all that she said. They witnessed the awesome wine cellars when in the basement area, however, there was one room that was marked strictly out of bounds. Rydeesa would only say that it was for storing private family documents and only her husband had access. Funny thing was she seemed very anxious not to be in this area for too long. 'Interesting,' Caren sighed out loud. Slightly odd and strange circumstances to keep family documents she thought when most of the family history appeared to be in the library. Rydeesa gave her a slightly off look that meant 'none of your business.'

Caren first met Rolando, Andre's father for dinner that evening. Tall and elegant in a manly way, charming certainly and full of Spanish smouldering good looks, there was something else, something perhaps unconventional about father and mother. One thing was for certain, they were both highly desirable human beings on many counts. Andre was from top stock!

Both of Andre's parents were very keen to gather some more background on Caren especially considering the age gap with Andre. It was nothing sinister but Caren had the feeling that snap checks were being conducted and that other more formal checks would be carried out in the background; she just sensed it. Still, they could do all of that and they would find nothing because apart from a fruity personal life she was clean. Dinner passed off well and after a few drinks in the library everyone retired to their bedrooms. When they got to bed Caren and Andre were highly aroused being together in this huge stately home together for the first time. For Caren the novelty of a four poster was fun and they had not seen each other for over a month. With a fair amount of champagne and port running through her veins, her mind was running wild and the centre point of her fantastical imagination was not the man below her, it was his mother Rydeesa who she could not get out of her mind. It was hard not to try to smell that perfume all night at every opportunity. Andre commented that he thought Caren had appeared to have made a real impression on his mother having caught her staring at Caren on more than one occasion. The lovemaking was as good as it had ever been after such an exhilarating day and became quite noisy in such a cavernous room and certainly by their normal standards. They were at the height of passion when Caren heard a sigh by the bedroom door as they were finishing. She got up quickly noticing the door was now ajar, which she was pretty certain it wasn't when they got into bed. Naked, she went to the door and looked into the vast corridor just in time to see Rydeesa, wearing only the sheer tights she had on during dinner, dash back inside her own bedroom. Andre had told her that his parents had their own rooms and came together for certain nights of the week. They had told him it was about sleep patterns. 'Of course,' Caren commented. 'Ah, interesting,' she thought!

Caren was on a roll now and had been planning 'stage two' all evening. She put on her mini she had been wearing for dinner and pulled Andre, still naked, by the hand and they crept down the stairs into Rydeesa's quiet room where they spent an exhilarating couple of hours in front of the pictures. Her particular focus of attention was the one of Mobola Yemba, the athlete, world champion sprinter and more importantly Yevana's muse, taken at a fashion shoot. 'Why are you so taken with this photograph?' asked Andre. Caren sighed. 'She is a perfect specimen human being and reminds me of an old friend of mine,' she sighed.

The following morning the men went out for an early morning jog and the ladies started breakfast early in the orangery. Dressed in a risqué pair of tight bright yellow shorts and a lace top, Rydeesa was quite chatty.

'Dreadful night's sleep,' she commented, 'I had something on my mind which wouldn't shift.' I noticed, thought Caren; your son and I making out. Teasing her, Caren replied, 'Yes, I was very hot; I think it might be the change of climate as it has been quite cold in the UK of late.' Her hostess replied, 'Well, next time you come you must stay for a few days and bring your costume as the pool is lovely any time of year. Some evenings we even discard them; such freedom, darling,' and on that note she finished her toast and coarse cut marmalade before making her excuses and vanishing into the house. Caren shortly followed her inside and once Andre had showered and taken breakfast they said their goodbyes then she left, alone, in the chauffeur-driven car back to the airport and travelled back to the UK.

Caren arrived back later that day and quickly got to work instructing a private detective she knew with a very good reputation, to bring her a summary of life in the Correntis' household.

In recent weeks she had become aware of the ever-burgeoning company owned by Yevana and her partner Toby; Y&T Entertainment.Inc, and she was looking for a way in and she had a plan! Over the previous few months since she split from the now deceased Julie, Caren knew she wanted revenge for the callous way she was discarded from the love of her life. Nobody had matched Yevana and she knew now that nobody ever would. They had a bond and it should have been unbreakable but whatever the future held and no matter how well her own business career was developing and it was growing extremely well in partnership with others, she could not let it go; would not let it go. Sometimes Caren wondered if she was going crazy but perhaps it was impossible to recognise that yourself. She didn't care! For now, though she had to let her plan mature and that would take time; patience was required.

Many weeks later a private detective called John Dexter reported back with a detailed diary of events complemented with a 'live' video. These were indeed busy people with non-stop commitments and a 'social locomotive' heading for the buffers. It comprised of family, committees, charity fundraising, business, parties and wife swapping including some 'big tricks'. Bingo – Caren was in! 'I am not sure what you were expecting but after a couple of weeks I was about to call it a day until a series of events encouraged me to stay on and it delivered, big time. These people will burn out living at this speed and taking these risks or perhaps they don't care.

Either way the pictures are sensational if that is what you wanted,' he finished. Caren sat in silence watching the footage on the video and having scanned the report and some digital pictures stood up and offered her hand. 'Thank you, JD. I do not need your services any longer.' This was exactly the opportunity she was looking for and although she was entering very dangerous territory she would now have Andre in the palm of her hand, where she would need him; for now. Any love for Andre would never last now, not that it was ever intended to in any case. She wasn't in love, and her priority was revenge against her only true love Yevana and that was non-negotiable. The video was explicit. One interesting party of evidence of their eccentric lifestyle seemed very funny, as the private detective had got into this particular party with a 'friend' and everybody had been happy to pose; brilliant, you can't teach that, thought Caren. You would have thought that they would have screened the clientele more thoroughly. Some of the figures filmed were senior Spanish dignitaries. JD had supplied a list of attendees which included some pretty famous people and others such as a wealthy Russian couple by the names of Yurenev and Yurini Caspanov for example, that she had never heard of. As far as Rydeesa was concerned, the word insatiable would be very appropriate. The best was in the next film which had been recorded in a downtown motel room. It became obvious that his mother had a liking for black men, of which one was a part time boyfriend apparently, young men more generally, her husband, sometimes all together and on this occasion the detective videoed a group sex party where Andre's parents had hired a low-cost downtown room for the night. Andre's father appeared naked tied in a crucifix against a wall and Rydeesa had been tied to a table on her back with her head dropping over the end, with four men, including her boyfriend, a man named Leon. They had cut all her clothes off except her heels and left her panties at her ankles. One man went to his father and brought him to a climax whilst the others used her mouth as sexual target practice. When his father came the young man dropped the contents into his wife's mouth and the next man rammed it down her throat. It all looked quite painful, however, the evidence suggested that she couldn't get enough! Not once was the rest of her body touched and after they had all finished they walked out after untying Mr Correnti. Rydeesa was crying for Leon to make love to her which in doing so excited her husband who did the deed, in situ, much to her disgust and out with her ability to stop him. He dressed and went out and bought her some clothes so that they could leave the hole they had hired! Caren found the whole episode quite spectacular and found that Rolando, his father, had a sense of humour because the photos of them leaving the hotel had Rydeesa in a mini skirt, heels and a short white vest looking horrified and cheap.

Caren considered her strategy and took Andre for dinner when they met up in London a couple of months later. Without showing any emotion she laid her cards on the table as bluntly as she could, giving him a summary of the detail without being too descriptive. She smiled and considered that perhaps she had a heart after all, then on reflection, perhaps not! 'Do as I say and carry on as usual and nobody will ever know what details I have. I can tell you that your parents and many of their friends take part in wife swapping sex parties and with some very senior dignitaries; I have the evidence but I will not show you or anybody else unless you do not co-operate with me. Do you understand me?' 'Yes' replied Andre, slightly crestfallen. 'Caren, why do you need to do this as it seems you must have had a bad experience to even consider using this sort of information to get whatever it is you seek. You should be careful as I know my parents have some very dangerous and influential friends who as you say in England, ''do not take prisoners''. I hope you know what you are doing.' Caren thought for a moment and replied, 'I do know what I am doing but it is my problem and I know the risks. It is not about your parents it is about how you will help me and if you play my game it will all work out in the end and cause you no difficulties.' Caren could not be sure of that of course but that would not affect her plan going forward. 'I do not wish to discuss it further,' she finished abruptly.

Over the next month Andre was not his normal self when it came to communication and Caren was getting a little anxious. She got the impression that if he started to cool the relationship with her the problem he faced would dissipate. A cancellation of a weekend in Paris was the final straw. She posted a picture of Rydeesa and Leon her boyfriend taken in a Parisian five-star hotel, taken through a long lens camera in a very compromising position and there was no doubt who the subjects were. The note attached said, 'See you as arranged but next Saturday instead.' The satisfaction Caren got from seeing Andre enter the room and immediately mount her from behind in a most aggressive and I hate you type of way turned her on, no end. They went for dinner in the hotel restaurant and settled into a better atmosphere. 'I need your help Andre and it would be better if you went with me instead of making it difficult.' 'My mother is really stupid getting involved with people like Leon; it will end in tears,' he moaned. 'What do you want me to do, Caren?'

Moving onwards and upwards

Yevana and Toby were drifting apart when it came to their personal relationship which was becoming ever complex and far from conventional. They were still sleeping together but they talked business most of the time and rarely socialised. Both understood other relationships were going on in their lives and could cope with that so long as their main focus was with Y&T. Yevana quickly grew to hate Christina but did not want to lose Toby so she was happy knowing that if she knew he had been near her, she would always have sex on his return as a matter of ownership. Psychologically, this mattered to Yevana and only once did she speak to her. Yevana waited for Christina to leave her office one day and had arranged for one of her trusted company security staff to meet her there and open Christina's car door. Yevana trusted her security agent to deliver good staff but she knew they were from the fruitier side of life and what they didn't know wasn't worth knowing. Later at the end of the working day Christina, in semi-darkness, approached her car and as she went to open the door she saw Yevana. 'Get in,' said Yevana, 'we need to talk.'

'What? How on earth did you get in here?' replied Christina.

'It's not important,' said Yevana, 'listen carefully. I know about you and Toby and that is fine. But if he ever leaves me without my understanding, I will make your life very unpleasant. Do you understand me?' she said angrily.

Christina looked shocked and slowly replied, 'Yeees.'

'Good. I am glad we understand one another, Christina,' replied Yevana. She then leant over and whispered in Christina's ear, 'I always clean up directly after he has been with you; I have a taste for it now.' Then Yevana grabbed a handful of blonde hair and bit deep into her lower neck and left a sizeable bloody bite mark, opened the car door and left. Christina sat back breathing heavily unable to move. She was in a state of shock but was determined that she could deal with it and more worryingly felt a tinge of excitement which she felt unable to explain. In fact, Toby had taught her a lot and brought her out of her shell which left her with the thought that she would reciprocate somehow. Christina worked quickly and informed Toby the next time he intended to make love to Yevana he was to let her know beforehand and drive over directly afterwards for 'a clean-up' as physiologically this was now important to fight fire with fire. He had sussed what was going on, didn't want to know how or why and just played the game as stupid as it seemed. They did just as she asked and to Toby's delight Christina was on an insatiable high on each occasion and 'she had a taste for it'. She was concerned that she was even considering doing this never mind she was doing it! 'Toby, what has made me do this? I do not recognise myself. Christina exclaimed.

'It is Yevana, she has this effect on the people she meets; be careful Christina, she bites.' Christina placed her hand on her neck and smiled nervously.

As the recession bit deep they hung in there and worked hard on advertising, pricing, value for money particularly and service, which was so important in these desperate times. Incredibly their foresight and undeniable belief allowed them even in this difficult period to dream of their next complex and they planned to make it happen as soon as they possibly could. In time, they knew they had survived. Business picked up and full signs were posted often as the clientele had endured and the complex prospered where others had withered. Regular clients were greeted as friends and this attitude across all departments of Y & T was decisive in a name being made that would be known way beyond Manchester.

The next step was to travel down to London on a regular basis together and start to build a set of contacts that would help them finance the dream. New accountants, bank managers, solicitors, property developers and estate agents were instructed. Bob Ray was on board as he wanted to continue as an investor and definitely wanted to be a part of this business as it grew. One early visit they made to town coincided with Bob being there which they used to good effect. He was able to open some doors to the City including some of his own business associates who in turn opened up their address books. Another useful bonus was that the beautiful Mobola was now not only an international athlete and the new world record holder over 400 metres but had also been delving into the sports and fashion world for both sponsorship and status. She was now cover girl material and had access to A list celebrities and the best parties in town. Obviously she had given up her work in the Luxury Club due to pressures of athletics and other more lucrative offers some time ago. Yevana was now used to viewing Mobola with her latest muse in the tabloids and weekly magazine covers and most recently they were all men. Yevana was her alternative interest having ditched her rich married lover – when she wanted it that is – which for Yevana was not always enough but it was always worth waiting for. Mobola would be very useful when they got a foot in the door of this wonderful city and Yevana intended to be there to make the most of it.

When the time came to expand and make the next move, they decided to keep their complex in Manchester rather than sell it. They were advertising through recruitment agencies to put a management team in place with a view to upgrade that site with the cinema club that it was missing, in due course. They would continue to modernise and keep its well-earned reputation. There was also a feeling of pride and nostalgia related to this project as their very first, especially as they had had to fight to keep it open during the recession. The current aim through investors including the banks was to buy and develop a £15 million hotel complex which would include their dream layout: two hundred rooms at five-star. They were already doing well with Bob having secured £10.5 million in Switzerland and London from several institutions based on the design drawings. Because they had done so well in what was becoming a premier hotel complex and night time entertainment site in the North of England, investors could see into the dream.

Whilst trawling property pages Yevana had found a suitable site just outside Kensington but near enough to be in the best area in terms of postcode and they got the prestige number in any area and that was No1 in Tudor Square. It was perfect as it had previously been a three-star hotel that had closed down and was next door to an old church that had also become disused and had stopped conducting Church of England Presbyterian services some years ago. Toby normally arranged to meet the estate agent on his own whilst Yevana looked after things in the north, until he was keen on a site after which he would arrange for them both to visit. To this point in time, they had not been able to come to a joint decision as there had always been issues with size, area or gut instinct, particularly where Yevana was concerned. On this occasion Yevana had to make the first viewing on this building as Toby was attending an event in the north for hotel business leaders. She walked through this dilapidated ten-storey building of 1920s structure and decoration in just a few minutes then exited through the rear into the garden and stood looking out towards the church immediately beside the old hotel. She turned towards the estate agent and said, 'I want to view the church now. Can you arrange that today, now?'

Looking slightly surprised the agent replied, 'Of course, madam. I will get right on to it.' He leapt away and started chattering on his phone before coming back through the rear doors and turning towards Yevana. 'My man is meeting us at the doors of the church in five minutes with all the details, although I can confirm you would get planning permission to reuse it. There was an original plan for residential/commercial use that a developer failed to get funding for in the end.'

Yevana looked at him and just said, 'Good.' This was a huge place with bags of potential and she was getting excited but not showing it. However, she had another idea as they were walking up the steps and into the space that could become their space and the best entertainment complex in London, in due course. They walked across to the church doors which were unlocked by the estate agent's 'man' and the double doors creaked loudly as if they had not been opened for some time whilst simultaneously they witnessed the glorious sunshine beaming through the stained-glass windows onto the isle seating and a group of birds fluttered across the roof space. She pulled her phone out of her coat pocket and called Toby. 'Darling, get down here as soon as you can, I will be waiting, and I have found our new London complex; you won't be disappointed.' She hung up and said to the agent, 'Arrange another viewing on both properties tomorrow morning and let the owners know we will purchase the properties, and I expect to arrange this by the end of next week.' Smiling, she turned back and walked out of the church without seeing anything else; she just knew. They may have struggled to agree on a property thus far but this was non-negotiable and in any case she knew he would love it; it was special, just special. Yevana called a taxi and met Mobola for a pre-arranged romp in her flat in Soho after Mobola had called her current top model boyfriend and told him she was unavailable for the night out. Mobola actually wanted to say no to Yevana but when it came to decision time she just couldn't say it. During the evening at a time when she had Yevana in some form of stress position Mobola picked up a text from him which read, 'I know who you have there in your flat and so, you are dumped, goodbye, lover.' Mobola had been in this relationship for some months which for her was a long time, so this was a bit of a shock and the net loser in terms of pain over the next few hours, was Yevana.

The following day Yevana got herself together after an hour's sleep on the floor applied minimal makeup and put on her shift dress and heels before legging it in a taxi to King's Cross railway station where she met Toby at nine a.m.. 'You look tired out Yevana, have you been playing adult games with a friend?'

'Darling, we are all well and we must go straight to the site where the estate agent will meet us shortly. Did I tell you I have already agreed to purchase?' she added with a smile and a warm hug.

'No, you certainly didn't' he replied, but don't let that stop you, will you?' he continued with a sarcastic statement and smile.

She went on, 'It is the most wonderful idea and you will love it I am sure. Wait till you see what it actually is.'

They jumped in a taxi and were soon on site meeting the estate agent. Toby shook his hand although Yevana snubbed him as he looked far too greasy and slimy for her liking; she was once again instinctive on these things. He was slightly embarrassed as his hand hung in mid-air facing her already departing back, whilst she did utter 'Good morning, sir, I take it you carried out my instructions.'

'Indeed, madam, I did and at the prices we agreed would be suitable,' he replied as he hastily followed them both up the steps into the hotel. 'Both prices were agreed by the relevant owners.'

'Both!' Toby blurted out. 'Both, what are you talking about; what have you done Yevana?'

'Darling, calm down all will be revealed and you will be happy, trust me,' she responded in a most calming manner.

'I do hope so,' he whispered tentatively as they walked throughout the building talking and comparing areas and potential. 'Look at the bedrooms, they are all such a good size which with just a modicum of imagination you can see the en-suite and decorating potential here, don't you think?'

Toby was opening cupboards and pulling wallpaper. 'Yes, it looks really promising but let's go back into the main function and public rooms.' They walked down into the reception area which is what sold it for him. There were large areas of intricate art deco plaster mouldings and wood which with the original marble flooring gave this shabby looking unloved property its history and potential. 'This must have been such a brilliant place in the Twenties, I can imagine the splendour and we must have it,' he stated bluntly. He walked out past the marble pillars that gave the exterior its superior feel and looked up and smiled to himself. What he loved though they would not own and that was the square opposite which had a dozen one hundred-year-old oak trees, park benches and was surrounded by wrought iron railings which for him framed this area and gave it a tremendous wow appeal. He made everyone wait for two minutes whilst he sat on the steps and looked out dreaming of what it might look like then raised himself and took Yevana's hand. She stared up at him and they smiled. Looking out for the rapidly following estate agent he called out, 'Now, I love this and I agree you have done well but the only issue is, is it big enough for our design and aspirations?'

'Follow me,' said Yevana. They walked around the corner still holding hands and stood in front of the church.

Stating the obvious, Toby said, 'It's a church, I didn't realise this was in the design or that we were adding a spiritual wing in the complex!' He laughed loudly.

'No, stupid' Yevana laughed. 'It will be joined to No1 by a glass tunnel and then we have everything. Planning will not be an issue as there were plans already which we will change but in principle it is okay as the local council and church organisations want the area rejuvenated in keeping with its past.' To the estate agent she said, 'Let's go inside please.' Toby loved the massive doors on entry and was taken aback by the vast space inside with its beautiful windows and ornate masonry.

'I don't need to see any more, this is it, this is definitely it and you have excelled this time Yevana, you really have. I will get on to our developer immediately as there is no time to waste, we must have these buildings as they are terrific, really terrific.' He gave her a big bear hug and after wrapping up business with the estate agent, took her via Von REVA the most delicious lingerie shop in London Town and bought her a yellow basque with a quarter cup and took her to her hotel suite and rewarded her for her efforts! This had been quite a couple of days for Yevana but she returned to Manchester by train with Toby, feeling on top of the world; what a victory, what a future.

Their property developer could get both sites with planning for a joint venture for £7 million plus £10 million to rebuild. Another £4 million would be required to set the complex up ready to open. This was a massive jump and so working to capacity was going to be required on an almost constant basis to get profits up and investors happy. The property once developed would be worth possibly twice as much so this was a project everybody was keen to get involved with. There was still work to do though which was both exciting and nerve racking. Of course, there were going to be highs and lows along this fascinating journey and they both knew that this project would be no exception.

After several months of negotiations, planning and fundraising, they were soon in a position to get packing ready to hand over the daily business at Y&T Manchester to a new team of experienced entertainment industry managers. A husband-and-wife team called John and Joy Jarvis were put in place and with no children decided to live on site, which Yevana thought to be perfect. John and Joy had been looking for an opportunity like this to be sitting managers and not have to worry about properties of their own as they were quite nomadic by nature. She was a slightly overweight woman who nevertheless enjoyed looking smart and was definitely wearing the trousers in the relationship. Before they departed Toby found out by accident, that Joy had a young lover in the south which only he had picked up on. Toby overheard a conversation about a future visit to Manchester and wasn't even sure if John was aware or perhaps it was an arrangement of some sort. He decided not to mention it to Yevana in case she started having second thoughts, which was too late in any case as contracts had been signed and there was no clause about infidelity included!

As they were upstairs at Y&T packing prior to departure from Manchester Toby asked Yevana, 'Are you scared of making such a commitment now that we have reached this point?' 'Are you,' she countered?' 'Do you have doubts that we can fulfil our dreams, darling?'

'No, I want this; we are going to nail it. If we don't we will be able to say we tried for our dream and gave it everything. We have done well but we will and can do even better; set a standard.'

'I agree,' Yevana replied. 'I am glad we've agreed to immediately rent some office space away from No1 Tudor Square before construction begins as the project will take nearly two years to properly set up and that could not be done from Manchester. Most importantly, it will allow us to recruit the initial management staff as it is too big to do alone, even at this early stage. We must also make sure we get the right people as they will be useful to us in the future as we progress and loyal staff that know or can help the business is so critical.'

'Totally,' said Toby. In his mind, he pictured Christina and was cognisant of the fact that Yevana didn't know he was bringing her to town. He had too as he loved his time with her and likewise, she was smitten with him even though she knew she was sharing with Yevana. Christina would pretty much do anything for Toby by now.

As if Toby was waiting for the moment and as if timed to perfection, Yevana finished packing her cases and her last box for the removal company to transport the following day, then asked Toby what he was doing about Christina. 'Darling, what of Christina?'

'She will move to London and join her parent company office there. She is part of a large multinational group and so with her talents they were able to sort it out without any problems, thank goodness.' He replied without looking up from the task in hand. Yevana stopped what she was doing taping the box and looked up into his eyes with an element of surprise because he used the phrase 'thank goodness'. She thought to herself, 'What did he have to say that for? She was only a cheap shag surely.'

He continued, 'As you know she is playing a key role in our project by assisting Barry Jones, the developer with the project, in order that the drawings are carried out to the letter; there will be nobody more trustworthy than her as far as I am concerned, she knows how we think and you know that Yevana.'

Yevana was roused though and blurted out, 'You are not leaving me, Toby' she said angrily.

'I know darling and she knows. I told her you and I have 'friends' but we have been committed to one another from day one so she shares or we separate. Christina accepts that situation and does not want to lose me,' he replied. 'In any case I don't see you as somebody who is going to be pushed to one side by a rival.'

Yevana smiled. 'Good, too right, gorgeous, because I will not accept anything less and I don't care what it takes.' They smiled at each other and finished off the last of their packing.

That evening and their last in the complex, Toby had to spend a few hours with Christina as she was not coming to London for a couple of weeks. He did not spend long with her though as he promised Yevana they would sleep together on this last night in Manchester. He did eventually get back around eleven and had one last brandy before going upstairs and spending the night with Yevana. Toby eventually fell asleep exhausted and couldn't help thinking why he had got himself into this position with the two women, a position most men dream of.

The following day Joy allocated tasks to staff who would take care of the needs of the owners and all that they wanted to ensure a smooth send off from the complex. At midday their longest serving staff came and took their remaining private and personal baggage to the lift and down to the cars whilst the remaining larger items and boxes were left for the removal company who were waiting outside the main entrance. They said their goodbyes to the new managers John and Joy then walked out to their car and given a rapturous send off. As Toby drove away Yevana looked back and said, 'Darling, I love what we have done and how we survived here in Manchester; we should always own this place if we can, but if not, always come back to remind ourselves of many brilliant times.'

'Of course, babe, it has our mark in every room and we will continue to ensure it gets better.' Toby knew they would never look back though and he accelerated out of town in a most determined fashion. On the radio the old Seventies hit *Love is like oxygen* graced the airways at which point Toby placed his left hand on Yevana's leg and even sang a line of the chorus which made her smile.

On the drive south Toby caught himself thinking about all sorts of things and he decided to ask of Mobola and how often she and Yevana were meeting one another. He had made a mental note that Mobola had been splashed across many of the periodical magazines and newspapers and mainly with a string of young men. 'Yevana, how is your relationship with

Mobola, for although you see her now and again I note that she has male companions most of the time she is seen in public?' Yevana was fairly dismissive of this question.

'Why do you ask?' she came back to him, slightly rattled by the unprompted question. 'She is a good friend and I see her when I am in town which will be more often in the near future. She likes my company and me hers; we are suited as very good friends.' He left that subject there before the atmosphere turned in the car as he was also aware that Yevana had not heard from her for a while which he knew tended to annoy her.

Another hour into the journey and Yevana was woken from a little nap by a message on her mobile. It was from Mobola of all people; talk of the Devil! She had not seen her for months and this gave her one of those electric shocks and standing hair on the back of her neck moments. It said, 'Party in London tonight, taxi will pick you up at nine p.m.. Dress is four items plus two-inch earrings for a thirtieth birthday party. Bitch, do not disappoint (M) xx.' Yevana could not believe it, here they were moving to London town where they had to settle into new rented accommodation, and she had now been ordered to attend what would almost certainly be an all-night party. She looked at Toby and with a sigh said, 'I won't be around for about twenty-four hours darling as my friend has summoned me to attend a prestigious birthday party. I will have to help with the arrangements at the flat when I get back. This will be a good chance to meet influential people now we are permanently in town.' She looked ahead staring into the distance thinking about what to wear and what lay ahead, then she relaxed and closed her eyes and sunk back into her seat and slept. Asleep, her body was whizzing at one hundred miles per hour; her body was in ecstasy as her dreaming mind started to play out scenarios of how the night would develop. Toby just acknowledged, 'Yes, babe, there is no rush.' Okay he thought, instead of working in the flat to set it up and just settle in he considered what to do if he felt inclined to go out. He picked up his phone and really enjoyed pressing 'Christina' and saying 'hello, darling, did you decide to come to town to see your sister yesterday? He sensed Yevana wake up but she kept her eyes closed.

'I did indeed,' she replied, 'just in case you missed me and needed me,' Christina exclaimed in a jubilant manner.

'I am free tonight; shall I come over to you?' Toby said in some delight. Yevana very gently leant into the centre and heard Christina say, 'Oh yes, that is fantastic, Toby. I have a new skirt I want to go out in and I have a new toy in the flat; can't wait, shall I...'

Toby interrupted 'no, nor can I' then cancelled the call before she could say more. In one fell swoop he had teased two women! Yevana shuffled sleepily back into the centre of her seat and in a resigned manner dismissed Christina and decided she was going to enjoy London and how!

London

They arrived late afternoon at the location of their new accommodation about five minutes' walk from Tudor Square. It was a loft apartment with two bedrooms, a bathroom and a spacious living area including the kitchen. It was big enough for them and with their rented business space in one of the commercial areas on the ground floor it was ideal. Toby opened a bottle of Brut Champagne once they had unpacked their essentials and toasted the 'next step'.

'Yes, darling, the next step and just what will it bring? Success and prosperity I hope,' she suggested.

'Yes, Yevana, let's go out tonight, have a great night, then come tomorrow we shall unpack our belongings when the removals company arrives, but on Monday we will focus our lives on London and Tudor Square; the super complex where we will entertain a generation of five-star clients.' Toby was on a high, in fact he really hadn't realised how much he was attached to Christina although he was getting the feeling Yevana had.

'Yes, darling, the lull before the storm!' she sighed not looking at him, 'tonight, we can relax and forget what's ahead.' She tailed off the conversation and picked up her drink.

Yevana took her glass of bubbly into their bedroom and sorted out in her mind what she had to do before she went out to meet Mobola. Top of the list was treating herself to some beautiful new gear. Under instructions it obviously wasn't going to be much but what it was had to count. She slipped on some heels, fresh bright red super tight jeans, loose white light jumper and a pair of white shades before kissing Toby and departing out the front door and into the lift. The doors opened and she stepped in giving herself the once over in the mirror and she had to admit she liked what she saw, whilst in a moment of devilment just raised a finger and brushed it across a nipple that immediately sprung to life; naughty but wonderful she decided although she wanted to go further but decided against it. The doors opened on the ground floor and a young man in his twenties stepped past her into the lift, and as she brushed past him she was watching him scan her as he passed. She knew he was watching as the doors closed so slowly and adjusted her posterior movement to suit.

Walking into Kensington, which was only a little walk away, was a delight after a day in the car travelling to London. She popped into a cafe for a strong coffee before browsing and buying the new gear she had imagined in her mind earlier whilst whiling away the hours in the car. It was important she got it right as this was her first night out in Mobola's company in ages, which she needed to impress if she was to maintain some sort of relationship with this beautiful woman. She had serious competition these days. It was a mystery exactly where they would end up tonight but Yevana knew that as it was Mobola it would involve walking on the tightrope of life, well, night life in any case. She decided on designer labels to impress the crowd as they would be people who would probably be wearing similar 'out there' type clothes.

She began by buying an eight-inch Volta deep emerald, green mini skirt although she did step back from a very daring six inches. She fell in love with a six-inch pair of heels from the same exquisite designer, coloured mainly yellow with sequins giving it a dazzling Saturday night glitz and the final item was a loose blouse in a yellow shear material that hung at the waist, which she bought from a different boutique that was also very popular with ladies in town. She tried them all on in the last boutique and looked stunning. Her mind was racing and she could not wait to see Mobola's reaction. That was the four items she had been tasked to wear and she was ready, but although tempted, decided not to wear them home as she had to clean up first of all. Risqué indeed, but at the party she was going to nobody would be wearing more. Yevana walked back to the flat and initially walked past the champagne bar on the way then thinking about it she decided a quick glass would lift her into the night; she did and it did!

On returning to the flat, Toby had already gone and left a note which just said 'Enjoy xxxx.'

'Umm, Christina must have delivered herself early, ah well' she reflected as she looked out of a window across a now dark but well-lit London night time skyline, then dropped all of her clothes onto the floor and stood naked considering the probable excursions that lie ahead. She could change her mind and have a quiet night, she thought, but she shouted out, 'bring it on' and walked straight into the shower. When she'd finished she pulled on a short robe and took a bottle of water from an almost empty fridge, then drank thirstily before subsequently putting a Rachmaninov piano concerto to play on their record player. She then clipped one of her treasured Cuban cigars before sitting in an old armchair in this rented space and sat with the lights off for a blissful half an hour.

Getting up, she stood in front of the mirror, allowed the robe to slide to the floor and checked that she was properly shaven in the places she expected to be. Yevana was a master of applying makeup and considered that she would have been a brilliant makeup artist in the entertainment industry should she have found the pull in that direction. She sat naked applying her makeup for that evening and her mind wandered in the mirror as she questioned why she was travelling down this most potentially perilous of journeys with people like Mobola Yemba. In truth, it was something she could reconsider again but Yevana knew she was made for risk taking, it was part of her being. What excited her, turned her on, she supposed. The eyeliner was sharp and dark as was the red lipstick. She briefly admired her work, stood, picked up her sparkling emerald, green loop earrings and pierced them through her nipples. Next, she picked up her shear blouse and pulled it over her head then pulled on her short but fitted emerald skirt and after zipping it tight, she grabbed her shoes and slipped them on and once again checked the goods in the mirror and satisfied, decided she was ready to deliver herself to London society. Out of the blue and with a smiley face emoji Yevana received a text from Mobola, 'Taxi now ten p.m. been at a fashion shoot this afternoon so delayed. Return message with what you intend to wear, bitch.' Almost flustered, Yevana quickly replied with the very brief detail. 'Good.' Mobola came back. 'Now send a picture but only from the neck down.' Yevana wasn't sure whether Mobola was in fact already at a party and this was just another part of a game. Yevana did as she was told and placed the camera on the side table in the bedroom and took the shot then sent it. Mobola called. 'Bitch, you look a million dollars and look ready to be devoured tonight. It will be long and plentiful I assure you' and she called off. Yevana waited patiently and the taxi eventually arrived just a little late. In the darkness she hailed the taxi and slid in gracefully, as any movement in her skirt would show too much and held a phone and some cash in her hand to pay the driver, one way! Her skin was on fire, almost red hot with anticipation as the time in the taxi seemed to play out in reverse; she was so excited.

She arrived at what turned out to be St John's Wood and the home of a young and successful oil executive who was celebrating his thirtieth birthday. The place was bouncing, almost literally, as she could hear and see through a large sash window, a throng of mainly bright young things who were hard at it enjoying their party. Yevana stood patiently outside having rung a large black electric doorbell on the most amazing old wooden black door. She'd considered calling ahead but thought better of it and wasn't sure anybody would be able to hear a phone inside in any case. The door opened, a well-heeled gentleman in his mid-forties welcomed her in and after enquiring told her where he thought the 'stunning tall black girl' was. 'Most beautiful I have ever seen,' he commented.

'Thank you,' Yevana replied. 'Your pulse would go through the roof if I told you what our relationship was based on.' As she walked past other revellers along a narrow but modern hallway, the heads of both sexes turned to follow this beautiful woman that spirited past them. Yevana was not out of place at this party as all of the women were wearing no more than four items, so there was little left to the imagination in this mosaic of fantastic beauty, colour and eccentricity. She eventually found Mobola who looked stunning in a white bikini and heels in the kitchen dining area. Yevana briskly and confidently walked straight over to Mobola who was busy talking to a small intense looking woman wearing a top hat. Mobola turned towards Yevana, held her wrist and pulled her close and kissed her on the lips before turning back to her conversation and Yevana joined the group of friends from what looked like a variety of backgrounds.

The evening was thoroughly enjoyable and flowed nicely as Yevana met lots of interesting and charismatic people who were just genuinely chatty, interested in her project and recent success or wanted to take her home with them, as usual male and female! Mobola stayed very close though as this was very definitely her territory and as a slender but strong companion she stood her ground like a predator over its captured prey. She also had well laid plans that could not be altered. One young female journalist in her late twenties called Jennie Mire dropped her twenty-four-hour news agency card in the top of Yevana's skirt which Mobola spotted and confiscated. It read, 'I live here and will fulfil your dreams xx.' Yevana had thought a reputable journo, which apparently this woman was, could have been useful for the business but did not get the chance to discuss anything as Mobola dismissed her in no uncertain terms. Much later in the night Mobola caught up with the journo in the toilets and made her eat and choke on her personal card given to Yevana in rather unpleasant circumstances, with others stood by watching; apparently the journo wasn't popular. Mobola's last words were, 'and I will fulfil your nightmares, bitch.' On hearing this story from a bystander, Yevana wondered whether the power of the pen might bite back one day.

Around two a.m. Mobola brought Yevana to a part of the house in the very modern more dimly lit basement area where they joined what seemed to be a select group of men, older than the average group at the party, probably in their forties who were from Russia and Saudi Arabia. The basement had rich multi-coloured wallpaper that reminded you of the 1920s by design but with wonderful atmospheric lighting on walls and ceiling. On the walls were portraits of African men and women wearing war like face paints and looking sinister and menacing which added to the dark atmosphere in the room. Apparently they were painted by the famous African artist Mumbacka Densolian who was killed when one of his subjects, a tribal king, took exception after finding out the artist had sold his portrait for thousands of dollars to a British aristocrat. Certainly, a sad ending for a man who had gained a considerable reputation across the world for his distinctive artwork; the crime was never investigated and in fact rather strangely, it was listed in the South African press as 'death by natural causes.' Yevana smiled on noticing the king was cross-eyed and that it might have been the first time he had seen a picture of himself as a proper reflection.

There were other women of various ages and nationalities amongst the group chatting, but they were not an active part in real terms, only bystanders ready to pamper the men as required, Yevana looked on rather drearily. Why did so many women seem so docile at times? Perhaps that was the way of the world and people should accept this as life. Perhaps women sub consciously wanted this role in society. Was she one of these women or was she a 'real' woman of substance? She actually considered she was half woman, half man, but would not be able to explain it to anyone else as she believed you are who you are and that there was no proper definition of who a woman should be; it was evolution and she firmly believed the female species was in change, which would develop over many future generations into a different form and already there were signs of more male-like traits in work, lifestyle and strength, which included both physical and mental aspects.

Caspinov

Two of these gentlemen wearing very casual but expensive attire, were introduced as Yurenev Caspanov and Prince Masood. It turned out that Caspanov was a man of substance in many parts of the old Soviet Union and particularly Russia where he was involved in anything from oil to cosmetics. He was wealthy beyond trying to calculate wealth but was widely acknowledged as being in a different league to the average billionaire. Yevana was eyeing him as he conversed with her, trying to tie down why he was at a party such as this and she also focused on the guy looking menacing behind him; private security, no doubt about it. Yurenev was of seemingly mild disposition with a well-toned body, whilst being very aware of his potential for any selected suitors, of his choice of course! He did spend some moments respectively giving Yevana the once over but did not linger, showing a degree of interest but good manners in one. Having dark smouldering looks and being around six feet, he was neither very tall nor small but had an intimidating presence which was not because he was being protected, it was deeper than that; something you could sense but were not able to explain. Interestingly, though he was married but she was not apparent here. Yevana noticed an occasion when his right hand found a discrete opportunity, he was prone to slide it across the back of Mobola's rear and hesitate momentarily in a brief moment of romantic or rather sexual unison which she seemed to ignore but not discourage. Intriguing, Yevana thought. Where would this lead?

    Yevana was soon engaged in a general conversation about such things as life in London, some politics and a little personal minutia, when something shocking happened. Yurenev had been distracted by another male in the group and moved to speak to him when Yevana saw he had received a text message and to her shock and surprise his screen showed a picture of herself from the neck down. He looked back towards her in a very matter of fact manner as he answered the message and carried on a conversation with the prince and his aide. She said nothing as she was caught off guard somewhat but looked at Mobola for reassurance who just ignored her. Why had Mobola asked for and passed on the photo? What did it mean? It all seemed very strange but that feeling of excitement ran through her veins and more questions would wait for another time. Nevertheless, in the main event Yevana had talked for some time to these men about her business ventures and aims for the future, particularly what the financial plans and aspirations involved. Both the prince and Yurenev said they would be delighted to investigate any opportunity to invest in the high end of the hotel and entertainment industry in London Town. Yevana was really intrigued by the way that the conversation was being conducted especially with her current dress state, as she saw it, of near nakedness. Most encouraging was that even like this it seemed that she was being taken really seriously. It was as if they knew they were dealing with a female 'player' in the fullest sense of the word. They understood the general idea and thought there might be an investment opportunity that was worth exploring at this early stage.

    Elsewhere at the party Yevana witnessed the ruthless side of Mobola that night, at first hand. As well as a plethora of men at the party another woman, not Jennie Mire, had continuously been trying to separate Yevana from Mobola all night, but having denied her advances she thought nothing more of it. This tall, elegant and beautiful model of a woman had the hots for Yevana, which was obvious, and she did not waste time or words in making her point. She was the white version of Mobola; perfect! Yevana under other circumstances may have shown more interest, however, when she paid a visit to the bathroom later in the night, it was frequented by a couple of women powdering their noses when she heard a noise of anguish in the toilet cubicle. Yevana went to see who if anybody was in some trouble, only to find to her horror, Mobola pushing this blonde good looking women's head down the loo and flushing it. She then ripped off the delicate lime green silk mini top she was wearing, flushed it down the loo with her head still forced into the pan. To finish she warned her off future dalliances with friends of hers, telling the unfortunate woman, 'don't mess with my chick, get it?'

    The woman spluttered 'yes' as her faced resurfaced.

Mobola sensing somebody was behind her at the doorway of the cubicle turned and saw Yevana. 'Get in and shut the door.' Yevana looked back down the bathroom towards the other women who were hurriedly packing their makeup and dashing out back into the party. She did as she was told and slid the catch closed and looked down at the woman who was shivering with her head in the bowl. 'Bitch, scratch her back, raw, Now!' she growled staring into Yevana's eyes with her piercing gaze. Yevana did as she was told viciously digging her long nails into the woman's back until there were long blood marks down her back. Yevana felt the fighting male in her or was it the female bitch coming to the fore, with adrenaline pumping viciously through her veins and mixing intoxicatingly with the night's alcohol. It felt like an incredible high, but Yevana knew she had moments like this in her. When Mobola was satisfied she said, 'enough, let's go.' Yevana turned, slipped the catch and walked out of the cubicle briefly looking back at the woman who was desperately trying to retrieve her top from the toilet. On leaving the cubicle Yevana stopped to wash the blood off her hands and as she finished she looked up into the mirror and saw Mobola was stood behind her just as she was placing her wet hands on Yevana's thighs wiping them slowly, sensitively and purposely down her firm inside leg. She quickly stopped then opened the bathroom door and left after which Yevana followed. It was not long before they saw this broken, dishevelled, soaking wet and apparently married woman wearing her retrieved wet top, walk out of the flat. She would have some explaining to do! Interestingly, nobody at the party seemed to take any notice as most were past the stage of caring anyway.

They both went back to the group they had generally been with for the past couple of hours. Yurenev definitely had the hots for Yevana, that much was obvious and unbeknown to Yevana a deal had been struck earlier with Mobola. The deal was that Mobola would escort Yevana out to a weekend in Monte Carlo on his super yacht, where they would talk investment opportunities and more, much more. They eventually got around to discussing this and Yevana was absolutely delighted, especially as the numbers being talked about would more than secure the London project and as long as the terms of the deal were good she knew Toby would jump at it. He would be delighted as deals such as this were not to be sniffed at. She gave herself a pat on the back and she thought what a clever girl she had been.

Yurenev said, 'Yevana, I want you and Mobola to come out next weekend to Monte Carlo and join me on my yacht. Please bring your partner but only if he brings his girlfriend Christina. I do not want him around for the fun bits. We will do a deal; you will be happy; I can assure you of that. Yevana smiled as this was both shockingly open but fun and Toby would be delighted, she hoped. Even more shocking though was the fact that he seemed to know all that there was to know about them. How the hell did he know about Christina? Yevana had to suppress a little jealousy again. Mobola was free out of racing season so she jumped at the opportunity that, let's face it, she had facilitated!

'My private jet will collect you all from Stansted next Friday evening. Please don't be late or it will leave without you and any chance of a deal. The boyfriend will not be permitted to board the aircraft without his girlfriend. It is up to you.' He finished giving Yevana a long stern expression.

'Indeed,' she responded. 'We will both be very excited about being able to work with you. It is important to us.'

The party started to slow down approaching dawn and people were sliding into corners or bedrooms or leaving. Mobola jumped up from a sofa where she was lounging with an actor she had met that night and said, 'We must leave!' Yevana slowly stood up and was joined by Yurenev and Masood who wanted to say their personal goodbyes. Yurenev gave her a gentle and warm kiss on her mouth and the prince, holding her waist from behind, kissed her neck and Yevana shivered with anticipation of this hedonistic sandwich-type hold. Prince Masood whispered in her ear, 'You will love the delights of being a prisoner at sea.' That caused another shiver and several other sensations. Mobola being impatient grabbed her wrist and pulled her from this grip of desire and off towards the front door. The girls got in a taxi and headed for Mobola's swanky new pad in Canary Wharf. Yevana was feeling tired from the move to London followed by no sleep that evening and so let her head fall into Mobola's lap on the journey across town. She lapsed into sleep for a short time before the taxi pulled up and Mobola shook her to get out. 'Come, gorgeous we have some catching up to do.' They walked into the very new East End tower apartment block and requested a lift to the fourteenth floor. After pressing the electronic code on the number pad, they walked into the space that through the lounge wall to wall windows they had a clear view of London Town. This was for movers and shakers on the London scene as these did not come cheap, thought Yevana, as she surveyed the premises.

'Who's a lucky girl then?' said Yevana. 'What a difference success, sponsorship and influence make.' Mobola said nothing but just took Yevana and pressed her against the tinted glass windows with the City offices in the background and slid down onto her knees. Yevana closed her eyes and drifted off to somewhere else. No matter what the circumstances Yevana knew she was in love with Mobola; this person put her in a delirious state at times, as her beauty produced neurological exotic unreality that could never be properly explained. It wasn't real, it couldn't, no, wouldn't ever be and one day she would let it go, however, for now it was an addiction she did not want to cure; her knees buckled. There was nobody there this time, so off and on they indulged for the next twelve hours or so. She could only fantasise about next weekend and what it would bring for them. She considered how Toby would react and hoped she was correct that it would be as positive as she had suggested to Yurenev.

Yevana had also made her mark so far as Mobola was concerned as she now had Yevana's name tattooed across her lower back in rather tasteful italics, which Yevana thought really showed Mobola's feelings towards their friendship although she never really showed them.

The following day she booked a taxi and returned to their flat across town totally exhausted. Toby joked, 'Blimey I tried to call you, thought you had done a runner, babe. You look shattered, is everything okay?'

'I had turned my phone off as I was tied up' she sighed, 'but yes, I am whacked and need to top up my energy cells.'

'Nothing untoward I trust,' he commented as he turned to pick up the newspaper, as if only partially interested. 'Was Mobola well?'

'Yes, darling, Christina?'

'Oh yes, fine thank you, she sends her regards and as you know we will see her this week on site,' he said with a wry smile. They both smiled then walked into the kitchen and made some tea before settling down on the sofa to catch up properly. 'Team meeting,' he joked.

'If you like Toby, but don't forget it is a two-man team!' she responded.

Toby acknowledged, 'Only room for two, babe. Who else could be tolerated or indeed be brave enough to deal with ourselves?'

'Indeed,' ended Yevana's input into this, as she saw it as meaningless conversation.

She decided to move on and get straight to the point as there was much to organise ahead of the coming weekend. 'Everything is fine and I have had a very encouraging introduction with some influential people courtesy of Mobola that may secure our outstanding finance. However, we have work to do which includes a busy weekend ahead, darling! The nub of it is, that we will be going to Monte Carlo this weekend and accompanying us must be Josh for obvious reasons and you must bring your bitch Christina with you for your entertainment as Mobola, who will also be there, and I, will be setting sail once the business is taken care of and you are not invited my darling. Sorry, it's orders.' she continued rather cattily. 'I have been busy indeed and so you see we have much to discuss and prepare.'

Toby was delighted with what he was hearing and especially the potential multi-million-pound deals that would secure the London complex in its entirety. He considered Yevana must have been working the room in her inimitable style as only she can, which he knew only too well was most impressive. He wasn't stupid, there were going to be strings and the way the Russian had gone about arranging the deal reinforced this. However, he trusted Yevana and as things were if it included Christina, then it had the potential to be an unbelievable weekend although he could sense the game being played here, and he was game. He looked at the clock on the wall then turned to Yevana who had fallen asleep against his shoulder. He picked her up and put her to bed still clothed then quietly slipped out of the flat.

They recruited new staff during the following week, in a new office close to the prospective London complex site, which was currently under offer whilst separately, they waited for funding and their initial application for planning consent. The first person they employed was a woman by the name of Summer Rules a bubbly, sweet and intelligent twenty-six-year-old PA who would work for both of them, who was followed by a secretary ten years older than her called Janice Baytree. Youthful and vibrant and in her mid-thirties, she brought with her proven experience, a ruthless streak and bags of enthusiasm. Both couldn't wait to get started on such a project for such an aspiring partnership and company. Oh yes...both were single and good looking. Yevana smiled in a moment of consideration and sensed that the Christmas parties might be fun! Not that she was going down that road she reminded herself!

First things first and Yevana got them at it, initially asking Summer to book a taxi for the trip to the airport to take herself, Toby, and their new accountant Josh Solbar. He was their new accountant in London who was needed to agree any deal in principle over this important weekend. Christina, particularly, but also Mobola would have to make their own way to the airport as they separated business and pleasure. Josh came well recommended and any deal would have to be agreed based on his exceptional financial acumen. He was a smart man in many different ways and was one of the few happily married men that they knew which brought a semblance of normality that they weren't used to. He talked about normal life, where normal people resided, that they seemed to live outside of these days. Yevana inwardly laughed and thought that one day they might get there; on the other hand, that scenario wasn't even making it into her dreams right now!

From Toby's point of view, it all sounded almost too good to be true, however, he had spoken at length with their friend and mentor Bob Ray who made various enquiries and he told Toby, 'The names you have given me are kosher mate and in fact I wondered why they were bothering with this project, as the deal you speak of seems to be pretty small fry, relatively speaking, I guess there must be another agenda. These are seriously wealthy individuals who generally deal in big business mega deals. It is up to you but be careful. Once you take that first step into that world you are committed as these people don't like to be dropped or their services dispensed with at the drop of a hat. They decide when business is completed and to offend has its consequences. They will not entertain failure. As I said, the money is definitely there but be very careful how you play this game and trust your instinct.' Bob cancelled the call on that note somewhat eerily.

Toby took the next opportunity to talk to Yevana about his conversation with Bob. 'Darling, Bob tells me this is small business for these guys, what do you think they are interested in?'

'Okay, Toby, cards on the table; Me. Yurenev has a picture of me on his phone wearing my party clothes, taken by me as requested by Mobola, which is a long story, but he is very keen, I think. He has not said anything directly though as I have only met him at the one party. But bear in mind the plane doesn't return until Sunday, we leave here Friday and our business meeting is Saturday a.m.. I know he has plans for Saturday and Sunday with Mobola and I but I don't know anything other than that. I do know that Mobola has been told that we should be prepared to meet you all at Monte Carlo airport on Sunday for the trip home and oh yes, he is married,' said Yevana. 'It would be fascinating to meet that woman I must admit.'

'Got it,' replied Toby, 'I suspect you are going to party at sea with a whole host of his friends flying on board for the night. Be careful, darling. Are you sure you don't want me to escort you over the whole weekend, Christina will understand?' 'No, Toby, you can nail your bit on the side at your leisure! We will get the best deal we can out of this and then I will enjoy my cruise, if that's how it turns out. In any case I am under strict instructions to ensure that other representatives at our meeting on Saturday depart the boat when alongside in Monte Carlo before she sails at midday. Basically you, Christina and Josh are not invited, sorry.' Yevana laughed, but inwardly she was excited about both the deal and the unknown elements of twenty-four hours on a yacht adrift at sea with some very strange people, which in her view also included Mobola.

On Monday the real work would start in earnest and their growing ambition should take off, as they were due to meet the developer to properly outline more project detail, find out whether they were likely to get a favourable planning permission decision and continue to drive through the finance with Josh, hopefully to a successful conclusion. For now, the new staff had some work to do in their absence but otherwise everything would wait until Monday morning.

Monte Carlo

They met Josh his wife Mary who Josh had requested to accompany him to Monte Carlo as an opportunist short break abroad in the sunshine together, Mobola and Christine at Stansted, where the Jetstream was waiting at the private departures gateway. Mary was a rather shy and demure young woman who was clearly uncomfortable in unfamiliar company and had no intention of competing with the likes of Yevana or Christina, who looked and spoke with power and focus. She dressed in comfortable clothing for the trip albeit she felt underdressed compared with the others. Josh leant over whilst walking sensing this and commented rather unhelpfully, 'don't worry, darling, different league.' If looks could kill then Josh's weekend just took a turn for the worse. He tried to explain but got no further than 'but...' as Mary launched ahead out of his grasp.

This route through the airport departures was exclusive to those that paid for the privilege of riding a private jet, which meant the least amount of fuss and bye, bye to the cattle in the terminal. Yevana loved this, it was such a privilege. 'Toby, I could handle this lifestyle, darling.'

'Yup, I bet you could!' Does this mean you will want to spend more time with Yurenev?' he chided.

'No, but you will do it for us in the future, oh Mr Toby,' she said with fun in her voice. Christina who by now was holding Toby's hand as they made their way to the plane, gripped it harder to remind him that he was with her this weekend. No problems encountered, straight on board and off they flew heading south across the English Channel. It was a twenty-seater aircraft with luxury seats and a relaxing area with a drinks cabinet should one care for some time out of one's seat. There was a French waiter serving a light continental breakfast and after half an hour one of the pilots came back and introduced himself. He was a Sauvé French gentleman with long grey hair which made him seem very distinguished. Not quite a hippy but nevertheless longer than you normally see on a fifty- five-year-old pilot.

Toby was loving it. This was the way to travel. Was this really their future too? Looking around him in the aircraft there was that feeling of abnormality, fiction or just plain madness. Here he was with Christina, his constant companion and sometime colleague sat next to him and his live-in lover and business partner and her girlfriend sat across the passage. It seemed a bizarre arrangement. Funny thing was it suited everybody at this time. They all had their space to breath, there was no pressure and whilst they were certainly not all the very best of mates, there was a level of acceptance. Toby was very happy with the current arrangements and not keen to change things too much, although he could see that the nature of their couplings might change some circumstances in time. He did wonder what Josh and his wife Mary thought about this group of people they were travelling with. Toby could see that they were looking around in confusion as they tried but couldn't quite work out how it all worked. Still, not their problem, he thought to himself, but intriguing nevertheless!

Yevana sat holding hands with Mobola who were both dressed in business attire wearing sun glasses and motionless staring directly ahead as if in a trance. Yevana was wearing four-inch heels, a long three-quarter length pencil skirt and black top with huge fake pearls tight around her neck. Mobola was in similar but with a shorter skirt; Yevana in grey Mobola in orange, yes orange, stunning bright orange. Those two women felt connected and natural when they were together. There cannot be two more beautiful women walking the earth, thought Josh and Toby separately as they surveyed the cabin space. On entering the cabin for the first time Toby noticed the look of amazement on the French waiter's face when he saw these two women and all that they represented in his mind, sat in front of him: priceless! Once again Toby just smiled whilst Christina elbowed his ribs. He was sure that for such a small space and so few people there was enough to talk about that would fill the average novel.

Mobola had tried not to show her feelings for Yevana in the past but was finding it much harder as they spent more time together. Mid-flight during a quiet period when people were snoozing, she had been looking at her lover and felt a real pull of emotion. She couldn't help it, the emotion had been building for some time and at that point she could not stop herself, so leant over to Yevana's left ear lobe and out of nowhere said, 'Darling, bitch, I will stab any 'New Lover' if you dare to finish with me.' Yevana didn't open her eyes, she just carried on resting and felt the kiss on that lobe that accompanied the threat which sent a pulse through her body to all the right places. How extraordinary, so now she had got deep inside the real Mobola; this raw woman had feelings, deep rooted feelings. There was currently no other lover except Toby but this normally strong woman had used this moment of venerability to make a stand of ownership. Yevana however only felt the sexual excitement not any fear.

They arrived in Monte Carlo around midday and were met by a white limo that collected them after they were escorted through private arrivals and passport control and sat in eerie silence in the sound and bullet proof car. Clearly Yurenev was taking no chances in his life, probably had too many enemies or potential enemies with his substantial assets. Toby considered that you didn't get where Yurenev was without treading on weaker people on the way.

It was only a short journey to the magnificent marina full of super yachts sparkling in the sunshine. As they approached what turned out to be their home for the weekend the size was awe-inspiring. Yevana thought there must be smaller battleships which probably don't have helicopters on board! A group of staff were there to meet the business party and weekend guests. All of the baggage was taken on board and the party was led onto the boat and shown around for orientation purposes. Yurenev was not on board and sent his apologies and requested that everybody make themselves comfortable until dinner at nine p.m. The rooms were sumptuous, the epitome of luxury and sound proofed. There were super king-size beds, satin sheets, mirrored ceilings, erotic human artwork, luxury towels and other bedroom clothing and cosmetics. To top it off the rooms were full of bright and beautiful orchids.

Christina didn't even wait to shower. She noticed as they were shown to the bedrooms that Yevana's room was next door and the bed headboard was up against Yevana's room, so she opened her case pulled out a pair of handcuffs and tied herself to a bar which made up the top section of the headboard. She got on all fours looked back towards Toby and said, 'screw me, and damned hard, so that she can feel it through the wall.' Although he couldn't quite see the point, Toby didn't need asking twice and jumped on board! His mind was next door!

Next door Yevana could sense something in the wall coming from Toby's room and knew Christina would want to make a point and was doing her best already. However, she knew how Toby's mind worked and he would be thinking 'what is Yevana doing?' Well, she was relaxing as she knew, sensed, that this would be a tiring weekend. Getting a deal done to help realise their dream and a twenty-four-hour party 'imprisoned' at sea sounded fun but would require energy. Hanging her clothes in the wardrobe she found a bag with two packages inside neatly and expensively wrapped as presents. The small one in silver paper was a box. It took a little while to undo the string and pull out some cotton wool but she saw it contained the most gorgeous emerald diamond ring about two cms in circumference and shined like a star; 'Wow', Yevana exclaimed in an instant of viewing it. 'Wow, weeee.' It was massive and again looked mighty expensive but there was no message, although she looked carefully again to try and find one. More surprisingly it fitted her index figure like a glove; it was perfect and she loved it. How strange Yevana thought and wondered what everybody else had received. Mobola was in a separate room so it would have to wait for later. It wasn't long before, perhaps with more trepidation, she started to pull the gold paper off the second parcel which was slightly easier to unwrap. Inside was something to wear with a message this time. 'Yevana, please accept these gifts and wear them for the party on Saturday as my guest.' It was not signed by anybody but she knew that you didn't need to be a rocket scientist to work out Yurenev was playing 'Father Christmas' on this occasion. Laid out on the bed the outfit was lacking in material! 'No surprise there,' Yevana said as she stared at it. It was a loose fitting and short halter neck shift dress, in a shimmering design of horizontal pastel colours with a few delicate green motifs carefully sewn in shaped like tiny leaves. There were several pairs of five-inch-high heels in the wardrobe that she could choose from to wear and they were all classic high heels in a variety of suitable light colours to match the dress. Well, that was for Saturday night so she hung the dress in the wardrobe and turned her attention to that evening and dinner. Tonight, she was teasing with red heels, black eight-inch tight skirt, white blouse, no bra, two-inch earrings, and bright lipstick, red. Their instruction on a note pad in their rooms was to be at the bar upstairs by seven-thirty p.m. Yevana also wore her Cuban signet ring for good luck.

The dining room was set in super luxury and could seat thirty people comfortably, wood was everywhere with leather coverings in the seating areas. The room's aroma was classic leather and oak; opulence and it smelt of money. At one end and slightly offset from the dining area was a magnificent bar area with a very happy-go-lucky Italian barman already producing fantastic cocktails as well as any other requests at the bar as he had the lot. It was not long before the business party had all assembled at the bar in jovial mood just happy to be in such opulent surroundings. Josh and Mary were first to appear and were appropriately soberly dressed for the occasion, Mary very smart in a white cocktail dress. Without being stunning she was definitely attracting complimentary glances from the male staff. However, what followed was an eye-popping short skirt competition won hands down by Mobola in six inches of very little! Christina in double that size was looking horny and stunning in equal measure with her key assets fully supported up front and Toby on her arm dressed in pink of all colours. This colourful scene was a prefix to what quickly became a good atmosphere and shortly they were joined by Yurenev and Prince Masood who was joined by what turned out to be a couple of his friends and their partners; two women. Talk was very general and there was a concerted effort to steer clear of business talk; that would be done tomorrow. Yurenev rang the bell and welcomed everyone to 'sleep tight' in his super yacht. But no chance of that raced through the minds of most in attendance. Yurenev went on, 'Please recharge your glasses and take your seats at the dining table, the night is young.'

The seating plan was set and Yurenev was already playing games to amuse himself. Christina was seated between Yevana and Mobola and Toby between Mobola and one of the other female guests. Nevertheless, the meal was going well and it was only during the sweet course that Mobola decided to play a future assurance card by putting her hand under the table and then very slowly slide it up Christina's left leg and very gradually near her crotch. She pinched her inner thigh at the same time staring into Christina's eyes whilst simultaneously, telepathically, telling her not to cry out, then leaned in towards her ear and said, 'Darling, we think Toby might already have the hots for their new PA, Summer Rules – a gorgeous bitch, darling, gorgeous, no contact yet but imminent, not good! You will want to sort her out, won't you? Warn her off personal contact with him, do you understand me?' With this she pinched her harder to cause a bruise. 'Don't let us down.'

Christina had turned a bright red. Mobola took her chance and gently rubbed across her knickerless crotch; wet! To Christina's credit she was tough enough now to be able to turn towards Mobola and whispered, 'This is not for you, you pathetic women, it is for me.' It would be done. Mobola withdrew her hand and turned to Toby for more gentile conversation.

Christina was not happy but she was not losing Toby to a PA, not now, and she knew that Mobola meant business. She could make her life difficult and with Yevana behind this she would be in a no-win situation if she didn't play the game. Toby asked Christina if her company had been okay during dinner, as they retired to the lounge bar for more drinks and coffee. 'Oh yes,' she said staring at him with a fateful look, 'never better, it was so good I could pinch myself.' Toby wondered what the hell she was on about but decided to let it go.

As the evening panned out Toby was fascinated as he watched Yurenev have piercing eyes for Yevana all night with Prince Masood practically transfixed the same from across the table. It reminded him of when he first set eyes on her and was soon dumping his long-time girlfriend. So much had changed since then and although they led very complicated lives the love still burned stronger than ever.

It would be interesting tomorrow both doing a deal and knowing what would happen when he had left. Would Mobola feel sidelined and had the prince no chance with Yurenev around? Time would tell. Even then it would depend on Yevana to decide how to play tomorrow out as she held all the cards, as in her world no matter what, her priorities were never straightforward.

Intrigued, about one p.m., Yurenev started to take his chance and dig a little deeper whilst chatting to Christina and Toby about their personal circumstances. 'Why do you not leave Yevana and live together?' he asked, teasing them both.

'I am happy, we are happy. I love both women,' said Toby.

'Well, I will be frank with you, when I am in London I want to see more of Yevana so therefore I want you to move out,' replied Yurenev.

'But you are not seeing each other,' said Toby.

'We will be,' he came back, 'and if we are to do a deal tomorrow and I can and will help your project, you must move out. Think it over. If the answer is no, talk to your group and leave the boat in the morning before breakfast.'

Christina jumped in looking rather worried, 'That may not be possible. Yevana has deep rooted feelings for Toby and I could be blamed and hence she will seek revenge against me; I know it!'

'That would not happen, I will assure you neither Yevana, the dangerous Mobola or anybody else will interfere with exposing their lives to huge amounts of scrutiny and risk,' Yurenev commented. 'Think it over,' he continued. Toby and Christina looked on as Yurenev departed for his cabin without as much as a goodbye. By two a.m. they were all in bed and Toby was feeling especially excited. Christina thought this was because they were probably going to live together permanently, however, as Toby held her ankles, bent her legs back to her ears he was only thinking of Summer, his next intended conquest; that decision had already been made in his mind.

Upstairs on the yacht Mary and Josh had said their goodnights and had disappeared at the same moment as Toby and Christina, of which Mary couldn't help but wonder why in such a hurry? The prince kept Yevana and Mobola occupied until Yevana gave her excuses and retired, whilst Mobola stayed on much later. A stylish husband and wife team in their fifties from Monte Carlo seemed intoxicated with their new black acquaintance but Yevana was not hanging around to see what might or might not happen. She certainly didn't want a part of any action tonight.

The Deal

The following morning, they all assembled for breakfast by seven a.m. ready for the meeting at eight sharp. Yevana met Toby aft on deck in the gorgeous morning sunshine looking over the harbour and Monte Carlo itself. She approached him stood against the railing and placed her arms through his for a comforting hug and her head against his back. He didn't move, just froze and enjoyed the moment. 'Tell me you love me, babe,' she whispered.

'Of course,' he replied. He turned, kissed her forehead and moved away just in time to see Christina approaching to do the same. He hugged her and she said, 'I love you.' He said nothing. Yevana looked down into the beautiful green sea and saw her reflection and daydreamed of swimming deep into another mysterious world of the unknown. No time to dream, she had to get moving and make her dreams reality and so within a few moments she was sat at breakfast with the rest of the party. Not much was said as people came and went in their own time. Yurenev asked Mobola what seemed like a loaded question. 'I wondered if you had had an early night Mobola, as you seem refreshed this morning.' Mobola thought he had probably heard the noises from his cabin sound proofed or not. Yevana looked at her and instinctively knew the truth; she knew her well enough by now and could see where it was going last night. She also noted that Mobola's new friends had not materialised yet which was probably testament to Mobola's stamina! 'Yes, I am fine thank you,' Mobola replied whilst eating her succulent melon.

Mary left the group to their meeting to sit in the Monte Carlo sunshine on deck, taking the opportunity to peel off her gown and lay out in her white bikini, new designer sunglasses on, totally relaxed. The others assembled in Yurenev's business lounge and prepared to talk through the deal. It turned out that Yurenev was taking the deal on his own with the prince explaining that if things went as well as they hoped, he would want in on the next investment opportunity in an international city such as Paris. The model was good and he could only see good things to come. Toby explained that Paris was an aspiration as was LA, New York and LA to mention a few. Josh was taken aback by the ambition here but was obviously more than a little excited by the prospect. Mary would think he was joking as this all seemed fanciful for her fairly normal but talented accountant husband.

The terms were good, Josh was very happy and relaxed. He leaned across to Toby and whispered, 'I can't find a hole in this investment opportunity, and in fact the terms are far more generous in your favour compared to many deals I come across.' Toby knew why! 'In short, he gets a good deal in future investments and profit proportional to his input and you get your project delivered and prove you are serious players in this industry. If all goes to plan you will soon be five-star entertainment market leaders, it's that good' Josh finished.

Toby sat staring at Yevana as the coffee arrived for a short break in proceedings. Yurenev's accountants and business consultants were going through the details on a draft agreement produced ahead of the meeting. She stared back over her coffee at him, too. He was thinking they were on the edge here and the other side was now a dangerous place, relationships were about to get more tangled and complicated whilst the business was going to be full on with much more travelling and separation. Does he 'pull the plug', should they stop this expansion and save their relationship or was it too late? He knew the way they were, conventional their relationship would never be, it was long past the point of no return and they needed others. She probably already knew that too.

Yevana sipped her coffee and stared across at her love, her one true love. My goodness she would do anything for Toby. It was true though that she would probably always need extras in her life; it was just the way she was. She also knew that this next chapter was unchartered territory, dangerous, exciting, elements of the unknown and what's more potentially massive in terms of where this project and new contacts could be taking them. It wouldn't work separately, she wouldn't want it anyway, and they would need to be together, it was written in the stars; however, she could see they might have to live different lives, at least for some time; room to breathe out of work. It may be that they would spend days and many, many hours in each other's company, have sex at the same levels of lust, aggression and love but not turn up at the same apartment by default every night. This thought was probably reality and she needed to get this; he probably already did.

The deal was signed for a multi-million-pound investment payable into their account on Monday at three p.m. GMT. Yurenev's accountant and business managers explained that there was an arrangement to be made with their bankers on Monday morning which was the reason for the slight delay in payment. Details of the current situation regarding planning and other funding were laid out by Josh and Toby, who also confirmed that all things being equal they should be ready to sign infrastructure contracts on Tuesday and the project could proceed. A meeting for Tuesday would be arranged between the bank, property developers and the Y&T team. With planning permission in the bag, it would be a very exciting time.

Of course, Toby acknowledged the unwritten clause in the contract that would be as he saw it, a small relationship 'road bump' in order to give the project the thrust they needed. It was only this sort of support that would take them out of the ordinary and allow them to keep Manchester as they wished.

They all stood up, shook hands and everyone was smiling, Yurenev thanked them all for coming and reminded those not invited to stay, that a car would collect them from the end of the gangway at two p.m. to take them to their hotels after a light lunch on board. He was moving on quickly, thought Toby. He wanted them off so he could prepare for that evening's festivities at sea. Yurenev though, quickly pulled Toby to one side. 'Do we have things sorted at home Toby?'

'Yes, we do. I intend to take other accommodation on my return. Please do not mention this over the weekend, but it will be taken care of in due course,' he replied.

'Christina will thank me for this,' Yurenev joked.

'Wrong,' said Toby, 'as she won't be moving in!'

'Oh, well that's a shame, never mind, as you English say, ding dong,' Yurenev muttered very matter of factly as he marched off into the heart of the yacht.

Toby wasn't happy but he actually thought that for now it would be for the best. They would both need time on their own in the next year that was for sure.

If Mary was fascinated before by this group she was fixed by what she saw next. She woke up from her morning snooze on the sun lounger on hearing voices, got up and started walking around the starboard side of the yacht having anticipated the end of the meeting and lunch. Suddenly she caught movement out of the corner of her eye inside one of the large portholes of the cabins below. She couldn't help but look in and she saw Yevana, only recognisable by her clothing worn at breakfast, bent over a soft chair with her arms by her side gripping the sides, dress pulled over her head and Mobola spanking her with her bare hands. Mary immediately turned bright red as Mobola looked up and smiled at her then turned and carried on as if carrying out normal practice; to her it was!

At two p.m. bags were taken to the rear of the limo and the departing group left the boat. Toby and Christina were arm in arm as were Josh and the still in shock Mary.

That night in a hotel in Monte Carlo Josh found the normal straight-laced Mary had a renewed sexual energy whilst making love.

'Josh let's go now. I'm feeling like an early nap, let's not waste those gorgeous satin sheets they have laid on,' she said with a wink and a smile. In fact, she insisted that they get back to the hotel early after a tour of the principality. Amazing, he thought.

'No problem, good idea Mary, darling.' She insisted on a spanking from Josh who was emotionally somewhere between terrified and extremely excited!

Yurenev left pleasantries to his staff, his interest had now moved on. They all looked back as the boat slipped its moorings immediately after Toby's group had departed, as if in a rush. In many ways Toby was pleased to get off; it all seemed too claustrophobic. Before departing he had said goodbye to Yevana in her room. 'Have a good weekend, my darling, be good and stay safe,' he said. 'I will lovely, I will,' she exclaimed. They both looked into each other's eyes and knew things would be a little different on their return but were not sure how different. The weekend would have already shaped that. Toby thought Yevana looked rather flushed then out of the corner of his eye saw a reflection in a mirror of Mobola hiding in the adjoining room which explained her condition. He smiled, as he guessed this would probably be the last time Mobola would be on her own with Yevana this weekend.

The Party

The rest of the afternoon on board was bikinis and sun cream whilst top halves were discarded, obviously! The trip out to sea was delightful, the blue green translucent water splashing against the hull as it made way for the magnificent beast of a super yacht. They spotted other cruisers and yachts as they sailed and noticed other very sophisticated owners and their families and guests in all manner of dress or what seemed to be mainly undressed! In fact, one such group were really at it in that they were participating in what Yevana could only describe as group sex and could not seem to care less that other boats were passing. Mobola also sitting up to view, just placed her right hand across onto the flat toned base of Yevana's stomach and then slid it back away again; Yevana shivered. For most of the afternoon they were the only women sunbathing and drew many glares and quiet whistles of admiration from the staff as they went about their duties. The senior male guests were not to be seen as they took a well-earned and pre-party afternoon siesta out of the searing sunshine. They could hear groups of other guests arriving by helo onto the flight deck all afternoon, seeming to be in very good spirits ahead of what was anticipated to be another great weekend organised by their friend or acquaintance Yurenev Caspanov. Yevana tried to consider the wealth of the different owners of the private helicopters that continued to arrive and wondered whether she and Toby might acquire this sort of prestige in the years to come. Yurenev also had his private helicopters transferring guests from Monaco for those arriving on international flights or private aircraft. Most were undressed and heading for the deck spaces as the evening festivities were not due to start until after ten p.m. It was a complete array of the great and the wonderful. Gangster types mixed with models, politicians, girlfriends-wives; both! Yevana wandered about getting drinks for herself and Mobola and also to get some exercise in the legs and in doing so became fixated by this world she saw around her. There was money, money and more money, the best clothes, helicopters, power and beautiful people. Yevana had a great moment later going into early evening when a tall, slim, stunning, flat chested News media star she recognised from the US, came and slid onto the sun lounger next to her. Before settling she immediately took off her one-piece white boiler suite to reveal only a small yellow bikini bottom then leaned over to Yevana, raised her sunglasses momentarily and said, 'darling come and see me later; I want to drink from the well of heaven.' Subsequently she leaned back onto her lounger, closed her eyes and said not another word whilst they were neighbours on the loungers. Later, she watched Yevana and Mobola move and just looked up repeating her offer, 'don't forget me, cherry.' Mobola took exception and leaned over the newscaster's head, took off the sun glasses throwing them overboard before grabbing her blonde immaculate bob, pulling it back over the edge of the lounger and threatening, 'Not for you honey, you haven't the right to touch it; be warned.' Yevana just kept walking and ignored what she was hearing behind her. In fact, she was back in her room before Mobola could catch up with her. There was a quiet knock on her door though, followed a few seconds later by a more stern and louder knock with accompanying words from a frustrated Mobola. 'Darling, let me come in; I want to say good luck before the party tonight.' For the first time with Mobola, Yevana found herself feeling that she had the upper hand in this relationship which she was enjoying in a way that was sexually exciting. She didn't move and waited for Mobola to go away. There was a long silence until Mobola whispered, 'I know you are on the other side of the door and I will make you pay you nasty bitch, you nasty, nasty little bitch.' Yevana felt her blood racing and although she wanted what was the other side of her door, the adrenaline rush was palpable. The US media star passed Mobola in the passageway just as she finished her rant with Yevana. As she passed, rather gingerly, Mobola grabbed her hand and said, 'hold my hand bitch and come with me.'

She did as she was told. This turned out to be both good and bad timing for this woman as she had the best sex she had ever had with a woman for the next hour; however, it came at a price because she was taken to the limits and did not emerge into the party until two a.m. when she had had time to sort out clothing and makeup that covered her scratches and bruises. Even then it didn't do the job.

Yevana had a long slow bath and had a brief chat with her PA on the phone who assured her everything was going well in London. 'Hi, Summer, how are things? I was wondering if the meetings with the developers are in place for next week. We must stick to the schedule if we are to meet the strict deadlines we have set out to achieve. The initial money we have to develop the idea from the bank will only last so long,' Yevana said in a very questioning manner.

'Oh, Yevana, you will be so pleased with us as we have done all of that and more. The meetings are all good to go and the developer has said that he thinks he has done a deal with the landlord for the planners to get on site earlier than planned. He wouldn't tell me how, he just smiled and said palms had been rubbed.'

'Exactly, Summer. Never ask awkward questions of our clients particularly where we benefit; we might not like the answer, or certainly want to know the answer!' replied Yevana.

'Sorry, Yevana, I didn't mean,' sighed a worried Summer.

'Don't be silly, darling, it is just a point to note, you have done a great job.' Yevana said in a reassuring manner.

A more confident and less crestfallen Summer replied, 'Thank you. Is there anything else I can do?

'Yes, stop working and go and find some fun tonight as we are here, goodnight Summer.' She cancelled the call. Yevana was all too aware of Summer's beauty and the attraction she knew Toby had started to feel, so coupled with the knowledge she just knew he was about to leave their nest there was a concern. Of course, this could be dealt with at any time albeit she would tread carefully.

Yevana watched some satellite TV, had a power nap for an hour then applied the evenings makeup and dressed. She still wasn't sure what to expect of this night but was sure she was slave to getting a deal done for their expensive and ambitious project. She felt healthy and was ready looking down at the emerald; magnificent it was. At about nine p.m. a member of staff came and knocked on her door and as she opened it she was confronted with a less than happy, rather frustrated Mobola, who had been called upon first of all.

'Madame, Mr Yurenev asks for the pleasure of your company.'

'Of course,' she replied,, 'I am ready.'

'Ah, you have found your key then' said a scowling Mobola sarcastically. At the same time, she scanned Yevana in her pastel and green shift which looked spectacular and knew she had somehow managed to hide her breast earrings inside her halter neck dress without them showing.

To add some spice Yevana held Mobola's hand and looked her in the eye with a soft reassuring glance and said, 'Shall we go and enjoy ourselves?' The young member of staff just looked on in awe as he led these most desirable females to Yurenev. He was looking splendid in an open neck white tuxedo and introduced the women to many others in his group then left them to wander for a while. Yevana thought there must have been at least one hundred and fifty people on the yacht and in the dim light of the Mediterranean _night sky it was a sea of sparkling jewels and summer colours mixed with the joyful atmosphere you associated with good times. She wasn't surprised to note that most women were only wearing a shift, heels and diamonds and not another stitch! She already had her attractors particularly one overexcited, overweight and over 'the limit' gentleman who was becoming persistent. He didn't seem to take a hint as he probably wasn't used to the term 'not interested.' Unknown to Yevana other eyes were on her also as this behaviour had been monitored by the staff. At the point of his third more drunken attempt to disrupt her evening with his charms, this rather large and unpleasant looking man was suddenly and unceremoniously picked up at the armpits by two very large members of staff and thrown directly overboard which was not only a long fall, but at night filled with alcohol and miles from anywhere a pretty dramatic occurrence. Some of the passengers looked overboard but knew better than to do so for long as this incident was off the radar. Nobody stopped what they were doing as the party was in full swing and most were oblivious in any case. It just seemed accepted that he got it wrong and paid an expensive price. It would also be obvious as a warning that Yurenev must have eyes on this woman and it became noticeable for the rest of the evening as suitors were conspicuous by their absence although not by their eyes. She, Yevana, was not to be interfered with or embarrassed. Yevana was wearing her rock, the emerald, and even in this crowd it stood out and she considered it was probably a Yurenev trademark; people knew.

Yevana found out the following day that apparently the nuisance gentleman got lucky and was picked up by another yacht four hundred metres away whilst screaming with all he had left in him.

The party was in full swing by midnight and there were already people in the pool skinny dipping. The oldest Yevana spotted was an eighty-year-old woman with the body of somebody fifty years her junior, whilst her most attentive Italian boyfriend was about thirty. There was certainly wine, decadence and song by the bucketload. Mobola, looking fabulous, walked up to the pool kicked her heels off and dropped her shift to the floor and dived in, swam a length and back and leapt out and got dressed again. She moved like a panther and certainly caused a stir. Yurenev came back to find them shortly after the swim and escorted them to his lounge area for nibbles and vodka on the rocks, his favourite tipple apparently. After a brief discussion of general chit-chat Yurenev suggested they move below decks.

'Ladies, please join me below, I think you will enjoy this fascinating private game of poker. It is a challenge between two very good players, follow me please.'

It was around one a.m. as they proceeded to follow. They walked down the wooden teak steps along a passageway and through a door kept open by a Russian minder, of fairly sturdy disposition to say the least. Yevana looked up to him and smiled; she wasn't surprised when he didn't reciprocate! There were seats to view from and about fifteen people did so with as many again standing of which Yurenev and Yevana were two. The room was air conditioned so there was that feeling of being cooled in a very hot atmosphere. The interior of the room had some very expensive looking oriental art screwed to the walls and the lighting was dimmed to suit the occasion. In various positions around the edge of the room were three and four seat sofas with bodies spread across them drinking and smoking fragrant cigarettes, which did not detract from the expectant atmosphere. The teak panelling also added to the aroma and sense of mystery that seemed to fill the nostrils at this heady gathering. The perfume odour was almost overpowering but Yevana was enjoying that intoxicating mixture!

'I normally play,' said Yurenev, 'but tonight the prince wants to take this other man on himself without distractions. It is what we call a duel, in the same way they used to shoot at one another in London a long time ago in order to settle a disagreement.' He leant very close and continued whispering in her ear. 'The other man is called Roy Walsterhome, an obese, very rich American entrepreneur. This match has been brewing for some time; should be interesting. The prince knows what he wants and has set a target.' She looked back at him and he just smiled, in that silent but deadly expression. They didn't have to wait long before even the untrained eye could tell that the American was losing heavily and sweating as much. He was breathing much heavier than when he started and fidgeted continuously, of course this could be a trick for all Yevana knew of playing poker seriously. His wife was a most stunning blonde twenty years his junior in her mid-twenties. Tonight, she was wearing a short one-piece halter neck with Japanese artwork and looked absolutely stunning. She stood directly behind him and showed no emotion as if she really didn't have a clue what was at stake, well perhaps she had seen it often enough, Yevana considered.

The fidgeting and sweating increased and then after about an hour things turned for the worst after a short break. The money on the table had reached serious proportions, even at this level and it was becoming clear that a big loss for somebody was on the 'cards'. The American got to the point where he could not lodge any more funds that he could repay if he lost. 'I have no more money to play' he declared in a rather shaky manner.

The prince looked over his shoulder and nodded his head towards his lawyer who immediately came across and listened to his boss. The lawyer nodded. The American pleaded to be able to carry on. The prince put his hand up.

'Enough, you may IOU your business.'

'But, but,' nothing else was said; he pulled a pen from his jacket pocket and wrote out the IOU on a gilt-edged pad that was put in front of him.

'Continue,' the prince called out and the game recommenced. Soon the American had written out IOUs for his business, his helo and his Californian mansion. That was his lot and he had lost the lot. Yevana couldn't believe that this man had put all he had worked for on a game of cards. All he had left was one thing. Suddenly it clicked, the penny dropped, the prince only ever wanted this! Yevana couldn't believe it.

'Okay' said Prince Masood, 'I have one last chance for you if you wish to get back some of your belongings.'

'Anything, Prince Masood, anything,' the American exclaimed seeking an opportuneity.

'Good,' he replied. 'Here's the deal and you can't lose. The next game, should you wish to accept the terms, you will play to win back your life. However, your new IOU will be your wife and its non-negotiable, so walk now with her or risk her to keep everything. If you win you win everything back and keep your wife. If you lose you win back everything but hand over your wife who will become my fourth wife; simple.' The blood drained from the American's face and he did not even attempt to turn to face his wife.

He replied immediately. 'It's a deal... I will win it all back,' the businessman said confidently, whilst sweating 'for ten men' and shaking uncontrollably! 'So be it,' replied the prince.

'Play then, deal the cards, please,' called the prince with a knowing smile spread across his face. 'By the way, sir, you will hand your wife over to me should you lose, but we must keep this dignified." The wife was stood fixed behind her husband and couldn't move, she felt paralysed knowing her perilous position. She had probably already worked out that lives were at stake if anybody tried to renege on the deal. Part of this game was the isolation of being on the boat; it added to the drama.

You could have heard a pin drop. This was like watching a cock fight in a sleazy joint in downtown Saigon; not one person there wanted the businessman to win, you could feel it in the atmosphere as everybody leant in to get a closer look when the cards were revealed on the table. This was human nature feeding off greed and evil excitement as if baying for blood. Yevana looked across into one darker corner of the room and saw one man step behind his girlfriend and lift her skirt from behind and from what she could make out, enter her, slowly, very slowly as she manoeuvred herself making no effort to resist him. To Yevana, the game seemed to go on forever until the last cards were dealt and over an excruciating last ten minutes the final cards were flipped. The business man showed three kings which was followed by a royal flush from the prince. The businessman's head slumped onto the table causing a shock wave of noise in a silent room where only air con was audible and momentarily he didn't move as if he had a heart attack. Suddenly though, he sprang upright as if nothing had happened and that he realised the gravity of the position he was in, knowing that two of Yurenev's minders stood behind him waiting to act as appropriate. He stood, turned to his wife and kissed her on the cheek, still in shock at what had happened at what was supposed to be a fantastic party. Having promised her as much earlier in the day, he was now taking her by the hand and to her prince who was sat motionless. Nobody dared move. Yevana thought that they might all start laughing as if part of some wild joke that everyone was party to; It was nothing of the sort, of course. The prince took her hand and made her do a twirl as if analysing a pedigree horse for the first time. 'You will be a good wife. Julian, come and take her to my quarters, I will see you later, darling,' he told his Greek assistant and his latest addition wife before adding, 'Please take this man away and get him off the boat.' The two Russian henchmen grabbed the businessman and marched him out of the room. He was given strict instructions by the prince's lawyer on how his marriage was to be dissolved then he was escorted off the yacht without mercy and driven by boat back to Monaco within five minutes; wifeless. In the dark corner the girlfriend and her man are pulling themselves together having 'sealed the deal.' Hot indeed, thought Yevana. As the gathering dispersed she noted that it was a jovial exit with everyone chatting about what they had witnessed. One woman said, 'shame about the young wife. She will be a sexual slave now, shame.' Interestingly, soon afterwards Yevana spotted the gent from the dark corner meet up with what turned out to be his wife on the upper deck! She was in her mid-fifties as was her youthful looking husband, but so engrossed in her various conversations and alcohol consumption she seemed oblivious that he seemed flustered and was sweating profusely.

Having settled back in the main reception area Yevana noticed that Mobola had moved across the room with a couple of middle-aged French politicians that she recognised from pictures in newspapers and television. Typically unfashionable, they seemed to love their assumed self-importance. Yevana was close hold with Yurenev and a few other friends of his. Eventually their group moved to another smaller room filled with all sorts of lively jazz music and shish pipes, she guessed filled with all sorts of substances. People certainly seemed happy and had assumed all manner of positions across seating and the floor cushions. Yevana took a pipe handed to her as they took to sitting on some rather smart but massive cushions on the floor spaced in a circle. An Italian next to her asked, 'do you smoke, Yevana?'

'No, not normally but I will try anything once.' She smoked what was said to be clean smoke and certainly there were no adverse effects she recognised.

'That is good,' he replied, 'it helps the body to relax.'

'I am as relaxed as one could be on this boat,' Yevana finished rather dryly. He was slimy and smelled rather awful. She quickly moved her cushion and sat next to Mobola and the Frenchmen.

The alcohol was flowing well and the vodka was having its affect. By three a.m. things were moving on somewhat and Mobola had disappeared with the two French politicians. Yurenev escorted Yevana onto a very feminine boudoir where there were several couples in various states of dress and undress. Yevana spotted Mobola in a dark space on the far side engaged with the two politicians; she was naked but for her heels. Yurenev didn't mess around as he pulled Yevana into a corner and danced a slow close dance and then spoke softly to her leaning close to her ear.

'On Monday the deal will be authorised, not by the bank but by me. You should inform me by text that you have made arrangements to live alone and have informed Toby and asked him to leave your flat with immediate effect.' There was no more to be said on this morning as the sunlight began to appear through a porthole on the horizon. He looked her in the eyes and said, 'I want you to meet two friends of mine.' Firstly, he proceeded to lift her arms up and removed her dress, revealing he sparkling earrings dangling in the soft light of the room. She stood there for a moment and sensed real freedom and anticipation in just her heels and earrings. He clutched her arm and led her into another corner of the room where they were joined by a husband and wife in their forties, who she recognised earlier as they had arrived in a giant Delorsky helicopter. It was from a Russian oil company which she couldn't remember but it didn't matter as she could tell they were players, real players. So Yevana spent the next four hours in this room in a jungle of bodies, noises and at some point into a more private room where all bets were off; this was serious endeavour! Mobola was not around as she was kept busy herself.

Yevana didn't know if she would get her dress back again and having moved from room to room in her heels, diamond and two-inch earrings hanging serenely from her breasts, was aware that most clothes had been dispensed with. Helicopters continued to come and go as people left the party having had their fill. At one stage she spotted her dress on a blonde with three men inside her; the lady noticed Yevana and smiled knowing who the dress belonged to. By mid-morning, Yevana had been with the oil executive and his wife alone for the past couple of hours and was eventually allowed to leave. Mysteriously, her dress was sat outside the room she was leaving. She slipped it on and walked outside to get some air, followed closely by diving head first into the pool and cleansing herself by swimming a few slow lengths. Interestingly when she got out she witnessed a beautiful striking individual talking to Yurenev who Yevana had not seen before. Yurenev had long since departed from their gathering in the early hours after he was called for by his staff. He actually left to join his wife who had arrived by helicopter for breakfast. She was a stunning blonde at around five feet eleven inches tall, legs to die for with an 'I am untouchable persona.' Yevana wondered what sort of life they led as a couple bearing in mind what she already knew about her husband's activities both entertaining and business. She was intrigued to find out and already guessed it was complicated when she saw her disappear below with a girl, aged no more than twenty, who had arrived with her holding hands from the helicopter.

After a few hours catching up on her sleep Yevana met Mobola in the dining room for a light lunch, both looking surprisingly refreshed considering the activities of the previous night. Others sharing the lunch areas were looking less refreshed and sun glasses were being worn inside and out and of the large variety. There was no further sign of Yurenev before departing as he was busy. When the member of staff told them this both women looked at each other and said, 'yeaaaah' and laughed out loud. He left a message with his staff though telling them to deal with all their requirements for departure. Mobola had some other news.

'Darling, I am not accompanying you back to Monaco as I have been invited to stay on board where I will be courted by Prince Masood.'

'But I thought your coach wanted you back in England for training on Monday?' Yevana teased.

'Darling don't be silly. He will have to wait as it won't hurt to take a couple of days off.'

Yevana laughed. 'That's rubbish and you know it. You will throw away all your good work. Remember what got you here; it wasn't your sexual appetite.'

Mobola was starting to get angry. 'That's rich from you, darling. I haven't heard you complaining lately. I told you it will wait. Now go and pack or you will miss your flight; it leaves in ten minutes.' She softened as she approached Yevana and gave her a big hug, whispering in her ear, 'Darling, next time we meet it will be special, you'll see. I love you. Bye, bye.'

'See you Mobola and take care.' Yevana finished with a blown kiss in her friend's direction as they went their separate ways. Yevana was worried about Mobola; she was in danger of drifting and if she was not careful it would be too late before she realised. She was typical of many talented people who lived on the edge but couldn't see it. They were both getting involved in a dangerous world and would need to try and watch each other's backs. Trouble was Yevana didn't trust Mobola to be able to watch hers so she would have to be doubly careful when isolated from Toby.

Yevana packed in quick time and was shown to the helipad and flown off the super yacht by the Yurenev helicopter to Monaco airport where she met the others, all of whom were in fantastic spirits generally speaking. Mary looked especially happy and as Toby pointed out later, 'it is as if she has had a moment of inspiration or seen something life changing. Whatever it is, it has caused Josh to look very tired.'

'How strange' replied Yevana genuinely not knowing she had been seen by Mary in the act of being spanked by Mobola. The others were like Yevana in that they all started to look tired as the day progressed and didn't want to say much, eventually sleeping all the way home on the aircraft. She looked at Toby and Christina and thought they looked happy together which although it pulled a bit, it was fine; it was just the way it was.

Ahead of their return Yevana had already made the decision to leave the apartment for one of her own. She knew that Toby had already also picked up the vibe and the way their lives were at present it made it easier. Through the smokescreen though, this would hurt her, hurt a lot. She had instructed Summer to have an apartment lined up for her to move into soonest and had received a note to that effect, which said that all was well and she could move in within a week of her return, at a location not far from the future complex. Summer managed to negotiate a really generous rent somehow. Toby, probably living with Christina in her old bed, did not sit well but she had not really lived in the flat yet so it wouldn't be as bad. In any case she would always have Toby if she wanted him and she would see to that. She drifted back to sleep dreaming of their London complex, its grandeur and the stars flocking to 'play' there. This was most important now and nothing could get in the way, nothing.

Josh was sat opposite Yevana in dreaming heaven. He had had one of the best weekends of his life and what a gas in such a fun town. Monaco was so vibrant and in such lovely weather he and Mary had loved every minute. He was fascinated that his wife had picked up a renewed sexual vigour that had obviously been lying dormant deep in her soul. She was already planning her next shopping spree to the lingerie shops, as she informed Josh sometime during the journey home. Then out of the blue, 'Babe, why is being spanked so exciting to people?' Josh spat out some of his drink whilst sitting bolt upright in the quiet cabin.

'For Christ's sake, Mary, take those headphones off when you want to say something and talk quietly,' he exclaimed whilst looking round frantically to see who heard the comment. An older lady, still awake and sat across the aisle two seats forward looked back and smiled. His face turned red!

He nervously cleared his throat and whispered, 'I don't know the answer, but suspect it is the element of the forbidden. Now settle down and get some rest.'

'Okay, babe, what fun though, I can't stop thinking about it!' she replied as she looked away with a beaming smile.

Josh looked across at Yevana and wondered what made this fascinating woman tick and tried to imagine the scene explained by Mary in the cabin, particularly as he fancied both Yevana and Mobola. No wonder Mary couldn't get it off her mind, because in fact, he was struggling too. Yevana was by far the most enthusiastic, diligent, capable and determined human being he had ever met and by some distance. He thought it must be difficult for such a person to get a high in the limited spare time that they allowed themselves. Other people took weekends off but not her, she was always working, just as this weekend had been a business trip. At that moment, a good-looking air stewardess breezed past and as he let her perfume drift across him and up into his senses he thought of her being spanked and started to drift off again, with a smile on his face.

Toby was feeling happy sat opposite, as he watched the others dosing and knew that Yevana would have been told of the deal and caveat that meant that they must live apart. He knew she would move out tomorrow and would have organised it already as she would not let anything get in the way of the complex plans, not even their relationship. Once Christina found out he knew she would be excited and immediately make plans to join him, however, unfortunately for her he had already made plans to the contrary; he was moving on. The major priority now was to get this complex started and completed to the exacting standards they had set themselves and nothing less was acceptable which is where he was completely in sync with Yevana. Christina would be upset but Toby could deal with that as it was better to deal with the expectation management now before it got messy. She was a girlfriend and no more which was the way it had to stay.

The aircraft arrived back in London and having fought their way through passport control, baggage return and then out to the taxis, they said their goodbyes. It was quite awkward as Christina said goodbye to Toby only to see him disappear in the taxi back to the flat he shared with Yevana. She shared with Josh and Mary but said nothing as this was a bad end to a great weekend. She had hoped he would come back to her flat for the night. When she broached the subject back in Monaco though all he would say was, 'No, Christina, I will be with Yevana tonight.' A crestfallen Christina sulkily replied, 'Oh.'

Single again

That evening as soon as they were back in the apartment, Toby and Yevana chucked the bags on the floor, made a filter coffee with amaretto and discussed the deal, the weekend and the future. Yevana spoke first. 'Toby, I am moving out tomorrow. We need space to grow, so apart, our ability to run the business and to meet each other day to day fresh and eager to discuss and plan the future will be healthier.'

'I love you darling but time on our own, well, I need time by myself, will only enhance what we have and remind us of why we are such a strong team. Living together, for now, will be too claustrophobic.' She wasn't lying she knew that, as it was not all about Yurenev and the funding, it was more complicated than that. She needed some more space and private space from anybody. This is what helped her tick.

As she had guessed he did not try to change her mind or sound shocked or chocked. 'I agree completely, it makes perfect sense. We need every piece of advantage we can glean over the next few years and this extra space will help. I will look after our flat in preparation for the day we share it or another home properly, which we have not been able to do this time.' Toby looked at Yevana and knew that they both knew why they were doing this but ironically although they were given very little choice it was still the right thing for many reasons and they would have their day again.

'I am not going to move Christina in here Yevana, which might surprise you. I don't want that and she will have to accept it although I know she has assumed this and will be gutted. I am not looking for a particular situation as you will understand. I wish also to have the space and some solitude away from building the business as you suggest. It is the right thing to do.'

'Okay, well I have asked Summer to find me an apartment immediately, which she has done in the immediate area of the complex site.

I can move in on Saturday; therefore, I will move to the Bay View Hotel for the remainder of the week, which is positioned well,' replied Yevana.

'Do you have to do it this week, can't it wait?' Toby tried to reason.

'I think we both know that is not possible Toby,' was all she really wanted to add but went on, 'but Toby' she sighed, 'I love you to the bottom of my heart and nobody else can replace you. We live fast and incredibly complicated lives that will test our wellbeing as we go forward, but we must trust each other and I know we will come back, definitely come back.' Suddenly she started crying and sobbing. Toby sat still, he could not afford to comfort her, it was not easy but he had to stay firm; they had to move on. She walked to the bathroom as he forced back the lump in his throat and a text message alerted him.

'Have you told her yet?' He replied, 'No need, she is leaving the apartment tomorrow. 'I will get ready to move in then and we can discuss the details in the morning my love. xx?' Christina came back.

'No,' Toby replied without hesitation, 'you will stay as you are we are not moving in together. I will explain tomorrow. xx.' There was no further reply. Toby could sense the desolation, almost feel it. Christina was a decent person who didn't deserve this. He stood up and walked over to the window and looked out into the London brightly lit night. He tried to understand how, when everything was going so well and had everything to live for, he had managed to get in a situation that both of the women he was having a relationship with and loved for different reasons, were in a distressed state. He could only hope it was worth it in the end. However, in reality he had never considered Christina to be long term and although he couldn't put his finger on why, it was just a feeling he had. She may be miffed now but he was convinced she would stay in the relationship; she enjoyed it!

Christina truly thought this was her opportunity and was totally devastated, throwing the phone straight out of an open window and three floors to the ground. She got up slowly from the armchair she had been resting in and walked across to the window and looked out and down to the pavement, but quickly jerked her head back into the room as she had spotted two people looking on the floor then up to the open window. She gently peered out again and she saw a man throw something in a bin. She hoped it had not hit one of them. She went out to retrieve the phone but it was smashed to bits but was lucky to be able to pick the largest bit out of the bin which housed the sim card; lucky! Having calmed down and smiled about the phone tantrum, she knew that this changed nothing because Toby was her rock and she needed him more than ever and loved their intimate time together and he was a great lover: the best.

Remembering Toby's reply and trying to reason why he didn't want her moving in with him, Christina, simmering with a little jealousy, but not so much anger, remembered Mobola's warning. She felt something she had not felt before in her life and that was some form of defensive tentacles, of a vigilante nature. This was terrible but if the new PA woman, Summer Rules, was moving in on her patch she would deal with it. She had no evidence, but worried now. She was not moving in on her man; she would sort it. Christina stopped looked at herself in the mirror in her bedroom and for a moment didn't recognise herself. She moved closer to the mirror and spoke to herself out loud, 'what do you mean Christina, what will you do about it?' She was shaking a little. 'If the situation arises, I will deal with it; I will take action, simple.' Christina walked away and knowing or realising she meant it, poured a stiff whisky and went to bed. She sat upright in her favourite satin sheets for a moment, drinking her delicious malt, then it became apparent, she was aroused.

Yevana walked from the bathroom, finished packing and called a taxi. She did not want to leave this bedroom which was supposed to be their new home and considered that this was a huge price to pay for their ambitions. However, when the plans were as big and aggressive as proposed, sacrifices were inevitable. Dressed in jeans and a T-shirt, she pulled on a coat and picked up her bag and case.

'I will come next week for other belongings,' she declared as she left the bedroom. He didn't reply. Toby was watching the news on a satellite TV station and did not look back as she walked past, not hesitating as she opened the door letting it shut by itself. She stood outside the door momentarily thinking about what she had just done. Was it right? Did they need to do this? Was she an idiot? Was this really temporary or would it be the end of their relationship? What was she doing? In a flash a picture of Caren Lords appeared and disappeared from her mind. The image made her feel weak at the knees before composing herself. Her mind was playing games. This moment passed quickly and she set off down the stairwell and out into the night. As she waited for her taxi to arrive she placed her bags down, sat on a step and took a deep breath then thought about how they had both just performed an act of denial, as it would have been good to have spent a proper first night in that flat. But of course, they knew it was better not to go there at that time; move on. The taxi driver pulled up and took her to the Bay View. She got out, the driver pulled her bags from the boot and he departed receiving a small tip. Before picking up her bags she looked up at the small hotel and all of a sudden felt lonely for the first time in her life, which made her bags feel much heavier as she walked up the few concrete steps and collected her keys from the rather old grumpy but leering fifty something male receptionist. Yevana could feel his eyes following her to the lift. His offer of assistance for her largest case was rejected. The sixth-floor room was fine and would be a good base for the next week. A little note on the bed from Summer was a nice surprise. It read, 'I hope this is okay Yevana, love Summer.' Yevana wasn't interested in the note at all but did put the card to her nose as she loved the strong scent. She said out loud, 'naughty!' and smiled to herself. Her phone buzzed which startled her in the silence. Looking down at it she saw it was from Mobola. 'Are you free?' was all it said.

'Yes,' was all Yevana replied. Yevana stared at the message and knew that Mobola was probably in a tryst. That would be form! At that moment Yevana wanted to be there! She wasn't, so she unpacked and naked slipped under the duvet and drifted into a deep sleep.

Toby waited to hear Yevana start walking down the stairs. He could not hear anything for a few moments and thought she might be changing her mind. Then she was gone. He looked down from a window and watched her get into the taxi. He popped his head back in and sent a text. 'Get over here now.'

'Get over here now,' was all it said. Christina jumped out of bed slipped on a pair of wedge shoes and shorts and a 'T' and left the flat.

Monday morning was a new day, a new era. Yevana was at the office at seven sharp. The others were there by eight. Toby was second in after Yevana and alone. She asked, 'On your own then?' Toby not sure if she meant it as a statement or question replied, 'Of course, darling, of course,' and he smiled his big beaming 'I am lying' type of smile and kissed her on the right cheek. Yevana knew him too well. He couldn't sleep on his own last night; it wouldn't have made sense to him.

The new staffs were brilliant, their enthusiasm would fast forward much that had to be done and their experience would make delegation easy at times in order to take some of the weight. However, more was needed so Summer had selected another PA who would be directly responsible to Yevana alone. She was due in for an interview at ten thirty. Tight schedule but it was essential. One of the criterion for selection of the new PA was having interior design skills and experience because apart from dealing with Yevana's every need he or she would help co-ordinate the interior design of the project that left Yevana free to make the very big decisions. Slightly unorthodox but it was what she wanted to do.

Her name was Fay Turner and she was five minutes early. Having rung the doorbell Summer went out to greet her outside on the street. What a sight! Summer had told her, smart but casual.

'Hi Fay, you look stunning, are you ready?'

'Yes, sort of,' Fay said with a nervous giggle.

She walked into the office suite definitely making a mark with her jet black very long hair in a tight ponytail, wearing a black pin stripe pencil skirt, waistcoat with high purple ankle boots and not much else from what Summer could see. She invited her inside and asked her to sit and wait outside Yevana's office door from where she would be called for interview shortly. Summer started to be concerned her work was flawed and that Fay might be totally unsuitable.

Having been notified Yevana looked up and waited until it was ten thirty before getting up from her desk and walking towards her door. She opened it slowly and came round in front of Fay and asked her to accompany her inside where Fay was invited to sit on a small basic plastic white chair in front of her desk. Fay went through a premeditated routine as she sat down slowly, crossing her legs and placing her hands together on a knee then slowly raising her chin upwardly and pushing her ample breasts out to focus on Yevana.

Wow, thought Yevana, what a statement. First impressions were that Summer had done well again. She took a long pause looking Fay up and down and was taken with such a strikingly confident young woman.

'Welcome to Y&T, Fay, I am delighted to offer you the job.'

'But,' Fay replied rather too quickly.

'No buts Fay, you have just found out how I work, which is dynamically, especially when decisions are required and of course I trust my staff. I am busy and so is everybody today as we have a meeting with the planners, architects, developers and Historic England in an hour. Without further ado I want you to meet our interior design consultant Justine Hauser, who unusually is actually a man regardless of his name and a brilliant designer as you will probably already be aware, who is desperate to be involved in our project in London. He will be at the Tate Modern top floor cafe at one p.m., so please don't be late. He is not sure what I wanted to discuss today or in fact who would meet him there. However, after you have read the same brief he has on your way to the Tate, which is with Summer out front, I want you to begin your friendship with him and come back here by six p.m. and back brief me on the plans as you both see them from the design perspective. Thank you.' She was being dismissed and she knew it as Yevana's eyes diverted to some papers on her desk.

For a moment Fay hesitated as she considered that she had not even been given the opportunity to say whether she wanted the job or even shaken hands at any stage. However, she could already feel the adrenaline was pumping through her veins and she couldn't wait to read the brief.

Fay stood turned and walked out of the office shutting the door. Summer was there as planned and handed Fay the brief.

'Happy reading, partner,' she said jovially as she returned to her desk without saying any more. The offices were busy as Yevana had pointed out and at this point Fay felt in the way so quickly departed out into the daylight. The folder was thick and had sketches and notes in various forms. She placed it under her arm and headed for the Tube.

Having had some breakfast in a cafe and taken the opportunity to start reading the brief, she settled down in a seat on the underground and closed her eyes for a few seconds to take in what had happened earlier. It was so quick it seemed unreal as she got up that morning not knowing if she had a chance of the job and was now thundering through the London underground with her mind racing like the various station lights as they flashed by. The person she was to have a very close working relationship with had not even conversed with her in any real detail before giving her the job, which was strange but exciting. Who was her boss? Well, most definitely one of the most attractive people she had ever met and for a completely heterosexual woman with a long-standing boyfriend, Fay had been stirred for which feelings she could not account. Staring into the dark walls outside the carriage, she considered that this next journey in her life might be spicy. It was several stops before her destination and she found herself drifting and had completely forgotten about the brief she was supposed to be reading when her stop arrived. As it pulled up she pressed send on the text to her boyfriend of two years. 'Moving on, sorry, please don't reply. I am not in love.' Message ended, she turned her phone off and she threw it in her bright mauve handbag. Fay knew she would be too busy and her priorities would not allow for a longstanding relationship. The fact they had not moved in together made this move much easier than it might have been. This was callous but necessary.

As the door closed Yevana knew Summer had found the most brilliant young designer, who would be a fantastic friend and PA. Later as they left the Y&T offices to travel to the council offices for a project development meeting, she lightly pulled Summer's arm back and lent into her left ear and speaking gently said, 'You have done very well Summer, please make sure you look after Toby.' Yevana, walked on ahead as Summer looked on in amazement. That was definitely a sign of approval if the opportunity arose. Summer smiled and ignored it for now; it would wait.

Summer was like her name suggested, sunlight, bright, colourful, fascinating, sexy, edgy, and damned gorgeous but romantic trouble if you were a woman with a man. She had very dark long wavy hair, lovely, muscled legs, a small bum and pert breasts. Best of all her lips were luscious. In fact, she gave Yevana the hots at times! Toby liked Summer immediately for all the right reasons and there was most definitely an attraction beyond business. That was a problem for Christina, thought Yevana, but not for her as Toby issues would wait; she had more important fish to fry!

London Project meeting

Yevana, Toby, Summer and Janice met Christina, Josh and their lawyer the hardnosed Julia Banks, in the local council chambers. There to meet them in the oak panelled room was a selection of people with all sorts of interest in this project. Last to appear was the confident and not to be messed with Developer Roger Watts. The meeting's agenda was a lengthy one which covered all the angles from the council's perspective. They wanted this size of project opening in their neck of the woods but they had to ensure the area could cope and that the Church would blend in and keep its historic beauty whilst being adapted to integrate with the project aims. Toby and Yevana took turns to brief plans and statistics whilst Christina described and showed detailed design images and drawings that were extremely impressive even to the most sceptical in the room. Yevana thought Christina was overplaying her part at times as she moved around the room in a rather flirty manner. However, she had to admit that the drawings were spectacular and had turned out better than she could have dreamed. The open tunnel linking the main hotel into the church was indeed biblical! It would be a circular glass structure of changing colourful lighting and images; spectacular. Over fifty metres long, it would be a journey of experience for its passengers, in 3D.

Not surprisingly the heritage and environmental lobby had a myriad of questions and wanted assurances for several issues they had with this project. They did hear concrete answers regardless of whether they agreed with them. One gentleman in his mid-sixties from the Heritage lobby was not a fan of this project and as it turned out later, had links to the local diocese and was a dissenter in terms of the church being used for other purposes. He claimed, 'This project has not been thought through at all and I cannot believe it has got to this point of consideration. This church in particular is an important monument of the Church of England.'

'What other plans do you have for its use then Mr Partridge? As I understand, it is in a poor condition with a leaking roof, woodlice and damp throughout. Your security or rather lack of it has let the vandals in to boot,' Yevana pointed out.

'Oh,' he replied rather curtly, 'I consider that having what amounts to an orgy in that space is an act of the devil. It will be like dancing on the grave of Jesus Christ himself; it's a disgrace and you should be ashamed.' Yevana and Toby noticed several of the other councillors and interested parties raise their eyebrows to each other over the severity of his comments.

'I can assure everybody here that we take the rebuilding or rather refurbishment to be more precise, of this site, as one of our highest priorities. As a small but significant example, there will be a couple of large skylights in the roof space which will open up the building to the stars and therefore hint at that religious route to the heavens. I would also like to remind everybody that this is a five-star entertainment complex that will deliver outstanding standards all round and of course business and jobs to this community.' Toby came back this time, taking up the fight in no uncertain terms. They were not going to drop to his level of argument as everybody had understood the brief which made it crystal clear that the Mr Partridge was way off the mark.

'Our pride is that there will be no equal and I look forward to you all attending the opening ceremony.' In saying this he made a point of looking at Partridge who by now was sulkily looking away. He was the type of person who saw no good in progress and certainly did not appreciate that they were his only chance of saving this church from near certain ruin.

The project was given universal backing and planning permission would be granted when proof of funding was delivered. They knew this was being sent that day so it was full steam ahead. As the meeting broke up Yevana saw Toby pull Summer to one side noticing they seemed in good spirits together. At Toby's request they followed him to the local wine bar and celebrated a significant milestone. With planning and the funding in place this fantastic project would put them on another level in this industry. Yevana was not participating in more than one glass of bubbly as she had here meeting with Fay and Justine later. Just prior to making her apologies for having to leave the impromptu party Yevana had looked across at Summer who caught her eye and winked as she stood too close to Toby for Christina's liking who was not looking best pleased to say the least. This was music to Yevana as Christina was not on her most popular list and although Toby and she did not have time for one another right now, she did not like the way Christina had grown so close to Toby.

Justine greeted Fay with open arms when she texted him to say she was in the cafe and they soon recognised each other from previous descriptions supplied by the accurate Summer.

'Darling, you are beautiful,' he commented. 'I love you already,' he continued laughing rather loudly. 'Sorry, that's not like me but I just wasn't sure what to expect.'

Fay laughed now.

'Well, what a welcome, you know how to make a girl feel great! I'll take it as a compliment then.'

'I am a gay man but please do that, as you are enough to make me reconsider! Oh, only joking let's get a drink. What would you like?'

'I would like an orange juice, please,' she responded.

Fay looked over to the bar and considered who Justine was. Without doubt he was a well-dressed man but with a feminine touch of very bright colours and of soft fabrics, in fact his shirt was practically see-thru. With his long wavy jet-black hair hanging easily over his well-built but natural shoulders he looked anything but gay and she considered most women would love him without reservation. This was confirmed when she noticed two good looking ladies in their forties eyeing his every move and noticing Fay watching them, gave her a cheeky wink. She smiled back and winked back, of course!

When he returned she was applying some fresh makeup.

'Who are you making up for then?' he teased.

'My new boss,' she said in an unconvincing voice. 'I think I fell in love this afternoon. In fact, on the way here, I finished with my boyfriend by text and it was done almost in a trance. I have never felt this way. Does that make sense?'

'Yes, I would be tempted by her. It is not right and I can't explain it either,' said Justine and continued, 'Perhaps we should seduce her together and get it out of our system.'

They both fell about laughing and then gave up as though it were a joke. Neither of them was joking!

They struck up an understanding of mutual appreciation that afternoon as they discussed the interior design brief and how they would work together. They were definitely on the same wavelength notwithstanding his superior experience and would be a good team in the delivery of this immense project. Fay was impressed by this most sensitive and intelligent individual who she could tell had a natural instinct for compassionate, physical and emotional design. Whilst being Yevana's PA would be time consuming she would use every other hour she had to learn from Justine. Design was her real passion!

'Okay' she said, 'Why?'

'Why what?' he followed.

'The name, stupid,' Fay replied lightly.

'I love it, it suits me and I don't care what it means to anybody else. Justin was fine but I am Justine; that is what my body tells me, end of story.' He smiled got up and turned away.

'Thank you, Justine,' Fay responded with affection. 'It's beautiful, really.'

He turned back, offered his outstretched hand which she took and he pulled her up and they left the cafe hand in hand. Looking over her shoulder she smiled at the ladies who shuffled in their seats; beautiful!

Back at their offices Yevana had enough time to make a strong coffee before Fay and Justine arrived to brief her on their views of the interior design plans. She stood in front of her wall mirror and put her black coffee down and applied a good layer of her finest bright red lipstick. Looking more closely, she added more mascara, inspected her piercing blue eyes and blew herself a kiss laughing out loud. Finally, she undid a button and sprayed her best Volta lavishly across her neck and breasts. At this point Fay and Justine arrived and having entered a code walked in and stood outside Yevana's office and heard the laughter. Looking at each other they considered whether to knock, as if she was still busy as there was nobody else around to ask. Then they heard the call and Fay took the lead and opened the door.

Yevana thought for a moment about the party at the wine bar and felt a little empty. At that moment she received a text from Yurenev stating that he was arranging a business meeting in London in the next couple of weeks and when he had tied down the arrangements he would let her know. That was it; she was basically being put on standby. This should have annoyed her but it had the opposite effect as she was excited, very excited.

Caren to London

Caren decided it was time to come down to London and find out how Yevana was living and help make up her mind to gain wilful revenge on her ex-lover. Andre had been and done some investigating and found out that Yevana and Toby had progressed with their business ideas and moved to London having done very well in Manchester. In its infancy they were building a firm base to grow a considerable business. Before she would make up her mind how to plan any further, Caren had to revisit her past and see Yevana again. It would be painful but it had to be done. She called Andre who was at his flat.

'Andre, please get me a return train ticket and hotel in central London for next week and the address of the Y&T office in London please,' spoke Caren in a most gentle manner. 'Andre!' she shouted in a less understanding tone.

'Sorry, Caren, I was watching TV.'

'Well, darling that was your first mistake, don't make it again or I will be really, well you know,' she said dismissively. She repeated herself rather agitated and left him to sort it out.

On the journey south she questioned herself on the point of doing this errand. Was there a point to it? What was she going to get out of it? Was it just spit, or did Yevana deserve to be punished and it was up to Caren to nail it? On reflection she accepted it was the latter and in fact she was going to revel in dealing out 'the good news' as Caren liked to put it.

When in London Caren purposely decided to dress down and only brought the clothes she was wearing which were a dour trouser and jumper outfit with a hood for the cover up when she got in close proximity to Yevana.

It did not take long after some careful enquiries to find the location of the Y&T offices but before she went out to locate them, for her satisfaction, she lay naked in the comfort of her darkened hotel bedroom and made the call.

A few minutes before Fay and Justine were about to arrive at the offices the phone rang on Yevana's desk and she answered as she always would. 'Y&T London, good evening. Hello, hello, okay!' Nobody spoke, Yevana pondered that it seemed a bit strange as if there was somebody there but she closed the call and forgot about it. In any case a random call on telephone systems these days particularly from random call centres was not a surprise.

Yevana looked into the mirror and looking at herself shouted, 'Come in, please.' She had not heard them but...

As they entered she spoke again, 'Come in you two, you are on time. That's good. Come on in and sit down.'

They heard her clearly and quickly walked in smiling politely and sat in the seats in front of her desk. They were sat upright like two school children in front of the headmistress.

'Relax people,' she joked, 'we have much to be happy about, don't we now?' Yevana came round and sat on the front and centre of the desk. Fay was now finding it hard to concentrate with this immaculate set of stockinged pins in a short skirt no more than two feet away from her. The perfume was intoxicating to the point that it felt like it was done on purpose. For a moment Yevana's first words sounded distant and unreal.

'What do you have for me then, Justine?' Yevana asked in a businesslike and frosty tone.

'I like the concept and I have pencilled onto the drawings the comments and suggestions I wish to make and other issues Fay and I have discussed this afternoon. It has been most useful to have her input' he added. 'Mainly, I would like to be more modern in the reception hall which will complement the grand structural design better. Your theme is of landmark individuality, style and comfort in splendid luxury. To get this right I believe we need to be flexible in order that we don't get fixed and appear stagnant. Flexibility is key! I have some wonderful ideas which I can show you tomorrow. The approach to the VIP Club should be one of opulence that is more white than red as lights will generate the soft and secluded atmosphere as necessary, but you want to know what she is wearing, not have to ask her! It is important too, that the female feels touched by the circumstances she finds herself in, don't you think?'

'Thank you, Justine, I do indeed, I certainly do. Please arrange a design meeting with all the main stakeholders for Thursday in my office. Ensure that Toby is able to be here before inviting everyone else.'

'Now, Fay, what do you have to say as our latest employee? Am I spending my money wisely? I mean on employing you,' Yevana said rather pointedly.

'Of course, you are Yevana. I have had a fascinating afternoon, thank you. My view is that there are too many quiet corners full of furniture which Justine and I have discussed. If furniture and decor is flexible then we will be able to rearrange to suit an occasion. I would like to allocate and decorate an executive business-only bar area positioned off of the main bar for weekdays only. It should have all the best business utility but in a relaxed atmosphere. I don't believe we have achieved that here as yet. Otherwise, I love it, really love it; I can't wait to get started.' Fay breathed!

'Okay, guys, thank you. We will review further as I have said but in principle Justine please carry on with refining this plan and Fay please assist alongside as time allows. You may go now. I will see you tomorrow.' Yevana turned and looked out of an office window and decided that Fay was naked and beautiful under that suit. Fay stared for an extra second at Yevana's back before moving.

Caren lay there transfixed all of her hairs on end, her skin had massive goosebumps and she had adrenaline running rampant through her veins. The voice came over loud and clear as she said her name, it was Yevana, the only one on the planet like it. Yevana put the phone down. Caren had a tear running down her right cheek. She had just heard the only, the one love of her life. Her phone did not break as it hit the window which luckily took the force of the impact. Almost immediately her mobile started to ring but on getting up and seeing that it was Andre threw it against the bedroom wall and this time it broke up. She laid there for a few minutes but noticing the time decided to get over to the office now as this might be the only opportunity to see Yevana on this visit as she had to leave for Europe the following day on business.

Within fifteen minutes she was stood opposite the Y&T offices in a narrow alleyway far enough away from the exit doorway of the building where the company offices were situated. Lights were on in only the ground floor commercial suites which must have been Yevana's if she was still there. Caren decided to wait for up to an hour before departing that night. She would try again in the morning before her flight if she was unsuccessful. She was here for a reason and that might be to leave it all behind; at this stage she didn't know.

It wasn't long before two people left the building, one a long haired good looking male and a tall stunning Amazonian female. Caren didn't know if this young woman was an employee but she did see beauty and knew that Yevana would be tempted by such devastation on two legs. She had an idea but that was for another day, and would need a lot of work but hey, what else was Andre for? Caren was jealous and if nothing else this made her mind up. Eventually the lights went out and Yevana appeared from the entrance and Caren felt her legs go weak and also felt herself choke. She felt sick. How had she lost this specimen of such beauty? Even at a distance and in dim street lighting it was suffocatingly apparent. Caren came round quickly as she noticed that Yevana seemed to be looking around as if she sensed something was not right. Caren shuffled forward, and then decided to move in case Yevana came over. She didn't look back just walked at speed up the road and into a side street and ran as fast as she could and into another alley where she stayed sat on her haunches in case of needing to get away quickly. Whilst there, initially out of breath, she felt a feeling of light depression come over her. Why couldn't Yevana have taken her on her journey? She had accepted her lifestyle. She wasn't greedy, she just wanted to be with her. Eventually she got up, looked both ways up the street and walked away and back to the hotel.

Yevana finished what she was doing and turned off the lights in her office and the outer office and locked the door before walking out to the street, now lit by the street lamps and a full moon. Something was different though. As she looked about her she sensed something strange and so stood and looked about her. There was the odd car driving past, one of which slowed down in rather dubious circumstances which Yevana blatantly turned away from, and a tramp in a furniture store doorway opposite, but otherwise nothing to alert the senses, yet... Then, out of the alleyway opposite, a figure moved, firstly just to change position but then to get out of the shadow and walked quickly off up the street, down a side street and out of sight. She could swear it was a woman by the way she walked, in what looked like women's shoes but Yevana was not sure from that distance, in the street light of the city and because of the hood the person was wearing. Yevana stood fixed for a moment wondering what this meant. Was she jumping to conclusions or was this person waiting for her? Surely not, she told herself. What for? Puzzled, she turned and walked up the street and the short walk to her hotel room. The most worrying thing was that for the first time in her life she felt vulnerable. On arriving in her room, she slumped into a sofa throwing her bags onto an armchair and sat staring out of a window, thinking for some time. Something was familiar about that person, something familiar, something! She was woken from her thoughts by a text from Toby.

'Great night, babe, missing you.'

'Damn liar,' she exclaimed out loud. If he is excited enough to be sending text messages at ten p.m. he must have a new babe with him.

'Who is it?' she blatantly came back.

'You are so forward, lady. I sent Christina home; see you early doors xx'

Yevana needed him tonight; she felt fragile on her own in these circumstances but no, not tonight. Over the coming weeks she would have to be careful and aware of her surroundings especially when on her own, particularly if she had been correct and she had been watched. It did occur to her it might be something to do with Yurenev but she doubted that somehow as there was no real ownership of any kind at this stage. No, it felt more sinister!

Fay and Justine went out into the night and walked to the nearest bar and had a couple of drinks to finish the day off. Fay had had the most life-changing day. An unforgettable day had seen her hired by a female boss she had immediate strong feelings for and had dumped her longstanding boyfriend without caring too much. Whilst sitting with Justine at the bar she turned to him and said,' one hundred pounds my boss seduces me.'

'My god, you are joking,' Justine replied. 'It will never happen; she is too busy and has far too much on her plate for that sort of thing.'

'You're wrong. She practically undressed me in the office earlier. I know it.'

'You're on. You have flipped; I can't lose. Joking apart, Fay, don't be foolish as this is a good job and a wrong move will see you out and my senses tell me these people are loyal but make bad enemies!' Be careful, darling.'

'I will, Justine, I will, I'm not looking for it,' she replied with a sense of purpose.

Before departing she hugged Justine, her new friend and she watched him call down a taxi and depart.

Fay walked for a while then out of the corner of her eye she suddenly saw Toby swaying slightly with a girl on each arm as they staggered down the high street. Fay pulled back against a wall and made out from her dark shadowy place, that it was Christina and Summer he was escorting somewhere. With a wry smile she thought this looked either complicated or interesting! Not knowing them she was interested to get this momentary glimpse to the life of her other boss who had his PA on one arm and architect on the other. Both beautiful and sexy, she considered it to be a theme at Y&T. She thought that perhaps that was why she was taken on but thought better of it as Yevana seemed to be more disciplined than that; this business mattered to them all too much. After a short while Toby hailed a taxi and he shepherded the women in making sure her new friend Summer was last and it was she who got the most delicate hand into the cab.

Fay walked out of the darkness and back to her flat where she hurried in and bolted the door then turned and stood against it before taking off her suit. She stood for a minute then walked into the shower and cleansed her body in stone cold water just in case it had all been a dream and so wake her back into her old world. Her one answer phone message confirmed reality!

Toby drew up in the taxi outside his flat and got out leaning back in and paying the taxi driver and giving him Christina's address where he was to wake and drop her off. He and Summer were holding hands as they went on up to his flat. The next time his phone rang he noticed it was Christina who would be in a rage having made an educated guess at what had occurred in her slumber.

The following weekend came and went with all parties receiving assurances as appropriate with confirmation that the money was in, developers given the green light and of course that Yevana had moved out and into her own flat as a newly single woman. Contracts were signed and the construction company gave notice to start on site within a month. This was so exciting for everybody associated with the project. Yevana and Toby were getting on as well as ever leading separate social lives, which surprisingly for her was a pleasant experience as Yevana found she really enjoyed the solitude.

On the following Monday morning Yevana, Fay, Toby, Christina, Josh, Dan Mason, and representatives from the property developer, construction company, council, bank, English Historical Heritage, Heritage of English Churches Council and a representative of Yurenev Caspanov met on site. Having agreed the deal previously and had outline planning agreed by the planning authority this was a final check before the bulldozers moved in the following week. The construction company, in fact, were already on site as the first portacabin was being lowered onto the road outside.

'Good morning, Toby, who was keeping you up? You look tired darling' said Yevana.

'Good morning, Yevana and thank you. I had a very light but comfortable night,' he teased. 'You?'

'Quiet, thank you.'

'Toby, can we have a look at the garden with the developer as I want to confirm the limits of the encroachment, because the garden will be important to me when we are completed? I don't want it overlooked. I see it on the plans but I want a guarantee on the ground now.' Yevana was adamant and in stating her requirement you could hear a pin drop even at this hour of the day in this part of London.

'Okay, darling of course. You got that, Dan.' Toby called back to the planning consultant who had been listening.

'Got it, Toby,' he replied.

Off they went into the old hotel and eventually into the gardens of both the hotel and church. Whilst in the church garden the guy in his fifties representing the Heritage of English Churches Council took the general pleasant, good nature Fay had displayed and in a lull in proceedings took the opportunity to very, very gently brush her rear with the lingering palm of his hand. Today she was wearing a tight pencil skirt and had been writing for nearly two hours as Yevana and Toby gave out their exacting orders and took advice from the group representatives. The last thing on her mind was this but she felt it and didn't react immediately. Once Toby and Yevana were happy the group split and as they did so down the old steps of the hotel, Yevana noticed Fay out of the corner of her eye swing her arm with some energy, stabbing the Churches Council guy in the rear with a razor-sharp pencil. He buckled for a moment and winced letting out a whimper, then carried on down the steps nearly collapsing, not looking back once, but limping off down the street calling a taxi as he went. Yevana sensing what had occurred looked across at Fay and smiled. 'You okay, Fay?'

'Yes, thank you, I had trouble with my skirt,' said Fay.

'Oh dear, I hope that poor chap is okay,' Yevana joked.

Fay smiled. 'I couldn't care less,' she replied. Yevana was not smiling any more as she stared into Fay's eyes. 'Shall I have these notes ready for you today, Yevana?' continued Fay breaking the slightly uncomfortable silence.

'Yes, please, I will be back at the office later today; have them ready when I arrive. Let's go please, Toby, we have a ten o'clock with Bob Ray.'

They walked off in the direction of the nearest tube station as other construction staff appeared on what was about to be a very busy site for the next eighteen months at least.

As they sat on the tube Toby received a text from Christina whom he had pretty much avoided during the time on site. Yevana could just make out the contents. 'Darling really missed you last night. I was so drunk but wish you had not sent me home, it was such a shock to be dropped off by the taxi driver on my own.' Yevana inwardly laughed at the next line. Christina continued. 'I trust Summer got home okay, too?' The question mark was a statement not a question of course.

Yevana watched as he wrote, 'Summer was fine, I took personal responsibility for her wellbeing, thank you.'

Yevana could feel at distance the massive sense of disappointment.

'Okay, what about this evening, are you free?' Christina replied dreading the answer but was not ready for the reply she received.

'I am taking Summer to the theatre; will you join us? Be at mine by seven-thirty p.m.,' Toby replied very nonplussed.

Christina came back quickly with a crestfallen 'Yes.'

Toby looked at Yevana and smiled as he noticed her interest.

'Be careful, darling, this is business and you are playing with fire,' was all she wanted to add to the matter. She leant back and closed her eyes to clear her mind in the silent yet rushing tube train and Mobola, then more interestingly Fay, slipped in!

No.1 Tudor Square

They met Bob at the Savoy, his favourite place to work or play in London as it just suited his style. He was not a flash sort of guy but liked the nice things in life and he could afford them. They met for lunch in the Riverside restaurant with Yevana getting the full embrace as they always started proceedings when they met, whilst similarly Toby got a bear hug also.

'Darling, Yevana, I still cannot understand why we have not married, it seems such a waste.' He immediately looked at Toby who smiled and injected a comment for them both.

'We are not together, if that was what your look indicated. We are too busy but I have a couple of numbers of people who you might find suitable though. Yevana's new PA is delightful.' Most surprisingly to Toby, Yevana came in with some haste and not looking that impressed with his comment.

'Sorry, Bob old boy but Fay, that's the woman Toby refers to, will and is far too busy for the likes of you right now, we have a superior entertainment complex to build!'

'Ouch!' replied both Bob and Toby in unison. Toby looked across at the rather strained looking Yevana and sensed a new interest was growing. He made a mental note to watch this space. He was aware that both of them having relationships with their PAs should be off limits, however, with a firm amount of control it should not become an issue. As he reminded himself, their relationship started in this vein and so what did he expect?

They started lunch and talked over the business, particularly his support alongside Yurenev.

'I can't say I like being involved with this type of individual. He gives me the creeps and by the way have you met his wife?' They shook their heads.

'Well, she is a vampire. There are stories of people becoming business associates and going missing under dubious circumstances, but under the umbrella of the 'Eastern Bloc States' enquiries have come to nothing. As I indicated to you previously the money is good money but I would not want to second guess where all of it materialised from. Be very careful they will ask a lot for their rouble! My dosh is good and my investors like what they have seen and so it is all systems go. Now about that marriage Yevana, you are single?' They all smiled and he proposed, a toast.

They raised their glasses. 'No 1 Tudor Square – the very best in class, top class!'

At that moment two texts arrived, one from Fay on a variety of small matters and one from Yurenev saying he would be at his apartment by seven tonight and she should be there at eleven. Yevana stared down at the phone thinking about what that meant. Well, she knew him well enough to know it meant she would be tired for the eight-a.m. meeting the following day!

'Problems?' commented Toby.

'No, just Fay with some updates. They have found a three-hundred-year-old religious transcript associated with the church under the pulpit. How wonderful is that? We shall have it encased and placed in the entrance hall in London, pride of place. Brilliant! We must have history; it gives perspective.'

Her mind was already racing. What was she to wear? He had a penchant for the group so would he be alone? Importantly, when would the wife appear, as Bob suggested she was never far from Yurenev and his business affairs apparently? Should she postpone the meeting scheduled for tomorrow morning and ensure she was in her comfort zone? Yevana felt that familiar adrenaline rush as she sat in the restaurant which answered her question. She didn't do comfort zones!

'Bob, I have got to get back but thank you for lunch and we promise to come out for a weekend in Geneva soon, hopefully to be introduced to the love of your life!' Yevana reflected on his current lack of love interest but felt she was offering some hope. Bob was a fair looking man but he did need to shave off a few pounds if he wanted to compete with the six-pack brigade. He had a heart of gold and Yevana made a note to herself to do what she could to repay him for what he had done, by finding the woman of his dreams. Unfortunately, it was not going to be her and anyway he would probably be unhappy about some of her leanings!

'Indeed, Yevana and I have the template,' was the only response he could find to fit the bill.

'Come on then let's make tracks,' said Toby as he stepped in before it got any more intense on the love theme front. Bob was soon in conversation with the staff and reading e-mail traffic. He did not have to discuss the bill as it was sent directly to his account with the Savoy as a privilege customer of note.

Back at the offices Toby and Yevana were absolutely delighted to see Janice, Summer and Fay working full steam ahead with other staff and project customers. In their shared office Toby and Yevana took briefs on current issues and gave direction as necessary. At one point their lawyer Julia Banks dropped in with some paperwork to get signed off relating to both the Manchester and the London projects. Toby knew there was something unsettling Yevana so whilst he was working he came straight out with it without looking up.

'What's up, darling? You don't seem yourself this afternoon, is there anything I can do?'

Slightly irritated and certainly feeling irritable and vulnerable, she replied, 'No, nothing and I am fine, thank you.' Feeling guilty about the impatient and frosty tone of her reply Yevana felt the need to tell him more.

'Well, actually Toby I am slightly stressed. Yurenev is in town tonight and he has asked to see me later. I am okay but nervous and not sure what to expect. Silly really because I can handle it.'

'Look, I told you before whatever we have said for now, I do not want to see you at risk and if that means this project has to go down the tubes then so be it.'

'Toby, no chance. I am fine. In fact, I have to tell you I am looking forward to it notwithstanding what I have just said.' She called in Fay.

'Fay, book me a taxi will you? I need to go home and get ready to go out later on tonight.'

'Anywhere nice?' asked Fay.

Yevana almost choking and noticing Toby smirk said, 'None of your business, thank you, Fay! Taxi please!' Fay disappeared at a rapid rate of knots chastising herself for being too familiar.

Yevana didn't wait for the taxi to arrive before walking out of the office past the staff and out onto the pavement. She felt she just had to get out and get back to her apartment as in this mood she was not good company. As she stood under the day's grey sky she felt the odd drop of rain that rapidly turned into a fully blown downpour. Her reaction to standing out in the open whilst making no attempt to get out a coat or umbrella and get completely soaked to the skin, made her laugh out loud. A passer-by watched in wonderment as she overtly took deep breaths of this refreshing air in the often-smoky roadside environment. The taxi drew up and she got in the rear seat which was a raw sight for the driver as her white blouse was now see through revealing her half cup red bra. Yevana had that sticky moment as the wet blouse stuck to the leather seat when she made any movement.

As she got out the driver gave her some advice. 'You'll catch your death out like that, luv, you need to carry a coat this time of year.'

Yevana smiled. 'I love the fresh air and love getting wet; it is so refreshing don't you think? Thank you.'

As he watched her disappear into her apartment block he noticed the coat poking out of her bag! 'I shouldn't be surprised any more, not in this town,' he said to himself as he raised his eyebrows and drove off to his next job.

Yevana took no time to get scrubbed up for the evening and was soon back out on the street again as a courier had dropped off a highly prized ticket for a seat in a box at the Royal Albert Hall to see Andoria Rosenta the world-renowned Slovakian opera singer. The note accompanying the ticket read, 'Darling Yevana, please take your seat by eight p.m. You will be met by a member of my staff who will see to your needs. I will catch you later at the Grosvenor Hotel as planned, Yurini xx.'

Yurini, wow! Well, it looked like the evening may be different to that expected and she was going to meet the wife. This was disturbing for Yevana as she had thought through all of the scenarios and cancelled out most of the wildest options in the, 'no it can't be they wouldn't' category.

Yevana wasn't sure she really wanted to go out to the theatre tonight but she would go with it this time as she wasn't in a great position to reject these plans.

The pictures of Andoria adorning the outside of the Albert Hall showed off the considerable assets of a beautiful well-proportioned lady of smoulderingly beauty. Her long dark and shining hair swept down over her pale complexion and fell onto her considerable breasts. Yevana knew nothing of this stunning singer and had never heard a note she had sung before.

Yevana took her seat and looked left to see she was alongside the Royal Box and the next in line to the throne, Prince Albert of England and his delicate wife Juliaetta with some aides sat in the rear. In Yevana's box were an assortment of men and women who did not seem to be part of a larger group. In fact, nobody so much as noticed Yevana take her seat which was only minutes before the concert started. She opted to wear a tight plunging neck-lined orange dress 'LBD' and stacked black wedges, with very little for the imagination to work with. The middle-aged man sat in front of her with his wife turned around to see who was behind him and looked pretty taken with the view but just smiled, meekly. The old lady sat next to her in a full ball gown looked much less impressed with the effort Yevana had put into her dress options for the evening!

The concert was a night of fantastic theatre and a singer performing in a magnificent vocal paradise. Her costume changes were dramatic and complemented the show brilliantly in timing and spectacle. As the concert reached its conclusion Yevana was ushered out of the box by her minder in a surprise trip down to witness the behind-the-scenes activities and unbelievably she was told she had been invited to meet Andoria. Passageways are a frantic mix of fast-moving sweaty minders, producers, stage hands, aides, and other staff belonging to the artiste and the RAH. Standing in a passageway against a wall, Yevana suddenly heard Andoria's finale top of her voice crescendo as she finished the main part of the show. It was like an electrical charge back stage as a form of madness ensued. She likened it to the appearance of a Messiah and it felt like a stampede as a group of heavy feet came charging around the corner. Then it appeared. A group of minders out front and flash bulbs going off as press pass holders captured the scene that would occupy copious pages in the following day's newspapers and the following week's glossies. Amazing, thought Yevana, as Andoria approached in what felt like a vacuum. She was taken aback by the singer's beauty and remembering the posters knew they hadn't got close to doing her justice. Her black hair was like a lioness's mane glistening with cosmetics and perspiration, over this most porcelain of faces. A male assistant was running alongside as she walked trying to mop her brow to little effect as he got in the way of the forward momentum and minders. He was nearly crushed at one point as he stumbled and fell against a wall which ultimately saved him from a messy situation; nobody seemed bothered in any case. In the wake of the main entourage other staff were giving orders and preparing for an encore.

The crowd in the full house were stamping their feet as the lights were dimmed. Yevana caught a glimpse of the superstar's eyes as she drew close outside her dressing room, noticing that her eyes were fixed in a sort of trance as if she had been given a drug but Yevana considered that this level of performance and adulation was like that.

As Andoria reached her door the minders backed off and an Oriental-looking young woman aide handed her a bunch of flowers with a card attached which she accepted with a smile. The door was opened and closed for her as she walked in on her own. Looking back down the corridor at the general commotion, Yevana was certain Andoria was in no position to see anybody until after an encore. However, all was about to change. Her minder for the evening was talking to the Oriental aide who came across and took Yevana's arm and said, 'Andoria would like to meet you now Yevana, so please come with me.' They approached the door and knocked twice and walked in without a word from inside. The woman held the door open and Yevana walked in and the door was closed behind her. How strange this was just the two of them. Andoria was stood with her back to the makeup table and wall to wall mirrors looking at Yevana. The room was awash with flowers of all types, but mainly lilies of varying colours, which looked magnificent. The aroma was intoxicating, almost suffocating, but somehow Andoria's energy, adrenaline and presence was apparent above this. Over on the far side of the room stood a rail of the most exquisite dresses of which two were laying adrift on the floor.

She spoke the only words of this short first acquaintance and pointing, said, 'Look over there, the Stanley knife, bring it here and cut my dress off, quickly.' Yevana caught off guard by this strange request did as she was told and grabbed the knife whilst sliding the blade forward.

'Start in the centre at the front and straight down,' Andoria ordered.

Yevana very gently put her left hand on the dress with her fingers touching the left breast as she pulled the dress material away from the skin and started to cut very gently downwards, noticing Andoria's eyes roll upwards. The material was a stretch silk and easy to cut. There was no bra in the way as the tight dress did the job and soon Yevana could see there were no panties. The dress fell away easily as she got on her knees to finish the lower part. When she came to the lower stomach she caught a tiny nick of flesh and looking up saw Andoria wince but no more than that. Yevana finished the job and the dress fell to the floor. Above them the crowd was making even more noise in anticipation of an encore but in the dimly lit dressing room the atmosphere was taut. There was a little trickle of blood running down the singer's lower belly in front of Yevana who remained on her knees.

'Lick it!' Andoria demanded.

Taking it on her tongue Yevana cleaned the surface wound then Andoria instinctively leant over and kissed her with her soft red lips, sucking back her blood from Yevana's mouth. Nothing else was said. Yevana dropped her head and took her lips down between Andoria's legs and drew in her sex. Sucking it between her teeth she felt Andoria's legs twitch as she teased, then gently bit the target whilst digging her finger nails into her rear as she took hold. Looking up, Yevana noticed the weight of Andoria's ample bosoms forcing two large nipples down in her direction but she did not touch. No more than twenty seconds later there was a double knock on the door and two Oriental women came straight in and selected the next dress, a purple sequined number. Yevana was locked in position between her legs as Andoria held her head tightly by the hair. In a second though she cast Yevana aside and the two women pulled the dress over her head and replaced the shoes she was wearing. Without a sideways glance the three women were gone and Yevana was still on her knees in relative peace and tranquillity; how bizarre she thought.

The door opened again and by then she was on her feet and escorted back to her seat to see the final pieces of music. As she had turned towards the doorway she read the note that was sent with the flowers she had seen and it read, 'Enjoy this beautiful gift, darling, your friend Yurini xx.' It was obvious that this mysterious wife of Yurenev was a connected lady of substance who had a wild imagination.

There was certainly a funny side to this as she looked across at the Royal Box and thought of the royal guests waiting for their encore without a clue what the star of the show was getting up to 'below deck!' As the show finished Yevana waited in her seat until the other occupants vacated theirs and then as she followed them a gold note card was handed to her which she opened immediately. It read, 'Please join me at the after-show party at the Grosvenor Hotel tonight. A.'

'Wow!' Yevana exclaimed. This evening is unravelling and she didn't know what to expect next. Yurini's man escorted her down to the luxury car in which she was whisked to the Grosvenor where she was ushered into the private party that she had been invited to. The party room was full of people, many famous, with waiters handing out drinks and food. The colours of the women's dresses on show were a kaleidoscope of the most dazzling design par excellence. On the other hand, Yevana thought there wasn't actually that much material on show! But it was the beautiful and the glorious once again. Andoria was already in situ and talking to a skinny blonde woman of earthy beauty. The Oriental aides were by her side but now dressed for the party in eight-inch skirts, T shirts and seven-inch heels. What a sight! They were stunning although they looked much younger than their years. Suddenly having entered from a side door, she spotted Yurenev who, having seen her, came across and embraced her.

'I see you are making headway with my money already. Site clearance has started and all agencies are on side, brilliant. I am very impressed. Tonight, is a good chance to mix and make influential people aware of the special facility you will be delivering in this town. Did you enjoy the concert? We are so sorry we couldn't make it as we always try and join Andoria before the encore if we can.' He seemed to be in high spirits and very happy to see her. Yevana could only think of what 'we' meant and what that entailed at the encore!

'It was a fantastic concert and Andoria is unbelievable, I love her voice, it is breathtakingly powerful. I adore her already.' Yevana commented smiling whilst continuing to scan the room.

'Good,' he replied, 'I believe she invited you in before the encore for a couple of minutes and commented on how much she enjoyed meeting you. You must have made an impression as she is choosy and has specifically requested to meet you again. We will see to it of course.'

'It would an honour. I have thought that she would be ideal to open our complex and sing in the main lobby from the marble staircase. I will not be happy unless I book her; nobody will fit the bill for the grand opening like she will,' Yevana said somewhat in desperation.

'We shall see, now I would like you to meet my wife, my beautiful wife Yurini.' He was already holding her hand and leading her to the group Yurini was hosting on the far side of the room.

Yurenev interrupted the gathering and the others moved away as introductions were made. Yurini held back looking Yevana up and down lingering on her legs of all things. Slowly she allowed Yevana to lean forward and kiss her on both cheeks. Yurini seemed to hold and linger taking a breath to smell Yevana's fragrance which she appeared to approve of.

'Yevana, darling, did you enjoy my arrangements for you this evening? I am most interested as Andoria is hard to pin down and having persuaded her it is important that you enjoyed her,' said a very relaxed but pointed Yurini whilst sipping a strong black Russian cocktail.

'Yes, thank you Yurini, you have been very generous, I could not have had a better evening and enjoy her I most certainly did.'

Yurini was a six-foot tall Russian with long natural blonde hair, a skinny frame but a muscled body. She gave out a strong, aggressive and 'doesn't suffer fools' persona. She was wearing a white front zip dress with the zip undone to below the rib cage and with no breasts that were apparent, was happy to take her chance. In her significant heels she towered over many people in the room which magnified her towering presence.

'Darling, I am very busy helping our friend host right now but please join my small girly gathering at two a.m. in my suite. You are most welcome.' Yurini leant over and pretending to whisper in Yevana's ear bit her lobe and was gone.

Yurenev didn't speak to Yevana again that night which was a surprise because he had arranged for them to spend the night together. However, on the plus side she had made many acquaintances here that would be of enormous value in due course. Around one a.m. she started to think about calling it a day as although it had been a wonderful evening on several levels, she could see the benefits of leaving now. Did she really need a private party in the middle of the night? Who was going to be there? The trouble was Yevana hated missing out and to annoy Yurini now would be stupid as she could see how influential she was by the people who were queuing up to speak to her. This coupled with any action she might take for being declined wasn't worth it, so she thought better of it and stayed on.

At this time the party was in full swing and showed no signs of petering out anytime soon. Yevana, sensing a change in the direction the party might be about to take up in Yurini's suite, decided it was time to visit the Ladies and apply some fresh lipstick, powder and her Volta perfume. When you are moving in these circles you sense the opportunities and dangers ahead and Yevana, having had a fair share of the champagne available, was happy to prepare for what might be on offer. She made her mind up to go for it. There was another lady refreshing her own makeup in front of the mirrors, but ignoring her, Yevana slipped out of the top half of her dress, removed her bra, threw it in the bin and pulled her Mobola earrings from her clutch. Having inserted them in her nipples, she reviewed her work in the mirror then pulled her dress back up. The lady was watching this scene in the mirror and had stopped what she was doing, mouth wide open. Having straightened her bright orange dress, she looked in the mirror, blew a kiss to herself and said, 'Let's go and enjoy.' She wasn't expecting to be disappointed!

The stairs to suite 444 were wide and magnificent with original portraits of famous aristocrats adorning the walls and pieces of antique furniture placed out appropriately. For some reason Yevana wanted to walk the stairs rather than taking the lift and now she was grateful she had as she got to learn more about style and choice and what could be achieved in a place like this. This wouldn't be No.1 Tudor Square but elements would, for certain. Eventually she reached the fourth floor and room 444.

Standing outside she listened for a moment to try and get a feeling for what was inside but to no avail. Gently, she knocked and in a moment Yurini answered the door and invited her in.

'I am so glad you could join us Yevana, we have been waiting for you, darling. Come with me.' The main room had several people lounging around drinking and chatting but Yurini took Yevana straight through to a bedroom and before entering said, 'It is so good of you to wear the huge emerald my husband gave you; he is delighted. Now turn round and let me unzip your dress. That's it, let it drop, someone will take care of it. Go on in.'

Inside was Andoria stood wearing only a black dildo and heels with the two Oriental aides each sucking a nipple. On seeing Yevana they stopped what they were doing and came across and placed her in handcuffs and guided her to the other side of the bedroom where they tied her to the bottom end of a four poster on her hands and knees. One of the girls then turned up the music very loud which would muffle the screams.

At about five-thirty she was free to go and so made her way out of the bedroom with the sole aim of finding her dress and heading for her office and the eight-a.m. meeting. The scene in the lounge area of the suite was now quiet with a few couples lying around although most had gone. Yurini and Yurenev were nowhere to be seen. There were other items of clothes on the furniture and floor but she struggled to see her dress. Then out of the corner of her eye she noticed a woman asleep with it half on, half off. She was a small woman, about the same age as Yevana with a small coat slipping off which looked as though it had been acting as a sleeping blanket, by her side. It was clear to see she was wearing no knickers and bra but did still have a pair of leather high heel boots on. Yevana walked across and spotting a half full glass of wine grabbed the woman's nose and poured the wine in her open mouth. Yevana sat on her calmly as she choked and said, 'get my dress off bitch or there is more of that.' At that moment Yevana unclipped one of the woman's heels and stabbed her in the thigh whilst she pushed the coat in her face to mask the scream. To make it easy, Yevana unzipped the dress off the now very frightened and hurting woman and walked out of the room, dressed; well, enough to get home she thought. Yevana called a taxi and once she was in it took a few moments to look at some of the marks on her wrists, which she had to admit looked sore. The love bite on the back of her neck might take some explaining also if she didn't cover it up. However, it did bring a smile to her face when she thought about the position one of the most photographed female singers in the world had been in when she delivered it to Yevana!

Yevana actually found time to go via her apartment before the scheduled meeting at the Y&T offices, where she changed and bathed at quickfire speed. On the walk into work, she received a message from Yurini for the first time on her mobile, which she must have got from Yurenev as they had not had any sort of direct contact before. It read, 'You silly, silly bitch. You have really hurt and frightened my Poppy, my very dear Poppy. I am going to send you her address and you are going to send a large bouquet of flowers and an apology card or I will give you a lot of big, big trouble, Yevana. Don't mess with me darling, you will not like me angry. End of message.'

'Wow!' said Yevana as she walked, somewhat surprised. Clearly, Poppy was a close friend of hers, to say the least. It suddenly occurred to Yevana that psychologically she was linked to Poppy due to the fact she was wearing her dress, which may have been a sexual link to Yevana for Yurini. Why otherwise did Poppy take her clothes off to change into Yevana's smart dress? What to do next? She could ignore the threat but create an issue with Yurenev and so potentially the project or do as she was told.

Poppy opened the card accompanying the single red rose which said, 'I am not going to wash my dress for a week, it smells so good xx.'

Within an hour of receiving the note Yurini was back on message absolutely livid with Yevana. 'You are not good with taking orders which will come back to bite you.'

Interesting to Yevana, Yurenev did not contact her at all but she knew the next get together with them would be edgy, whatever that meant! She also knew she had played a risky game here, one that needn't have been played but Yevana liked to play on the wire, it was just the way she was.

An Item on the agenda for the internal progress meeting that day was IT for which Fay had a number of organisations that she thought would be suitable for the business. A new contract would have to improve on the service they already had in Manchester and be able to cope with the requirements of the London complex, whilst being able to build in future opportunities as they developed. Toby was particularly keen that an IT business partner would buy in to the Y&T DNA which was important. One company in particular whose HQ was based in Madrid seemed absolutely perfect although a proper screening would be required to establish their long-term suitability.

Yevana was impressed with Fay's work but added a note of caution. 'Fay, this is very good work but be careful we don't jump in here, as there are some real cowboys around. Toby, please ensure the guys in Manchester have some involvement before you and I interview potential companies.'

'That's fine,' he replied. 'Fay will take the initial procurement a stage further. I have briefed her on the requirement and how to deliver the preferred candidate process.'

Fay was smiling as she was so keen to impress her boss for a variety of reasons and this was another great opportunity even before she helped Justine on the interior in London. This was turning out to be a life- changing experience and she was determined to maximise it.

Spanish influence

The company Fay favoured most was run by Andre Correnti the son of very wealthy Spanish aristocracy, whose company was very keen to get into expanding the business with global reach aspirations. She had three suitable companies lined up to see Toby and Yevana but Andre's was her favourite candidate for numerous reasons. On her first meeting with Andre in an office at Y&T London she was bowled over by his attitude, experience and enthusiasm to succeed.

'My company can easily take up this contract and be more than capable of helping deliver the vision of your project. I will give you all the evidence you need to scrutinise my company but more than that I can promise you dedication, no one provides better service as a guarantee.' Andre knew that these comments were slightly exuberant, but he was desperate and so had to tread that fine line between confidence and desperation. In his case he was definitely in both camps!

Fay was struggling somewhat. She was desperate to get this right and did not want to let anything get in the way of delivering this task as specified. However, this typically, dark, smouldering, gorgeous man with long dark shoulder length hair and a strong masculine body was sat in front of her and his aftershave was more powerful than her fragrance and she was weakening; fast! It very quickly occurred to her she was single.

'Thank you for coming to see me Andre and for being forthright about your company, what it is capable of and your aspirations that indeed, would if selected, suit our vision. You will understand though that it is not for me to say. Just prepare your case for Toby and Yevana our owners.'

'Thank you,' he replied, 'when and will, I get the opportunity to be interviewed? I have heard so much about Yevana Narvik particularly. Apparently, word is she is the most energised of businesswomen, who should not be messed with,' he finished laughing rather nervously.

'Well,' Fay was not sure where he was getting this information from as Yevana was a very private person.

'My bosses are very dedicated is all I will say on the matter.' It was a rather frosty end as Fay wondered where he had got that impression from.

'Now I will bid you farewell and I will be in touch, good day to you Andre.' She extended her hand which he accepted and it felt as smooth as his looks. Not working class but definitely lady killer!

He took a deep breath and took his chance whilst clearing his throat.

'I am in London for a few days. If you are at a loose end, call me, I would love to buy you dinner.'

As he turned his back and walked out she spoke in a low tone under her breath and out of his earshot, 'No!'

As he was leaving Yevana came out of her office and glanced towards Fay asking, 'Anybody I should know?' Fay took that to mean; I would like to know.

'He is a candidate company for our IT contract and is very keen with good credentials and whilst on the subject, I will have prepared the brief for all three companies for you and Toby by this evening.'

'Great,' Yevana said excitedly. 'I want to get on with this, so please arrange the interviews asap and if there are any issues and we take a view not to interview you can cancel, okay?'

'Got it.'

Fay's adrenaline started to rush as she anticipated calling the companies involved and especially Andre. Again, she said, 'No!'

Fay quickly called the candidate contacts with interview dates and times which would be conducted over the following week. After calling off from Andre she received a text from him. 'I booked a table at the Astoriana restaurant East London for eight this evening see you there.'

Fay stared at her phone. 'No!'

At five minutes to eight Fay, wearing stacked heels thick black tights and a very short dress that was practically a T shirt, with a tight pony tail falling over one shoulder, stood outside the Astoriana which was a gentleman's club! 'No!'

She turned to walk away but couldn't. She was single and glad to be and this was very exciting, so exciting for somebody wanting to experience more in life. The option of going back to her apartment to watch TV or read a book was a non-starter as far as she was concerned. She took a breath and walked into reception.

'Hi, I am here to see Mr Correnti please.'

The male receptionist looked her up and down and she could tell he initially thought she was a dancer at the club or that she should be.

'Follow me, darling, he has already taken his table. Have you been here before?' he asked.

'No never, but I am intrigued,' was all she could think of to reply.

'You ever thought about dancing?' he replied with a rather dodgy smile. She did not reply.

The place was dimly lit and a pole dancer in a minute bikini was already in action on the small stage off to a flank. The woman was beautiful and looked like she was made of elastic as she entwined herself in so many positions on the pole. As they approached Andre's table which was near the pole dancer stage, he got up and embraced Fay with a warm kiss on each cheek. As they took their seats he looked up at the dancer and spoke. 'A beautiful thing don't you think?'

She knew this was a test and her response was suitably immediate.

'Yes.'

He didn't speak until the woman had finished although a waiter had taken a drinks order for Fay.

'I love the beauty of a female, so much grace and elegance. It is very disagreeable that so many waste this opportunity to be special, don't you think?

'As I said, yes, I like beautiful things.' Fay's response was from an uncomfortable point as this was not something she had ever really considered. Lately, things were conspiring to affect her thinking. She had felt her first leanings towards the female sex with her growing feelings for her boss and now Andre was teasing and testing her emotions. He called over the dancer as she finished. After whispering something in her ear the Russian slid over and climbed over and sat across Fay's legs like a child would an adult. She then leant across with the side of a full breast rubbing against Fay's chin and slowly moved her head lower and kissed her left ear, sending a visible shiver through her body. Standing up, quickly, without looking back, the Russian was gone walking with the swagger of somebody who knew they had it all.

'She liked you,' Andre stated. 'You look beautiful tonight. I like what I see.'

'Thank you, sir, I appreciate that, but I am not here to shake your bones! I am a purely professional woman and intend to make sure we instruct the right company taking care of our IT and in house media; fact.'

'I know, I understand that but I do have great thoughts about your bones shaking!' he chided, laughing. 'I tell you something, I know you already. But I will be with your boss before you. I know you feel for her; I know it. If you want to get there be quick because I will be there and soon. Now, another drink?'

Fay wasn't happy but for some reason she wasn't angry. She liked Andre for better or worse. He was a character, one of life's enigmas, a lover, fighter, dealer of sorts.

'Fine, we shall see but you certainly have a very active imagination,' Fay responded unconvincingly. 'I don't imagine myself with my boss thank you. It is inappropriate,' she lied.

Andre was serious, 'Okay, okay, okay., I find someone telling small lies exciting, and you excite me Fay. Another drink before dinner?'

It was a good evening from that point on and as far as Fay was concerned she was happy with their relationship going forward and anticipated them working together in future. She believed he would win Toby and particularly Yevena, over. He was very happy that they were on the same wavelength and that he had cemented his relationship to help get the contract. As they went to leave at the end of the evening and walked out to the waiting taxis he commented, 'Take care of those bones.'

She winked as she opened her taxi door. 'Don't worry they are in good hands!' Fay finished.

They had agreed to meet again though and she recognised that she was hooked on something undefined and wanted more; of something. As she was taken away in the taxi she looked back and watched the Russian walk from a side door and join Andre at the next taxi.

Fay slumped back in her seat and said loudly, 'Brilliant. That is what he was engineering. One was not enough.'

Moving On

Andre's company was expanding and under direction from Caren applied and competed successfully to become the main IT and media support contractor to the rebranded Y&T entertainment Global. She was in! Caren was absolutely delighted. He had done really well and he had fascinated her with his description of the negotiations with Yevana and Toby. She insisted that he gave her a blow by blow debrief on everything he heard and saw and she had a hundred questions. Andre had said that they seemed dedicated, lived for the business and were in love but lived separate lives. At the moment Yevana was single although there was a hint of nocturnal activities and a most beautiful black woman popped into the office during one session they were conducting. Caren turned red with jealousy and rage that she couldn't suppress, as she knew full well who that was: Mobola Yemba.

'Don't like her, don't like her one bit,' was all Caren said on that matter and moved on.

'Andre, what is the position of the company in terms of growth?' asked Caren. 'Y&T is a booming company and destined to be a serious challenger in their market place. Both the owners have what it takes to know what their target client at the top end of this business wants and how much they are prepared to spend and where. They are even preparing to launch in the States and the plan looks massive,' remarked Andre.

'Okay,' replied Caren in a sinister tone. 'You have done well but remember I hold the aces here. Did you do as I told you?' 'Yes' he said in a low voice. 'I got on particularly well with Fay, Yevana's PA and certainly got the idea and feeling that both Toby and Yevana were very happy. Yevana was very flattering and I sensed some attraction. On the day of the contract signing, we celebrated with a business lunch and she couldn't take her eyes off me, in fact she asked me to meet her for dinner at the Savoy in London, that particular evening. It was a lovely dinner; she looked a million dollars and was incredible to spend time with. After about three hours we moved to the Savoy bar and had another glass of wine when she leant over and handed me her room key and stood up asking me to give her five minutes to prepare herself! I didn't wait long instead I asked the concierge to call me a cab, handed him the room key, then went to the Hilton where I was staying instead.' 'You did well,' said Caren. So far as Andre was concerned it had eaten away in him since, as Yevana was the most beautiful, mesmerising and although potentially dangerous person he had or would ever meet, he found that intoxicating. It was also a strong statement considering who he was telling this to; whatever happened between them they must have had a hot partnership. It had occurred to him that he was sinking into a deep pool of icy water! That was two days ago. He jumped as his phone beeped and Yevana's name popped up on his phone messaging. The message said, 'great doing business and look forward to engaging again in two weeks' time to confirm the plan going forward, P.S. thank you for dropping the key off; I owe you one!' 'Shit,' thought Andre, 'what does that actually mean; I'm going to get cooked.' He was sweating and having seen the message Caren started laughing. 'Don't worry young man, she will eat you alive; what a pleasure!' Andre was wondering how the hell he had managed to get caught up with this group of lunatics! The trouble was his company was now in a contract with the most fantastic company courtesy of Caren and if he pushed her away, his parents and their high rolling acquaintances and friends' activities, would be outed and cause a storm of disgrace across Spain and other parts of the world. Caren was not in the mood to feel sympathetic as this was as she had planned. She said, 'Reply, saying, can't wait to progress and pay off my debt!' He pressed send and Caren remarked, 'Perfect, go and do your business. You and I will only meet in the future in this cafe until you've established a strong and binding relationship with Yevana, after which we will become lovers once again. Concentrate on the job in hand but be efficient and don't drag your heels. You must become friendly with Yevana and gain her trust which will be hard but she has taken to you, which is a good start, especially considering how your last meeting ended.' Caren smiled as she could only imagine how frustrated and humiliated Yevana would have felt at the time, although she also suspected that Yevana liked a game and she knew there was to be only one winner. Andre knew from his point of view he was now playing with fire, in fact he felt like he was in the fire! His company, his life, his parents' lives and everybody he was associated with could be swallowed up by these people and there was not a single thing he could do about it. Caren concluded their conversation by saying, 'When I say tell me when you are engaged, I mean you must have arranged to marry her; I want a date. My plans involve humiliation.' Andre replied, 'shall we say good bye properly before I fly back to London?' Caren picked up her phone and pressed call. 'Hello Rydeesa, it is Caren Lords, how are you and how is Leon?' 'Sorry,' coughed Rydeesa, 'what do you mean, who is Leon?' 'No, I am sorry, Rydeesa. Sorry, wrong person, I meant Rolando your bullfighter of a husband, how is he?' 'He is fine,' spluttered Rydeesa, 'what are you doing? Are you with Andre?' Caren pressed loud speaker. 'No, he is very busy, doesn't have much time for me at the moment, in fact I wondered whether he was with you as I can't get hold of him, but don't worry, got to shoot, ta, ta.' Caren was enjoying herself.

'Get out of here Andre and don't let me down. We are finished as an item but as I have indicated, we may have another day in the sun if you do well; it's up to you or rather me,' she laughed. 'I am meeting a lawyer, a lovely woman called Dreana Martel in exactly five minutes and she has promised me an exciting evening having just won a stellar case in the high court, therefore I cannot afford to be late.' She then opened her compact case and added fresh lipstick, admired the job in hand then replaced the case deep in her bag. Caren stepped off the stool, pulled her skirt down fully, grabbed her clutch and replaced her sunglasses, something she very rarely left home without. As she got to the doorway she looked over her shoulder at Andre, turned and she was gone. Andre watched her leave and cross the road with some grace, where she then met another woman, a petite brunette, carrying a leather briefcase. Not even a kiss goodbye, he thought. This must have been her date; you could just tell as the welcome kiss from Caren was on the neck and the woman looked to the sky as Caren threaded her left arm inside the woman's coat. They quickly disappeared up the road and out of sight. Andre felt empty as he had grown to like Caren for all her faults, but she was cold and remote especially when they were in bed; her mind was elsewhere in a fantasy world of sexual intrigue and mystery that was blocked to all comers. As he called a cab and stepped in, he began to wonder what would happen next because failure was not an option so far as Caren was concerned. He was locked in this situation. He could go to his parents and warn them and try and bring the police in and start a bribery investigation, but he could not risk this because he was hooked in with Caren which did not sound sane and if his parents found out, they might or probably would disown him. More importantly, he was at a point of no return with his business which was taking off and progressing on 'rocket fuel'. He was in, full stop.

Andre was soon back in London and took a rental on an apartment in Swiss Cottage as he required a residence in which to base himself whilst his company built its business with Y&T in London for at least twelve months. He took the weekend to prepare for the journey ahead and bought himself new clothes and shoes to freshen things up in order to brighten the outlook ready to start, including playing games with his target audience; Yevana. He was feeling slightly sensitive about his relationship with Caren effectively ending so easily and if he hadn't shown it, he was feeling bruised as he had really liked his time with her; It was electric. Once in town he went into a top-drawer hair salon 'Rupert's salon' and had his shoulder length dark curls tailored to perfection; 'gorgeous,' whispered Leslie, the young voluptuous receptionist, as she slipped him her number whilst he paid and departed. He ditched it at the first bin in the street; he did not want the distraction.

The following day he was at the Y&T offices in central London with his business partner and some staff conducting the planning going forward, which was mainly with Toby. He liked Toby; he was easy to work with and had a bit of fun about him whilst remaining relaxed and in control, which seemed essential regarding his relationship with Yevana whether business or otherwise. Yevana didn't come in until later that week as she had been doing exploratory work in the United States. The sight of her caused him to catch his breath. She was wearing a twelve-inch skirt suit by Volva, like Yevana, his mother's favourite Spanish designer, in bright yellow; stunning. She came over to him later in the early evening and asked him to join her and a group of friends for dinner at the Dorchester. 'It will be good to catch up,' she smiled. 'Indeed,' he smouldered purposely.

Earlier Yevana had walked back into the office in London and had drawn a sharp intake of breath on spotting the gorgeous Andre. She had remembered the night he had stood her up. After half an hour and confirming with the concierge that Andre had departed she was so wound up she had called her recently acquired friend, a Spanish gigolo and dancer, Leon who was in town with a boyfriend who came and entertained her. They were officially in town with his boss, well ladyfriend; the Spanish aristocrat Rydeesa Correnti. Yevana had wondered if Andre was any relation to her but it had not been mentioned and as she and her husband were such high profile, you would think it would have been. She did know that the only work Leon did for Rydeesa was service her every need and that was not for the faint hearted. Leon had given her the eye-watering details, in full.

Andre went via his hotel room to smarten up and relax then called a cab which took him to the Dorchester Hotel for dinner. Before departing he had viewed himself in the mirror and was mildly assured that he was ready for Yevana if required.

The huge tree outside the Dorchester was such a landmark and helped give it its distinctive character and status. He stood at the steps looking back into the windswept branches for a solitary moment, took a deep breath, swept his thick black hair back from his face and launched himself up the steps and into the hotel. Yevana and friends met him at the bar where introductions were taken care of. There were about twenty others all told and Toby was not there on this particular evening. They were a bright and breezy gathering at ease enjoying each other's company. The plan was to eat and then move to an exclusive club in the east end at around three a.m. Long night then, he thought, which was fine by him. Yevana and the other women were wearing top end black patent high heel boots, black stockings and suspenders that showed at the slightest movement of the legs with various brightly coloured skirts and tops which happened to look fantastic. They all joked that they needed the air! Andre was inspired but laughed, almost nervously. They gave the air of girls on a mission. The food was good and Andre had enjoyed the company as they rotated places during the evening to engage fully; a great idea his parents always encouraged at their sumptuous dinner parties. They eventually went out east as planned in a string of taxis and up to that point he had not engaged with Yevana as she had spent much of the evening with several others in various conversations. At one moment in time, he noticed Yevana looking over as Neya a very polite and delicate looking Persian woman sat next to him, was getting fixed on Andre. As a 'table rotation,' was announced, with a smile in his direction Neya whispered, 'catch me later, darling.' Andre just moved round. It was later nearer six a.m. that Yevana eventually engaged with Andre in the Labrador club which had a jazz type theme. They started by catching up on what he had been up to of late.

'You look fantastic at six a.m.' she declared. 'So do you Yevana, you look absolutely delicious, which is what Roger there has been trying to tell you all night no doubt' he guessed. 'What happens for breakfast?' he joked. 'What do you eat?' 'You,' she replied. At that point two men looking deadly serious and the sort that tell you 'your names not down you're not coming in' and not part of their group, came across and the taller man whispered something in Yevana's ear. She stood up and excused herself and disappeared out of the club in a moment; gone. Andre was taken by surprise as she did not waste time on goodbyes with anybody after such an enjoyable night. Yevana just left.

Yevana was escorted to a smart hotel suite back in the West End where she was taken to a pre-arranged room. She was shadowed into a suite by the two escorts where she was told the Spanish socialite Radeesa Correnti was tied to a bench in the centre of the room. She was only wearing a skirt and of course heels which she wouldn't be parted from normally. Yevana, already on a high from an energised evening out with friends, was ready for more fun. She walked quietly into the room and glided over in front of Rydeesa's head which was blindfolded and facing the ground. A young man was indulging at the other end and quite noisily as Rydeesa sighed in unison. Rydeesa sensed somebody else had moved close and most probably the waft of strong Volta fragrance on many parts of Yevana's skin was being sucked into her nostrils. She tried to lift her head and her long wavy dark hair fell by the side of her face once again. Instinctively she moved her arms to feel what was there and touched Yevana sending an electric shock up Yevena's spine. This woman had certain magnetism of that there was no doubt. Rydeesa's hands found the knees and slowly slid her hands up the outside of Yevana's stocking legs all the way up inside her short skirt feeling the luxury of her suspenders and skin that both felt sheer. Yevana kept herself at arm's length therefore Rydeesa couldn't get a grip even if she tried, which she did. The other guys in the room were watching and motionless as Yevana hesitated whilst Rydeesa tried to pull at the knicker elastic. You could almost hear a pin drop apart from some whimpering, but before Rydeesa could try any harder to achieve any level of success Yevana turned around, bent down and gently and sensitively whispered in Rydeesa's ear. 'I am Yevana and it is my knickers you are trying to pull down.' The guy behind her seemed to be getting ever more heated, or perhaps overheated, she thought, smiling, so she proceeded quickly. 'I would appreciate a friendly ear when my business Y&T.inc Global takes a business opportunity and it is due to very soon into an area near the Royal Palace in Madrid.' She said no more, she didn't need to. Gently, Yevana pulled Rydeesa's hair in a ponytail, lifted it and rubbed her nose against Yevana's pants between her legs and then instantly, unceremoniously let go. On the way out of the room she dropped a card into Rydeesa's handbag. Yevana looked back on the scene in the room and said, 'We must have tea one day.' Radeesa had said nothing and was already in no position to be able to reply! Yevana winked at Leon.

Over the coming days in London Andre was very busy and tired, not just recovering from a hectic and sleepless first twenty-four hours, but because the planning was intensive. He was concentrating on the business with his team in London and because the previous system in Manchester had become very dysfunctional he had little time to get the work done. With Y&T expanding time was of the essence as he sought to prove their undoubted capabilities. He had had no contact with Caren; she was now off limits and he had his instruction which had been explicit. It was over a week later before he and Yevana caught up again, in the London office, when she apologised for her rapid exit that previous evening at the Jazz club. 'I am sorry,' she said, 'but unfortunately I had to accompany those guys to speak with another business associate over a hastily arranged breakfast which was a shame as I was hoping to conclude some unfinished business with you.' 'Don't worry,' replied Andre, 'but thank you for inviting me, it was a wonderful evening.' Yevana coughed and cleared a 'frog in her throat.' 'Excuse me,' she smiled.

'Yevana, I know you are busy but as its Friday I wondered if you were up for a short trip this evening?' 'Perhaps, where?' she responded politely. 'I am flying out to Tunisia for a short break tonight, with a friend of mine for a bit of North African fun. If I put him off would you fancy something different?' 'I will let you know,' she laughed. 'What have you planned?' 'It will be a mystery ride,' Andre whispered, 'but I am leaving for the airport in thirty minutes, so yes or no?' She started walking and replied, 'I will text you in three minutes.' In two minutes, the text said, 'Cancel the friend, I have booked myself and my companion, Mobola, on your flight. See you at the airport, oh yes and absolutely no baggage!' Andre was confused but interested. What a weekend this might be. He rebooked the hotel which was a flea pit in downtown Tunis. He couldn't wait to see the reaction when they pulled up outside!

Tunis – an experience

They all met at the Go-net Café through departures at the new six runway London International Airport. Andre had obviously seen Mobola a lot on TV but nothing prepared him for her beauty. Tall, slender and strong was how he would describe her, and even more beautiful than he was prepared for. She looked complicated and was already complaining about being out of the UK when her coach wanted her to train on Saturday; he was not impressed apparently. She was even less impressed that Yevana had ordered that no baggage was to be taken on the trip except a handbag. They were both wearing different patterned hot pant suits, which were very interesting to say the least and causing a lot of distraction in the cafe. Mobola smelt gorgeous too, although he was not sure what it was, it was mesmerising. Yevana did the introductions as they kissed cheek by cheek. 'Andre, this is Mobola my good friend. She is accompanying us for the weekend; I hope you don't mind?' 'Not at all' he replied. 'You are very beautiful and the pleasure is mine.' 'Well, let me be the judge of that.' Yevana laughed then looked into Mobola's eyes with a sigh of intention. 'Yevana you both look stunning but you do realise you will need to cover up when you arrive in Tunis?' he said. 'Darling, I am not stupid, we will buy some cloth at the airport in Tunis, although they are more liberal than in past times.' Andre watched as the women took a seat and talked some girl talk quietly until, to the surprise of the admiring audience, Yevana picked up Mobola's hand and entwined their fingers tightly then rested in silence. Andre found the reaction funny as many, especially the men, had become mesmerised by these beauties. He guessed this would have a more general reaction in many bedrooms the following evening!

They got on the plane and in a few hours were in Tunis buying something suitable to cover up. What came next was a real shocker. Yevana moved across to a stall holder and paid for two black burqas and two yellow and blue jilbab, then took Mobola off to the toilets. Minutes later they came out and Yevana walked over to a bin and ditched the clothes they had been wearing. Andre exclaimed in a quizzical but light hearted tone, 'What are you doing?' 'They are not required any longer, so take us to our hotel.' Although tradition is that the clothing must hang loose so that the shape of the body is not apparent, he could easily make out their body shape and they still managed to looking stunning without showing their faces or any flesh; unbelievable. They boarded a local taxi with a driver not as accustomed to hygiene as they! The women sat in the back and said nothing. Andre sat alongside the driver looked in the rear-view mirror and stared at the staring pairs of eyes in the burqas not sure what they were thinking. They headed downtown under Andre's direction noticeably away from the central visitor and business district, eventually arriving at a very grubby small hotel that looked in particularly poor condition. The taxis driver asked for a slightly inflated thirty dollars of which Andre gave him twenty and a promise to ask for him for the return journey, which he accepted, probably because he realised he had met his match with this customer. Yevana leaned forward at this point and said softly, 'You are joking aren't you?' 'No, get out,' he replied. They did as they were told. Standing outside the hotel they looked up into the neon night sky. Yevana commented, 'No clothes, no toiletries, no towels and no security, brilliant, what have I done?' The hotel frontage was a grubby, pealing yellow colour, with bits of masonry and plaster having broken off or in a poor state of repair. Some windows had curtains which were hanging in different variations and one or two had broken window panes. Andre said, 'Follow on ladies and let's book in.' They walked up a short set of steps through a creaking set of wooden double doors and into the hallway where they met the male proprietor. This scruffy looking individual who was aged about sixty-five, although he could have been younger, checked their names and allocated a single room and one double, pointing up the staircase with a dirty, horrible smile. Andre looked at them both and said, 'Who wants the double room?' 'I will,' said Yevana. 'That wasn't what I was expecting,' he replied. 'Good' was all she replied. They walked up a barely carpeted staircase to their rooms and as previously arranged by Andre, a male and female couple with skills and equipment to relax the intended 'targets' were in the single room waiting. They pushed the door open and what they saw in front of them was very basic indeed. There was another very drab, bare and grubby carpet that had definitely seen better days, a cracked mirror above a dirty looking sink, a wooden dining chair and a single metal bed with a mattress and sheet that looked used and dirty. The window was small and cracked with no curtain. They were ushered in by the woman and sensing what was on offer Yevana joked, 'you did have a busy weekend arranged and we mustn't waste it, must we.' She stuttered nervously looking at Mobola. They closed the door and before anybody could say any more the muscled and fairly large women dressed in only a burqa and thigh high boots, walked over to the other women and took off their jilbabs and threw them in a corner leaving them in just their burqas. In reasonably good English she said, 'If you do not do as you told they will be destroyed, but do not remove your burqa.' The scene was decadent and murky as they stood with heels and the burqas plus the large hoop earrings Yevana was wearing! The strapping male dressed in shorts and a mask came across to Andre and placed him in the seat and tied his hands to the rear legs and said, 'Just sit and enjoy, Andre. 'They will pay for being disobedient to our country's dress code and for Yevana standing you up.' This pair had Mobola crawling around like a cat and Yevana screaming like a banshee during several hours of punishment. The final act had Mobola and Yevana tied together on the bed still in headdress for the rest of the night, to be released in the morning ready for the flight home. The proprietor came into the room at six a.m. and untied the women with a look of pleasure in his dirty eyes. They did not see Tunis.

Andre had already returned to London on an early flight by the time Yevana and Mobola had taken their seats on the scheduled flight. They didn't speak to each other and luckily were covered from head to foot, although they revealed their identities whilst passing through customs at both ends of the journey. From the taxi into town Yevana sent a text to Andre saying, 'Thank you for our weekend in Tunis, I must say it is a lovely city. Remind me to repay you at the earliest opportunity as I don't feel we have had the chance to get to know one another properly yet. Mobola says she is not going to train until Tuesday as she feels tired and sore, and we thought she had stamina; poor darling.' She finished the text with a double kiss. In the taxi she leaned across to Mobola and said, 'you are pushing your body too hard Mobola and if it takes its toll you will lose your coach and athletics which have got to be your priorities; don't waste your talent babe, love it!' Mobola continued looking ahead and just said, 'You have no idea,

Yevana, no idea, let's leave it at that.' Yevana said no more. The taxi dropped Mobola off at her flat and then Yevana went on home.

Yevana and Andre didn't actually get together for over another month because of business in the UK and abroad. The Tunis trip never got a mention and Mobola seemed to be more and more estranged and appeared dishevelled the last time he saw her. She was obviously struggling with balancing a hectic social life and athletics career coupled with demands on modelling due to her exceptional beauty and the money she could earn. He also heard rumours of dalliances with a Russian businessman with a high profile and demanding by nature. It seemed to be a dangerous game if it were true. In any case Yevana was consumed by her business activities and especially the proposed move to the United States. When they did meet it was in very different circumstances to that last trip to Tunis. After discussing some work issues, she took Andre for a cream tea at a local cafe where she came across very normal and was consumed with the work, love and life issues generally, like any other person. This did not lull Andre into dropping his guard as he did not trust Yevana. She was lovely but dangerous, very dangerous. You could never tell from her expression what was coming next and that was what was so fascinatingly attractive about her. He had never even kissed her and considering why he was there; felt something he had not felt for another woman before. He had to have a word with himself though because he needed to change that feeling quickly because it was akin to holding a primed hand grenade, in his current position. He could only imagine the consequences of going back to Caren and telling her he was in love with Yevana; not good! They left the cafe and walked down the Strand making their way to the Thames, across Westminster Bridge and over to the South Bank where they walked and talked for some time. 'What drives you Andre' Yevana asked in a matter-of-fact sort of way. 'I love life, I want to experience success and love and lust but without commitment; it seems to me that love ties down flexibility!' 'Very inspirational indeed, sir' she replied, 'what of you Yevana, what is in your bag of life?' 'I do not anticipate what I will do tomorrow and that excites me.' 'Touché!' 'You are something else and it would seem that we are two plusses perhaps in mathematical terms,' Andre observed. 'Indeed, and that may prove dangerous,' Yevana confirmed. 'Well, I think we should walk up to the Nordic theatre where I have two tickets to see the latest hot ticket in town, The Doorman, a sensational story of murder, treason and life in a notorious prison in Arctic Norway in the twenty-second century. I had a date which I have cancelled and you are the beneficiary, she will wait; lucky boy!' He laughed out loudly.

The show was terrific and hand in hand they were chatting away as they came out into the evening street lights when Yevana was stopped in her tracks by the sight of a woman stood looking stern but vulnerable, if that is possible. Yevana broke away from Andre and walked over to the exceptionally tall woman and whispered something into her right ear which didn't take more than a few seconds after which the rather forlorn figure turned and walked off in the opposite direction into the evening. 'Who is that and what did you say to her?' 'My date and come to my place at five a.m. I am grooming her. I will not answer the door at five a.m. but I will text her at nine a.m. on Tuesday during an important modelling assignment; her choice.' They walked on to The Room wine bar where after an hour or so Andre informed Yevana that he had to shoot, as he had an early start. 'I would like you to reconsider and come back to mine, perhaps.'

'Not today, Yevana, I have to be at my best to get this project where it needs to be,' he warned. He went to kiss her cheek but she turned her back on him and he waited a moment, got the message and departed. He looked over his shoulder and knew this game was the most dangerous he could play especially with Yevana. She had gone.

Over the next few weeks Andre started dating a bank executive called Relensa Tolgan, a Swiss national he had met on business in Paris. She was a beautiful, delicate and loyal woman who had started to bond with him. As far as Yevana was concerned she had left all work issues relating to Andre for Toby to deal with as she was not doing a particularly good job of hiding her annoyance with him. The next time they were in the same room was over a month later for a dinner in a restaurant near the Y&T offices in London, when during the evening Yevana started to have a long conversation with Relensa and Andre. 'You must come over for dinner one night and I will tell all about Andre,' joked Yevana. Andre nearly choked on his brandy. He interrupted before Relensa could say yes. 'Unfortunately, we are very busy at the moment but I am sure we could more easily arrange an evening for dinner and include your latest flame.' Relensa was a little taken aback by the interruption but she trusted his reaction and didn't add anything further. At that point Yevana realised she was wasting her time and so excused herself and carried on circulating.

Viper

The turning point in the relationship between Yevana and Andre came the following week when he received a note, which certainly couldn't be classed as a letter, from Caren. In short, it read, 'get on with it!' Caren was obviously monitoring things from a distance and had found out that not only were they not an item but knew Andre had also struck up a relationship with another and considered his efforts on the task in hand to be 'pathetic.' This was a shock to Andre who had put the whole thing on the back burner because of work commitments and his latest relationship both of which he was enjoying; He did not wish to disrupt his life with what would be a good deal of angst. What next? He had to act but how, was his first question and when, was the second. The third to consider was that if he started a relationship with her what of Rolensa? He decided to move it on and arranged to be in the London for a celebrity party night that they had both been invited to attend in the West End. There was a copious amount of champagne in the VIP area and about two hundred people crowded into the main bar. Having arrived quite late he could not see Yevana in the crowd to begin with and so he circulated chatting to a couple of popular male singers who were eyeing up the females in the room without disguising their efforts! Eventually he spotted Yevana and he was not prepared for what he saw. She stood out from the colourful crowd and most men were circulating around her at every opportunity and this over some very influential film and TV stars.

Yevana had her hair, which had been dyed jet black, tied in a pony tail. She was wearing a bright green suit in the form of a short skirt and wool top with black sheer stockings and high heels. Complemented by various black jewellery it was a sensational mixture. Their eyes met and he smiled whilst she turned away. She got a signal though and to his surprise within an hour he was slipped a card by stewards, which read, 'meet me in the No. 2 VIP guest room at one a.m., and don't be late xx.'

It was a good evening and everyone was enjoying the considerable benefits of unlimited champagne, then when one a.m. came round he made his way to the No. 2 suite. These were sumptuous rooms where VIPs could have guaranteed privacy for as long as they wished. A chaise longue covered in large cushions was a central feature with a private bar and TV screens for use as appropriate. The lighting was set to soft and romantic with several large candles lit. This hotel room must have been hired by Yevana and prepared in advance of their meeting. Andre walked across to the music system and switched to his favourite musician; Barry White; so smooth. He continued sipping his current glass of champagne until he heard the door open when in came Yevana. She set his hairs standing on end and the atmosphere was palpable, like static electricity coursing through the room. He walked over to her and they embraced and slunk down onto the chaise longue with Yevana on her back. They started kissing passionately although Yevana found time to look up and see the red light on the en suite camera flicker on as she had prepared, which caused a smirk across her face in anticipation.

Andre felt a tinge of sadness but there was no going back and in this case now he was in the moment and it felt mesmerising and adrenaline-charged. His next move was one that all men plan for, dream of and never get tired of. His right hand made contact with Yevana's sheer left leg and what a feeling as his nerves tingled like an electric shock, his skin felt hot and his blood was rushing everywhere and fast.

Yevana felt Andre's hand touch her stocking leg above the knee and start to slide slowly and carefully up the inside of her leg. Her body shivered with excitement as nerve endings came alive and her blood felt like it was at boiling point.

Andre had time to consider this moment as his hand slid up inside her skirt; a moment all men should experience at least once in their lives but one which when experienced you feel you must return to. No other experience in life comes close, he thought, especially if it is a woman of substance, beauty and fortitude and he most certainly had his hand on that person right now.

Her eyes rolled high and the anticipation was giving her a high. Andre made that next movement as his hand slid from the sheer leg and he touched first the suspender hook and onto the warm, soft and smooth skin high on the inside of her soft thigh. His hand felt warm and soft to touch and as it moved to its intended destination it sent shock waves as her nerve endings went haywire!

Andre made his move.

Rolensa was sat in Andre's office one lunchtime having received a message from his e-mail to meet him there. She had tried to call but he was in a meeting. She sat contentedly looking about the room when the TV set on the office wall crackled into life and a picture came onto the screen. Very quickly, all she could see was a semi-naked man who she could see was Andre having anal sex with Yevana on all fours pulling hard on her pigtail, on the chaise longue in a plush hotel suite and at that point Yevana turned her head to look into the camera as he climaxed. Rolensa stared at the screen and a tear of extinguished love slowly rolled from her left eye and down over her cheek. She stood up without wiping it away and walked out of Andre's life and on receiving a barrage of calls from him, instructed lawyers and thus the relationship ended. He was gutted, but obviously not surprised as that is what happens when you play with vipers!

The next few months went well for Yevana, Y&T and Andre. Toby, the love of her life, was happy elsewhere and Andre had not sensed that they had been together in any sense. Yevana was still seeing the model from time to time for reasons of power, greed and wanton desire which was like a food to Yevana. The young woman had lost her latest modelling contract after twice leaving a shoot in response to 'come now' texts from Yevana. Caren had sent an encouraging note and now Andre was poised to push things further having bought a sparkling engagement ring! He was upping the ante but an engagement was a big step for Yevana; he was going to need a lever.

Over several weeks he started to bring contracts and getting itchy feet into conversations and showed less enthusiasm for some of her latest liaisons with the model. In fact, Andre was pretty convinced that she had more feelings for the model than she let on and had started to sound jealous from time to time. He picked his moment and took Yevana away for a weekend in Paris near the Moulin Rouge where the less salubrious of nightlife hung out. To his shock and amazement, she invited the model and he did not know until she took her seat opposite them on the plane. 'Yevana, this is supposed to be a romantic weekend for you and me to enjoy the city and all its life. I have decent restaurants arranged, some shopping and a surprise or two. I don't believe it, I really don't; it's as if this whole thing is a big joke to you. Look at her, what is she going to do all weekend and where is she staying?' On that ending Yevana looked at him eyes open wide without saying a word. 'No way' he shouted. 'No way is she, in fact I can't even bring myself to utter those words.' Darling, it's about time you were introduced as I am very fond of her as you have probably guessed and I want her to join our relationship more formally, which is non-negotiable, darling. So, I suggest you rearrange everything to include Rolla and make sure you have lots of stamina for tonight because you are going to need it.' Andre was not prepared for this and his plans were in tatters. That evening though turned out for the good as Rolla was just brilliant in bed and for the rest of the weekend.

Andre changed tack and started dating somebody else and stopped dating Yevana. There was no chance of any meaningful relationship, he was going to have to manage Caren the best he could, which would be another unwelcome juggling act!

Ru Carter

Yevana was soon to meet a woman of influence, a Texan oil billionaire widow by the name of Ru Carter. She had lived a completely different life since she lost her husband of thirty years two years earlier. Before, she was a typical housewife of the rich and famous carrying out charity commitments, gala dinners and afternoon tea with suitably rich friends. The most faithful of women, it knocked her for six when she became single again. Nobody knows what happened but soon afterwards she cancelled all meetings and invitations and suspended herself from most committees with immediate effect. When one acquaintance questioned why she needed to cut herself off so, she frostily deleted the woman from her contact list! Having given her apartment in New York a twenty first century single person makeover with all manner of modern and erotic art, she set about re-inventing Ru. This only went so far though as she would always have her default uniform of three strands of pearls, hats, huge glamorously lavish jewellery and of course her most fantastic designer dresses, albeit with this more youthful outlook. She couldn't look any thinner as she was by nature but where she could she showed her curves more than she had done for a long time.

On one particular trip to London, she met Mobola through mutual acquaintances and they became friends and had met on several occasions since which they both enjoyed. Ru observed with interest the power Mobola had over her prey!

Ru eventually met Yevana at the London gay nightclub Free. This is one of the world's most renowned and opulent clubs where the great and the good came in their droves to enjoy a very heady atmosphere. On the evening that Yevana was introduced to RU it was an exclusive and private male and female topless function and one of extreme decadence. This was the first time Mobola and Yevana had got together for a while and both were in good moods especially as Mobola had just won gold at the world athletic championships in Copenhagen. Mobola and Yevana travelled to the club and straight to the cloakroom on arrival. Yevana quickly removed her see through stocking top and out loud said, 'Bring it on, darling, bring it on!'

Mobola smiled and said, 'Later baby, later.' She had plans! Mobola removed her short coat and revealed no top! Yevana laughed and shook her head acknowledging a typical Mobola statement; it wasn't a surprise.

Ru is sixty-years-old, completely flat chested, 5'8" tall and beautiful, very beautiful. She has dyed bronze straight hair to her lower shoulder blades that shined like gold in the club lights. Her skin is still tight for her age and white, very white. This evening she was wearing a pink and black corset sitting below the navel, black stockings and huge wedges. Additionally, she had a diamond neck chocker that had a chain attached that ran down between her breasts and disappeared under the corset, leaving onlookers to guess where it ran thereafter, which of course is the desired effect! Whilst they are introduced and enjoying getting to know one another Ru was inundated with people who knew her and men especially, who wanted to. She was polite but firm, no thanks. The great news for Yevana was that they get on really well and this woman knew Andoria as a best friend and promised she would ensure that she came to sing at the Grand opening of No.1 Tudor Square! Yevana mentioned they had met but did not give all the details!

'Yevana, darling, I promise you Andoria. She owes me all sorts of favours and I will call one in. In fact, I let her borrow my Oxford undergrad toy boy recently and not just one night but the whole weekend. My goodness yes, she owes me big time and she knows it. Leave it with me but send some dates over. I am also interested in your relationship with Mobola. Come and see me and explain will you?'

'Of course,' said Yevana ,'it's quite simple.'

'That's good but I want detail,' she replied in a sultry, sort of how does it work type of question.

'Okay, I can do that, anything for Andoria's booking!' They laughed loudly. Then more seriously she remarked, 'Yevana I like your business plans also and would like to help you explore the US, say LA, Texas and New York; I have friends you know. I need to get back to work again and this could be an interesting project to be involved in, with people I like. In fact, plan a trip out to New York to see me; soon!'

'Got it,' was all Yevana could muster; this was brilliant as this was the opportunity she was looking for and couldn't wait to brief Toby who would be delighted. At that moment Ru witnessed Mobola slide in behind Yevana and in a hugging motion, she slid her hands onto her inner thighs and inside her mini. Ru looked on and down then commented, 'I look forward to the detail; I am interested!'

At two a.m. Ru left the club after her beau Simon, the twenty-year-old undergrad turned up with friends. Yevana admired Ru, she was a 'can do, will do' type of person with huge influence and Yevana liked women like that.

The story about Simon was relayed later at Yevana's apartment by Mobola. Apparently, she met him at an art expedition in New York where he was displaying his first pieces to the public and he was good at just eighteen. Having taken him back to her modernised apartment and satisfied her desires for the rest of the weekend, she decided on impulse to sponsor his place on a History of Art course at Oxford University in England. His parents who were from a modest city background, think he had won a competition in which a very private art philanthropist would pay for the education of a talented US student; well, it was sort of true; she was a philanthropist and he was talented!

Whilst in his second year there Simon got brave and although he was booked in to have one of his regular visits to see Ru in London, he decided he had better things to do and so skipped off with another female undergrad he was seeing. On this occasion though his mistake was to underestimate Ru as he came back after the weekend to find himself booked in for an interview without coffee, with his college professor of art – a good friend of Ru – who informed him that she was most upset that he wasn't taking his studies seriously and thus the professor put him on a warning for dismissal! Simon couldn't get to speak to Ru for over a month, after which she arrived like the Queen in Oxford for an update on his studies and on being satisfied that she did not need to stop supporting him, took him away for the weekend to a top London hotel. Although he could have a separate private life outside of his loyalty to Ru, he had to do as she asked at her behest. He has not missed another appointment! He was a top student, brilliant artist and good-looking dude who attracted the attention of all the finest and most affluent of the female college. His favourite was a Dutch princess brought up in Malaysia who had a taste for the wild side. Her tastes were from an eccentric family background that he found hypnotic, addictive and often involved group sessions! He was keen to introduce her to his rich 'Mummy' at some stage in the future and see where it led.

Interestingly, Mobola also told Yevana that night after the club that Ru was exercising her long held fantasy that had been locked within a safe marriage, now being played out at random intervals in downtown Sao Paulo, Brazil.

Mobola commented, 'No details, she will tell you about it if she wishes, but enough to say, Ru Carter was now Ru Carter the second coming! The woman you met tonight half naked would have shocked the old Ru.'

Work on No 1 Tudor Square was already going at full steam ahead. It looked like a bomb site and a massive clearing operation was ongoing causing a major disruption to that area. Toby and Yevana decided to take a walk down to the site and general area without hangers-on to get a feel for their project and its place in their imagination. As they left the offices Toby looked back and said to Summer, 'I have tickets for the opera tonight. Do you want to come? Don't worry if not I'll ask somebody else.' The central office fell quiet as everyone including Yevena stopped to listen for the answer.

'Don't ask anyone else. I love the opera, of course I do!' In fact, she had never been before and Toby guessed that but didn't care. 'Oh! but don't forget you have a meeting with Christina at her office at five p.m. though which is programmed for two hours,' Summer called out as he was going out the door.

'Cancel it, tell her I am engaged but reschedule for next week please. See you at yours at seven,' he replied rather dismissively.

'Okay.' Summer quickly got on with the task of giving Christina the good news! She knew Christina would be peeved as Summer had heard her telling him that they would go into the West End on completion of their meeting.

Summer got through to Christina's mobile quickly. 'Hi, Christina, bad news I'm afraid.'

'Summer, don't mess with me and don't tell me, you of all people are cancelling my appointment with Toby tonight, okay?' Christina was feeling low and sensed the timing and subject.

'Christina, I am …' the phone went silent and the dead tone came into her earpiece.

She texted Toby to say that the meeting was cancelled but had not had chance to rearrange the next meeting but would explain later.

'Toby, whilst we are walking to the site, can you tell me what you think of the new additions to our staff? I am quite pleased but it is important that we have a joined-up approach going forward. It does have a feel for being female top heavy although I am sure this is not a problem from your point of view!' remarked Yevana as she tried to gauge an impression from his expression.

'On the contrary, darling, on the contrary, I was just thinking about this the other day as it can be overwhelming at times,' he joked as he jumped a punching distance from her whilst laughing loudly. 'Honestly though,' he continued in a much more serious tone, 'we have selected well and I believe we have the right people. The IT and media company are super good and the most immediate staff are the right people at the right time. Fay seems to be a real find, isn't she? I am most impressed with her capacity.'

Yevana looked a little surprised as if he had taken too much notice of her and was therefore surprised at the little moment of jealousy his comment provoked, then replied.

'Indeed, and I intend to take a personal interest in her development.'

Toby looked on and smiled. 'I am sure you will!'

'Yevana.'

'Yes.'

'I have concluded that you are the nearest thing the world has seen that can be classed as properly bi-sexual in the real sense of the word. You are both a male and female of the species. The dissection of your brain would be a true piece of Frankenstein work, if you take my point.' Toby tailed off on that conversation and carried on walking having made a temporary halt to make his point. Just tailing behind again, Yevana replied, 'That may be so Toby but it is not a choice I feel I have and I just wonder where it will end. I do enjoy my life and the choices I make; in fact, I love my current solitude but that does not mean I do not miss our time together and I am convinced it will come back.'

They got off that subject and made brisk progress to the site.

Christina was there with a local authority planner, construction site manager and a director going over some planning issues to be resolved. Christina saw them coming and broke off to greet them.

'Hi Toby, Yevana, isn't it looking good already, although it does look like a bomb site having had so much gutted from the interior in particular?'

'It looks great actually,' Yevana commented. 'I can see the shape of things to come and it is exhilarating to see progress on this scale.' Yevana then broke off and left Toby with Christina whilst she discussed issues with the project team.

'Toby, I am so looking forward to this evening; where are you taking me?' Christina asked in a forthright manner and pursed lips.

'Don't be clever, Christina, Summer cancelled tonight as I am busy which you jolly well know,' replied a frustrated and put on the spot Toby.

The innocent-minded Christina was fighting her corner. 'No, she didn't, she called but got cut off darling, and it seems very unfair to cancel on me at this late stage.'

'That is rubbish and you damned well know it. Look, Christina, I have a meeting later and I don't know when it will finish, it's as simple as that, so we are cancelled tonight. Look,' he continued whilst putting a comforting arm around her briefly, 'I am not happy about it but we can rearrange for Friday if you like.' This statement went some way to placating Christina who stepped back from his arms and shrugged.

'So, you are not going out later then?'

'No, I am not and that's the end of it.' Toby's voice was raised and the others looked over which he was less than impressed about. He turned and walked off to the project group. Christina headed off to her car and did not rejoin them.

Something was worrying about this, thought Toby, as he watched her throw her briefcase in the back of the car; he saw something on her mind and her eyes had gone crazy-like. This was not the Christina he once knew as her love for him coupled with his apparent malaise about his feelings towards her was something she was struggling to cope with.

Toby acknowledged himself that he was getting very close to Summer both at work and at play without taking it farther than a meal and some time together as he had still been openly seeing Christina. So, although there hadn't been much play so far they both knew that moment was getting closer. Their first stopover at the recent after the office get together was purely platonic although Christina was sceptical to say the least and had started brooding and harbouring dark thoughts about her colleagues.

It wasn't long though before Toby was in a relationship with Summer. They had been seeing each other off and on discretely for about a month. Yevana knew and was fine, because as time passed she was busy in mind and body on anything other than her relationship with Toby. Her life was in a good place both businesswise and socially. Her friendship with Ru Carter was gaining momentum and remained platonic and business centric with a social spin! She enjoyed her company and as a much younger person was keen to learn from such a smart, wealthy and can-do woman. Mobola was still her favoured partner if and when they had time together, which wasn't too often. Yurenev came through irregularly which Yevana tended to enjoy as they had similar minds with no attachment on her part!

Toby, on the other hand, was having severe difficulties with Christina as this previously balanced and good-humoured individual became more and more eccentric in her pursuit of a more substantial relationship with him. He had recently twice cancelled dates with Christina and periods of intimacy with her were becoming more and more irregular. In her frustration she had recently taken a toy boy lover on a weekend break hoping to form some sort of jealousy but to no avail, as Toby was so busy he had just been relieved that she was not around. Actually, it did make him a little jealous but he had now moved on and would not be going back on what he had told her about their future, or rather lack of one!

The Friday following Christina's jaunt to the country with her lover, Summer was invited to Toby's apartment to complete some work briefly after which he would escort her to a music gig in town. Christina had been put off by Toby that evening which seemed dubious to Christina for some reason – woman's instinct – and made her feelings very clear which caused Toby to lose his patience, something nobody saw too often. They were at the contractor portacabin at the London site. Seeing where this conversation was going he grabbed her arm and took her into the entrance to the old hotel out of sight of the builders. There was a look of shock and horror on her face as he slammed her against a stone pillar.

'Christina, you don't get it, do you? We are not doing it any more. You are a brilliant architect and lovely woman who I have been lucky to have had a relationship with, but I told you before and I will tell you gain now, I don't want it. I am going alone and you and I are finished in terms of being a couple, finito, done, not happening. Comprehend?'

'Toby, you are in denial, darling, you will regret letting me go. I am the only woman that would allow you to carry on with Yevana in the way you do as if it were normal, turning a blind eye. You need me. You will be lonely on your own.' Christina was scrambling to get the right words out and it showed as her face went red and her breathing sounded rushed.

'I have tickets for Covent Garden tonight, why don't we go together and back to mine afterwards?'

'No. We are not.' Toby let his emotions get the better of him and blurted out his plans for the evening.

'I am taking Summer out to a gig this evening as a thank you for all the hard work she is putting in for us at present, so no, not going to Covent Garden. Thank you,' he finished off, calming down and lowering his tone. 'Now let's get back to work, I have to be on my way by five. Oh, and by the way, I am not sleeping with Yevana.' He let go of her arm, which he had not realised he had gripped rather harder than he would have wished to, then turned away and set off back into the contractors cabins.

Christina stood fixed and slowly rubbed her arm which after the event started to feel sore from his firm grip. Under her breath she replied,' I hate that girl and she needs to be reminded of her place in the grand order of things.' Christina was done for the day, so she walked back behind Toby collected her things and set off home in her car. Before setting off though, she text her toyboy, 'Get over to my place for seven.'

Christina had made an immediate plan in her state of rage. She guessed what Toby's arrangements would be for the evening and set off via a stop to grab some clothes and a swift gin before parking near the underground car park at Toby's. It was already dark outside and the weather was a typical British temperate bad day. Although questioning her morals and sanity for a moment, she adopted a disguise with a black wig and face mask, large coat and roll neck jumper and pumps. At around six she saw Summer's car pull up outside the apartment block of Toby's rented flat and slowly turned in to negotiate the tight concrete entrance. As the car disappeared she got out of her car and followed her into the underground car park watching the red lights come to a halt as she had driven directly into a tight space in the far corner. Christina was shaking. Conscientiously she knew she was having an out of body experience as this was not rational, this was not the Christina people who knew her would recognise. It didn't matter she wanted to do this; give this woman a warning to leave her man as Toby had not fallen out of love with her, no, he had been taken by Summer and that was out of order. She watched as Summer pulled down the sun visor and opened the mirror flap before applying a last coat of red lippy. Christina could see why all the guys loved Summer as she was rather annoyingly delightful. Summer finished preparing herself then opened the car door and got out. As she did so she felt a foot violently kick into the back of her legs behind the knees which caused her to crumble and fall onto the ground, dropping her keys and handbag. Christina quickly fell onto the collapsed body and in a gravelly voice, fit for the occasion, whispered, 'It is not in your interest to scream so keep quiet, don't make a sound, bitch,' she growled in a male like voice. 'And don't look round. Face the floor.'

She grabbed her hair in a bunch and dragged her into the damp smelly corner of the dark car park which was only a short distance away. There was a dank smell of urine associated with many spaces like this in most car parks. With a surge of violence raging through her veins she acted, pushing Summer's head against the ground and into the very corner with her nose up against the wall. Simultaneously she pulled back her soft shining and preened blonde hair and pulled out an electric head shaver. With a couple of easy strokes, she shaved a central path through the middle of her hair line leaving the opposite of a Mohican-like gap on her head. Summer was gibbering from the cold and the shock whilst her head was spinning and her brain made defining noises she didn't recognise in this almost silent space. Summer's above the knee skirt had pushed up towards her waist and therefore her legs felt cold against the stark concrete of the underground surface.

Christina spoke for the second and final time, 'You have been warned, don't move until I have gone and do not get close to him. You have been warned.' She said no more and got up, turned away and disappeared out of sight. Summer gave it a couple of minutes and sat up firstly still shaking but getting herself together before standing up, brushing herself down and taking stock. Her shaven hair was scattered on the ground by her feet and brought the stark reality of the situation into view. What next? Did she call the police? Of course. No, she decided, whoever this was she felt it couldn't be anyone she knew yet there was something familiar, but she had no idea who at this stage. That would wait for another time as now all she wanted was to go home and deal with this in her own way. Getting back in the car she got out her phone whilst looking in the sun visor mirror again. This time the lippy was smudged, her mascara had run badly and there was a black mark on the right side of her cheek from her face being pressed to the ground. The hair shave had left a very ragged line which she knew meant shaving her hair once at home. A tear ran down from her right eye, which she duly wiped away before turning the key and reversing out of the bay and leaving the car park. The text to Toby read, 'Sorry, had to change my plans. Mum coming over and she needs to chat some things over which can't wait apparently! Boyfriend trouble I think. I am gutted but please forgive me. Don't call, I am too upset S xx.'

Something happened to Summer in that car park. She arrived back in her flat and sat at her dressing table and although what she saw in front of her in the mirror was frightening, she came round quickly, sat upright and found that this soft girly girl was made of stronger stuff than she had imagined. The word revenge came to her, the thought of hurting somebody came at her like a wounded animal. 'I will deal with this,' she said out loudly to herself in the reflection in the mirror. 'I will get you.' With that she stripped off and with a mix of shaver and razor took her hair off and ran a bubble bath sinking into its depths with Vivaldi, at some volume, soothing her pride. Afterwards Summer found a suitable headscarf and played with how it sat best on her head as she was going to work like this and would make a story fit. Quite what it would be, she wasn't sure yet!

Christina arrived back at her apartment and was disgusted with herself and to such an extent she was physically sick down the toilet pan. What was happening; she was not brought up to act in such a violent manner. She took off all the clothes she had been wearing and dropped them into a nearby bin out in the next street. She had a few minutes before the toy boy arrived which was part of her alibi, albeit a bit lame but she would instruct him on timings. Still shaking, she rang Toby for a chat which she knew she shouldn't but had to. His voice always soothed her nerves if she was having a bad day and this was one such occasion.

'Toby, I am so sorry but I just had to talk to you and apologise for today, it was so unlike me but work has been hard and I have missed our time together.'

'Don't worry, Christina, I love you, you know that, but things change and as I've explained I want time and space at present. You understand that. Anyway, tonight was ruined because Summer had to rearrange, as she had to see her mother who was not very happy about something.'

'Okay, I am coming over,' Christina responded with authority. 'I will bring dinner and wine and I will not take no for an answer.' She called off as she was not going to give him the chance to say no. A decision had to be made on the toy boy and having been schooled by the Yevana and Toby way of running on the edge, decided on a physical evening if she had her way; and she intended to. Firstly, she ran a salt bath and soaked whilst her mind was soothed by some classical piece on the in-house sound system.

In fact, she hurt the toy boy in the act of sex, who on completion, ran out of the apartment as though he had escaped and this wasn't long after he arrived. Christina subsequently drove to Toby's to find he was gone; he had had it with Christina for now!

The following day Summer came into the office and was flippant although apologetic about missing the meeting the previous evening which once again surprised her. This felt like another change in her attitude. It was very easy to see something had gone wrong so to cut the explanations to a minimum Summer told them all she had had a nightmare with some cheap curling tongs and so the hair had to go. On taking off the headscarf Janice shouted out, 'I love it babe, I love it. You are the only person I know who could get away with that,' and she burst out laughing as did the others in the office. When Toby noticed her head had been shaved and Summer explained to him how it came about he was not so taken with the explanation; it just didn't add up somehow but that would wait for later. 'That is very odd, Summer, you must be more careful,' was all he could think of to say but he was thinking, Christina? He wouldn't believe it and turned that thought off; for now.

Progress

No.1 Tudor Square was progressing well as the design and structural work on the complex took shape. Toby and Yevana were stood in the Y&T offices looking at the latest photos and drawings with the construction team.

Yevana was very excited by what she saw on the latest artistic impressions, photographs and plans which had all been approved where alterations had been concerned.

'I love the atmosphere I am picking up from these images and you have given us the prospect of a fantastic garden. Well, not that there was much choice of course,' she said as she looked up and smiled at Christina, who returned her stare with a nervous smile and replied, 'Of course, Yevana. The garden designer is renowned and will deliver the best garden for your clients to both relax and dine in.'

'Mmm,' replied a content sounding Yevana. 'Toby, you happy darling?' Christina twitched at this question not liking anybody else calling him darling particularly as he most definitely was not viewing herself in that way at present.

'I love it; we have a fantastic idea and it is coming to life. Christina you have excelled.' She smouldered thinking perhaps he was softening towards her again but as she smiled and tried facially to message her intentions he immediately looked away and ignored her for the remainder of the meeting. In fact, it got worse as once the main issues on design had been discussed she was dismissed by Yevana.

'Christina, thank you, that will be all for today. We want to continue with Dan and Barry on some issues that are not relevant to the drawings and design. If we want more we know where you are.' Toby did not look up but carried on a conversation with Dan and Barry.

He was actually still seething with Christina over Summer and didn't like being in the same room as her. Christina wasn't stupid and sensed something was different between them which meant she needed to stay well clear for a while after which perhaps he would come back to her if he missed her enough and got bored with Summer.

The church was going to be a fantastic structure consisting of cinema, club, private club and casino. It was having a glass roof added that was seen as a fitting link to its past history and a view of the heavens. Toby had already named this part of the complex as Heavaniana – Transport to the Stars – from every room the night sky would beam in and put clients in a spectacular space making them feel like they were a part of the solar system. Décor and lighting would help facilitate this mood.

Viewing the photos, you could see from the outside of the main building that the basic shape and feel was one of grandeur and this was epitomised by the fantastic entrance, which took you back to the days of the Empire and the grand palaces of the Raj with, in this case, a mix of Portland stone and marble. The new marble columns were spectacular even now amongst the building site that they currently sat in and had started to transform the area. The stone steps leading up to the main entrance were laid also and quite steep which added to the dramatic effect. Moving to the plans they looked closely at the move through from the main concourse holding the restaurant, bars, cafe space and reception. In another direction through from reception the gym and swimming leisure club area appeared. The photos once again showed this was already taking shape with impressive high ceilings and dynamic futuristic multi-coloured lighting embedded into walls and the pool areas. The developer was on schedule to deliver the project within the eighteen-month deadline although there were issues as always with infrastructure projects, of which this was no different. Toby and Yevana were pushing hard and getting results and had also decided to recruit some of the staff required early, to assist in much of what had to be done in advance. This would ensure that they were all trained to the highest standards of service delivery and accountability expected of a superstar residence such as No.1 Tudor Square. Another interesting input from Justine and Fay was to collect as much vintage furniture as possible which meant they had to hire a warehouse to store it. This would ensure whether it was bathroom equipment or lounge furniture, that there would be a feeling of class and history to complement the fresh new feel of a vibrant and nostalgic atmosphere.

About six months into the build Toby and Yevana had only really been engaged in business matters, purposely not meeting socially, whilst Yevana had noticed that her concerns over Summer being in a relationship with Toby were unfounded as they were very discrete in whatever they did. Of course, unknown to Toby, Yevana had given a gentle nod of approval to Summer; anything to stop Christina. She was also working as hard as she could to develop all parts of this business which included future growth after London was completed as she would never sit still; she couldn't. Only one thing was eating away more than anything and that was not having seen Mobola in a few months since the party at Free, as she had been away training hard at altitude. Having got her act together – she had even given her Saudi prince the cold shoulder – she responded to her coaches' demands to buck up or be deselected for the next Olympics. To say Yevana was frustrated was an understatement. She loved Mobola and sexually she gave her what she couldn't even dream of with most people and that included making her feel desperate; and she was. It would not last long though as although a real talent and a world beater, Mobola had addictions and they would come back to dig at her soul eventually.

The following month Yevana had planned to attend an international entertainment industry seminar in New York and hoped this trip would give her a much needed break away from London as she would be able to spend some more time again with her new very good friend Ru Carter, the philanthropist. Yevana missed living with Toby and had not seen Yurenev for some time which, considering his motivation to have her as a London prize trophy, seemed strange. But that seemed typical of him and he had a very active life of course! His wife in particular was a real influence and more so than many people gave her credit for.

Toby was as busy as ever, working hard but playing very hard also. He managed to get off to Geneva to meet Bob Ray and have a long weekend skiing whilst partying at Bob's chalet. As there was work to be done on the trip he took Janice to carry out some secretarial duties as firstly, she could crack the majority of work he had planned in a series of meetings on the Saturday and secondly, she could ski and was also good company. She was no trouble and deserved the break having worked her socks off to help get this project off the ground. But what a shock he was to have. They did their work on the Saturday in question, went skiing and later went into town with

Bob and friends for the evening. As the evening progressed Janice got talking to a group of people younger than herself and eventually moved on with them saying she would see them all tomorrow morning as planned. Toby thought no more of it as she was staying in a local hotel, which had been her choice. On his way back to the chalet whilst passing Janice's hotel, he heard some noises under a set of steps out of sight and decided to investigate as he was unsure what it might be in these cold temperatures. As he approached them he saw a white female face appear out of the dark and two young men gyrating, one at each end. The woman was stood bent forward with her large breasts hanging out and her ski pants nowhere to be seen – Janice! Those two guys were no more than twenty-two years of age and Janice from where Toby was standing, loving every second. He quickly scooted off without being seen and rejoined Bob and friends on the walk back to the chalet. He was laughing to himself and quietly out loud he commented, 'Good on you girl, good oh, mmm, very interesting.'

Toby asked Janice to join the guys at the chalet for breakfast before they headed off skiing and he asked, 'Good night, not tired I trust?' 'No' she replied, 'I was in control' and winked. They laughed loudly together. When they were sat on the ski lift later that day she leant across, put her arm on his lap and said, 'Never mix business with pleasure but if you want you can come and watch again at midnight tonight, probably same time, same place.' She winked, jumped off at the end of the chair lift shooting off down a red run in some style and speed. Toby was so impressed with her enthusiasm and determination.

The two guys were well built and very good looking. Janice dressed up for effect that evening in her hotel where the ski group were all eating, in standard jeans, blouse, and chunky boots in which she looked delicious. The evening was fun when around midnight and after a few bottles of wine between them, she made her excuses and put her arms through Toby's who had offered to escort her to her room. The two male 'friends' looked up and although they looked surprised to see her escorted by Toby, they left the group they were with and followed her as she had arranged earlier in the evening. At her room door she led Toby in and briefly paused to kiss her friends goodbye; they weren't required tonight. They looked crestfallen but she couldn't care less. They were young guys and they would get their fill later in the local clubs. For the rest of the night and on the plane home Toby started another relationship with certainly no strings attached! This one would stay very discrete and serve its purpose. Janice led a fairly adventurous sex life in London and although careful, she was not inclined to tie herself to one relationship, as she didn't enjoy that and had been bitten once too often in the past. This was perfect for Toby because he was running similar thoughts himself.

The following weekend back from Switzerland Toby was invited to a lunch at the SWAY restaurant Notting Hill; a swanky number for a get together of old rugby pals from uni. It was a mainly male affair but with partners if you wished. Toby would ordinarily have gone alone or on some occasions he had taken his current muse to this type of get together and of course being Toby, it was normally a hot date and had been Yevana on a couple of occasions. In this case he had thought he would be taking Summer but at the last minute decided not to take her, instead he took Janice! That day, Christina still brooding from being unceremoniously dumped, texted and left an answer phone message telling him, 'No more messing around, you are dumped. You are not dumping me. You are a low life who does not deserve somebody like me. You are pathetic. You can have that slut; she is all yours.' There was a minute's silence then the call was ended as if she had wanted to say more but couldn't muster the words required. He also told Yevana he was meeting his chums and that he was taking Janice and not Summer. She did not have a view choosing to remain silent, just raising an eyebrow. The evening as usual was a hoot and Janice went down a storm amongst this group. Later, back at Janice's apartment they nailed it, whilst playing back Christina's rant on answer phone – wicked!

By the following January the No.1 Tudor Square structure was in good shape and Yevana was happy, in fact, looking forward to going to New York for a fairly important seminar on hotel/leisure to focus on trends, the competitors and enjoy a mini break; she needed it. Yevana arrived at the hotel and was delighted to see several beautiful note cards accompanied by bouquets of flowers, informing Yevana to expect their arrival that weekend also. These were separate notes so they were all unaware of other imminent arrivals. Yevana unpacked then opened a bottle of champagne and sat sipping her drink whilst reading the note cards.

'Darling, glad you could come to NY. I will call you on arrival; I have some friends you should meet in the business. Ru Xx.'

'Babe, I am in town on a fashion shoot as we discussed. I will pick you up later and I have a great night organised downtown. Don't wear much! M xx.'

'Yevana, darling I am in town on business (isn't it always!) and I have somebody who needs to meet you, properly! I will see you downtown I am sure. Yurinev x.'

Wanting to completely relax she spent a little time unpacking before stripping off completely and laying back on the chaise longue, in this gorgeous room reserved and paid for by Ru Carter. It was one of brilliant modern colours but complemented by classic original furniture. This was a stylish mix of modern and classical which was actually difficult to pull off. Yevana drifted slightly into another world, concluding that it could be a very busy few days so this peacefulness, sipping wonderful zingy champagne whilst listening to Elgar would be money in the bank. Ru had had a Cuban placed for her too. In fact, it was not long before she was woken from her thoughts by the room phone springing into life, like an alarm bell.

'Darling how are you; I am so glad you have arrived safe and well and I trust you are already settled into that fine suite and those fine views of an autumnal Central Park. If it is not right I will talk to the manager,' Ru commented in a rather thrilling manner.

Yevana feeling the champagne seeping into her soul was very happy to hear from her relatively new friend. 'It is fine Ru, darling, I could not be better served; you did not have to book me into this superior suite; however, I have to say it is wonderful and appropriate to what we will deliver in the Y&T chain. I am relaxed and swimming in my own world which feels like the first time in a while, thank you.'

'Oh, thank goodness, I am very happy in that case. I must say I have missed you Yevana, I must be honest. Not sure exactly why but I have. Now I've got that off my chest I must let you know that as I indicated on my card I have some significant friends I know you will be interested in meeting who can help meet your business vision of the future. They have been told all about you and are very eager, one in particular. But not now that is for later. When are you going to be available?' Ru was very excited and Yevana was now trying to think fast as all of a sudden everyone seemed to be descending on her. What should she do? Knowing Mobola, she would turn up unannounced and want her full attention and although they were good friends neither Ru nor Mobola had mentioned to the other about this visit and Yurinev was a wild card in any case.

'Ru, I am available, what did you have in mind? Yevana responded.

'Well,' Ru paused, 'I will have my driver collect you at nine. Is that okay?'

Yevana looked up at the classic wall clock which looked like it had been removed from Waterloo station, it was that big. That gave her two hours; perfect.

'I will be in the foyer.'

'Ru sighed. 'Can't wait, darling, see you at the restaurant; I shall be seated. Ciao.'

As Yevana said 'see you later' the call ended before it was all out. How strange she thought as she replaced the receiver.

Yevana drank the whole bottle of champers and soaked in the most adorably deep bath, letting the Radox soak in deep. In anticipation, she shaved fully and adopted a severe ponytail for the evening. Dressing was simple as she chose a full length flowing emerald coloured dress, tucked at the waist and a deep V neck with patent black heels; nothing else required. Stunning would not do it justice. She thought about a handbag but decided she didn't need it.

Outside the hotel the paparazzi jumped out in front of her as she walked to her chauffeur-driven car thinking that she must be famous. The driver was not surprised as he had not seen a more beautiful specimen for some time! Yevana was on a massive high having downed the bottle of champagne and just ignored them as she knew they didn't have a clue who she was.

The Galaxy was the No.1 restaurant in New York without doubt, based in the premises of an old Bank that had moved on to more modern facilities that suited their requirements of the modern banking era: High ceilings and superb architecture. Ru knew that Yevana would appreciate this place and she certainly did. They greeted one another like long lost friends.

'Yevana, ooh how I have missed your company. Please tell me all,' uttered a very eager Ru accompanied by a huge hug and kiss on both cheeks.

'I am fine, really fine. You look beautiful, darling,' Yevana commented as she scanned this slight, delicate but strong woman. Ru was in minimalist mood also wearing a red one-piece mini shift and black patent stilettos. As they embraced Yevana noticed a Hollywood A lister she recognised look past his wife and smile; she did not respond. He could dream on.

They settled down to eat and the conversation soon turned to Mobola.

Yevana couldn't resist it, so mentioned her probable appearance as Ru seemed oblivious to the fact she was in town.

'Mobola should be in touch later as she is shooting in town but of course you will know that.' Obviously not from the look on Ru's face.

'No, I do not know that, how strange.' Ru was slightly irritated which was the first time Yevana had noticed this.

'Yevana, is she calling you later?'

'I don't know. I have not got my things with me so she cannot this evening. I am with you.'

Ru smiled a lovely tender smile, and then sent a text and the reply was instant.

'Mobola is in town and has been trying to call you. I will reply and let her know you are busy.' It was a matter-of-fact statement but firm and without a smile. 'To be in town and not let me know is very rude; it is unacceptable.'

The text read, 'Mobola, I am very upset that you chose to ignore me whilst in New York. Do not track down Yevana this evening, she is busy. Come to see me in my office at one p.m. tomorrow. Don't be late and cancel whatever you are doing to be there.' She then looked up and smiled once more at Yevana.

'She is busy and won't be about this evening. What a shame.' Instantly, they smiled at one another. They knew what that meant as they were on the same wavelength. It was a delightful evening of two likeminded people and on its conclusion, Ru looked up and out of the blue asked, 'Yevana, I love you in a way I have not noticed during the rest of my not inconsiderable life. I want to share my bed with you tonight without sex. Is that okay?'

Yevana was taken back but certainly felt a desire for Ru. Holding back in that situation would be a challenge. She stood up walked round the table, offered Ru her hand and they departed hand in hand. The A lister had an open jaw moment as Yevana read his mind engaging auto drive as they drifted by his table! Even his wife looked over; perhaps…she thought and laughed at herself.

Ru's apartment was opulent which was as Yevana expected with some of the most expensive art work imaginable and magnificent wall to wall glass panelled views over Central Park as a backdrop. The library was full of volumes of the classics and apparently, according to Ru, first editions to boot! A modern wall of windows on one side gave the evening light from the city an added edge which helped provide the heady atmosphere Yevana felt once inside this wonderful space.

'I used to have this apartment as my individual space as our main house was in Cape Cod. Weekends there were fantastic, such a party, but so relaxing. Here though I had my space and from time to time we would come here for our own version of a dirty weekend; special.' She glazed over slightly but quickly snapped out of it.

'But you don't want to know about all that, it is gone and cannot be brought back. I am a new Ru Carter now and equally enjoying helping people and living a different life. On that note did I tell you, you look beautiful tonight? Well, you do darling, you do. You make me feel different as though you have switched on a switch I didn't know I had; it feels invigoratingly strange!'

They didn't linger once inside though as Ru not being shy got on with the job in hand immediately. Firstly, she picked up a remote and instantly an immaculate sounding *Faithfully* by the band Journey drifted out of an invisible sound system complementing the heady atmosphere in the apartment. Ru reached up and stretched behind to unzip her dress letting it fall to the floor and stepping out of it and her shoes, she then walked across to Yevana and without saying a word, walked behind her and did the same. Yevana stood transfixed as Ru slowly, very slowly, teased the zip south. Then holding her hand, she led her to bed where Ru slipped in behind her and slowly wrapped her hands round onto Yevana's flat belly. Yevana sighed but didn't react further before they closed their eyes and proceeded to sleep like babies.

The following morning Yevana planted a meaningful kiss on Ru's forehead but left her sleeping, as she was up and out quickly with the New York early birds wanting to get cleaned up at her hotel before the international leisure seminar that day. Ru had arranged for an early cocktail party the following evening post seminar at the Greaves Club in Manhattan, where Yevana would be introduced to potential investors as Ru had promised. This was an exclusive club for people of a certain wealth and they were from all over the world.

The conference centre was massive and there were some two thousand delegates from all corners of the world trading tips and strategy in order to drive business forward. Although Yevana did not see this as the most exciting group of people gathered in one place, she conceded they knew their stuff and had a huge knowledge base. Most incredible but not a surprise were two enquiries about how she could spend the following evenings whilst in New York; both married! The trouble was even when she dressed down; in this case, in a high-end trouser suit she still looked hot.

Back at Ru Carter's residence she had called forward to the company using Mobola in the current underwear campaign and had it cancelled with immediate effect. Influence was everything in this town. Embarrassment was intolerable!

'Ru, I am so sorry, why are you being so cruel?' was the immediate response from Mobola calling at pavement level on Ru's apartment block intercom.

'Mobola, don't harass me and don't do it again. You are not as great as you think you are, now go away and concentrate on what you are good at: running fast! I will see you later,' was Ru's curt response.

Mobola walked off and sat in a favourite bar and drowned her sorrows for the afternoon. She did though text Yevana soon after arriving there.

'Yevana, I am really upset, I must see you later. Do not let me down.'

Yevana read this during a lecture being delivered by a seminar guest speaker. She considered a response but thought better of it although it pained her, partly, as she needed Mobola's kind of love badly but was cognisant that whilst in town she would have to tread very carefully with Ru and she knew how mad she was with Mobola. After half an hour without replying another text arrived.

'I know you have read my text; you bitch. When you need me I will remember this.'

Yevana was aching; she needed Mobola. She didn't reply.

On completion of the seminar, the following day, Yevana headed back to her room which was actually in the vicinity of the conference centre, where she bathed in a huge spa bath ahead of the evening cocktail party scheduled later, across town. Ru arranged a dresser for Yevana to arrive at six-thirty p.m. with a range of couture outfits specifically for that evening. Two women arrived, one sophisticated and glamorous in her mid-thirties and one fresh out of college. They helped Yevana get in and out of several beautiful garments before she settled on a cream pencil skirt and black skin tight, roll neck jumper that they paired with an emerald, green pendant and earrings. This matched the rock given to her by Yurinev on the boat that she had insisted on wearing that night. A glorious pair of black wedge platform shoes completed the look. The service was so personal that they would not leave until, as instructed by their client, Ru, they had personally dressed her and that included bra and tights. They asked about panties but she chose not to, and they did not comment on the misplaced loop earrings that she had already inserted after her bath! They placed a belly chain with diamond centrepiece around her waist and just told her that Mrs Carter insisted. There was a moment when the young woman on her knees and her face as close to Yevana's hip as it could be without touching, fastened the chain into position, and Yevana looked down and their eyes met; not today, she quickly looked away! Yevana enjoyed this prelude to the evening because although it could have been intimidating, she trusted the fact Ru had organised it and the feeling of being very intimately dressed by these two women was potent! Of course, the seed was sewn and such a service must be available at No.1; it had to be.

When discussing this event later that evening Ru pointed out the success of that business was based on complete trust and no touch.

'It's essential darling and has allowed Rosemary Hooney, the owner, to blossom into the top dresser company in New York. She is now a dear friend and I can assure you, you had the best there is there today. They come to me once a month and on special occasions and they never fail,' Ru declared with enthusiasm.

Chuck

Yevana arrived at the cocktail party by a yellow New York taxi and was met by the gorgeous Ru resplendent in a yellow jump suit unzipped to the midriff.

'Darling, you look fantastic,' commented Ru whilst kissing Yevana and then leading her by the hand into the grand looking Greaves Club. Momentarily, Yevana looked back and up at the Empire State Building which more than anything helped fix her position on the planet at this time and she shook her head as if in disbelief of how quickly things were moving and in what fantastic company she was now keeping.

'Darling, are you okay, you look like you have just seen a ghost?' Ru asked as she noticed Yevana look back and hesitate.

'No, Ru, just pinching myself.'

They looked at one another, got the moment and smiled.

Ru quickly ushered her into the foyer where they were asked if there were any belongings to be secured. 'No thank you, she travels light,' was Ru's response as Yevana had no handbag, coat or even a mobile once again on this occasion. Yevana had picked up quickly that on these occasions and in this company money was not traded in any shape as it was about 'the account' or you were looked after.

The room they walked into opened up into a high-ceilinged lounge with bar, very art deco with staff in abundance. Yevana noted that there must have been about eighty people in the room and eventually only about another twenty arrived after she had. The age group was senior and executive and you could virtually smell wealth. The women were generally of the same ilk and mainly wives who were dripping in diamonds and pearls. Yevana noted that it was clear the surgeon had been busy!

Her tentacles stood on end immediately when she spotted Yurinev, his wife and Mobola stood amongst a mix of American and Middle Eastern businessmen on the far side of the room, but far enough away to have not noticed her yet. How convenient, she thought, as she was introduced to Chuck Bush a Texan oil tycoon and his wife Sarina who were most charming. Sarina was conservatively dressed but smart and shapely which was normal for an American wealthy woman in her sixties supporting an influential husband.

He continued his conversation with another American, in this case a markets trader, whilst Sarina wanted to know more of Yevana.

'Darling, you are more beautiful than Ru told me. How long are you staying in New York?' She subtly looked her up and down and perhaps she was conducting an initial assessment before Yevana would be given access to her husband.

Yevana responded whilst sipping her G&T. 'Just a few days for a leisure seminar but not really much time to see or do much more than that with my commitments back in the UK. I must say I am enjoying myself and of course it is a chance to catch up with my friend Ru.' They all smiled.

Sarina soon showed her conservative leanings when enquiring about Yevana's relationship status. Perhaps this was the safety net survey before she allowed anybody to near to her husband.

'Is there a man on the scene warming the fires back home as I see you are not wearing a wedding ring? I must say you are young though and you have time. I though married very young which has been most agreeable, but I have to confess that is about finding the right man.' She looked admiringly to her husband Chuck who did not notice as he was embroiled in political conversation. Sarina laughed obviously alluding to the fact that, wait too long and Yevana would be past her sell-by date. Yevana didn't take umbrage just calmly responding whilst understanding the company. She did think that the exterior seemed fine but under the surface she had probably always had to accept being an understudy as part of the package!

'I am single at present and find very little time for such things whilst building a business with my partner. I am lucky as I have some fantastic friends though who look after me which is enough for now.' Yevana looked across at Ru and gently touched her arm. She felt Ru shiver and thought about last night and what a shock Sarina would have if she knew of last night's sleeping arrangements. It turned her on just thinking of it. Ru cleared her throat and looked at them both as another G&T arrived.

'Indeed, friends are so important,' Ru added. 'Now Chuck,' she exclaimed interrupting his conversation which she clearly had more authority to do than Sarina, who suddenly looked sidelined.'

'Hi, I trust my wife and Lady Ru have kept you entertained, sorry ummm.'

'It's Yevana,' She interrupted also acknowledging the emphasis on the Lady when talking about Ru.

'Oh, so sorry, age and all that, brain not what it was,' he lied to make basic conversation that was not his forte, which was followed by a deep hearty laugh.

'You must be a very clever lady to have engaged Ru Carter. Her husband was a best friend of mine,' and losing the smile becoming slightly sinister continued, 'I subsequently consider myself a guardian.' At this point he touched Ru's arm and stared at Yevana as if to say, 'take note'.

'Anyway, enough of that, I understand you have a business in the UK that has promise and the concept could do well here in the States. I am always interested in good things and helping those individuals or businesses that add value and have the enthusiasm and ideas to make money. I don't deal with losers.' This again generated a spout of uncontrolled hearty laughter. Carrying on, he abruptly concluded, 'My people will contact you then please brief them as required. Your idea will work in a number of States here and I have the contacts to oil the process.' He put his hand out, shook hands then he tipped his Stetson, which apparently, he wore almost everywhere, then quickly turned and continued his conversation with the dealer.

Ru pulled her to one side and Sarina started a conversation with another wife in the group in the blink of an eye; it was clearly form in this peer group.

Ru was happy and took the moment.

'Well, darling, are you happy? It doesn't get much better than that when it comes to contacts. He has an ear on the hill in DC and can make waves when required.'

'I am delighted. As you know we have a way to go in London but we know the model and it can be replicated anywhere with the right backing and we want to move as quickly as we can. Toby will be so excited, in fact, I can't wait to get back tomorrow.' She noted the disappointment on Ru's face so came back quickly, 'Present company accepted, but you must come to London soon. I might be getting cold, it's winter,' and gently, very gently, moved closer and pressed Ru's front zip against her stomach then turned and moved with her towards Yurinev and company.

Yurinev greeted them both warmly introducing other members of the wider group. 'So Yevana, Ru, how good to see you both.' He called a waitress over and recharged their G&Ts.

'How long is it Ru since we met in UAE with your late husband? I was sorry to hear of his death, what a shock.'

'Thank you, Yurinev but not really,' said Ru. 'He suffered several ailments for many years that ganged up on him and there was nothing the doctors could do in the end.'

'Well, I am sorry to hear that.' He soon changed the subject.

'Yevana, I hear you are here to learn but also look to take your business to America? That is good news as my stake feels very secure in your capable hands. Now talking of good feelings what of this evening? I have designs on a good old fashioned New York knees up.' There was a general nod of agreement and chinking of glasses in this abundance of good humour and enthusiasm. After about another hour Yurinev called his staff who would arrange onward transport.

Of course, Yevana did not require any further introductions with Yurini. She was a Russian woman of substance in her mid-thirties who looked every bit Russian and very obviously who you would expect to be the partner to Yurenev. Tall, pretty, blonde, legs to die for and solid high cheek boned features. They conversed for a short while, not mentioning the last rendezvous at the party in London and that intro to the Great Andoria. However, she did consider that there must be something else to this woman as she knew Yurenev's tastes and everyone close to him had a reason to deliver and she would be no different. She also sensed that she was strong and had an edge. Not long before they departed The Greaves Yevana noticed Yurini being touched with a double tap on the hip very slightly by a passing Arab which she didn't react to. That just about confirmed her suspicions. The dress she was wearing in gold had triangular gaps below the bust line and another at the lower belly area teasing above the panty line with just a small piece of material dividing and certainly very striking.

Yevana looked at Ru.

'Are you coming down town Ru,' asked Yevana who was hoping she would say no as she knew where this evening had its potential and was not expecting to be disappointed.

'I don't think so. My darling toyboy is back on Monday and I need my energy, he has some years on me you know,' she sniggered then continued, 'you go on and have some fun. I will call you in due course but as soon as possible. I will see you in London and if not before for the opening of No.1 in London. Don't worry, Andoria will be there, trust me!' As they said goodbye in the foyer, Ru moved forward, gave Yevana a large hug and very gently placed her bone china like right hand on Yevana's rear, touching the wafer-thin skirt and feeling the belly chain, automatically sending a sexual shock wave down Yevana's legs. Ru sensitively lingered as she withdrew it and they stared into one another's eyes, messaging something! Yevana whispered in Ru's ear, 'Darling, Ru, come to my bed in London,' then she immediately turned and walked back in to join the group and Ru walked to her waiting car.

Yevana rejoined her friends and they were soon arm in arm walking out to the cars waiting for their departure. Mobola grabbed Yevana's arm and they walked out together.

'I am very angry with you Yevana, I really want to punish you.' Having said her piece, she walked away from the car Yevana got into and accompanied Yurini. What a couple they might make, she thought, black on blonde. It occurred to her that she would be shocked if there was not some sort of need being met. She knew Yurenev and Mobola intimately and knew their desires and needs so Yurini must be involved, too.

They hit the town together firstly at a club called Hope and Luck and a bucketload of cocktails, vodka and champagne were scuppered as they all danced this Saturday night away. But as with everything involving this group and particularly in Mobola's world it wouldn't be simply a good night at a club, there had to be some planning to drain every last opportunity out of the evening. It was a glamorous night out and the whole group of about twenty looked wonderful together feeding off the group energy. They moved on to a celebrity gay club where Mobola had arranged to meet a couple of US female athletes who eventually disappeared with a couple of the men from the Middle East, which raised a wry smile from Yevana as she decided that they hadn't disappeared to go and discuss a sponsorship deal! Their group were not there long as they soon departed for a house party located in the vicinity of Central Park. The house which was huge belonged to a Russian friend of Yurenev's who just happened to have his wife back in the homeland, which allowed him time to arrange a party for his American girlfriend for the weekend. She was a young Asian-American broadcaster of notable beauty.

It was a very relaxed atmosphere with josh sticks, candle fragrances and all manner of other aromas drifting through the air. The time was now reaching three a.m. and so many amongst a house full of guests, were sat congregated on a variety of cushions. As was usual at any party at this time, the lights were dimmed and it was starting to become a place of decadence. Some couples were in close embrace on the floor and others disappeared for long periods. Her first trip to the toilet was met with a very resistant door. After a five minute wait a woman came out adjusting her waistline to normal, except that as Yevana went to move in she was nearly knocked over by a man pushing past replacing the buttons on the front of his jeans who smiled and said, 'Sorry we had an issue.'

Yevana in her style did not reply but returned the smile!

On completion of her ablutions Yevana sat talking to Yurenev and Yurini for a while mainly about the business but also about Mobola, as everybody was starting to have concerns that she was straying off the chosen route as fame was affecting her and perhaps worst of all her ambition. Having said this Yevana could tell that it wasn't sincere on their part as they were part of the problem as she saw it. This would become much clearer shortly afterwards. Yevana was feeling a little weary by now as the effects of a long couple of days in the seminar and a skinful of alcohol was taking its toll. She was laying back on a huge cushion with her legs stretched out and enjoying the ambience when Yurini leant over and in front of a group of eight people, also lying about in all manner of positions of relaxation, placed a hand on her thigh inside her dress and said, 'Follow me Yevana, we are going somewhere quieter.' Well, it was relatively quiet there but she got the drift. Yurini led the way up a flight of stairs and opened a door into a bedroom suite of enormous proportions. Mobola and Yevana followed closely behind into the suite where Yurenev poured a prepared bottle of iced bubbly into some glasses. In a strange turn, Mobola took his hand and looking at Yevana with a note of nonchalance, took Yurenev into a bedroom and shut the door. Almost like it was in slow motion, Yevana turned her head to look at Yurini's reaction and saw that she was playing with a remote control as if nothing had happened. At this point a large painting of two Greek goddesses lying on cushions scantily clad looking up at their warrior, started to move on the far wall. A huge one-hundred-inch TV screen replaced it and as she pressed another key, what was obviously the bedroom Mobola and Yurenev had entered, burst onto the screen. Yevana watched transfixed as Yurini, Yurenev's beautiful wife, stood and watched as he tied Mobola to a bedstead and ripped her clothes off tying her short dress around her mouth. Yurini turned off all the lights from a remote control then put her hand out and led Yevana over to the sofa in front of the TV. At first slowly, taking off her necklace and wearing it herself, and then more aggressively Yurini ripped her black jumper off, then tied Yevana's wrists to a chair, pulled her skirt down and quickly and aggressively set about gorging on her orifices, various; over the next couple of hours, she made Yevana reciprocate. The adrenaline rush on being manhandled by this expert, whilst being made to watch the black leopard that is Mobola being well and truly abused, was sensational. Yevana thought Yurini had the longest most slender legs ever and not a hair anywhere other than her head.

Eventually, they both fell exhausted onto the sofa. Daylight was seeping through the curtains and so before there was movement in the bedroom, Yurini gave Yevana her personal mobile number and two large diamond ear studs in a small box as a gift.

'I can't have my husband as the only person to give you a gift,' she said as she looked at the emerald. 'My husband informed me that he owned you. He owns me though! Don't be a stranger.' Yevana had another fan!

Yurini picked out a top from a bag and through it to Yevana to leave the party in!

She pulled on a new pair of knickers from the same bag, slid on her heels then told Yevana, 'Let yourself out' and walked into the bedroom where the twosome had played and would obviously play some more. Fascinated, Yevana pulled on the spare top then waited for a moment and witnessed the TV images come back to life and Yurini getting onto her knees and sinking her considerable white teeth into Mobola like a hungry leopard! Mobola appeared to twitch but was in no position to scream.

The flight home was uneventful and gave her a chance to get some well-earned rest and do a self-appraisal of the seminar which she decided had been a good chance to meet many key individuals in this environment and understand and implement some useful practices to No.1 and more importantly, eventually, worldwide.

On her return the building was being driven at an extraordinary rate as the weather and supplier availability were playing ball and helping the constructor to at least keep to the programme. Toby was happy and very interested in the US developments.

'Babe, you have done well I must say. Was it all work or did you get some time to yourself?' Toby asked with sincerity although they both knew he was doing some background fishing as well!

'The seminar was quite long and tiring but first class in content and delivery,' she replied. 'However, I was looked after by Ru Carter as you know, who was absolutely charming as ever. Her short but important introduction to the Bush's was worth the North Atlantic trip on its own. He, Chuck, is as influential as you get in the States. Otherwise Mobola and Yurenev and his wife were there and we had a good night out to complete my weekend.' She left it there and added no more. Looking at Toby though, she knew she needed a man again and soon, but that would wait.

Opening

The following summer came and with the improving English weather came the final touches to the London complex; it was truly magnificent. Marble and opulence was the norm, like the setting from a Middle Eastern palace. Chandelier after chandelier, decorated the larger rooms sparkling in the light but settling into their surroundings with ease. Expensive modern art was scattered everywhere in various forms from life size statues to huge paintings or murals that seemed to leap out at you as you approached them. Some of the best young artists of this generation had taken the opportunity presented to them to display their work and use No.1 as a gallery, which in itself became a media talking point. This had actually been Fay Turner's idea whilst working on design elements with Justine Hauser and Toby thought it a master stroke. The leisure complex had turned out to be fantastic and the design had been adapted so that an extra tunnel took customers from leisure reception to the main bar and club in the church wing without going back through reception: Costly, but worth it. The original plan was for Toby and Yevana to take a top floor suite permanently but they decided not to take up the option based on two reasons. One, they were not together and so two rooms was out of the question and two, the initial bookings were exceeding expectations and so all rooms were required and this was looking likely to be a long-term trend.

Before opening, the marketing company they had instructed, who were leaders in their particular field, had worked wonders. Membership schemes were another key element of this project and specifically for individual functional areas of the complex. In the event, the schemes had been taken up in large numbers for the first year with some taking a five-year option as incentives had been set out intelligently in this wonderful space. The fact it was London and they had good transport links nearby as well as affluent areas within walking distance were key factors. Good people had been employed as managers and in other staff positions as the word had got around that this would be the place to be seen or to relax in private, which allowed for all types of celebrity. Staff rules had already been set for automatic dismissal for anyone who allowed privacy to slip to the media or any other purposes.

Well in advance of opening night Toby and Yevana got together to organise the VIP guest list. Their investors, friends, certain MPs, minor royalty, the Mayor and celebrity A listers would be treated slightly differently to other good looking eye candy who would nevertheless still attract the attention of photographers and thus get the project media space from the evening's entertainment. The majority of the details though were in fact left to Janice, Summer and other the senior staff to organise with only some minor issues to resolve. Yurenev and Yurini, Bob Ray and all associates had confirmed as had Mobola who was coming with Prince Mahood. Ru was coming unaccompanied but couldn't stay as she was meeting a friend in Sao Paulo the following week.

The night before opening Toby and Yevana came back after a final walk through with staff that day and went up to a booth in the private members club and poured a series of G&Ts. They dimmed the lights then sat chatting for ages about how they got here and particularly how relatively quickly. Out of the blue Toby asked about somebody that had never been mentioned since the end of their uni days.

'Yevana, darling, do you ever think of Caren Lords?' he reflected rather uninterestingly.

Yevana looked up looking rather surprised. 'My goodness, where did you drag that name up from? That seems such a long time ago doesn't it?'

'Yes, I suppose so. I was surprised you left her, you seemed so in love. Do you ever think of her?'

'Now and again. She was a teacher of love and sexual expression like no other but it came with a price tag. I can't explain it, so I shan't try, but there was something that told me the only way to leave this relationship was to leave dramatically. That's it. I don't regret it. It's just the way I am. Let's leave it, eh.'

Toby studied her as she spoke and wandered what Caren was doing now. 'Okay, babe, just came to me, that's all.'

Yevana came across to Toby on the red velvet designer sofa and he cradled her in his arms as she settled across his lap. They continued talking for a couple of hours before Summer texted him saying she was at his flat and thus he departed with a kiss on the forehead for Yevana. 'Love you,' he declared.

'Love you too,' she replied as he moved away. All very matter of fact but that is how it was.

As she heard him exit the executive bar area she had a flash. No, she didn't want to wait on this epic of nights, she needed spice in the form of sex. She pulled out her mobile phone and called her ravishing Spanish IT consultant, the good reliable Andre. She knew he was in town as he was on site personally managing the transition to opening, but he had mentioned he was expecting a female guest to arrive who may come along with him to celebrate at the opening ceremony tomorrow. He, Andre Correnti was quite a slippery character but whether by design or not he had kept Yevana grasping for the fly!

'Ah! Andre, it's Yevana, are you at a loose end, darling? I am getting really excited and wondered whether you wanted to settle pre-opening nerves and join me for a drink. What do you think?' She blurted it out but hoped the more she talked the more time he had to agree.

'Hi, Yevana, that's funny you didn't mention that earlier today at work,' he came back struggling to think on his feet as he looked straight ahead into the clear blue eyes of Caren Lords. This was the first time she had paid him a visit for an update on his romantic situation with Yevana and had not been impressed to see he had not progressed due to the business being so busy, Yevana being non-committal and away for protracted periods. Placing his hand over the receiver he mouthed in a light whisper, She wants to see me now for a drink, what do you want me to do?'

Caren replied, 'Get over there you flippin creep.' She got up and started nervously patrolling round his flat. 'I spoke to your parents the other day and they seemed to be enjoying life. I know Leon and has been very busy, apparently!'

Nervously, he quickly uncovered the phone to listen to Yevana.

Yevana pushed quickly saying, 'I know, but I am now and as I see it you owe me Andre on many counts. Be here in the executive area in twenty minutes,' then she called off.

Andre wiped his brow thinking about what a mess he found himself in at that moment. He didn't know what Caren would do next and was not sure what awaited him at an empty No.1 the night before the grand opening.

All Caren said before he departed was, 'Bring me back a memento, Andre. Oh yes, I think I will come as your guest tomorrow but don't worry I will be in disguise, Oh, how exciting!'

Obviously, Andre was not as happy with the situation he found himself in but had no choice. He thought Caren might have got over this previous relationship in time, particularly as she had pointed out the beautiful diamond ring she was wearing that her barrister girlfriend had bought her for their third anniversary together. However, he registered that she mentioned this as a matter of fact with little if any emotion and Caren had not reciprocated.

'Okay, see you later, Caren.'

She leaned back and switched on the TV ignoring him as he left.

Yevana got another G&T and poured one for Andre, too. They had not been together for a little while, so under the circumstances this would be exciting and aggressive; she just knew it; wanted it.

Andre got the tube across to No.1 and was let in by the hall porter as security on the building had been in place for some time. He walked up through reception and across the darkened glass walkway to the church complex looking out onto the road outside as London life went about its business. He walked up past the main club bar area and restaurant then pulled open the doors to the private members club where Yevana was sat drinking her favourite G&T with one sat opposite. He walked up to her, picked up the other drink and threw it down the front of her blouse, took her drink, had a drink then did the same, this time aiming at her short silk skirt. He was immediately taken by the moment and the darkened atmosphere was only enhanced slightly by the wall lights. Grabbing her wrists, he threw her onto her back on the sofa, jumped on top and pinning her down took the opportunity to pull her small knickers to one side. Within what felt like an instant he had mounted her, choking her throat with one hand at arm's length whilst ripping open her blouse and biting her breast, eventually leaving a deep purple bruise. It did not take long and when he'd finished he pulled back then remembered his last instruction before leaving the flat.

'Ah, nearly forgot. I need these.' He bent down and pulled off her knickers and pushed them into his trouser pocket, zipped himself, turned and walked out, saying no more.

Yevana lay there for a minute and rubbed her throat which had been held very tightly for as long as it had taken, looked and gently touched her bruise and memento from this energetic encounter before tucking her blouse into her skirt and pouring one last drink. She thought of Andre and was definitely interested in him but for what she was not sure, but he was good at what he did. He was decent, well-mannered and sexually he definitely did it for her and she looked forward to testing his experimental side in due course! As she sat down again with her drink, she looked about her and felt at home and just knew that the customer would also.

The exclusive nature of this establishment with the financial backing they enjoyed, would ensure the longevity, she believed. Yevana finished her drink, walked across the glass walkway and walked back into reception where she met Toby and the delectably attired Summer who had just walked in. Seeing her made Yevana feel awful knowing the state she was in; post being beaten in the dark.

'I just had to have one last look in the quiet hours before the storm really! This place will never have this moment again until it is closed or destroyed,' was his immediate remark on seeing his friend, business partner and ex-love of his life, walk in.

'Correct. I was having a last walk round myself.' Yevana sighed as she walked across and stood up against one of the internal marble pillars.

'I will see you outside,' said Summer as she spoke softly into Toby's ear before turning on her heels and disappearing.

'I am sure I just saw Andre walking towards the Tube. Was he working late?' Toby asked as he took a seat in reception.

'Yes,' she replied not wanting to discuss it further.

As she walked closer to him he noticed her poor attempt to cover up her ripped blouse and stained skirt as he put two and two together. Blimey, she has only gone and christened the place, he thought. Should have been us not some Spanish IT consultant.

'Isn't it just amazing that from these steps inside the reception area tomorrow, from an idea we had some time ago, the top opera singer in the world, Andoria Rosenta, will sing and announce this fabulous creation?' She was jubilant about what they had achieved.

'Indeed, it is the most amazing thing, and I am so glad I have done it with you Yevana.' He stood up and held his hand out then led her to a point halfway up the steps and turned around to look into this beautiful cavernous space. Still holding hands, he turned and looked her in the eyes and said, 'I love you Miss Narvik.'

Yevana's eyes watered slightly as she drew him close and kissed him once on the lips before withdrawing and leading him back down the steps in silence, which she thought was appropriate for this occasion. At the bottom of the steps, she stopped and he kept walking and didn't look back as he walked through the entrance and out into the London night. Summer was waiting and they called a cab and were gone.

A slightly dishevelled Yevana followed shortly afterwards and decided to walk in the rain then take the Tube and join the peaceful, random, night life back to her flat.

Andre arrived back at his flat and was looking forward to ending this evening with some well-earned rest. He put the key in the lock and quietly turned it so as not to wake Caren. The room seemed to be mainly in darkness except for a side light in the corner of the lounge area. He crept inside the room and slowly and carefully shut the door behind him. There was only one bedroom so knowing Caren as he did, he knew she would have taken the bed, which they hadn't discussed, although he knew she hadn't bothered booking a hotel room, so, he had planned to sleep on the sofa that night in any case. As he crept across the lounge he suddenly noticed a pair of legs poking out from the armchair with its back to him. As he drew alongside and looked across he saw Caren, naked except for a pair of huge heels and a bra, sat looking straight at him and smiling.

As she expected, Caren noticed that he, Andre, looked white faced in shock as he obviously thought he would be coming back to slide beneath a blanket on the sofa. How wrong, not yet, she had other ideas!

'Come here!' she demanded.

'Caren, it's been a long day and I am tired,' was all he could think of, albeit that was the truth.

'Tough, get over here and unzip!' Caren was in no mood to mess about and didn't want to be up any later than necessary either.

'Did you get what I wanted?' He had, of course, and duly pulled out the tiny white panties from his pocket. As he handed them over and he continued to unzip directly in front of her, Caren sniffed at the wet material and slowly teased them into her mouth before pulling them on herself. She made so many different noises of satisfaction and anxiety in the act, as Andre was just a prop for the satisfaction Caren gathered from tasting and smelling her ex-lover on his person.

On finishing orally, he tried to pull out but Caren instinctively punched him hard in the stomach forcing him to double up momentarily as she took him deeper causing a scream of agony until nature abated. She then got up, pushed him aside and went to the bedroom and slammed the door.

Andre fell onto the sofa opposite and didn't even get the blanket until a couple of hours later when he felt the middle of the night chill on his skin, but even then he just threw it over and continued sleeping; he was tired.

First thing the following morning Caren was up and had gone for a run in the local park and had eaten her Weetabix before Andre had surfaced from his sofa. It was quiet in the flat again with just the breakfast news on the TV and some traffic noise buzzing as normal outside. Caren was soon out into town for some last-minute shopping whilst he got up, showered and grabbed a breakfast at the local café, before arriving at No.1 to help in last minute prep before that evening's festivities. The media facilities had to be ready and in particular the bespoke facilities for that evening. The first person he met in reception was Yevana who greeted him as any other employee. As he walked off out the back to the new complex offices he had received a text which read, 'I want my panties back and, oh yes, you to fit them please xx.' He stared at the text and for a moment he thought more of the same about how he could get out of this situation with Caren, but then his mind started to turn. He looked at the phone and started a reply to her text.

'Do you know what, Yevana? I want to do that and soon xx.' He smiled and walked into the IT/media hub facility. He did like her, well who wouldn't, which might make this situation easier. Dangerous but exciting, probably more exciting than he needed but exciting nevertheless, was his final thoughts on the matter.

Yevana heard the beep and looked down at the message on the screen. 'Umm, excellent.'

Her final text said, 'Volta, yellow, Petite, please!'

This was shortly followed by a text from Caren, 'Andre have two tickets delivered to the Bedford Hotel as I will now be coming with Tab this evening who has arrived in town. Ignore me; enjoy the evening, I shall!' she finished drily.

'Great!' he declared shoving the phone in his pocket. He couldn't even begin to think of all things that could go wrong. What he did know was that Caren would enjoy his misery and predicament.

Toby woke up, pulled the blinds and in stormed a bucket load of bright sunshine and it seemed a perfect start to what could be the best day of their lives. He was alone now as he had asked Summer to leave after they had been to bed on their return from No.1 the previous evening. She didn't argue as she knew how important it was for Toby and Yevana to work together and have no distractions on opening day.

Toby looked at his phone and noticed he had already started receiving messages of good luck. First was from Christina. 'Can't wait for tonight, so excited. If you want to celebrate after, then I will make myself available.'

'No chance,' he muttered as he deleted the text. He still had significant issues with the attack on Summer which still had to be dealt with so far as he was concerned. But that would wait. Next was a message from Janice, which he laughed at. 'Hi, have a great day, can't wait, you both deserve it! If you want to have five minutes with me afterwards before you enjoy Summer, then I am free, well for you anyway, any time, lol. Of course, if she wasn't my colleague I would join i…' He laughed loudly to himself. He had a real affection for Janice, she was fun and on message with a real personality. He preferred it as it was though and kept his dalliances with her from Summer.

'Thank you, I will look at my schedule!' was his humorous reply. Last one so far of any real importance was from Yevana.

'Feeling lonely but focused in my apartment, thinking of you, us and wishing you an unbelievable day. To the future. I love you xx.'

Toby sat down to compose his reply considering how best to articulate his response.

'Still the best a man could have. See you soon xx.' He didn't need to say any more. He did believe their day together would come again albeit it wasn't clear how it might come about with their complicated lives.

As Toby arrived at the complex he stopped to admire the newly refurbished structure in the sunshine of the early morning; it was magnificent. The stone pillars were stood as icons of another era back to their resplendent best. The main large black doors were shut, were shining bright and keeping the secret of what lay inside. The small garden spaces to the front had had a major makeover and gave the whole area a facelift, particularly the long-standing variety of beach and oak trees which gave real life to this area. Walking up the considerable steps and past the doormen the first person he saw was Yevana already looking busy on her phone.

'My goodness, you never stop,' he joked.

'Hi babe,' she replied as he planted a kiss on her cheek. 'In fact, I was just placing a personal clothing order!'

'Anything interesting?'

'No, not really just some underwear,'

'I am always interested in women's' underwear,' he responded again, grinning, before walking off towards the complex offices out back behind reception.

'Hi, Andre,' Toby called out on seeing him in the office suite. 'Not you on the phone already as well, nothing urgent I hope.'

'No, no,' Andre remarked nervously. 'Just matters of a female nature but all sorted now.' Having sent his final acceptance reply to Yevana he made his excuses and went with his own staff to complete the checks on all media facilities for the opening night.

The Y&T business staff HQ was still off site around the corner as this would continue to be the business centre for Y&T Global which would be the newly created company name. The London complex like Manchester was now in the hands of newly recruited management staff and a workforce that had been in place for a number of months, recruiting and developing the most up to date procedures required to run a business on the forefront of good practice and technology, which this complex was most certainly about. This would now allow Yevana and Toby time and space to concentrate on the new parent company and the proposed worldwide operation.

Yevana ran through the opening programme with the complex manager, Jim Guy, a focused and astute person who had a vast experience in this field and spoke several languages which would help in managing an international staff and client base. Well into his forties now, he was celibate for reasons he did not explain and would live on the job. His nature was friendly and forged a popular but firm stance in these early days. He called his bosses by their surnames which suited them all.

Having completed her rounds of the complex Yevana went for lunch with Ru Carter who was already in town but staying at the Dorchester as the only suite to be used this evening was for Andoria Rosenta, the international operatic singer. Ru preferred to quietly stay off site out of the way which Yevana appreciated.

'Darling, so good to see you, you look magnific! How do you do it?' Ru almost shouted as they embraced in the restaurant. 'Take a seat, darling.'

Yevana, at her naughtiest, slipped her right hand under Ru's loose top, gently onto her porcelain skin above her skirt which caused Ru to shiver, as she reciprocated with a kiss on both cheeks. On purpose, but sensitively, Yevana was making sure that Ru was firmly caught on her emotional hook!

Ru was interrupted by her phone and looked down to read a message. 'Andoria Rosenta has arrived at Heathrow from America and will be at No.1 around two p.m. She has her two PAs with her and asks that you are there to meet her on the steps, front of house. She wants a maid on hand for the next twenty-four hours also. She does not want you to worry about her PAs as she will take care of them.'

I bet you will, thought Yevana, smirking as Ru carried on reading before looking up having finished.

'I will see to her needs,' was Yevana's immediate reply not knowing whether that would have a deeper meaning before the night was out.

'Now let's order our lunch. I don't expect you want too much as your nerves must be on edge.' Ru, however, was insistent regardless and they were soon tucking in to a healthy lunch.

'Interestingly, I am not feeling too nervy, as I feel that we have done our work and earned a certain level of confidence. We are also very excited about the future plans of our worldwide business which already has shoots of development which you have kindly helped us to progress in the US.' Yevana placed her hand on Ru's hand and held it there for a moment.

'It was nothing, darling, I am delighted to help in any way I can. It keeps me busy.'

Yevana took the opportunity to change the subject as she took her hand back and placed it on her lap.

'Who is your guest this evening?'

'I took my time and thought I might go alone but on reflection thought better of it,' she laughed, 'my toy boy, he had to accompany me this evening. He will be here at about five-thirty. He is only staying the night as I am off for a short cultural trip to Sao Paulo, Brazil tomorrow morning. Have you been there?' she enthused.

'No, actually. What am I missing?' Yevana teased having been told by Mobola that Ru had 'interests' there.

'Oh, it's so vibrant. Perhaps I will take you one day.' Ru was actually quite keen to get off the subject of Sao Paulo.

'I am sorry we cannot spend an evening together this time but it will wait,' Ru remarked as she reciprocated by placing her hand on Yevana's whilst looking sympathetic, perhaps even longing.

'Enjoy this evening, Yevana. Please look after Andoria well, or it will cost me dear! I will see you there.'

After lunch they embraced and Yevana departed back to the complex to finalise instructions for the opening.

Toby had finally decided to set up the media area for a series of TV, radio, and newspaper interviews in an executive suite out of the general hubbub of preparation for the opening later that day. Magazine, general lifestyle and industry magazine interviews would actually take place over the coming days although all main leaders had obviously been invited to the launch party.

The first interview was for an afternoon lifestyle and current affairs show, a very popular satellite afternoon programme on air weekdays. The presenters were David Eckel, a smooth-talking male in his early fifties and Jane Marks who was an intelligent and quiet serious female in her late thirties. They were to be the first on later in the day and were being shown around the complex by Janice before lunch. Janice picked up pretty quickly as they walked and talked that they were going to run a slightly negative line asking, 'Does London's need this type of establishment, was it over the top and would it be affordable?' This was not good news as they did not want negative lines from such a positive day especially when they had no substance. However, about threequarters of the way round Janice took a call and left them on their own in the garden out back. When she returned from a different entry point to the garden she saw the TV stars embracing out of sight, or so they thought, and David had a hand nestled between his colleague's legs. She had her eyes closed. Janice moved quickly and took a photo on her phone and passed with a short message to Toby.

'Toby, they are running a negative line generally speaking, as they think this will stimulate more debate. Does London need such extravagance? Be warned they are not the easiest to talk to.'

His reply was instant. 'Brilliant, you are a star, what quick thinking, thank you.'

Janice smiled and coughed as she entered the garden and they soon followed her back on the tour.

Back at the executive suite after lunch Toby was introduced to the TV presenters and had a light conversation where they confirmed what Janice had surmised, a frosty outlook for some reason.

Toby pulled Jane Marks to one side and enquired, 'What was your overall impression, Jane? Looks terrific don't you think? I will have to introduce to Yevana, my partner who has such passion for this business and is actually at dinner with Ru Carter the philanthropist at the Dorchester as we speak but should be back soon. We have plans to take this worldwide which I will be only too happy to discuss. Anyway, Janice told me you liked the gardens, I must say they are quite romantic!' As he finished speaking he raised his phone as if to view a message then turned the screen in order for Mrs Marks to view it. She looked in horror as he left it long enough to do a double take then pulled it back and moved off without another word or glance back to see her look of shock and horror. She was obviously knocked back knowing that this image was out there.

The interview went like clockwork with both Yevana and Toby taking part in the interview to be recorded for transmission the following day. It was light hearted and very positive! They were both invited back for a live show in the future when they launched Stateside, which they accepted.

'Toby,' he heard his name and turned around to see Jane Marks stood behind him looking very meek and worried.

'I hope you feel we were most positive about this fabulous project; we wouldn't have wanted to be seen otherwise after all the effort and risk you have sunk into this venture.' Jane looked him in the eyes and stuttered slightly, 'Would you delete that image for me please, I beg you?'

'No, Jane.' Toby was adamant. 'I like insurance policies, they give one comfort, don't you think? But I look forward to viewing the programme tomorrow and accepting your invite in the future. It is very exciting and thank you for the opportunity. Now I must get on. You have nothing to worry about.' As he left he lent over, touched her hip and kissed her cheek, whispering, 'Lucky man!' He didn't smile or smirk; he had this influential woman where he wanted her. Eckel didn't get involved and it was obvious he was getting the blame for this problem.

The good news about this incident, as explained by Yevana, was that these people had felt so comfortable in this place to let their guard down so easily.

'Darling, how typical of you to spot the positive story from that potential trauma and of course you are correct, Toby responded'

Yevana and Jane got on very well and seemed to have a lot in common but the subject was not broached by either.

The interviews of varying duration concluded at around four p.m. when the last checks were conducted on all equipment and routines for the evening before Andoria and her entourage arrived at the front door as planned. Yevana had taken care of these arrangements and had the most suitable maid on standby to assist. Most suitable but not shy to fend off unwanted clients. Although young and good looking she was strong, experienced and Russian! They stood on the steps as Andoria arrived in a black cab, her preferred mode of transport in London as she liked the chat with cabbies. She got out and looked stunning for somebody who had been travelling from the USA for the last twelve hours. Her Oriental PAs helped her adjust her footing onto the pavement and Yevana was soon there at her side.

'Yevana, isn't it?' Andoria asked bluntly. 'You don't know how lucky you are to have me here tonight. I have been so unwell this week. This is my maid, yes?'

'Yes, Andoria, she is at your service for the duration. Please feel free to address your requests to her; she can also be reached by text or through the reception. Her name is Katina. Now let me escort you to your suite, I know you will love it. Katina, bags please.' Yevana then turned and led the way up the steps. Andoria struggled in her trademark high heeled boots but was propped up by her girls. Resplendent with her black mane sweeping down over her shoulders Yevana felt a weakness for this beauty fall over her as she was taken by the aroma and beauty as it drifted past her. Her spray-on leather trousers were a sight that none of the assembled staff could take their eyes off. Andoria lived in a world of her own though and it was obvious she noticed very little going on about her. As Yevana delivered her to her suite and she started to enter, Andoria looked back towards Yevana and said, 'I believe we might catch up later, perhaps after the show.' It was largely statement partly request.' Yevana looked her in the eyes, didn't answer and the door was shut.

The thought that she had perhaps got under the skin of this heroine to the rich and famous took Yevana by surprise although she could understand that there could have been an impression left on conclusion of that first coming together. 'Must get on,' was her comment as she pressed the lift button for the reception.

Yevana walked back into reception, collected her bag from one of the receptionists at the front of house, threw her hair back as if refreshing herself for the outside world then departed through the front doors. On reaching the bottom of the steps she asked the doorman if Toby had departed and he confirmed he had.

She had not booked a taxi and looking at her watch decided she needed the walk and so off she stepped.

Toby disappeared by taxi to dress and was soon in his flat where he picked up good luck cards from the post-box. As expected, Christine's was first and to the point. 'Enjoy, Toby, you deserve a great night, love always C xx.' He laughed to himself and thought about how much he actually admired her persistence. Next was from Summer as expected really, then lastly from Janice who shocked him slightly. 'We touched on it once recently. I don't know about you but I think that if we get the opportunity we should deal with our issue of justice. Have a great one, Janice xx.' Toby put the cards on the main window ledge and went to get ready for the event.

Yevana was soon back home and soaking in the bath, she really loved a soak and with the bath salts it made her feel a million dollars. She had decided what to wear that evening and it was black, long, silk and slinky as it tightened around bust and waist. It was delivered direct from Volta HQ in Spain and was a class cut and obvious who it was designed by. A huge black pair of heels, one long necklace with diamond pendant nestled at the approach to her bosom with suitable earrings completing the look. As always she went out minimalist. In some ways, it didn't seem appropriate to be at such an event and not be escorted which added complications for overbearing pursuers. However, this should not be an issue this evening as she would be with Toby for large parts of it or otherwise she would deal with the problem! In her case it normally came on two fronts! As the time approached she was ready as the taxi called to collect her and within a few minutes they had arrived at the complex. It was looking magnificent as the daylight started to fade and large outside lights beamed light onto the frontage. It was quiet and there was no fuss as she made her way inside where she met Toby.

'The lull before the storm,' he declared looking about as he greeted her. 'You look too good to be here. I should be taking you out somewhere, treating you like the Duchess that you are.' 'Now you are going over the top darling, come on you smoothie, let's have a look round. Have you spotted our singer yet,' she replied in a spot of sarcasm.

'No, not yet all quiet on the western front! Apparently, she has made some requests to room service about her dietary requirements, but nothing untoward.'

'I am glad that's all it was,' Yevana remarked, thankful it wasn't worse. Andoria was not coming down until she was due to sing.

Toby allayed her fears. 'Her PAs would escort her onto the stage and Andre was ensuring the technical equipment was up to spec. Any problems and she would walk off, but rehearsals without her had gone well, so I know it will be okay.'

It wasn't long before the guests were arriving up the steps and into the main building where they were met by welcome drinks, canapés as well as many tour hosts and hostesses who had been employed for the night. There had been more than five hundred invitations delivered to all parts of the industry, London nobility and selected VIPs. Together they met the first batch before separately dealing with the VIPs and other notable guests as they arrived. Certain individuals were selectively brought to them by Janice, Summer and Fay as directed on a pre-prepared list.

First special to Yevana was Mobola and Prince Mahood. What a fine couple they looked. The only surprise so far was that she had not yet become Mrs Mahood number five.

Kisses all round were dished out until Yevana opened the conversation.

'I wasn't sure you would make it in the end as I thought you would be at the International Diamond League meeting in Geneva this weekend.'

Mobola, whilst looking around, replied in a rather lazy manner. 'I, I, wasn't going to miss this, don't be so silly Yevana, anyway my prince insisted.' She looked up to Mahood and then back at her again. Yevana saw something that worried her in Mobola. She recognised she was spending more and more time in the Middle East and had recently changed coaches as she became more unreliable. Her coach was reported as having given her an ultimatum but Mobola told the media that she wanted to freshen her approach and she needed a new coach to take her up to the next level. Considering she was world champion and undefeated in the last two years, that was difficult to understand. There were several rumours circulating about her social life and her habits. Yevana looked at her and dressed in minimalist black hot pants, displaying her fine shiny skin and standing taller than her escort, gave Yevana a shot of adrenaline. It had been too long but it would wait; everything could wait.

Toby was soon in conversation with the Mayor and his wife when he noticed Andre escorting two feisty looking women through towards the glass walkway having collected a drink and something to eat. They stood out because they appeared to be an item, although he conceded with women you could not always tell friends from lovers. One of them had a large mop of hair covering her face and as their eyes met briefly, for some reason, there was a familiar feature he seemed to recognise although he quickly let the thought go.

'I am sure Toby clocked me,' said Caren as Andre whisked them off down the glass walkway.

'Come you two, I told you not to look at them and stay out of the way. If you are spotted and associated with me, I have had it.' Andre was so nervous he would have to settle down as he had lots of important responsibility for the rest of the evening.

'Calm down, Andre, it will be fine. Where is Yevana?' As they approached the main club bar area in the church Caren spotted her talking to some business executives.

'My goodness, she has got more beautiful. She stood staring for a moment and dropped the hand of her lover who looked slightly crestfallen. Andre moved them away through to the Private Members Club and continued the tour.

Ru did indeed arrive with her toyboy, her delightful Simon and didn't bat an eyelid, in fact she was getting a lot of envious glances from other women of a certain age! Looking stunning in a red tight fitting ball gown for the evening she had insisted he wore jeans and a sports jacket so she felt like she was with a rugged looking young man.

Yevana was soon engaged with Yurenev and Yurini in the gym area where she eventually caught up with them having got away from the industry execs who were drooling over what had been achieved here. They had left cards to discuss how they might help in taking their plans forward. Yevana was not surprised either to see a personal mobile hastily handwritten on the rear. One part of the conversation had started, 'May I say, you and your, is it boyfriend? have done a massive job here.'

'Yes you may,' was her reply, followed by, 'No, he is not my boyfriend I am happily single at this time and far too busy to play those games.' Whatever she meant by those games, she did not mean she didn't play when the desire took her, in fact far from it. They were sniffing but were politely dispatched! That did not distract though as there were important conversations to be had with these people and others like them.

'Darling, so glad you wore my earrings tonight, I would have been so disappointed if you had not,' was a sharp and pointed note of ownership from Yurini.

'Indeed,' replied Yevana, 'we owe you both a great deal of gratitude for your continued support and we hope it brings about many good days in the future.' 'I'm sure it will, darling,' Yurini sighed, 'in fact I'm certain.' Yevana smiled as they started to move off into a position to get the best view of the great Andoria, their friend, as she was due on stage shortly. As Yurini moved past the rear of Yevana she let her right-hand fall and slide very gently along her bottom instantly noticing that she was bare. Leaning into her neck and touching her ear with her lips, she made an offer, 'Yevana, please feel free to catch up with us afterwards as we are off to a club, then a party at ours if you like and I expect Andoria to be in attendance! It will be hot I can assure you!'

It was an offer that she would think on and probably, no definitely, find hard to refuse. Not replying she walked off in the direction of the temporary stage on the reception hall steps to await 'Lady' Andoria's arrival.

Nobody was disappointed to see the two PAs dressed as ballet dancers in white tutus escort Andoria who was dressed in fantastic long sparkling boots, a long skirt and a silk top, handle the microphone and immediately start singing firstly, Madama Butterfly Act Two *Un bel di vedremo*, then *Suspicious Mind* followed by *Jerusalem* as a brilliant finale that brought the house down. It was truly magnificent and reverberated around the entrance hall and moved many to tears. At one point Toby looked up at the chandeliers which were shaking!

Caren was enjoying the moment in this most delightful of places and with such exalted company that for a short while she forgot about her Yevana, that was until they nearly bumped into one another. They didn't and as there had been no recognition, Caren remained standing silently behind her but near enough to touch, as Yevana talked to a Russian couple. She held her girlfriend's hand and stood taking in Yevana's aroma which she felt was totally intoxicating to her.

Andre was absolutely delighted at the success of the evening so far, Andoria had just finished to rapturous applause when he turned away smiling until alarm bells started banging inside his head when he saw on the far side of the hall, Caren, stood just in his sight line with the girlfriend immediately behind Yevana.

'Jesus,' he exclaimed, 'what the hell is she doing now?' He moved over as quickly as he could but was stopped by Toby for a quick chat after which he steered the women away from an imminent disaster.

'What are you doing Caren? It's madness, this not part of your plan. I don't get it. Actually, I do. It is just a kick to you. I'm off, just stay away from her on her big day.' He was angry now and they knew it but he was right, Caren was savouring the moment and was getting a kick from taking the risk. As she moved away she brushed Yevana's back as did her girlfriend although Yevana was so engrossed in her conversation she did not seem to notice.

Toby did the honours by thanking everybody for attending. The mass of people below him in the reception hall seemed to be buzzing which was fantastic. He noticed Yevana standing next to Mobola and that they were holding hands. The singer was with the Russians and Janice had a group of youngish execs around her! Of no surprise to him was Christina near the front staring up at him.

'I hope you enjoyed the tour and the singer.' The audience laughed at the term singer for the international superstar. 'Andoria, you were fantastic, thank you,' and then there was more rapturous applause. She smiled and tried to look shy and waved off the attention whilst clearly loving it! 'I trust you have seen enough to know that this is a serious business hub and leisure complex to facilitate any need you may have in central London and may you and many others return here for many years to come. Lastly, the people who made this a reality: Yurenev, Bob, Prince Mahood and our construction team and our fantastic staff without whom…' he waved his arms towards the group, 'and lastly my partner, the distinguished and guiding light driving Y&T, Yevana Narvik.' His final 'thank you' was drowned out by the cheers and applause as he walked down the steps and walked over to Yevana and gave her a big hug, whilst quickly being handed a huge bunch of lilies for her. He then started shaking hands with some of those mentioned and saved a bear hug for Bob who was supporting a big, big smile as the one man who got them on the road in Manchester. Like the ending to any cocktail party this signalled the end to proceedings and people started to drift out into the night and in this mood a good night on the tiles in town for many.

Yevana moved away from Mobola to say goodnight to Ru who had collected her coat and was leaving.

'Be careful on your hols, darling,' was Yevana's cautionary farewell as although she didn't know exactly what the circumstances of her activities were there, she was showing some concern.

'Thank you, Yevana, but don't worry,' she replied as they both noticed that the toyboy had eyes for a young woman he was stood with a short distance away.

'I have made changes to my life and there is far more risk involved,' she subtly eyed the toyboy and smiled, 'but based on age I am content. I am happy and will be as careful as I feel the need to be. As I said previously, if you wish I will invite you to come with me on a future trip perhaps. We shall see.'

Yevana enquired as to who the people were her boyfriend Simon was talking to.

'Oh, a couple of professionals, they seem like good company. He is quite taken with the younger one, a barrister I believe. He hasn't realised yet that she is as gay as they come. They seem good company though and so we are going to move on with them for a drink before calling it a night. Want to come?'

Yevana was already drifting and watching her own group getting ready to depart. 'No, darling, in fact I have to get going myself. Do take care, Ru.' Big hugs and kisses were delivered and off they went. Yevana watched, briefly, as she joined the others and as they walked out of the building there was something about the couple of women that seemed familiar but she could not and did not ponder.

Andre did not venture near Caren again, he just stayed away as he had had his fill of her for today.

Yevana saw Andre as she went to collect her bag.

'Andre, we are moving on to celebrate will you join me?'

'I don't know, I am feeling a little tired, a bit weak I know,' he smiled.

'Don't worry, Andre, I am a good battery charger. You're coming then?' she smiled in return.

'Yes,' was all he added; he couldn't say no! He looked at her and wanted it; they both knew it.

The guests started to disperse quite quickly and decisions were rapidly being made on who was leaving with who. Yevana had accepted the invitation from Yurini and this group would include Andoria's group and the prince with Mobola. As they left the complex Yevana was actually arm in arm with Yurini closely followed by Andoria. Yevana and Toby didn't even speak again after the close, it was done, tomorrow was business as usual notwithstanding they were open for the first time; they would both be there at eight, no doubt about it.

Goodbye, Christina – After Parties

Janice, Fay, and Summer had done the honourable thing and invited Christina, a major player on Y&T projects, to enjoy the party they were planning in town. There was no way she would get near anything Yevana was doing socially, although professionally Yevana thought Christina was brilliant, but that was another matter. She was once just a very nice professional person who was great company. They all accepted whatever happened between her and Toby had had a major effect on her character and life. Toby was happy she was with them tonight as she deserved a good team night out together. In any case, it was a case of the more the merrier tonight. Leaving the complex after the majority of guests had left, they jumped in an eight-seater taxi and off they went, starting at an East End bar before moving on to a club of dubious reputation. It was in a dungeon-like basement, had dancing girls and it was jam packed with sweating bodies. By four a.m. they were getting pretty wrecked and nobody had shown signs of leaving with anybody. Summer was playing her cards close as were the others, mainly in case others departed and left Toby for themselves. At around four, Janice took the opportunity with the alcohol pumping wild through her veins. She grabbed Summer and briefed her on what they were going to do next and although Summer was not that happy, she knew she had to do this; it was right. Toby was instructed by Janice to get Fay on the dance floor for the next couple of tracks. Janice asked Christina and Summer to come outside for some fresh air as she was starting to feel lethargic from the lack of oxygen. They all went outside and then Janice led them round the corner into an alley which was very dark. As they started round the corner, Christina stopped.

'I don't like dark places like this, they give me the creeps.'

Christina was pushed forward and before she could shout, Janice covered her mouth.

'Christina, you are about to take your medicine for what you did to Summer, we know it was you! Struggle and it will be worse,' Janice demanded in the most sinister of tones as she forced her victim onto the damp, slimy, concrete surface.

'Don't dare move Christina or trust me it will be worse for you. Summer, here is a small knife, cut off her clothes, now!' She shouted in the lowest tone she could to get the petrified Summer active as she handed it over to her. Christina was wearing the most gorgeous bodycon in black and beige that with her current long blonde locks, had had all eyes turning that evening.

Summer quickly, albeit nervously and with some hesitation, started to cut away the dress followed by her bra.

'Now,' Janice demanded. 'Pull off the knickers, it's more degrading, she deserves this.'

Summer slid her fingers under the elastic waistband of the minimal material and pulled them down.

'In her mouth!' She did as Janice asked forcing the material into the frightened and tightened mouth. Christina was shivering by now, frightened, humiliated, dirty and in fear of her life.

'Christina, you are lucky we are leaving you with your pants, so don't move until we have left. Janice threw Christina's heels over a large wall with her ripped garments. Lastly, they forced Christina flat on the grubby alleyway that had all of life sprayed all over it without being washed over decades. Then, without emotion, Janice stabbed Christina in the rear once then hacked off a length of hair and handed the knife back to Summer. 'Do it Summer!' she told her in no uncertain terms. Summer bent down and whispered 'bitch' in her ear then stabbed her right cheek. The two women walked for two miles and didn't look back before hailing a cab back to Janice's to get changed for work. No sleep on this night out.

Christina was in a really poor way although nothing critical and eventually got up and was able to call another passing woman, who handed her a coat and called her a cab. She was dazed and confused and unable to get home, so the driver took her directly to A&E. There she stayed in hospital for several days. She would not speak, and various police enquiries came to nothing. She was eventually released to a psychiatric unit where she was to stay for over two months before being allowed back home. It was a sad ending to her time with Y&T who would not utilise her services again. There were no long-lasting injuries, and she knew she had now paid her dues. She had made a mistake and paid for it; finished, move on.

Christina eventually confronted her demons and was soon living with a theatre director and relative happiness albeit she continued to watch Y&T develop from a distance. On random days out walking in the capital she often walked past No.1 Tudor Square London; it was her baby. Was it Toby? No, it was the building, 'well'...

Toby understood what was taking place that night as he had been warned by Janice that it was time to 'sort it-put it to bed' as she put it. It was rough Justice. The upside for Toby was that he was left with Fay and he may on any other occasion, have taken the opportunity but not tonight. He didn't want this. He had enough going on and they had not selected the staff to seduce although he had already crossed that boundary but enough was enough. So, as they arrived at Fay's, he leaned over kissed her goodnight in the taxi before going their separate ways to get ready for a busy day. As Fay walked across the pavement outside her apartment block looking stunning in her short dress and heels, he chastised himself then laughed causing the taxi driver to smirk as their eyes met in the rear-view mirror; he knew!

Ru led the group out to the waiting cars and invited the others to get in with her. Caren and her barrister girlfriend got in splitting the group up meaning that Simon sat between them and not Ru.

'Simon, have you had enough of me already? That would be so unimpressive, I must say.'

'Of course not, Ru, that will never happen,' he responded just as Caren moved her girlfriend's hand onto the outside of his leg and out of sight of Ru. Dreana didn't look pleased but left it there or she knew she would see the worst of Caren later.

'You will, Simon but only when I allow it, and only then,' she concluded. Caren then took the liberty of informing the driver that the top West End jazz club was their intended destination.

'Ru, tell me, how well do you know Ms Narvik? I do find her an absolute trendsetter and she seems to be such a class act and brilliant businesswoman. Of course, I do not know her, but she has forged such a reputation. She must be doing well to have befriended you Ru.' Caren was being careful to allude to a business relationship rather than anything more intimate, although she knew Yevana was capable of both.

'Yevana is indeed a friend of mine and first and foremost I am helping her build her contacts in the States and really no more than that. After that, in helping her after being brought together through mutual friends, she has become a good friend and one I very much treasure. Her attitude is spot on. Do you know her, Caren? Or were you just a business guest tonight?'

'Just a guest,' Caren jumped in quickly. 'I have never met her before but perhaps we will in future.' As she finished speaking, she leant over and placed her friend's hand between Simon's legs and sat up herself to cover Ru's view. The driver was now being distracted as he watched the performance on the back seat. Simon was going red in the face but enjoying every minute. Dreana was not impressed but did not retract until they pulled up outside the club.

The club was full and as vibrant as it could be with a great soul band getting everybody on their feet most of the night. The four of them were getting on great and certainly extending the time Ru intended to be out and had drunk more than she normally allocated herself. Caren's girlfriend Dreana had been given instructions on a visit to the toilet.

'Dreana, get Simon into a drunken state, I don't want him in the mix when we get to wherever we end up, hopefully with Ru in tow. If you cock this up, then you get him for the evening! Don't let me down, Dreana.' Caren had a plan and this was the first part. She knew Dreana would do her bit as the thought of a man inside her had never occurred, had definitely never happened and would not want to start that tonight. She was desperately in love with Caren and this meant she would do anything to ensure that continued which meant she intended to carry this out to suit them both.

Simon was getting very high on the alcohol and atmosphere as Dreana continued to supply him doubles and more of everything all night, whilst dancing him into the ground. He was very tired and drunk by the time they hit the fresh air again. Ru looked on in giggles but as it got later more in wonder of the youth of today, so easily led. She was slightly surprised at how well he was getting on with the young lady but thought no more of it in this playground.

Caren was making sure Ru had strong levels of alcohol also as they danced in tandem with the others. As they hit the early hours the music slowed and Caren, in her expert manner, that not many could master like she could, gently pulled Ru onto the dance floor and led a slow, firstly, slightly detached slow dance until for the second song they embraced, and then Caren's left hand slid down onto Ru's rear at just the right pressure to cause a stir in her partner's lower body. As they carried on into the third song and the lights lowered further, Caren directed the movement into a darker corner of the dance floor away from the stage and moved her right hand through the waist high slit in Ru's gown and lifted her pantie elastic and pushed her thumb gently into the space. Ru's head slumped forward almost in shock.

'Uhhh, Uhhh, I...I...,' Ru tried to speak but Caren took it deeper and with a subtle movement.

'Shuuush baby, shuuush, you'll wake the neighbours!' Caren joked, which was a very dubious moment for humour especially not knowing which way this would go. 'Enjoy the moment. Is it your first time with a woman?'

'Yes, well,' thinking of her night asleep with Yevana, 'I have slept with a woman but not in that way,' she continued before Caren interrupted.

'Shhhush, quite.' Caren whispered as another smooching couple drifted by.

Caren knew immediately that she had slept with Yevana. Perfect, she would enjoy this even more now.

As the current song was drawing to a conclusion Caren leant forward and pulled her hand from Ru's sex.

'Bite it hard!'

As Ru carried out the order Caren pulled Ru's dress to one side on her flat chest and bit her next to her left nipple causing a small murmur from Ru but no more. Caren suddenly walked off to their seats to meet the others. Ru pulled herself together adjusting her dress and panties. Caren approached her girlfriend saying,' 'Suck this clean,' then gave her thumb to suck for a moment, as she laughed at the good job she had done with the now prone Simon. An obedient Dreana looked up and watched Ru approach looking flush and slightly shaken as she took her seat again and shakily taking a big gulp of her drink. Dreana knew this was the result of that dance.

Caren pulled her thumb away as Ru approached and got Dreana to help get Simon upright.

'I suggest we leave now, perhaps a nightcap at yours, is that okay, Ru?' Caren asked standing, looking down at Ru in a matter-of-fact tone, expecting a negative answer.

Ru looked up, as if in deep thought, then a smile appeared.

'Absolutely, why not indeed? What about Simon? This is our only night together before I head off. Not going to come to much is it?'

'You don't need him tonight Ru,' and Caren smiled as she looked at the bite mark that just protruded from Ru's dress.

'Let's get out of here.'

Caren and Dreana got Simon to his feet and managed to manoeuvre him to the car where the driver took over and dragged him into the car and eventually into the flat before his services were dispensed with.

Caren sat in the car holding hands with Dreana and even had a snog at one stage. Ru did not take any notice.

Whilst the car thrashed through the London night Ru was considering her next move. Should she change her mind or was this another risk being taken at the increased levels she had adopted after the death of her beloved husband, who, if watching her from above now, would be horrified? Importantly, she did not believe in the afterlife and so this was her life part two; different, more exciting and if it had to be, downright dangerous!

The driver despatched Simon into the bedroom and slung him on the bed, took a tip and departed with instructions from Ru for the morning trip to Heathrow.

As he left Caren followed shutting the door then turning off the lights so that only the outside streetlight intruded the space. She walked over to Dreana and took her clothes off except her shoes and as she did this looked across at Ru, who was still standing, looking for a reaction. There was none, just a long stare as if she was trying to adjust to the circumstances. 'Ru, please remove your clothes except your lovely dangly earrings and your shoes then sit on the sofa.'

Having did as she was told, Caren came behind the sofa and spun Ru round so that she was laying across the length of it, but pulled her hands over the arm and tied them to another chair with her dress. Dreana approached from across the other arm without instruction and slowly, very slowly kissed her way up the inside of Ru's legs until she found the intended target. As she did this Caren turned around with her rear facing the sofa, and as Dreana hit the spot, she looked over her shoulder and her eyes met the wide-open space in Ru's eyes. She could see something happening inside her brain that was being tested where it probably had not been in her life before, ever. Caren turned her head back and slowly lifted her short tight dress up over her suspender belt and hips, lifted one leg over Ru's outstretched arms and then lowered her torso onto the victim's face. There was a noise on impact but it was muffled. After a couple of minutes Ru's legs twitched as if there was a struggle and then Dreana pushed them down hard as if in rebuke. Caren raised herself a little and then sat again. This went on for some time leaving Ru in between ecstasy and pain as she struggled to get air. Caren was by now wanting more.

'Bite me, Ru, bite me,' as she repositioned her anal passage to meet Ru's lips.

Eventually, both women climaxed. Ru was left on the sofa for a few minutes breathing harder than ever, before she could consider moving. Interestingly, the first thing that came to mind as she came around from this experience was that she wanted Simon and of course he was still out of it on the bed.

'Ru, come over here, please.' She hadn't finished as she had a girlfriend to think of. Take off your earrings and place them into Dreana's nipples, come on, quickly!' Ru did as she was told but was finding it difficult as the target was now bent over a chair.

'Good, well done. Now, spank her very hard until I say stop.'

'Caren, I have never hit anybody and I am so weak it is pointless,' Ru couldn't believe she was about to do this.

'Nonsense,' Caren remarked. 'Just start and you will get it when you see the satisfaction it generates.'

Caren got into a position underneath and started sucking. Dreana took a deep breath and waited on the thrashing. The first blow was weak and the second not much better.

'Get on with it, Ru, you are pathetic, harder much harder.'

Ru raised her hands higher and as Caren got angrier and she heard the moans from Dreana, Ru started to realise she was enjoying it and got quicker and quicker, harder and harder and even though her hand was becoming sore and ached she started to feel moist again herself. Ru couldn't believe that this night of all nights was ending like this. What a sight, three women in the mix. Dreana now standing with a bright red posterior soon came into Caren's mouth as her legs were only stopped from collapsing because Caren's head propped her up. Almost instantly Caren then moved between Ru's legs and finished the job off. For a finale, they bent Ru over the sofa and took turns to spank her until she was red raw and pleading with them to bring her off for the third time. As she lay bent and stooped over the sofa exhausted Dreana placed her business card on Ru's backside and the women very quickly dressed and walked out.

'You will want to find us,' said Caren as the door shut.

Ru looked up and watched them close the door before moving. She was in pain but felt something she had never felt before…and wanted more. The earrings she was wearing that night were a very expensive present from her husband and hence she thought about whether she would see them again. However, she had the address card.

She walked into the bedroom and woke Simon who was struggling to make sense of what had happened to him. What happened next was a game changer. Ru made him have sex twice before letting him sleep and insisted he missed next week's college as she wanted him in Sao Paulo; she booked the flight then went down on him again at the thought.

Before departing that day, she texted Yevana. 'Wonderful evening/night/morning! Met some exciting new friends and want to catch up with you sooner than I thought xxx!'

Yevana heard the text as she walked past the doormen down on the pavement. She pulled it out of her bag and saw it was Ru. 'Wow' was her reaction, 'she must have had some night with her boy!' Replying, she teased, 'Miss you, darling xx.'

Ru looked at the immediate response and sighed; she loved Yevana, she just did, it was something about her personality. Things were changing; things were getting complicated, which she had not considered in a life that was free of responsibility, as a contrast of her previous existence that had been planned, stable and …as she now considered it, boring!

The cars filled up and as she got in her car Yevana noticed Andre jump in the rear car as it was about to pull away.

'Who is that charming creature?' Yurini asked.

'Oh, it's Rydeesa Correnti's son, beautiful, isn't he?' replied a serious Yevana.

'Yes, darling, can I be introduced?' Once again, there was no question being asked here these women were making statements!

'Of course, Yurini, as you like.'

They all congregated in a ritzy cocktail bar for the rich and famous where clothing was normally worn in its minimalist form and this group were doing well on that front. Andre was mingling and had found a soulmate in Yevana. He loved the limited time they had had together, even before their brief liaison the previous evening. He knew she was not somebody to be messed with though and this was a problem because he also understood that there was something about her that meant if the chips were down, she would deal with it, whatever it was and that frightened him!

'Andre, can I introduce you to Yurini?' she delighted, as Yurini approached where they were sat chatting.

'Hi,' was his brief response. Oh no, he thought to himself. He looked at Yurini and saw trouble, trouble he could do without. This was yet another woman who definitely got what she wanted. His burgeoning ability to attract these people was starting to worry him.

'Darling, you must have a drink with me later and discuss your business. My husband and I are always looking for talent.' Simultaneously, both Yevana and Andre looked at each other and thought 'I bet you are!'

Eager not to be seen to be rude or perhaps indeed lose an opportunity, he accepted the offer, 'That is so kind of you, Yurini, it would be greatly appreciated.'

It was soon time to leave and the final destination was Prince Mahood's London residence. Once there, Andre watched as the gathering grew and all manner of people arrived in all manner of states, from the drunk to the semi-naked. Although there seemed to be so many people they appeared to disappear quickly in this heady atmosphere. Staff waited on their particular group within this smoky atmosphere of incense and perfumed body odours, but it was not long before Yevana was led away upstairs by Mobola and Yurenev without a look or a word to explain where or why. Not long after he was approached by Yurini who just picked up his hand and led him upstairs and again nobody batted an eyelid. She said nothing until they approached a door on the fourth floor. 'When we enter, I will lead you.' She opened the door and Andre could not believe the sight before him. Yevana was on a lounge chair in the corner of the room wearing only her heels, some large loop earrings through her nipples and a plastic mask with just a gap for a mouthpiece to breath. Her ankles and wrists were cuffed to the chair and it was clear to see a white substance was dribbling down her chin on the outside of her mask onto her chest. Yurenev and Mobola were naked and making love in the far corner and Andoria on her knees, fully dressed, was feeding from Yevana's chest and eating between her legs with her back to them all. Her Oriental PAs were stood beside the chair.

'Wait!' came the call from Yurini as Andre drew closer to Yevana. As she said this, Yurenev pulled out of Mobola and came across to the chair and deposited into the space in the mask. Yurini moved forward and took back her husband's deposit and swallowed. She then led Andre over to Mobola who was now on all fours.

'Fill the gap, Andre.' She undid his trousers and he did not need to be told any more getting down on his knees and started to play this game until its natural conclusion on the chair.

Everyone left the room and Yurini threw him the keys.

'Up to you now, Andre. You'll need to find some clothes though. We ripped the dress off, shame I liked it on her. Yevana, darling, we'll call you, toot toot!'

Andre walked over to take off the mask, when Yevana spoke for the first time.

'Don't remove the mask. Take off the cuffs and get inside me, I want it, you, now, darling!'

'Okay, if that's what you want Yevana.' And so, he pleasured himself in her which wasn't hard under the circumstances.

Next, he looked about the next two rooms and found a dress in a wardrobe which he took to Yevana who didn't seem that bothered she was so fearless and without much choice!

'Thank you, Andre, now let's go home to my place.' They calmly walked down a hallway noticing a room full of men and women; a proper orgy, including Andoria and PAs, with all the lights on, too! They didn't linger though and descended the stairs past the room they first came into, where the others were now dressed and in group discussions again as if nothing had taken place upstairs. Nobody noticed or cared that they were leaving. Andre was aware that Yevana wasn't bothered, her mind was now on the first day of opening proper and there was only three hours to go. Having pushed past a couple of wasters at the front door they jumped down to the pavement where it was now raining and stopped the next taxi driving past.

'Andre, come back with me and wash me off, cleanse my soul, please. I want you to bathe me.' She laughed but put her hand on his and leant back in the rear seat and closed her eyes for the remainder of the journey.

She opened the door to her apartment and went into the bathroom and ran the bath whilst Andre made a breakfast tea in the pot as Yevana had asked, her favourite drink of any sort, so soothing. He heard her get in and a gasp that accompanied it.

'Oooohhhh, I feel love,' she sang the Donna Summer song out loudly followed by a call to arms for Andre.

'Darling, please come and clean me.'

'Coming...well.' he laughed at the term.

'Kneel there, will you? There is the sponge.' She leant back on the edge of the bath closing her eyes and waited for his gentle touch, which duly came in the most masterful yet delicate way that soon had her aroused once again.

'Not this time,' he teased, 'we are going to work, this is cleansing,' and so he moved back and brought her a bath towel and wrapped it round her as she stood out of the bath.

'You are a hard taskmaster and tease, Mr Andre.' She reached up to the tall Spaniard and kissed him on the lips.

'Come back tonight; I am staying in.'

He looked at her. 'Of course, I am free!'

'Good, now get lost,' she joked as she showed him the door.

'Thanks for the tea,' she declared as the door closed on him.

The previous evening's huge success was soon matched by the opening day which saw at least ninety percent bookings taken across the business and had seen a huge take up on membership where it was available, in a variety of schemes. Staff were performing well and the management had a grip on everything, managing issues quickly to the clients' satisfaction.

Yevena took the call from Andoria to be escorted to her car and met her at the suite.

'Andoria. I assume that you are satisfied and that we can look forward to seeing you at Y&T again soon. I must say it has been a pleasure to have you.' They looked at each other focusing on the end of Yevana's statement.

'Indeed, I am satisfied. I very much look forward to staying with you again and tasting all of the delights London has to offer.' Once again they smiled at each other. They both knew how to translate what was being said.

'Yevana, my staff and I would like you to join us in LA soon, we have great facilities you know. We will treat you like a Queen. Don't let me down. I think you owe me a small favour and this will suffice.' Smiling not very genuinely, she started walking out of the suite closely followed by PAs and porters. She had enough cases to stay forever! Yevana laughed to herself when she noticed the PAs seemed to have very little.

Down on the street, Yevana said her goodbyes and waved the 'singer' off. The paparazzi were there waiting and delighted in capturing Andoria posing with her beautiful assistants. Yevana recognised, although quite painfully, these profile players were essential for all of their future projects. This was the evidence as it was these pictures that would give free publicity in tomorrow's papers and next week's magazines.

One week later and everything was working like clockwork. Yevana booked three flights, one to Vegas, one to Madrid but firstly to the Alps in France.

'Andre, I have booked us a flight to the Alps, skiing, going tonight. Pack a bag and meet me at mine,' was all the text said. Yevana wanted to have an uncomplicated weekend away with a man and she needed Andre. Next week the trip to Vegas was with Toby and the next phase of the master plan to start in the States followed by a trip to do the same in Madrid where they already had plans for a site in the centre of the city, where they also hoped they had the substantial support of the Correnties to ease any complicated planning issues.

He looked at it, looked up and informed his business partner that he was going away for the weekend at which point he darted back to his digs and packed. It occurred to Andre having stayed at Yevana's four times that week after the opening night that she liked what he had. She wasn't sure what that was or why but by luck or judgement the task given him by Caren might, almost by accident, be falling into place.

The skiing was fantastic and liberating. Yevana had told Toby she was not to be disturbed over the trip away and Andre was given the same order; they didn't see their phones all weekend until at Gatwick on the return. The difficulty for Andre was you could not read Yevana and if you tried to, you had already made your first mistake. He found this the case on the following night back in London. After work he thought he would surprise her and come to the apartment with flowers as a thank you for a great weekend. He pressed the doorbell and waited a couple of minutes until just as he thought she wasn't in, the door opened and Mobola wearing nothing but a strap on and a mask opened the door leaving the security chain attached and shrieked, 'Yes, can we help you? Oh, Andre it's you!'

'What a shame, Andre, I will tell Yevana you called, darling, she will be sad she missed you. Unfortunately, though she is engaged at present and will be for some time!'

She smiled and shut the door almost before she had finished, leaving him standing looking at it in a moment of disbelief. Mobola looked both ridiculous and beautiful under the circumstances.

He didn't get a word out. Almost robotically, he bent over and left the flowers immediately against the door then turned, went home and didn't see Yevana again socially for some weeks.

As he took a cab back to his flat many thoughts ran through his mind. What was it about these people that made them so different from people he had met before? Why him? He concluded that Yevana was indeed different and like Caren was practically impenetrable, so if he held onto that belief he would be in a far better position, particularly emotionally. These types of women had needs just like any man and in fact he thought Yevana was more of a man than many men and with a streak of steel to match except, there was no other more beautiful creature on planet Earth, which gave her enormous advantage. These were the reasons men and women chased her. They also saw something beautiful like delicate porcelain, a piece of fine art or perhaps the most treasured flower. Yevana blossomed and it confused women about who they were and where their true desires lay, but, most important of all they quickly felt helpless and that was more akin to being in quicksand! Andre tried to decide if he was sinking or swimming amongst this tidal wave of intrigue and beauty. He didn't know, although at least he recognised the problem but for many reasons he felt powerless to walk away; he was up to his neck!

As Mobola left the apartment she turned and kissed Yevana goodbye stepping over the flowers.

'Who called at the door earlier Mobola?' asked Yevana.

'Ah, oh yes forgot to say, sorry. It was poor old Andre, looked quite shocked actually. Bye darling, love you,' and she blew another kiss as she disappeared into the stairwell.

Yevana picked up the flowers and took them inside where she filled a vase and arranged them as she liked to do, taking her time to enjoy them. They were beautiful and she knew they were given with sentiment for a great weekend. She shrugged and went back to bed, removed the restraints, and this time went to sleep.

John Dexter – Private Detective

Caren had started planning already for her next move. She called John Dexter, her private detective.

'John, I have a job and it is immediate and you must drop whatever you are doing,' she declared sounding more desperate than she wanted to.

Sensing this he was slow to respond. 'Sorry, Miss Lords but I am a busy man and I cannot let down my other customers. What service is it you require from me?'

Caren started laughing. 'JD, I am well aware of what type of work you deal in generally and I am sure your tax return is in date and accounts for all your activities. I understand one of my colleagues has your account.' The gap she left gave enough time for him to jump in.

'Look, I am a good man, deliver for my clients and don't want any problems Miss Lords, now what is it you want?' He cleared his throat in anticipation of the task he was about to receive.

'Get the first flight out to Sao Paulo and track down Mrs Ru Carter and survey her activities there for the next week until you are satisfied you understand her business there. Do not inform anybody of your reasons for being in Brazil. Do you understand me?' Caren finished sounding deadly serious.

'Yes, Miss Lords, I do.' He was sounding exhausted as he enjoyed his normal tasks of following married men and women around the north east of England, however, Caren Lords' tasks were a whole lot different and on another level. He knew of Ru Carter; she was rich and big time!

Caren continued, 'Come to see me with your brief on her activities and with video evidence where it is possible. Don't let me down!'

'Of course, I will do my best,' was all he added before pressing the red button on his phone. Within minutes he was in a taxi to the airport and preparing to fly out.

Caren was intrigued. It was a hunch but it was clear this woman of substance was running a different life to the one people knew of before her husband died. She had just witnessed that first hand! Why Sao Paulo? She was convinced this South American 'outpost' held some sort of secret away from prying eyes.

Jon Dexter arrived in Sao Paulo and was soon making enquiries to track down Ru that turned out to be as difficult as you might think. Caren had told him that she had no lead other than the destination and Sao Paulo was a big place. Initially, doormen at the exclusive hotels drew a blank even after a few bribes were paid! They had not seen a woman of her description or by name. Seemingly getting nowhere at the end of his first day in town, he had booked into a cheap hostel and was having a beer in the bar when by a complete fluke he got chatting to a local who advised him that a man sat opposite knew most goings on as he owned a local five-star' taxi business that worked out of the airport although not exclusively. They were introduced and as normal in these parts he covered the price of the enquiry and went back to his seat. About an hour later the taxi owner came across with a piece of paper in his hand and an address where he believed a woman as described had been dropped off earlier that day having come in from London. Interestingly, she was easily remembered by her beauty and because she only carried a large shoulder bag which was unusual. It certainly added up and so John immediately got up and headed for the drop off point as described. He felt slightly crestfallen when he was dropped off by a taxi.

'Driver, this cannot be the address, it is a complete dump in the wrong end of town,' he pointed out.

In slightly broken, albeit intelligible English the driver was insistent. 'Sir, your hotel, this is where I was told, this is your place.'

'But this is a dump, downtown even for this place, surely you are wrong.'

The driver had had enough. 'I must go, you must get out now!' John paid the driver and hesitantly got out and stood looking about him in the dodgy looking downtown area of Sao Paulo. It didn't feel safe at all but he decided to check out that this was the correct location given him by the taxi owner. Walking across the pavement into the front of the hotel he approached a seedy looking obese male receptionist who just happened to be eating and drinking Coke at that moment late at night. This place was old, had not had any refurbishment since it was built and needed some urgent TLC. It wasn't easy to see in the foyer because the light was dim as several bulbs were broken. With his desk lamp shining brightly across his face the receptionist continuing to eat, looked up waiting for John to speak first.

'Hi, I am looking for a friend who told me she was booked into here tonight. She is expecting me. Her name is Mrs Carter or in fact better still here is a recent photo.' The guy did not speak and therefore he didn't know if this was a language problem or otherwise. They stared at each other for what seemed like ages then John put his hand in his pocket and pulled out some ten-dollar bills and put them on the ledge of the receptionist's booth. Unfortunately, this didn't have the desired effect, as the reception guy only moved to drink his Coke and continue his stare. John put his hand back into his pocket and withdrew another batch of dollars as though he were a cash machine, then placed them on the ledge on top of the others. The guy's eyes flickered as he picked up a bread roll and then the cash. Slowly and rather annoyingly as far as John was concerned, he counted them before looking up again simultaneously placing the dollars in his tattered shirt breast pocket.

The guy said something and pointed to 'Room 24' on the key holder. He then pointed to a worn diagram which showed it on the second floor. As quick as a 'striking slug' he then picked up his bread again and looked away as if enough dialogue had taken place. John turned around and looked across the hall and thought about his next move. He knew he had the right place but struggled to understand why she was staying in this dump in such a dodgy area, when she could afford whatever she wanted. Miss Lords obviously knew there was something to discover here and it looked like she was right. Although it was nearly midnight by now he decided to assess the situation from along the corridor where number 24 was located. Slowly and quietly, he walked up the stairs whilst being passed by some colourful looking men and women going down until he reached the second floor. He approached number 24 and listened up against the door and heard voices and sudden movement. He quickly moved into a recess and watched as a native in his fifties walked out of the room but Ru did not show. John followed the guy out and tracked him to a local bar across the street where he engaged with two young females aged about twenty, giving them what seemed like instructions.

This seemed like his chance, so over the next couple of hours he got into a situation where he was able to talk to this group and by the early hours after drink had flowed, of which he had paid his fair share, tongues were more liberally free to speak. The older man was happy to hear of any deal that involved more cash and so John remunerated him in dollars at an acceptable rate to achieve the aim of the mission as soon as possible and report back.

'Miss Lords, I think you will be happy with my work when are you available to see me.' John was feeling well satisfied with himself.

'I suggest you get over here now if you want your bill paid out in full in cash! Of course, that still depends on what you have for me!' Caren was excited as he had something which was a great start prior to any screening of information, whatever shape it took. 'Okay, coming right over, see you in an hour. Get the screen set up as you will like what you see,' he said rather excitedly.

Caren let John into her flat and sat on her sofa whilst showing him to his seat from where he could brief. He was soon describing the situation and the story as it unfolded until it got to the point where the young women went to room 24 and placed his day sack with built-in microphone and camera on a chest of drawers. At this point he sent a message to Caren's email with a video attached which she uploaded to play on her large screen in the lounge area. There was a silence as the image focused and broke up momentarily before becoming crystal clear.

'My goodness, she is so beautiful and what energy,' said a mesmerised Caren. John looked on in wonder thinking about that comment. Knowing what was on the film he questioned who all these people were. To him, it seemed they all lived in a mighty strange world.

Ru was stood in a room that had a wash basin, a single bed with an old quilt on it, some ropey curtains hanging on only a few of the hooks it should have been, no carpet and the chest of drawers that the camera in the bag sat on. Ru was stood in a bright red mid-thigh, sleeveless dress with a front zip and a pair of sandle high heels. The two young women walked out of the camera view and after about a minute approached Ru naked. The first shock on view was that they were well hung; she-males with mature looking breasts. One unzipped her dress letting it fall to the floor then slowly picking it up and throwing it to one side. On their knees now, they started at the ankle kissing and gently biting their way up the inside of her legs before removing her only other piece of clothing, her red small panties.

Caren sat motionless watching the scene before her. She had taken a shine to Ru but would not let that get in the way of her ultimate goal.

Ru had travelled a long way to carry on like this which was the one unexplained factor that was still bugging Caren as she watched the orgy of sexual fascination. About twenty minutes into the video something caught her eye. The men seemed to be aware of something behind them to the right but out of camera. Caren leant forward trying to make out what it was if anything.

John sat motionless still but now watched Caren as she scrutinised the video and clearly noticed something was not all that it first seemed in the room. Of course, he knew!

After the event in Sao Paulo the man who had set up the liaison in room 24, met with John back in the bar the following evening and gave him a memory stick.

'You will like this, even took a copy myself, hot stuff man, haa-haa, serious!' and couldn't stop laughing.

JD took the booty back to his downtown room and played the video on his laptop. Obviously, he expected it to be hot as the guy in the bar had alluded to, but this was better, particularly as the she-males were a complete curiosity to a simple man from the North East of England who had not travelled far in his life.

'Wow!' 'I need to get out more! Wait till I tell Dave and Rog down at the Tyne bar.' Sitting through it and getting very excited he did consider actually whether good, testing, very adventurous sex involving a sixty-year-old woman and some she-males was actually that extraordinary, even considering her position in US society. Indeed, was this what Caren Lords was looking for?

Caren leaned further forward and asked JD about the movement in the room.

'What is that; is there somebody else in that room?'

'Wait,' John replied smirking.

Suddenly the two women moved to one side and another man approached from the corner. He was a tall man wearing a Stetson. He gave a couple of orders and the women did as they were told. The next hour was compulsive viewing to say the least.

'My goodness,' exclaimed Caren, 'this is dynamite! That is Chuck Bush husband of the equally influential Sarina Bush, both stella figures on the US political and business scene. They are going to assist Y&T get started in the states, in cahoots with RU. Brilliant,' she shouted, 'flippin brilliant. You have done well JD.'

John couldn't stop smiling. 'Thank you Caren, my pleasure I can assure you.'

Caren counted out the bill and handed it over and showed him to the door quickly once she knew she had what she wanted and he was of no further use. 'Thank you; we may do business again, who knows?'

As he walked through the doorway he stopped momentarily. 'Something you should know. The next night I saw him come back with a local male dignitary but sorry no film or details. What a shame eh!' He disappeared out of sight and Caren went back to continue watching the CD. Later she rang Dreana and had virtual sex on her bed but promising the full Monty the following weekend whilst watching her new movie!

Caren had what she wanted which she knew would be explosive material as and when she deployed it for best effect. What she had here would cause widespread misery amongst America's elite social circles and particularly to Sarina Bush and Ru Carter who appeared whiter than white in magazines across the US. 'Hot, hot, hot darlings, whoop, whoop.'

The material would not be required yet; it would wait for the right moment when she would use it to reap her revenge. She decided it was time to call Andre via an answerphone message. 'Andre, I trust things are going well, don't forget to update me on how things are. I have been very busy! We must get together again sometime soon! Miss you!' Caren closed the call laughing out loud. 'Sucker.'

Andre picked up the message and pressed delete. He was busy and didn't need Caren's sinister messages. However, the thought of sensual contact with her again gave him a shot of adrenaline. He enjoyed her edginess if that was the right term to explain it.

Mobola

Several months on and life was hectic at Y&T. Both complexes were making large profits and all parties were very happy with the progress of this venture and profits. London was running twenty-four seven at maximum capacity in all areas and Manchester was not far behind in the North. Their image was spot on and since the last recession people had more money in their pockets and wanted to spend it. Consequently, the Luxury Club brand in London was a phenomenal hit, with top end A list stars also booking the luxury suites in the main hotel area ahead of many other choices in the City, who could not meet the challenge of the Y&T offer. With twenty-four hours opening and a very strict privacy policy it suited the needs of people who wanted top end and this was actively guarded by the management team. Toby and Yevana were very popular and seen regularly in the main complex areas but made sure that they were taken seriously and rationed the time they spent with any group or individual in order to stay impartial and as senior management only.

The offers they did receive though were unbelievable and ranged from 'I will buy the business and you can run it' to 'Give us a kiss, luv.' All were 'permission denied' of course.

On a more personal level Yevana was starting to pick up some bad news from close friends. There was news brewing that an international athletics star had failed an out of season doping test. Yevana didn't even consider it might be Mobola at first until Ru called and said that she had been tipped off in New York that indeed it was the case, even before an announcement was made.

Yevana sent a text asking Mobola to call immediately. 'Call me. Y xx,' was all it said.

The following day it was only stopped from hitting the media outlets, where headlines such as 'World champion drug cheat!' were typical, by Ru and her political contacts, but it could not be held for long.

Mobola rang Yevana crying like a baby and mumbling, mostly without coherence. 'It is me,' she said. 'What is you Mobola?' Yevana replied.

'The doping test, I have been stupid, but it's not performance enhancing, it's only drugs, recreational drugs.' She rambled on without real thought for what she had been saying.

'You idiot, where, when, why?' cried out Yevana even though she had had her suspicions about her lifestyle and in many ways this was not a surprise. She felt physically sick from the bottom of her stomach, she loved this woman but knew this would end her athletics career and seriously tarnish her image and her huge sponsorship deals. She would face a two-year ban minimum, and this could finish her.

'Yurenev and Yurini got me involved and I need it now, I am a regular user. It has been ongoing for over six months or perhaps a little longer,' she said sheepishly. 'At first it was just a bit of fun out of season at parties organised by Yurenev, then it just kept occurring and I was seeing them more often and it was tied in with more frequent sex game parties. I tried to stop at one point as it was affecting my performances but when I did this, they sent me a video with me explicitly sniffing cocaine from between Yurini's legs. They visited the next day and warned me not to be so stupid, that they were my friends and they had the influence to make sure I would not fail a test. Since then, I have been seriously hooked which I think is mainly down to the strength they have been supplying me, for that sole purpose. I need some every day now and of course some days I cannot get it and they don't respond to my calls when I ask, beg, Yurini for assistance. Two weeks ago, I had had a bad training session, my coach threatened to ditch me and I had not had a supply for four days, I think as punishment for missing a specially arranged party on a yacht in the south of France, with a special Arab client of theirs. It was punishment!' They supplied me a little after that but have held back again and I am desperate.'

Yevana and Toby had a strictly no drugs policy at Y&T and unusually perhaps, it did not put off the crowds of A-listers who played 'in that field!' They would rather the business collapse than turn their dream into seedy downtown motel type establishment and clients got it.

'Mobola, pull yourself together, you're not helping going off on one, where are you?' 'In London, in my new flat,' she replied.

'Okay, you are to come immediately to my apartment but you know there will be no drugs here, so forget that, you need a friend so get over here, now!' Yevana was angry but also acknowledged that in the world they travelled in there were risks and these had to be expected or you had to get out while you were in command of your senses. Clearly, Mobola had passed this point. The two of them had not been together sexually for some time now as Mobola was carried away with the attention and riches on offer in Saudi Arabia and Russia as she had highlighted, and eventually they had sucked her in and stuck her on a proverbial hook.

'Don't bring any of that stuff with you but bring enough clothes to last a couple of weeks until we sort out a way ahead. Do you understand me?'
'Yes,' Mobola replied, as if chastised by the headmistress.
'Yevana.'
'Yes.'
'I am not allowed to have sex with you,' Mobola declared like a naughty schoolgirl.
'Get over here, Mobola!' Yevana was not impressed and even less impressed with her apparent bosses, the Russians. The conversation ended and Yevana went about her apartment to accommodate Mobola for a short period. It was not what she wanted which was why she lived alone but it was okay for now; she was a friend in trouble.

For the first time since they had known each other Mobola looked shabby as she arrived at Yevana's. Her eyes were dark and hollow, typical of someone with her problems. Closing the door Yevana grabbed her bags and placed them on the floor. Then, grasping Mobola's hands and shaking them, she looked her in the eyes.

'You stupid, stupid, woman, when you play with fire you must understand the dangers and risks, and in your life drugs were an unacceptable risk, totally stupid, ridiculous!' said Yevana. She then proceeded to give Mobola a long, hard hug, sweeping her long black hair from her face and kissing her tenderly on the lips.

'I love you, lady' she sighed and continued, 'we are going to try and sort this out. But you have to want to. Simple. If not, pick up your bags and get out of my life for good.'

Mobola looked sullen and just nodded.

'Empty your bag onto the floor and strip,' Yevana demanded.

'I said no sex,' Mobola weakly responded.

'I'm not repeating myself,' said a frustrated Yevana. Mobola did as she was told and Yevana did the required search which was satisfactory,'

'Good, let's sit down and think.'

After Yevana poured a large vodka for them both they sat for several hours in the lounge area of the apartment and discussed what to do next and plan a way out of the mess Mobola had made for herself.

'Firstly, on completion of this discussion you will go back to your flat and collect some more things and return to my apartment and move into the spare room. You have rushed over here without enough kit. We need you to stay away from your place until we make some progress on a better lifestyle.

'We are not a couple and will not be until at least the time that you are clean and sort this mess out. Secondly, you will stop communications with Yurenev and Yurini. Thirdly, my lawyers will instruct the hold on this revelation to be lifted and you will face it. Fourthly, do not come near Y&T or be seen with myself or Toby until I say otherwise as it will have an adverse effect on the business. We have worked too hard for you to ruin that. And lastly if you ever take another recreational drug you are on your own. 'Got it?'

'Understood, Yevana,' was all Mobola could manage.

Over the next few days there were times when Yevana had to tie Mobola to her bed as the effects of withdrawal kicked in badly. It was agonising and it hurt Yevana, especially as she often left her all day in the apartment alone. The first few days were the worst as she would come home to see Mobola stricken with pain and fear, with saliva running across her ashen face and sore red cut marks where the rope had dug in as she attempted to break free. She cared for her, shouted and screamed at her whilst also cooking for her in what became a toxic atmosphere. Worse was to come though. As the news broke and the press pack got all over the story in search of the subject and more detail, they centred on all known contacts including Yevana. Eventually, having been told categorically that she was out of town, they accepted that she was out of the country in hiding keeping away from the media and getting help. She received the anticipated two-year athletics ban and lost her advertising contracts overnight. The only good news was that it was recreational and had been seen as self-destructing, performance destructing rather than enhancing, which went some way to explaining her recent poor record on the athletics track at the start of the current season. At least she was not being seen as a cheat and having victories scrubbed from the record books like some had which was a very small consultation.

Yurenev and Yurini were very angry bombarding Yevana and Mobola with calls and messages, even calling at Yevana's apartment one evening. Sensing this was going to happen, Yevana worked from home as much as she could during the first week and had Toby over for dinner on five occasions for extra presence in the evenings. Also, Mobola had her phone removed for her own good. On the third night the Russians turned up at the apartment, so Yevana didn't have much choice but to let them through the downstairs central security and up the stairs. Toby played his part quickly disrobing in the lounge in full view when Yevana opened the door. She was in a thin nightdress as if they had been in the middle of something, which didn't impress Yurenev at all.

'Yevana, where is that girlfriend of yours? She is in trouble and needs our help,' Yurini stated looking much less composed than normal.

'I don't know,' she replied hoping that there would be no noise from the cupboard they had bundled her into in the main bedroom.

'I don't know what is going on here Yevana, but it is very unimpressive from our point of view; we expected better! I suggest you quickly reassess your priorities and find Mobola before it is too late. I thought we had a strong agreement,' Yurenev finished then looked at Toby and back to Yevana.

'We do,' she replied. 'I do not have any current knowledge of Mobola and Toby is here for a shower and dinner after work. I have not been well this week and that is why I have been here all week. So, if you please, remove those spies outside the block if you would; it is annoying me and will start to worry the other residents. Yevana felt her anger growing.

'Now, please can I get on with dinner... for two!' The Russians turned and as they approached the stairs looked back and Yurini said, 'If we were to find out you had knowledge of her whereabouts, we will ruin you. It will be painful too; you have been warned.'

Yevana shut the door and looked straight at Toby.

'Sorry, darling, what a mess.'

'I always thought Mobola was trouble, but we are here now and she is supposed to be your friend. My concern is she will do a runner once you let her and run straight back to them as a virtual slave as she gets all her tricks with them, sex, drugs and otherwise. Athletics is actually the last thing on her mind at the moment.' Toby walked in and dragged Mobola out of the cupboard and laid her on the bed again still gagged and tied her up. She was swearing through her gag which they couldn't afford to remove for now with the enemy nearby.

Yevana was concerned that Toby was accurate but hoped she would see sense and put things right in her life.

Yurini and Yurenev to a lesser extent were hooked themselves and not exclusively on high end drugs but also on Mobola their leopard too. They wanted her back in their lives asap and were not about to give up without a scrap. The low-level surveillance continued for another week as Yevana moved around London before they eventually gave up. She now had to be vigilant as the secondary level; much less obvious would be there somewhere.

Yevana kept monitoring Mobola's phone but received nothing of concern until a message from Yurini arrived with a demand. She seemed very agitated and sent a message detailing a site where Mobola should view a certain movie 'she might be interested in.'

Yevana accessed the video site from an obscure e-mail account given to her as an emergency by Andre, for such occasions as this. She sat at the computer and using the given password and sat open mouthed as she watched Mobola sniffing what looked like cocaine from the anus of one of the leading gentlemen of the IOC, a well-known Italian delegate. It was proper scandal of the gold medal variety. Yevana sat back and sighed. 'What a royal mess this is,' she exclaimed out loud. Mobola needed help here that was obvious or did they just let her go and allow her to dig herself a deep hole in outer Mongolia somewhere, out of sight of the world's press? Yevana knew there was no choice. She wanted to help Mobola, after all, when it suited, they had been lovers. It wasn't regular anymore but it was fun when they did get it together and she loved her for all her faults. Yevana spoke with Toby and they agreed to discuss it the following day in the office.

Yevana had to concede that the video content was very, very horny to watch particularly at the point where another well-known international female athlete from Germany came into view and joined in. It had clearly been a stitch-up but for what reason she didn't know and quite honestly, she didn't care. It had been done and they needed to sort it out. Next door in the flat Mobola was playing Mrs Innocent tied up and sweating badly in the bedroom. Over just a few days she was looking tired and drawn having slept little and eaten even less. It was a shocking sight of someone so blessed in terms of body and soul. It would be some time before she was back in training let alone on any athletics track. She needed help beyond being tied to a bed in Yevana's flat because unless she got expert help the demons in her head would send her back to square one and the executive-drugged orgy lifestyle of her Russian and Middle Eastern lovers.

'Toby, darling, you have the awful detail and you know even if it is only on this one occasion as a one chance shop, we must help my friend. Under different circumstances we might agree to ignore it and let her deal with it, however, I love Mobola and I am trying to fix somebody before she has a very untimely death. Believe me, you know, that is the way it is going. The threat basically outlined, states that if Mobola does not answer their calls in the next five days and return to see them and put all of this nonsense behind them, a copy of the video would be sent to a tabloid newspaper editor in both the UK and the US whilst images would immediately be uploaded to the internet social network sites. The humiliation could, no would, be catastrophic for her career and life; there would be no lifeline afterwards as the images were too graphic and memorable. Careers would be shredded, destroyed for those involved and retribution would be the first item on the menu.'

'Yevana, you are right, we have to do the right thing here and I feel it is unchartered territory, even for us! Question is, is it worth it for us to get involved? From where I stand, I am worried about where this might lead. We must be careful or we will get dragged into a world that is unsafe and dangerous to say the least. Is she really worth it or is she just a dirty chancer who doesn't deserve our help? Our business must not be affected by association here as we have other factors to consider. Most obviously the Russians have helped fund the London project!' He wasn't happy about the level of risk but knew Yevana's feelings for this woman, which made the difference.

'That is a bit strong, but yes, I want to give 'this chancer' a lifeline; one chance. If she doesn't take it, I will cut her loose. And yes, we owe them but that is business. It might be based on a rather dodgy agenda of having me in their lives, but I can and will deal with that if I have to, full stop!' Yevana was a little irked by the terms he was using but knew exactly where he was coming from.

'Darling, what am I to do?' she pleaded.

'You must love this woman,' replied Toby.

'I do,' she replied, 'she doesn't deserve this; yes, she is a risk taker and she has been punished, but not this. I don't need Mobola but right now I still want her in my life.'

'Okay' said Toby, 'let me think, how long do we have?

'Five days.'

'Five days, right, I will get back to you later.' Toby left the office and moved quickly to plan a move that would solve the issue, for the time being at least. They had both been invited to a Yurenev and Yurini party in Moscow over the next weekend, which they had already accepted long before this incident had occurred. The invitation and party stood and would enable him an opportunity to solve the problem.

The following day Toby met Yevana in the executive area at No.1 Tudor Square where he gave her his plan to solve their problem.

'For what it is worth, I think it is a waste of time as she will not learn her lesson and we could come out of this as the long-term losers as well, when we don't need to. However, I understand your stand on the matter so here goes.'

Toby had spent the last twenty-four hours making a plan that would possibly allow them to eventually get even more from this situation. It was at risk, huge risk but he and Yevana were at their best at risk and this excited him!

'Good news on the wire is that Yurenev is away at one of his Serbian oil fields dealing with business until the main party on Saturday evening, so our best shot to sort the problem at source is to deal with Yurini before his return. Janice will travel with us and is a part of the plan. I have already briefed her and she is a willing participant and will do as we ask. The fact it excited her is a bonus!' At that point they both looked at each other and smiled.

'I still fully intend for us to all attend the party on Saturday unless we get the plan badly wrong of course.' They both knew this would mean getting out of Russia might be difficult!

'Umm, Janice. Okay, should be interesting. Not Summer then?' She enquired smiling once again pursuing a response.

'No, I am not getting her involved in this type of work. Janice is strong and will aid the plan, not hinder it from a morals viewpoint, particularly if it were to get nasty!' Toby looked away and saw a bright and breezy Summer approach with a set of notes she had been working on to do with the future planning in Madrid. Yevana got up and walked in the opposite direction back to reception. She had to work out what she was going to do with Mobola over the weekend. She could not be allowed to leave the apartment, so a Plan B had to be sorted.

Back in the office she called in Julia Banks, her trusted lawyer and friend, explaining to her what she was asking her to do as a big favour.

'Don't worry about Mobola, she will do as I brief her. She will be over the worst in terms of shakes and anger and will be free to leave as she wishes but she should not. I will tell her that's it's in her best interests. I just need you to cook and be there for the evenings until we return Sunday night. Does that make sense and are there any issues with this? I am sorry to press this on you, but we have to go to Moscow on business with Yurenev and Yurini, our investors.' This was only partially a lie. She didn't like being untruthful with a most loyal and valuable person, but it was in Julia's best interests.

'I will be delighted to help out Yevana, anytime; enjoy Moscow,' Julia replied.

Moscow

They flew out from Heathrow, business class on Thursday ahead of the party and earlier in the day than they had done to Moscow on previous business trips. They had all brought hand luggage only as briefed by Toby to enable quicker movement through the airport system at both ends. Janice was looking very relaxed but excited by this adventure, not worried by the chance of the mission going wrong. Wearing a short emerald suit, she looked smart and attractive and sat next to Toby on the aircraft. Yevana as ever was dressed to kill in yellow, this time in trousers in the next aisle. She didn't even acknowledge the others or the rather shifty looking businessman from the States sat in the seat next to her who was overly keen to strike up a conversation, or more, at least twice brushing past her inappropriately. At the point early in the flight that he was becoming very annoying, Yevana went to the toilet to coincide with the flight attendant delivering hot drink options. Viewing from outside the toilet she took her opportunity to get back to her seat when the American was being served. As she approached them she tripped into the back of the young, very courteous female attendant who subsequently threw scolding hot coffee directly into his face and chest. Toby woke to see the commotion over near Yevana's seat and the man next to her being given first aid and very careful treatment. The guy was in a state of shock and was taken to another seat near the stewards bay, to be monitored for the rest of the journey covered in ice packs. Yevana brushed herself down and had a comfortable journey from thereon in. In Moscow, the guy was wheel chaired through arrivals to the medical centre. Yevana smiled as she watched him have to hand over his passport at immigration control with some difficulty. The flight attendant was shaking even as she sat waiting to depart the plane. She had been traumatised by the incident and wasn't able to participate any further during the flight. Yevana looked down at her as she exited the plane and smiled. The young woman looked up in horror as she instantly recognised what had occurred, on purpose. He mouth just fell open.

'Thank you,' was all Yevana needed to say.

'Interesting flight, darling!' was Toby's reaction on meeting up again in arrivals.

'He touched me twice which happened to be at least once too often for my liking. He knows, he won't be playing those games for a while or perhaps again!'

'This weekend could be interesting with you in this mood.' Toby knew that Yevana had a lethal streak in her and you messed with her at your peril.

Arrangements were made to see Yurenev and Yurini on Saturday morning before the party and for a get together on the Friday evening with Yurini. Yurini would host at her private apartment in the city and might invite some other guests as it suited her feelings that day! Toby rang ahead to speak to Yurini to ensure that it was a quiet get together.

'Yurini, darling, how are you? It will be so good to catch up tonight.'

'Yes, Toby, I am so excited that I will see you earlier than expected and of course you already know my husband will catch up with us tomorrow.'

'Thank you, Yurini, indeed. We are coming early to view potential sites in Moscow, a sort of early feasibility study. We are interested to discuss further any potential joint venture we may take up once again and particularly where we might get support, especially in terms of planning and development.' Toby was laying this on thick as a screen for the actual purpose of the visit.

Yurini sounded as though she was getting more excited the longer they talked. 'I hope Yevana is happy and feeling relaxed as I always enjoy her company.'

'Yes, good point, Yurini. Yevana did mention to me that she hoped it would be a quiet evening of relaxation after a long flight and journey, with no other guests to have to socialise with.'

'Okay, Toby, she has her wish. I did mention it to a couple of friends but I will put them off and I will have the champagne on ice.'

'Good, thank you, Yurini. We will have Janice, my PA with us who will help us relax; she is good company and very trustworthy.' He tailed off and heard a small sigh from Yurini.

'Ohhh, that's good, you are trying to outnumber me,' she finished with a calculating sounding giggle. Toby had set it up; perfect.

They stayed in the five-star Beverley Moscow in the centre of the city and once they had booked in and moved into their rooms Yevana got a call from Yurini who obviously had influence even at hotel desk level.

'Darling, Yevana, I am so desperate to see you, please don't take too long and don't forget to bring that charming man with you. I know I have been a bit mean lately but it is the pressure, which you must understand. Yurenev has sent his apologies as unfortunately he had been delayed until late tomorrow afternoon. I have promised I will look after you properly until that time.' She laughed as she overemphasised the word, properly.

'Of course, I do, it isn't a problem from my point of view. I understand our friend is in trouble and you want to help.' She knew the problem all right and she was talking to it! If they were thorough and had a bit of luck the real problem could be sorted that evening.

'Don't take long now, Ciao.' Yurini cancelled the call and Yevana called Toby on the hotel system.

'Darling, she has called and has arranged for us to see her as soon as we are ready in her apartment as arranged.'

'Good,' said Toby. 'This is what we do then.'

Toby was staying in the same room as Janice so he was best placed to advise her on how to play the evening, so he gave her a running commentary on the outline plan and how to use her indomitable assets to maximum benefit.

'Be prepared to let go, as she has a high pain threshold and pain and enjoyment go hand in hand with this couple. Yevana will carry out the business end at the appropriate time whilst we concentrate on entertaining our host. Okay?'

'Yup,' was all Janice needed to say and smiled whilst pulling his hand and placing it under her very short skirt between her legs and kissing him square on the lips.

They all met down on the street, got in a taxi and were soon stood at the entrance to Yurini's apartment block entry system. As they stood like the three amigos looking at camera box, it burst into life, with a series of red lights and Yurini's face bursting onto a screen. Toby standing behind the women noticed that he must be the luckiest bloke alive. To be going into this lion's den with these most powerful, resourceful and erotic of females was true deliverance! He just hoped they could pull it off.

Yurini was delighted as she witnessed the sex on legs cued up at her den. 'An orgy,' she laughed, 'oh what have I said, ha, ha, ha, come on up darlings.'

The entry system kicked in and the doors opened and they were soon pressing fifty-five for the penthouse apartment on the top floor of this very shiny new block. There was an eerie silence as the lift shot up the building with just some soft buffeting and cable noises making them aware that they were moving at all. Yevana stood looking at her reflection in the mirror and was self-critical on several aspects. She noticed the others were doing the same and thought they all looked like they were space astronauts preparing to enter the cockpit at any second. Well, all except the raunchy outfits! The doors opened and they were greeted with a view looking out over Red Square and Moscow more generally from the lift lobby area.

'Wow, fantastic,' was the comment from an inspired Janice. They looked left and then right before spotting the only door on this landing. It had no visible marking that said who or what purpose it had on this floor. The camera in the top right corner twitched as the owner scanned the area outside to ensure all visitors were accounted for. It was obvious this was a high security environment for general civilian accommodation. A buzzer sounded and what appeared to be an outer door swung open and a speaker-activated voice barked an order. 'You are being scanned, please stand separately or you will be rejected.'

'Sounds dodgy,' Toby declared as they did as they were told.

'Thank you, you are cleared. Please proceed forward through the yellow door in front of you.' Immediately the door opened and they walked into a modern, mainly minimalist, light and airy feminine inspired apartment where, judging by the art work and literature lying around on the tables, sex was a prominent subject in the owner's life.

Like the waiting area the views were equally spectacular. Later when Yevana went to the loo she sat looking out over Moscow with uninterrupted views!

'Sorry about the security,' Yurini exclaimed as she bearhugged them all. 'Unfortunately, Moscow has progressed a lot since the revolution, glasnost, but not all is good. Don't be too worried by the body scanner, although Janice, it was nice of you to come with the full range of your jewellery!' Yurini looked down between Janice's legs. 'Now, drinks everybody?' Toby and Yevana looked at each other and knew they were both thinking alike. Yurini was almost certainly part of the 'not good' element.

They soon settled down with the music system blaring away and separate conversations engaged as the atmosphere became friendly and relaxed. It did not take long for the conversation to open up after a couple of bottles of wine and some stiff vodka, when the subject eventually turned to Mobola.

Yurini was clearly upset that they were not talking at the present time.

'I miss her dreadfully as does Yurenev who is mad, just mad. I must warn you that his temper turns very quickly at the mention of her name at the moment and he is promising to do horrible things to anybody who gets in the way of our reunion with Mobola. He sees himself as her father figure and gets very upset. I repeat, she refuses to see us at the moment, very stupid, he is very annoyed. He is taking it out on me and wants to find her very quickly. It will be bad for all of us if she continues to hide.'

Toby kept sipping his wine suppressing any emotional reaction, whilst Yevana did think to intervene.

'I don't know that anybody is interfering. I think Mobola is very upset about the situation she finds herself in and is trying to do something about it. We shall see when she decides to resurface. I miss her, too.'

Yurini got up and decided that as the sky started to turn, it was time to venture into more salubrious material by informing the group that, 'it is time to view a masterpiece of a video you will not have had chance to see. Mobola has been sent an e-copy although she has not confirmed to have seen it yet. I am not surprised though as you will see.' Yurini was very excited and eager to show them the video which had been made several weeks ago in a mountain retreat hotel in Switzerland.

'The main character in the "show" is a senior Olympic IOC delegate who does not know of the secret camera recording. If Mobola does not come back to us we will be sending a copy to this individual and we let him find Mobola for us; we know he will have the resources to do this and more importantly he will want to, trust me. Anyway, refresh your drinks and sit back and relax, enjoy!' Yurini pressed play on the remote and they all sat fixated watching the full movie until after three quarters of an hour Yevana stood up.

The alcohol had by now been consumed in a sufficiently large volume for Yevana to feel she could ask questions about the storage and distribution of the movie.

'Yurini, darling, to what lengths have you gone to protect the movie distribution? Is it just the copy sent to Mobola sent out so far? You wouldn't want to lose control of it would you?' Yevana was hesitant but very matter of fact as she thumbed a photographic coffee table book on famous designer dresses.

Yurini was by now losing some concentration as Janice's hand slipped under her skirt just as Mobola sniffed her first line from the breast of the other female in the movie.

'Don't worry, this is the only other source copy loaded from my computer over there.' She wagged a finger towards the corner of the room where there was a door to another room as her head flopped back as Janice hit a tender point!

The party was breaking into top gear now on the sofa as Toby joined the action ensuring that Yurini was drinking significantly more than they were. Yevana took the opportunity to go to the bathroom as the others were now hard at work. As Yurini had told them this was the only copy recorded direct to disk and there was only one copy on her computer. Having already deleted the copy sent to Mobola they could achieve their aim here, stroke of luck!

Janice whispered to Yurini that she wanted to try what was on screen guessing she would have some stock at hand and she was right. Yurini got up, opened a drawer and brought back a packet then lined out some of the powder to sniff from Janice's now bare, large breasts and nipples. Toby mounted her from behind and Janice continued to layer powder between her legs and her breasts.

Yevana came out of the bathroom and walked to the study to find the computer searching for the file in question. In this sparse room of little furniture and minimal art she found a computer and discovered that Yurini did not have a short time screensaver or security set up. It was still showing an exclusive shopping site for designer jewellery. No surprises there, thought Yevana, and no security. She had a reasonable knowledge of computer systems and it didn't take long to search for the file. Yurini was telling the truth, there was only one file, which Yevana took pleasure in deleting and again from the delete folder. She walked back to the lounge and watched for a few seconds at the organised carnage on the sofa smiling and deciding there and then that it was not for her tonight. Before going back in she gently poured her wine into the back of the computer until she noticed the screen start to look confused. Having wiped up the mess with a handy desk tissue she sat it back on the desk firstly making sure some fluid remained inside. Hopefully now she had done enough to kill this movie but lastly, she wanted to take away the video as some sort of insurance; it might come in useful!

Yevana walked across the room and turned on the stereo and played some dance music. Then she gently ejected the disc and inserted a blank disc she had found in the study, renaming it in the same manner. Hopefully this would delay any immediate recognition that something was wrong.

From where Yevana was now sat on a stool opposite the group on the sofa, Yurini looked miles away on a concoction of alcohol and drugs but in relative heaven. Janice was terrific, no wonder Toby liked her, she had guts and was a sexual legend. Yevana thought she must have been bruising Yurini's mouth with how she was ramming her into her sex. Toby finished by grabbing Janice in front of Yurini's face and allowing her to take the prize. Supper served! Yurini was lying on the floor spaced out and spent. Janice not feeling that 'with it' herself by this stage put her own knickers in Yurini's mouth, then placed a black stocking over Yurini's head and tied it off, tied her ankles with the other then they left; job done.

As they descended in the lift Yevana remarked, 'Toby, Janice, well done, only time will tell whether we have made a huge mistake here but it had to be done and it has been. Yurini will wake up with a stupendous hangover and Yurenev will have an almighty shock when he discovers his wife later today.'

Saturday flew by and the party was a breeze with everyone enjoying fun time in the normal manner associated with this Russian couple. When they went to leave at three p.m. Yurenev had a final chat with Yevana.

'Yurini says she enjoyed your company last night but can't remember much of it, so has your attitude to drugs changed for the better?' he enquired rather in hope more than anything else.

'No,' came back Yevana's rather frosty reply. 'I just watched; she won't remember that.' He looked pleased as he assessed her mood.

'She was in a mess when I freed her. It is fortunate that she isn't available to come tonight. But I reminded her of the English expression, "If you can't soar with zee eagles…"' 'I hope she has recovered as she is wanted by a friend of mine tonight. 'I will try to get to London soon, perhaps for a re-show but with my involvement next time. You owe me!'

'Perhaps,' said Yevana.

Janice was having a ball. She disappeared out into the lift for ages with a young Russian, eager to support the plan to the last!

Nobody mentioned the video or the computer that night which was a huge relief to them all.

On arriving back in the UK, it wasn't long before Yevana received a text from Yurini. 'You have stolen the video, I know it. I can't remember a thing about that night but you must have stolen it and I know you corrupted my computer. Yurenev has beaten me and has sent me to the Middle East for a month as a punishment. You will pay for this, Yevana, you see. Look out baby, look out.'

Things had moved very quickly though as they found out on their return to London. Yevana got back to her apartment and the door was unlocked and ajar. She slowly crept in trying to listen for any movement.

'Mobola, Julie, is anybody here?' Nobody. Searching all rooms, she came up blank with no sign that anything untoward had taken place. Mobola was missing, gone, where though, and with whom? Yevana was straight onto Julie.

'I left her this morning straight after breakfast, she was quite perky, even asking me if I wanted to join her for a bath. You will be pleased to know I declined,' responded Julie. 'Nice girl but not with it really, is she?'

'No, not ever but…oh hang on, found a note, I'll catch you at the office, bye Julie.'

The note she found on the bed read, 'The video within twenty-four hours delivered to 24 Maple Leaf Gardens, or Mobola will be sold abroad, you will never see her again. She has just had her first heroin injection and will be given much more and soon.' Yevana had to deal with this now, but how, was the question.

They all knew that a new recording could be made with a new subject, particularly with Mobola in her current condition but the key to the original was the presence of a senior high profile Olympic IOC delegate, who Yurini and Yurenev wanted on a hook for other reasons! Yurenev was obviously not happy with the way things happened and forgave Yurini as she had sorted the problem by herself. Her message to Yevana was, 'You owe me!'

This was now very hot property as there were others associated with the IOC delegate that could be pulled into the 'net'. Yevana considered what to do and perhaps she should call it a day and send back the video and let Mobola go as she was not worth the aggro.

'Yup, it is time to let go, I have had enough.'

Later in the street she stood at the mailbox and waited with the envelope sat on the lip giving herself one last chance to change her mind as this could condemn Mobola. She let it go, then went to a local café and sat contemplating as she looked out on a windy, grey London day. 'God, I love that woman but it's now a senior interference; I'm out!'

Mobola was released by the Russian hoods who had taken her in London and went back to her own apartment where her luggage had been dumped. She had quickly gone from celebrity world champion to lonely addict and her address book wasn't worth a penny as nobody wanted to know her now; she was finished. Worse, the heroin she had been given every day for a week had hooked her into a nasty habit which had to be paid for. She was given a supplier who was exacting in his methods of payment. She tried to call and contact Yevana but she initially refused contact also.

Dead

Yevana gave strict instructions for Fay to take no messages from Mobola and blocked her number on her mobile. The video was not released by the Russians and they carried on as if this episode was done with. Career over. However, the darker side of Yevana kicked in now. When the inclination caught her fancy and she felt she needed a Mobola fix, she accepted a call and arranged to meet Mobola. On the first occasion she went in her shortest Volta mini and the earrings and allowed Mobola to tie her up and screw her for all she was worth, with the background her latest accommodation which was downtown and pretty grimy. Her money and favours had gone and she was not her old immaculate self to say the least. She was high on drugs, aggressive and easy prey which turned Yevana on even more. The last time they had met Yevana gave her some money leaving it on her unmade bed.

'Mobola, goodbye, it was good whilst it lasted.' Mobola looked up in her dazed expression and said nothing. She made a grab for the notes which were her most important asset for the next few hours but from within and silently came the tears remembering better times.

Yevana walked the long way back to her flat and thought about what she might do to help her old friend.

A month later: 'Former world athletics drug star found dead in squat.'

'Yevana, have you seen the news today?' Toby blurted out as he burst into the office.

'No, what is it?' she replied.

'She is dead.'

'Who is dead, Toby? You are not giving many clues, are you?'

'Mobola, your ex-lover, for goodness sake.'

'Calm down, darling. That is sad but inevitable. You know she is a drug addict, what did you expect? I expected this. Now have you organised the girls to book the flights to Madrid for Friday as we agreed?' There was a silence as Toby walked across to his desk and sat down.

'Do you have a heart, Yevana?'

'Yes. I do'

'Okay and yes the flights are booked. I am going home, good night.' He was feeling slightly frustrated by her response but he did know her and once you were not required in Yevana's life you became irrelevant; that had not changed in their time together.

Yevana sat looking at the wall. Fay popped her head round the door to say goodnight and the offices eventually went quiet. It was dark outside and the eerie office silence descended like a cloud. Yevana leant against the window and looked out into the bleak wet night and dreamed back to good times with Mobola. Yevana walked over to her desk and pulled out a cigar, lit it and sat down to reflect. A small but significant tear slowly meandered down he left cheek. It was done.

Mobola's funeral was a sombre affair attended by a handful. No relatives, no athletes, no drug dealers just Yevana and a few others she didn't recognise. There was a wreath from Yurini to, 'Our friend' love Yurini xx.' Yevana laughed as they were probably the main reason that she ended up here, that is apart from her weakness to say yes to almost anything that involved excitement.

In the chapel Yevana looked at the coffin and said goodbye.

'I loved you darling, goodbye Mobola.' She placed some flowers on the coffin but did not attend the cremation ceremony.

Outside the chapel Yevana walked out to a waiting car and got in. Ru Carter held her hand and kissed her cheek.

'Take me home Ru,' she whispered solemnly.

Madrid

Yevana and Toby landed in Spain to work with a developer and city planners to gain necessary consents to purchase and develop their latest city location. Toby took the opportunity to relax in the hotel with a massage while Yevana worked on business arrangements ahead of a significant meeting in the capital the following day. She called Rydeesa Correnti to arrange the meeting.

'Ah, Rydeesa, good day to you, long time no chat. It is Yevana Narvik, how are things?' she asked in a rather light hearted tone. You remember me from that time that you were all tied up in some nice place. Didn't want to hang around then as you were obviously very busy. Shame we haven't had a proper chance to meet in more agreeable circumstances.'

'You didn't need to call, Yevana, I have made the appropriate calls and pulled in a favour or two. You will not have any barriers to the central old city television station HQ site. It was going to another developer who has been put off. Now, on another matter, I heard you were getting close to my son. Is that true?' There was a sense of panic in her voice as she felt growing pressure on her interesting lifestyle.

'I'm not going to discuss my private dalliances with you, darling, I don't have time for complex relationships, my life is much simpler than yours Rydeesa,' Yevana continued with some venom. 'You will know soon enough if I was moving in on your family. It would have its benefits, though but my inclination is you would not like it. It might be too much for you to cope with and I am very exacting. Now, just be available if we have any problems over the next few days as I want this deal done by Friday next week, do you understand?'

' Yes,' was all Rydeesa could quickly think to muster.

'Well, that's fine then,' finished Yevana who cancelled the call and then called Andre who was flying in specially the following day for the rest of the week.

'Darling Andre, are you still coming tomorrow?

'Yes, of course Yevana. I have taken the rest of the week out of London to conduct some business in Madrid as well as supporting your project. Do you need anything specific from me?' he asked sounding nervous in anticipation of a difficult task relating to his parents.

'No, I have the lovely, charming support of your parents which is fantastic, I really don't know why they are so good to me, I am so grateful. Now, must be going, see you!' And she was gone but as if by fate or magic (he actually thought tragedy) Caren's number glowed on his phone screen. The sound was set at the theme for *The Exorcist* which made him both smile and go cold.

'Hello, Caren,' he stuttered as he put the receiver to his ear. He had already started guessing what she wanted.

'Ah, Andre, darling, long time no hear, how is Yevana? '

'Actually, I am off to see her tomorrow in Madrid.'

Caren jumped straight in, 'romance, I hope?' It was more a question than statement.

'Not really, or perhaps a bit of both. She is hoping to conclude the deal on their latest project in the capital. My parents have helped arrange an easier planning passage. Y&T are going to develop the old television station HQ near the palace.' He didn't know why he was so readily volunteering so much information.

'That is great news Andre but first I want you to call your mother and tell her to delay the planning meeting and call Yevana also. Tell her there is a hitch and the meeting with planners is postponed. By doing this I will find out if she has something on your wayward parents. Call me when it is done.' She called off and Andre slumped into his office chair in London. He just wanted to be normal, run away somewhere, get out of his hole. He slowly picked up his phone again and looked at it as if finding the energy to make another call and rang his mother.

'Hi, mother, I am in town tomorrow on business but unfortunately probably won't have time to see you. Need a favour though, Yevana has really upset me and I want to remind her she is not bomb proof. Stop the planning meeting for the new hotel in Madrid. It is only a delay. Thanks, mother. Ciao!' He didn't let her come back as he knew there must be more to this. His mother had been got at probably as Caren had said. Might be similar to his predicament.

'Yevana, a hitch, darling. Your meeting has been delayed. My planning agent has told me there is an issue with this government-owned site. Last minute hitching I am afraid. I will keep you posted.' She cleared her throat and waited for a reply from Yevana who was listening with burning annoyance.

Yevana didn't get this or like it but reacted quickly.

'Rydeesa.'

'Yeees,' she replied like a naughty schoolgirl waiting to hear her punishment.

'Listen to me carefully.'

'Okaay'

'Meet me at the Turkish baths tonight at eight p.m.. Have a massage and I will catch up with you at some stage.' Yevana put down her phone and went to bed for a couple of hours post-flight rest.

At around seven p.m. as planned Yevana walked to the baths taking in some fresh air on the way to collect her thoughts. Toby was out for a beer with the developers which was fantastic and allowed Yevana to sort out the dirty work. Toby knew the whole situation with Rydeesa Correnti and was just as angry that she was suddenly stalling. The developers were mystified too as there was no warning or perceived problem with their contacts.

Yevana arrived at the baths before eight and paid extra up front to ensure that they both had separate massages in private rooms. She was soon on the central female wing hot stone slab, getting soaped and washed wearing the issued minimal cover lower body cloth towel. The experience of being in this mosque like building was a very special atmosphere. The Turkish attendant, a rather stern and robust looking woman with a menacing demeanour, was experienced in giving the best service and twice before Yevana had been here and felt lifted after the experience. The all-over soaping and cleansing with full buckets of ice-cold water was very therapeutic. Tonight, would be slightly different as she timed it so that she was out, off the slab slightly earlier ahead of the Rydeesa and into her private massage. Tonight, she opted for a full body massage after a body shave. Very discrete and mind blowing in this gentle, aromatic and warm environment where the gentle delicate female hands of a more feminine woman danced a merry rhythm over her limbs exacting deep pain in the muscle where it was required. Her eyes watered as she lay staring through the gap in the table and into the abyss. Yevana dreamed a fantastic world whilst in this position but nearly always Toby drifted in and out as a constant no matter how she tried to shift it. As one moment of pain in a calf muscle induced a low grunt, a face appeared that shocked her and she drew her head upwards slightly. The masseur interpreted this as hitting the target and dug deeper! It was Caren Lords and she looked fierce and angry with a real presence as if delivering a message. As quick as she came she disappeared leaving a strong impression, almost ghost like. Finishing off, Yevana dropped off the table and walked into the room shower then reappeared and stood still and let the masseur apply a full sensitive all body lotion and in closing her eyes noticed that power, in many guises, was a prominent thread!

Having paid the staff a significant extra in euros prior to her session, at the end of her most rewarding therapy another attendant entered her room and informed Yevana that the other room was in use and ready. Her attendant finished what she was doing then offered Yevana a small cloth which she took and tied round her waist. Slowly but purposely, she composed herself then walked outside her room and met the waiting member of staff who led her to Rydeesa Correnti's room. The woman opened the door and Yevana walked in gesturing the resident attendant to leave. Rydeesa was naked on her front as she listened to the wall music, oblivious, as Yevana took over massaging her neck as the door closed in silence; they were alone! Yevana moved round and pulled a bucket of cold water onto a low trolley below Rydeesa's head. Yevana then gently eased Rydeesa forward so her breasts moved closer to the edge and when happy, Yevana placed Rydeesa's arms down by her sides then tied two cloths to the bench quickly and tightly to Rydeesa's ankles. Yevana then moved forward grabbed the target's ponytail and pushed her head into the shallow bucket of cold water and held her face down in it. Rydeesa started to panic as relaxation and delirious satisfaction became nightmare and potential drowning. Yevana pulled her head up by her black ponytail and then slammed it back in again ensuring her nose hit the bottom of the bowl as Rydeesa spluttered gasping for air. The next time Yevana pulled Rydeesa's head out, out of Rydeesa's line of vision, she spoke for the first time.

'You bitch, you lousy piece of rubbish, you do as you're told or your social activities will be outed and big time, do you understand me? I will ruin you and your grubby husband.' Rydeesa's head and red swollen nose went back into the bowl then out and a few seconds later Yevana held it close to her lips again.

'Get that meeting back on and for tomorrow. You have disappointed me but for the last time. Get it sorted. Oh yes, I nearly forgot, I think I may be in love with Andre or lust perhaps, I have not made my mind up! We might become family -- Mum!' Finishing, Yevana turned and picked up a glass of red-hot chilli liquid she had brought with her that had been pre placed in the room. Using both hands Yevana dribbled it into Rydeesa's anus using her own fingers to make sure an element entered quicker, and satisfied, she departed. Soon screams were audible outside as Rydeesa attempted to keep her head out of the water, trying to kick her ankles free whilst trying with both hands to get the chillies liquid out of her anus as the burning sensation kicked in. The attendant waited for a minute until the screams became a nuisance and as instructed, went in, untied Rydeesa then stood her up. Bent over the bench and with medical gloves on, she washed out the offending liquid the best she could before leaving the room. Rydeesa couldn't speak any more and for a few minutes lay curled up on the floor of the flowing room shower naked and shivering from shock. She eventually got up, put the cloth round her and went back to her changing area, shattered. Dressed, she walked, awkwardly, back to her mansion but stopped on the way and sat on a wall as her legs were still shaky and she needed to sort things out quickly. She called those she had to and then texted Yevana.

'Good news, meeting back on as planned tomorrow.'

Shortly afterwards she contacted Andre. 'Andre, not possible to slow Yevana planning. Not sure why you wanted this, but I am not happy I can tell you. I won't be able to see you this week.' Andre knew Yevana had worked quickly and had got at his mother, who seemed upset with the text.

'Caren, meeting could not be postponed, don't know why but mother was upset,' Andre reported to Caren with some trepidation.

'Thank you, Andre, that is fine. You will have guessed that your mother's lifestyle is catching up with her. We shall see what comes next! Goodnight baby, sleep tight.'

Andre closed the message, threw his phone onto his apartment sofa and went to his fridge for a beer; he needed one!

Caren did not. She was having sex with the husband of a business client who had let her down regarding a property investment that had gone wrong, causing her to lose tens of thousands of pounds. Having finished, she got him to call his wife to arrange to be picked up from the end of her street, after visiting a so-called *friend* locally for the evening, for a few drinks.

The following day Caren requested the money from the husband by the weekend. Happily married he sorted it, job done; easy!

Yevana picked up the mail on her phone whilst sipping her G&T in a bar close to the Turkish baths. She smiled. She had viewed Rydeesa leaving the baths looking dishevelled and much less than relaxed. Going to the loo would be a challenge for the next twenty-four hours! It was an enforced way to lose a few pounds although Rydeesa didn't need to lose weight. She considered it cruel but necessary!

On arriving home, a member of staff greeted Rydeesa as always and to her horror was given the message she didn't want today. 'Mrs Correnti, your husband asked that you be told that he will be in the family *historical* room, in the basement.' Rydeesa's eyes rolled. She knew what this meant and declining was not an option. That evening the screams could be heard on the second floor of the mansion!

The meeting the following day went like clockwork. Their planning team, local planning authority, the developers, Spanish bank - Spain Bank 1905 and Prince Mahood were represented at the planned meeting, as the major stakeholders for the project, who, with others, all agreed that everything was in place and could proceed. The planning authority representatives said that they expected to deliver a positive outcome in writing within a week although there was still a procedural meeting to complete the formalities the following day. Rydeesa would ensure that this was not in question and that it was a formality now. It was to be a carbon copy of the London site where a stunning church-shaped structure would be built to house the executive areas connecting the main building. It was already a massive success in London and would be here too.

After the meeting Yevana and Toby went back to the intercontinental hotel and spent the afternoon by the pool with a cool cocktail and some sunshine to celebrate a great deal. Summer who had been at the meeting to assist in the post meeting administration going forward, joined them by the pool as arranged by Toby. As she approached them in their position near the pool bar wearing a tight above knee pink pencil skirt, having been delayed following some language issues in completing some details, Yevana felt a tinge of jealousy. Summer had perhaps the most perfect rear on planet Earth which was part of a truly beautiful body. Every red-blooded male and most women around the pool for different reasons, were desiring her or wanting to be her respectively. Yevana wondered how they had managed to employ so many beautiful people at Y&T. After Toby stood up and greeted Summer he got her a sun bed organised whilst he also busily sorted more drinks for them all. Summer quickly dropped her cloths on the spot next to her bed and lay out in her swim smalls only. On his return he looked down on these beauties dressed in very little wearing cool shades and causing a commotion. Some women nearby had moved! He stood for a moment and considered that it was indeed an incredible scene. 'Anybody want a drink then?' He stood laughing as they opened their eyes and they both laughed out loud in unison.

Sometime later that afternoon, Yevana stood ready to leave the pool area.

'Toby, I am staying on tomorrow as Andre is coming tonight whilst I will also conclude the planning formalities, but I shall meet you in London the following day for our monthly board meeting. It's important that we get the planning for the US in place. Do you think everybody will be there who needs to be to view the work done so far for LA?'

'I do, I have asked Bob to be there and I have one of the top LA architects, a guy by the name of Tim Robins flying in for the meeting. He is very excited and has worked with Chuck Bush on various projects throughout the USA and the Middle East. Chuck will be sending a senior business representative at this early stage also.

'Okay, Toby, that's fine. Please call me immediately if you need me in London earlier for any extra preparatory work.'

Yevana was delighted, this all seemed great. In real terms they had now moved from running a small hotel in Manchester to the beginnings of an empire that was to become global at some speed. She reminded herself that they should not get carried away as there was much to do and much that could go wrong. They would have to take risks but at the same time look over their shoulder at the inherent dangers involved.

'Got it, Yevana, it will be fine, I have it. Have a good couple of nights here, Summer and I are going to travel back later tonight, so not hanging around. Is there anything I can do for you?'

'No darling, enjoy.'

They all stood up from their chairs, dressed and kissed their goodbyes. Yevana teasingly and very subtly placed her right hand on Summer's right rear cheek of her pink skirt in full view of the 'audience' as they briefly embraced, taking that moment longer than necessary to remove it; naughty but ...Yevana enjoyed putting on 'the show'! Not for them, it was for her, the sexual predator surfaced, albeit briefly. Andre's number started buzzing on silent on her mobile. He had arrived at the front of her hotel just as the others left the pool area.

'Andre, darling, you are a saviour. Order strawberries and cream for room 666, get somebody to let you in and be shaved ready. I will be up in thirty minutes.' She didn't wait for confirmation; it wasn't required. Ten minutes later, she wrapped her towel around her cleavage and gathering her things walked towards the hotel and into a lift. As she entered her room she could smell aftershave before she spotted the very, very excited looking young man in her room.

Ru had flown into the UK and called Caren immediately.

'Hello, it's Caren, hello' then Caren called off. Ru tried again and left an answerphone message. 'Hi Caren, it's Ru, remember I said I would call next time in London. I am in today for three days at the Dorchester, would be good to catch up, perhaps you might call me back.' Then she rang off. Caren got on the train south to London and was at the door of Ru's room within twelve hours which was early evening. She had not told her lawyer girlfriend that she was coming to town. Ru opened the door dressed in a red designer shift, same quality shoes and some appropriate jewels ready to walk out for a dinner date. 'Oh, Caren, lovely to see you but I am out at a dinner party with the US ambassador this evening. I called you but as you did not answer or call back I assumed...'

'Good,' said Caren. 'Have a lovely time and whilst you are enjoying yourself you will be kept moist knowing I am sat here awaiting your return and that I have some things you will want to see. I will choose a suitable outfit from your things to prepare for your return.' She emphasised *things* as she walked past Ru, momentarily embracing and running her left hand a few inches across the inside of her right leg ensuring a slight scratch as she took her hand away. Ru sighed as Caren walked towards the bedroom and disappeared. Ru turned and walked out to her dinner party. She didn't want to; her head was already spinning out of control and was back inside that room of which the door had now snapped shut behind her. She considered she hardly knew this woman who had got under her skin so easily. Turning momentarily back towards the door as if she might change her mind, she kept walking. Departing the lift at the reception she briefly noticed a good-looking couple holding hands waiting to enter it. Ru wasn't used to noticing courting couples in her previous busy and limited circle of life. How things were changing.

Around midnight Ru arrived back at the hotel but first she checked for any messages almost stalling as if she was too excited or was that apprehensive about what lay ahead upstairs in her room?

'No, Mrs Carter you are all clear,' commented young Joy and Jenny the helpful receptionists.

Ru looked at the clock and for a millisecond debated with her mind why she should reject the possibilities available in room 520. A millisecond later she was already at the escalator and pressing five for the fifth floor! On the brief trip in the lift, she removed the emergency panties she had had to adopt that evening, as she had started to show signs, as a consequence of her erotic thoughts, on the dress she was wearing. Like most women there was always a spare stored in her bag for emergencies such as this. Ru stood silent as the lift came to a halt, and just briefly she eyed herself in the large surround lift mirror and applied a last layer of red lipstick gently rolling her lips to ensure the consistency. Pulling her dress tight in length, and sweeping her hair back behind her ears, the doors opened and she passed a smart gentleman waiting to get the lift down. He was her age and took a moment to give Ru the once over and she sensed him follow the line of her firm and beautiful bottom as she moved out of his sight. She heard the doors of the lift close as she came to a halt in front of her door. Her body was not her own at this stage. Her skin was on fire and every sinew was aching and moving in some way.

There was some noise inside which sounded like the tv, so she thought Caren was probably half-asleep waiting for her arrival. Ru nervously picked out the card from her clutch and slid it across the lock and as the green light flicked twice she pushed the door open leaning against the heavy fire door to move inside. What she saw next under minimal lighting was a huge shock to say the least. The fifty-inch tv on the far wall was indeed on but its feed was from what looked like a hastily arranged laptop feed and to her horror there were four people acting and it was an orgy! She knew what it was and from when! The suite desk chair was placed a few feet central in front of the tv obviously as a viewing seat for somebody. As she tried to come to terms with the shock and confusion of the film on screen, Ru had not noticed the noises from her bedroom in the suite. Was this some sort of joke? If so, she wasn't finding it funny and her body language was changing from anticipation to horror. Slowly, now wondering what she had entered into, Ru put her clutch on the large coffee table and carried on to the bedroom.

Caren heard the door spring open and took no notice but remained ready for the appearance of Ru in the bedroom doorway. She duly appeared looking ashen faced and unhappy.

'Darling, you took so long I thought I would invite some friends. Julie and Troy say hello to Ru.' The couple she vaguely noticed from the reception area earlier that evening could not answer as they were in no position to speak! Ru stood transfixed; things were not working out here and all of a sudden her change of lifestyle was starting to make her feel queasy and was slipping out of her control.

'Now, darling, just do as you are told and I will be back in touch in due course when we will discuss the movie. Go back in and watch your movie after all it is superb viewing, then when we have finished here, we will leave you alone. Oh, and thank you for the clothes they are gorgeous.' Caren climbed on top of Troy, a muscular beast of a man as Julie came around and on all fours and entered Caren also. Ru watched as Caren's eyes rolled as the group engaged. Caren had commandeered one of Ru's favourite mini-shift dresses and Julie one of her basque sets in which Ru had to admit she looked fantastic. She was your typical playboy bunny with the standard long blonde hair and long legs and the bunny breasts; standard. Ru turned from the now quite noisy scene and did as she was told and sat in the chair and started to watch her performance in Brazil and wondered how it happened and what the consequences might be. What she did know was that it wouldn't be good and Chuck being part of it meant trouble for someone if he found out, in fact, big trouble on a nuclear scale!

On completion in the bedroom Caren tidied herself in front of the mirror then walked straight out of the suite still wearing one of Ru's dresses and matching heels leaving her own clothes on the floor, followed closely by Julie, now dressed also, holding hands like lovers.

'I will be in touch soon Ru, but as a bonus for your complicity I leave you Troy! Enjoy!' was all Caren said before letting the door close behind them.

In the silence that followed, Troy walked out of the bedroom naked and lifted Ru from the chair.

'Get on your knees and clean me please,' a still excited Troy ordered whilst pushing her forcibly by pressing on her shoulders. She fell to her knees dutifully obliging. He stood rigid focused on the movie that continued to play to his front. The subject was to his liking. Having completed her task he carried her gently and took her to the bedroom and unzipped her before getting her to redress in Caren-perfumed short skirt and silk blouse from which point he seemed overtaken by desire and lust and took her for over two hours before departing.

Simon the uni student turned up out of the blue from clubbing in town at four a.m. but she wouldn't answer his calls or messages. She wasn't going to let him join her! He was relying on digs for the night at the very least but she didn't respond; she couldn't.

Ru fell asleep in position across her bed in a state of fatigue until around six the following morning having had no more than a couple of hours' sleep. Her suite room phone rang.

'Ru, it's Caren.' There was a brief silence of realisation from Ru before she responded.

'Thank you for Troy,' Ru remarked, cautiously, 'he was insatiable, which I have to admit to enjoying, although I have to concede I had to turn away my naughty toy boy at four a.m!'

When Simon arrived at the Dorchester unannounced he asked the receptionists if Mrs Carter was in and alone. The two girls looked at each other and spontaneously replied 'yes.'

'Yes, she is in or yes to both?' he replied.

'Both,' they replied in unison. They would not call her room at that hour so he called her mobile but was diverted to her answerphone message. As he unhappily walked out of the lobby, the girls giggled thinking about the random people that had asked for Mrs Carter's room number that night. They had commented on what might be happening up there because a man and woman had arrived holding hands but the woman had left holding the hand of the other female guest who had arrived before them.

'Don't mention it, Ru. Meet me for breakfast, at yours, at exactly eight a.m. in the breakfast restaurant. The table under the Battle of Waterloo oil painting would be perfect. Not that I am expecting a scene you see! See you later. Ta, ta!' Ru replaced the old-style phone and sat up taking a sip from her hastily made-in-room herbal tea. There was obviously going to be a *request* of some sort and judging by the amount of effort expended to get the movie footage, it was due to be significant and difficult. But she really had no idea at all. She couldn't understand what she could influence in any way as there was nothing in her life that got near to breaking the law. Of course, the subject was way too sensitive to call her lawyer, at this stage in any case.

Ru bathed the night's activity from her body then dressed for breakfast in an emerald jump suit and black wedge pumps. She wore her hair in a ponytail tied by a black pin-like brooch, in anticipation of a severe or rather pointed conversation.

She arrived five minutes early at the table taking a tea and orange juice to begin with, in order to be relaxed in advance of this confrontation. The room was busy but quiet, something Ru insisted on when poring over the latest news in the morning's papers, wherever she was in the world. Breakfast with the rustle of a brand-new fresh morning paper was non-negotiable, that smell! This room, like many in the hotel, had an historic feel just being part of such old and unique heritage. Even though it had modern aspects and was immaculately cleaned, the musty aroma of its heritage was definitely present and unmoveable. It was like a ghost in the room!

An old friend of her husband's from New York came across to her table, but she politely made it obvious she was meeting somebody and he soon went back to the table he was sharing with other businessmen. Ru continued to get a lot of attention as if people thought she was lonely and needed their company; she didn't and consistently looked away abruptly when she noticed. It made her smile to think of how they would react if they knew how her current lifestyle was panning out! She moved in her seat as she felt a slight soreness at the thought of it.

Showing exactly one minute past eight on the antique ever chiming restaurant grandfather clock, in walked Caren turning heads in unison as she sought out Ru seated on the far side of the breakfast room. It was like the black widow entering the room. Dressed head to toe in black, she certainly stood out. She was wearing a tightly tied neck scarf and a full length fitted black dress that looked stunning. A silver pendant nestling between her cleavage completed the look. The open back to the dress, reaching to her buttocks had every person in the room following her distinct movement until she reached her intended destination.

Slowly walking across to Ru's table under the battle scene, she took the seat opposite her, taking a brief moment to study an attractive blonde waitress bending over to pick a lone napkin which had fallen from a nearby table.

'Lovely specimen, don't you think? Perhaps it might suit your newly acquired taste, no?' Caren smiled at the girl who quickly and shyly turned away and disappeared out of the room on noticing the unsolicited attention from Caren.

'No, not what I was thinking Caren, not at all, thank you,' replied Ru totally unimpressed.

Ru jumped straight in not wanting to spend any more time in Caren's company than she had to.

'Now Caren, what is your business? I have business of my own to conduct in town today and so I do not have long. Oh yes, and here is your laptop. I have taken the courtesy to wipe the video. Now, tea?'

'Yes, thank you, and don't worry I have a safe copy.' Ru was not surprised at that and beckoned a waiter to order the tea.

Caren got straight to the point. 'Okay, I want to know all about the progress of future Y&T deals in Spain and the US particularly. I want to be kept abreast of negotiations and plans so that I can act as I see fit and at timings of my choosing. Any interference or lack of information or misinformation will mean elements of your movie will be released to a social media frenzy. It is up to you, but reputation is hard won! You have my mobile number, don't use any other media. Is there anything I have told you that you don't understand Ru, darling?

'Well, firstly it is not my movie,' said an irritated Ru, 'in fact it disgusts me that you stooped so low to record such private moments between adults. Secondly, why do you want to do this Caren? What can you get from this?' Ru looked perplexed and was finding it hard to deal with this horrible situation. This was a million miles from her previous life; it was ridiculous and had to be a bad dream.

Caren was unrepentant. 'Actually, darling, I think you will find the average adult finds your *private moments* quite strange and in fact disgusting, particularly with another woman's husband and of course those funny men, no women, well people.'

'Don't lecture me, Caren.' Ru looked down to her tea and took a sip feeling chastised. Caren smirked having noticed this and then thought about how many times she had enjoyed watching her personal copy! It was dynamite.

'Revenge, darling! She hurt me and badly. That is it, full stop, and Yevana will have to answer for her betrayal, simple as that. Don't be tempted Ru. I will bury you, humiliate you, trust me! I mean it! Now where is that tea?' Caren looked round nonplussed.

Ru stared at Caren and knew she meant what she said. Someone she knew who could help her against someone so ruthless was Yevana but...

Ru stood up, she wasn't hungry anymore, as her nerves jangled madly at the bottom of her stomach taking away any hunger she might normally have felt at this time in the morning. Ru started to walk past Caren towards the breakfast room exit. 'I am off, goodbye Caren.' Caren grabbed her wrist, tightly digging a fingernail into her skin as Ru attempted to shake it free.

'Not hungry then, okay, but not goodbye Ru, not goodbye.' Ru looked around feeling embarrassed.

'You keep me informed like I said, that's a good girl.' Caren looked Ru in the eyes and then looked away and released her wrist as her tea arrived. Ru walked off shaking the pain from her delicate wrist and went straight out to make her business appointment not looking back. She was more confused than she had ever been and only her husband could have helped her but of course if he was still alive she would not have been here in the first place!

Yevana had a very eventful next twenty-four hours in Madrid with Andre as she used him to facilitate extra meetings with the relevant authorities and his mother Rydeesa who was now conforming readily. Andre was also delivering on the energy front with Yevana in a particularly horny disposition. He was however hiding something as he seemed on edge but she put this down to the pressures of business and being involved emotionally with her.

At a meeting with the authorities the following day Rydeesa explained what a great asset Y&T would be to the city in terms of five-star executive accommodation.

'Ladies and gentlemen, I have witnessed the huge success of this project in London which has not been bettered by any similar facility; anywhere! Confidence is that high Yevana has already agreed a deal to take the model to LA; Madrid must be at the forefront of this type of attraction for both business and leisure. I fully commend it.'

She was speaking confidently and avoiding eye contact with Yevana who sat fixed on the gentlemen opposite who had to give the final nod with reference to the sale of the land for this purpose. There were rules in this city regarding property sale that were different. Rydeesa and her husband carried weight and key knowledge though and Yevana could sense that the city planner, a good-looking man in his fifties, was or had been involved with her. The meeting concluded quickly with the planner standing and informing them that all was well and the lease would be sold for one hundred and twenty years to Y&T Global. He came round and shook Yevana's hand and left the room with his small group. Rydeesa sat pensively and looked across at Yevana who looked stunning in a green skirt and sheer black blouse high on the neck.

Rydeesa looked across at Yevana looking very concerned as everyone left the room.

'You can't keep me on a hook like this Yevana, it will catch up with you one day and it is cruel. I don't deserve this,' she finished in a rather downbeat tone.

Yevana walked across to Rydeesa who remained seated and moved to stand behind her from where she placed her hands on Rydeesa's chest and slowly her fingers slowly opened her blouse then with a sharp jerk ripped it open. Violently she pulled her from the chair and pulled her flowery delicate small bra from her back and tightened it round her neck. 'You will do as you are told. I might not need you much any more but be ready as I may want to call you.' Yevana walked over to her seat, collected her things and left not looking behind at the shaking devastation on the floor.

Caren pulled out her phone. 'Andre, I have the cradle snatcher Ru Carter on the team, she will be most compliant! Now, I can't say the same about Mummy, can I? What are we to do about her?

Luckily, Yevana was getting something to eat in the kitchen area of their suite and had taken no notice of the call. Andre jumped out of bed and into the toilet. With some frustration at the timing, he listened and replied, 'I don't know, Caren. What do you have in mind?'

'Get over there and find out what changed her mind. I want to know the lengths Yevana is going to, to get what she wants. Now I have a date with my lawyer who I am staying with over the weekend here in London, so must rush. Bye, Andre and back to me within twelve hours with some information! Ciao.'

Andre got back into bed and smiled as Yevana came back to bed with the champagne, strawberries and cream. He didn't last long and was soon making his accuses.

'I have just had a call from Mother who wants me to come over for dinner tonight which I have accepted; alone,' he hesitated.

'Shame, I would love to have come to see Mummy,' Yevana commented very sarcastically. 'Do you think I should come anyway?'

'Absolutely not,' he replied. 'She is not herself at present and just wants a small family dinner.' Yevana contemplated insisting that she should attend but decided against it; there was little value in doing so.

'I would love to get together with your family again, but alas another time. I have some mail to catch up on and will take my dinner in my room tonight and take an early night for a change. Send them my love, please.'

Andre was gone in a whisker as he needed to get the information to Caren soonest and Yevana had worked him hard that last few hours. Yevana was sceptical about his reasons to leave so quickly but he was a young man and probably had another date later also in town. It had been a busy week so far and the rest would do her good.

Andre was soon back at his parents and having invited himself to dinner was quick to ask his mother what she was up to and why she had not stalled the client meeting as he had asked.

'Mother, what on earth were you playing at? Yevana is a good client for my business and you almost torpedoed the whole thing; thanks a lot!' He was furious and seeing her sat in front of him looking carefree really annoyed him.

Rydeesa suddenly looked really guilty. 'I have my reasons. You know your father and I are really passionate about the City and its architecture; it must be preserved. I was not sure if this project was right and wanted to give it more time to make a final decision.'

'That is fine, but you changed your mind so quickly again. Why?' At this point his father came in and they were called to dinner. His mother glared at him as if to say, 'don't say any more in front of your father'. He shrugged and went into dinner.

Dinner was a quiet affair with just general family chit-chat. On completion his father went to his study to complete some business in preparation for the following day, whilst Rydeesa and Andre had coffee in the library.

'Mother, tell me the truth or I will ask father why my friend seems to make you so nervous. In fact, I will also invite her to stay here next time we come and I will discuss it then.'

'No need, darling, don't be hasty.'

'Well?' he replied, 'What of it then?'

'Okay, she has something on me which I am not prepared to discuss with you as it is extremely personal, although you should know it is not something criminal. Do I need to say more? I hope not because you will not like it and nor will your father. We have our weaknesses and she found one of mine.' She looked away towards a window and drank her coffee. He decided he had heard enough and left the room and called Caren from his room.

Caren heard the phone buzzing in silent mode on the bedside table and leant across her lover Dreana, who was blindfolded, in a doubled-up position with hands and ankles tied together wearing only a pair of Caren's favourite high heels and answered the call from Andre. 'Yes, and be quick, I told you I would be busy.'

'Caren, I have spoken with Mother and she told me Yevana has something on her but would only say it was very personal but not criminal. As it is my mother, I hope you will understand that I did not want to know the detail.' Of course, Andre did have knowledge of his parents' activities but chose to pretend he knew very little for his own sanity.

Next thing Andre heard was the flat liner sound in his earpiece. He pulled the phone from his head and looked at it as if puzzled. 'Strange woman,' he said out loud.

Caren had heard enough and closed the call without saying any more to Andre. She would think about her next move. Slightly frustrated and thinking about other things, she pulled on the strap on that was lying ready on the bed and mounted the lawyer grabbing at her ponytails and thrusting with all her might. It was a frenzied assault on her subject who was powerless to respond. After five minutes or so Caren withdrew and looked down on her friend and lover who was breathing hard. She had won a case in court today prosecuting a man who had taken his sexual passion too far and hurt his female partner badly in the act. Here she was a forceful powerful prosecution lawyer by day but tonight tied up and being abused by her girlfriend. Caren knew this was Dreana's antidote to her tough working schedule. In fact, when they first met that evening Dreana had told Caren to be hard on her as she needed to be punished. To finish, Caren slipped off the strap on and slid onto her seat smothering Dreana's noisy breathing and then watching her struggle underneath. As Caren felt panic setting in below, she climaxed and slipped off and finished giving her a large unmistakeable love bite on the neck. She untied her ten minutes later and made dinner: it was love!

Caren was fidgety now and couldn't settle whilst she considered her next move in her attempt to get her revenge on Yevana.

'Dreana, darling, do you love me?' Caren asked as her lover came out of the en-suite having showered her sexually generated sweaty body.

'Of course, Caren, I always will,' she replied as she came across and planted a long soft and gentle kiss on Caren's lips. They parted and Dreana went into her bedroom and started to dry off her hair with a towel whilst seated at her dressing table. She is such a lovely person, thought Caren, which made what she was about to say even more difficult although necessary.

'Good,' Caren responded from the lounge whilst changing channels on the TV.

'You are to start a relationship with Brad Bush the son of somebody that can help me out; a wealthy American. I will get you the in, then you will integrate and relay the information I need. Do you understand me?'

First of all, there was a silence, then Dreana replied, 'No and no. I love you and I do not want a relationship on any level with anybody, particularly a man. It is ridiculous to suggest such a thing; I know you aren't even joking Caren, no!'

'Caren got up from her chair and whilst Dreana was still drying her hair with the towel, grabbed a chunk of it and dragged her out of the flat throwing her on to the floor of the cold, austere landing space.

Caren listened to the banging on the front door then persistent whimpering for an hour before she let Dreana back into her own flat!

'Sorry,' she said as she stood with just a small towel round her waist, shivering in front of her furious friend. 'I don't want to disappoint you baby,' said a pathetic sounding Dreana who was crestfallen.

'Good, now take that ridiculous towel from around your waist and bend over onto the dining table.' Still shivering, Dreana did as she was told then Caren walked to her bag in the bedroom and pulled out a menacing leather whip and after one fierce strike on the wooden table, proceeded to whip Dreana until she saw blood on her rear, after which they moved to the settee and made love again. Caren noted the following morning that sitting in court was going to be a challenge for Dreana. Caren smirked as they kissed goodbye on the pavement outside the law courts and Dreana walked smartly but tentatively to work. Caren wondered how she could possible hurt such a fantastic bottom as she walked off in the opposite direction.

Within a week Caren had texted Dreana her instructions and how and when to contact the young, brash, but gorgeous Brad Bush. It did occur to Caren that a heterosexual relationship might change her lover which would be a shame. On the other hand, she knew Dreana well enough to know she was going to hate every minute! Caren laughed loudly in the cafe where she was drinking her favourite Americano with hot milk added. The stately very dignified and elegant lady sat opposite, looked up at her and Caren winked; the woman left immediately! Caren laughed loudly.

Ru darling, Caren, how's your love life?' she joked on a mobile call to the States. 'I trust you have been behaving badly. I do admire your energy.'

Ru coughed into the phone and cleared a lump in her throat. 'Caren, what do you want? I don't have time to chat to the likes of you!' was her immediate and frosty reply.

'Now, now, darling, don't be hasty. I have a task for you which won't cause you any trouble.' Caren smirked and waited a moment sensing Ru's unease.

"I am going to send Dreana Martel, our friend,' she teased, 'to the States and I want an introduction to Brad Bush, son of, you know who, don't you?' Caren didn't want to reply. 'Not for discussion, darling, just make it happen and let her know directly, she is waiting. Ciao, baby.' Caren called off immediately.

Ru put the phone down and sat in her big chair looking out over Central Park.

'How the hell did I get involved with that viper?' She felt vulnerable but decided there wasn't much choice and it was a simple enough tasker. A fine malt settled her nerve endings!

Ru was on top of the requirement to get Dreana introduced to the charmingly good-looking Brad, which wasn't difficult.

It wasn't too long before Ru made the arrangements. She texted Dreana. 'Hi, Dreana, it's Ru, long time no see! Xx. Caren asked me to introduce you to Brad Bush which I have arranged for the end of the month here, that is the States, in DC where his father and family are attending a charity event. Details to follow Xx.' There was nothing else to say.

Dreana was very anxious but wanted to please Caren.

'Brad, this is the eminent London lawyer Ms Dreana Martel, could you entertain yourselves whilst I find a good friend of mine please? See you in a bit.' Ru was almost shouting amongst the throng of the gathering whilst moving off into the crowd waving her arms.

Through Ru, Caren had Dreana invited to the function in a swanky Washington hotel where the great and the good were assembled for an international Aids charity.

Dreana and Brad were soon conversing easily as she worked out what or who he actually was apart from Chuck and Sarina's son, and how quickly she could have him in her proverbial pocket! It took half an hour. Dressed in a ridiculously revealing skirt and blouse, the signals were sent and he had her in his room at the same hotel and was back downstairs again within the hour. She thought it wasn't as unpleasant an experience as she had imagined although he was selfish. Having arranged to leave the party much later, together, they spent the rest of the night in town dancing and drinking until the early hours. For her part, she made sure that her masterful prowess of giving relief left him mentally charged and wanting more of which she delivered in a passageway before calling her own taxi and leaving him her number *'in case she should be back in the capital any time in the future.'* The following day was Sunday and just as well as Dreana was feeling ill. Caren rang to discuss things but Dreana would not take a call as she felt disgusted and very low. Brad called as she expected but she did not answer him either; he would have to be put off for a while and become needy, if not desperate, to see her again. Two days later she did send a text. 'Hi Brad, wow what a night! You know how to treat somebody. Can't wait for a repeat. I'll call you when I have time after my next case in court. See ya D xx.'

Back in London Dreana had called Caren with an update on recent text and calls to Brad but seemed very upset as her current in-town girlfriend, a famous TV presenter, was treating her badly and she was feeling low and not sure she could make the next trip out to see Brad as arranged in three weeks' time. With that and a heavy work schedule it was inconvenient. 'Nonsense, what is the problem darling and who is it?' Caren asked.

'It is Drew Getisso, an Anglo-Italian news presenter on Channel GB9. We met at a party of a mutual friend who hosts influential parties now and again and by the end of the night, out at a West End club, we got it together. I took her to my place and we have seen each other quite often since,' Dreana confided.

'What is the problem and is there anything I can do for you?'

'No, Caren, leave it,' Dreana said as she knew her intervention could be brutal. 'Anyway, she stopped answering my calls and then out of the blue turned up on my doorstep after a few weeks. We get on great and I like her a lot but she is using me I think.'

'Okay, Dreana, I do think you should just let it go and drop her completely as it is obviously going nowhere.' Caren sighed, losing interest in Dreana's love life. Unfortunately, Caren could see this wasn't straight forward and she would need to step in to oil the wheels to get Dreana in the right frame of mind. This was a turn for the worse and the situation had to be addressed.

Caren came down to London on business having done her research with some help from JD and followed Ms Getisso to a London West End restaurant and once settled, approached her table.

'Hi, Ms Getisso, sorry to disturb you, but could I have your autograph for my friend please?' Caren thrust a card and pen with a picture of Getisso on TV and a message on it which read, *'Don't mess my friend around or I will out you!'* At the top of the card was written *Dreana* in italics and a smiley face.

Her husband and two young daughters looked up and he said, 'Do you mind!'

As Getisso signed the card she looked up and interrupted him.

'Don't worry darling, just this once, now can you leave us in peace to have our dinner please.' She looked decidedly unhappy. It had the desired effect though as she looked shocked at the knowledge of what had just taken place right in front of her husband and two young girls and in such a public place. Getisso actually looked frightened.

'Of course, and thank you, you are most kind, good day,' Caren replied matter of fact, as she retreated to her table feeling a set of questioning eyes piercing her back as she sat down.

Caren watched the family enjoying their meal but noticed they probably did not stay as long as normal as Getisso looked agitated and probably confused. As they went out of the main door she looked back at Caren then turned and got in a taxi.

Drew Getisso was the number one news presenter in the UK at this time. She was intelligent, had beautiful straight blonde hair and the most desirable long legs. Caren always enjoyed trying to understand what made people like Getisso, so prominent in the public eye and affections, dabble off piste. Was the risk worth it? Caren knew there was only one obvious answer to that. What she expected though after this shock was for Getisso to turn it off completely. Wrong! Caren received a call from Dreana two days later saying that Getisso had apologised about her absence and later that day after work, they had sex in a public toilet off Sloane Square. Dreana had come from court and was still carrying her legal files! Getisso who had turned up on her way to the studio with no dress under her trench coat, was on TV that night within two hours of their rendezvous, 'Dirty but nice,' was how Dreana put it, also mentioning that Getisso had given Dreana her mobile number for the first time, painted on her chest with lipstick. This was a bit of a surprise to her as Caren thought she might have frightened her off for good. That woman obviously had issues. Caren felt a tinge of jealousy having now met the beauty that was Ms Getisso! Dreana did not know of Caren's intervention but was now super excited to assist Caren again in the States.

The next meet was actually part of a combined holiday to New York with Caren. Dreana organised for them both to attend a gathering of business associates of his father Chuck, to celebrate a successful launch of his latest shopping mall success in Miami. Caren could see that Brad was very attentive to Dreana and considered that she must have done well. Of course, this was not a surprise as Caren was fully aware of her undoubted 'talents'.

Dreana, as instructed, ensured that Caren was introduced to Chuck by Brad. Caren, in anticipation, had dressed in a short red skirt, white blouse and heels that she knew would have Chuck drooling, which was indeed the case. His lovely wife Sarina swiftly turned and walked across to greet friends. She clearly hated competition and knew not to be around when her husband was playing! He couldn't take his eyes off Caren and started sending signals of intent for the evening. Of course, Caren had other ideas.

Dreana had Brad upstairs in his room tying him to the bed on all fours as they had planned.

After a few minutes of general chit-chat Caren moved Chuck to one side and pulled her phone from her bag and played him a thirty second clip of his performance in Sao Paulo. The blood drained from his face and he stuttered, 'What do you want from me and by the way you do know you are not only playing with fire, you are in it? I'm not used to losing,' he finished giving her a death stare.

Caren was not put off in the slightest, in fact she hardly blinked as she carried on.

'Okay. Simple, I want my friend Dreana Martel, a lawyer, to be appointed on the board of Y&T LA with immediate effect. I will instruct the moves to follow. Don't think your power will beat me Chuck as that will be your first mistake, trust me! Now, your son is at present being photographed in his hotel room upstairs being mounted by my friend. Don't worry though, I will keep that footage safe to. Ciao, darling. I will be in touch.' Chuck stood fixed as he watched Caren wiggle out of the room but had soon composed himself, then made his way upstairs to check on Brad. Caren met Dreana in the lobby.

'Sorted?' asked Caren.

'Yup,' replied Dreana, 'Your end?'

'Yup also,' Caren declared.

'It is done, you have done well, now, let's go and celebrate at a club,' Caren directed as she put a consoling arm around a relieved Dreana.

They walked out to the waiting taxi laughing loudly. Caren was sure that although dumbfounded by this shocking revelation, Chuck was probably immediately more gutted that his female target, dressed in *come and get me red*, had been lost for that evening and the wife might have to do!

Caren knew she was taking a risk here as Chuck could take all manner of actions to get out of this situation, the most obvious was violence. However, Caren was confident that she had the high ground as he would be nervous about who had the video to publish in case of such an event. Indeed, Caren had instructed her private detective to do just that if she was to be seriously injured or killed. The exact instruction was to 'send the videos viral JD, spare nobody!'

Dreana on the board

Back in their London offices planning was gathering pace as the board was confirmed for the Madrid project and things were moving quickly for LA. Strangely for the LA project, Chuck had insisted on a young London lawyer be placed on the board, a certain Dreana Martel. Apparently, Martel was a rising star, according to Toby's friend who he had asked to make some enquiries. It all seemed fine and nothing adverse came of it and so Toby confirmed and moved on. However, unbeknown to Toby and Yevana, Caren had ensured that there would now be a majority on the LA board that would react to her every whim. Ru Carter and Chuck Bush were both tied by their seedy Brazil tape and Dreana by her infatuation with Caren and the threat of outing her media friend. Ru had been a volunteer and serious investor but since Caren had appeared she had lost her appetite and was gutted that she would one day be letting down her dear friend Yevena.

'Yevena, are you content with the board set up to run the LA project?' Toby asked across the table at their weekly meeting.

'In principle, although I take it you have done some checks on the unknown?' she asked quizzically.

'I have no reason to doubt that she, Dreana, is friends with the Bushes having apparently won a small case for them recently here in the high court and they trust her.' Toby came back strongly, a little irritated.

'Sorry, darling,' Yevena replied noticing his position. 'I am just a bit surprised but not sure why.'

In concluding the meeting, they were able to confirm that all investments were secured and in place and the boards were agreed. Bob Ray was in attendance as their non-executive member and lifetime trusted agent. They all left the meeting and met at a local bar two hours later before attending an industry awards ceremony.

Christina had won several awards for her design of the Y&T London project both for interior as well as exterior architecture and was now busy planning future designs for a series of top projects around the world. She had not seen the Y&T team for a while and was not expecting their appearance, so she had prepared to attend with friends. Not more than half an hour before the start and before her planned acceptance speech after winning an award as the architect of the year, Toby, to Christina's surprise, pulled her to one side and congratulated her on her achievements and apologised for how things were handled on not being employed by Y&T anymore.

'Toby, I will always love you, you know that,' she went on.

'I am very happy now with another more considerate man; you know my number.'

Toby said nothing. He smiled, leaned forward and kissed her on the neck below her right ear and touched her gently on the ribs. Christine nearly collapsed. He turned and walked off.

Christine joined her table for the rest of the evening where she was sat with her new boyfriend of twelve months.

The following week Yevana took some time out to trace Ms Martel and just take a look at her and particularly her activities. She didn't know what it was but something didn't seem right. All of the people associated with their projects had appeared naturally as either advisors or investors but this seemed and indeed was different.

Yevana found Dreana worked long hours at her offices or in court and socialised with a number of friends. It was two weeks later on her third random outing following her from the courts that something out of the ordinary occurred. Instead of her normal route to the Tube she headed down some steps into a street side toilets. Yevana followed and noticed Dreana go into the far-right cubicle. Yevana waited a moment then washed her hands and at that moment she noticed another woman, businesslike, tall with straight blonde hair, walking quickly towards the far-right cubicle. Expecting it to be locked Yevana was surprised to see the woman enter without hesitation. Quickly, Yevana crossed to the adjoining cubicle, locked it and sat on the loo, listening in the quiet space. There was nobody else around and so every movement seemed amplified in this echoic space. Next door there was no talking just clothing being removed and then somebody was peeing onto the floor and groaning! She looked down in anticipation and in this rather murky underground light, Yevana watched transfixed as a trail of urine flowed into her cubicle and touched her shoe. She couldn't work out why she had just let that happen! Yevana considered that this was not groundbreaking but under these circumstances she would have to be aware that Dreana was a risk taker. The thought of, and sounds being generated by two very good-looking women next door, was arousing her and having heard enough Yevana unbolted her door and strolled across the room and walked out back into daylight. Two hours later watching the GB9 News Yevana came over faint as she saw the other woman from the toilet, Mrs Drew Getisso, a married mother of two. She knew she had been right; there was something to be unsure about Dreana, something different, although for now she would keep it to herself but be vigilant.

Over the coming months Yevana and Toby spent a lot of time in LA as they brokered a great deal on a prime site near a major motion picture studios. Andre had by now taken a back seat and been socially discarded by Yevana and as irrelevant by Caren having failed to get anywhere near to marrying Yevana. Caren wouldn't give up on this and constantly threatened to expose his parents.

Yevana was too busy with business and had conveniently found a young blonde beach bum in LA. On the night in question, Yevana wasn't short in letting Andre know they were finished altogether. After a casual dinner in a London bistro, he plucked up the courage and asked her to live with him as part of his plan to eventually ask for her hand in marriage.

'I can't and won't live with you or anyone else, Andre. You are a lovely person but things move on and I am saying from now on it is business only, I am sorry but that is the final word; I will not discuss it! Now stiff coffee?' Andre was not expecting this and knowing the consequences of this finality he just stood up, dropped some cash on the table and walked out. Yevana, pulled out her compact mirror case and added some pink lipstick. The waiter came across and asked, 'Is your guest coming back Ms Narvik?'

Smiling, Yevana replied, 'Never Gaston, never.'

'Caren, bad news. Yevana and I will not be seeing each other again. We are finished.' Caren was silent for moment then, 'pathetic!' and she hung up and never spoke to Andre again.

The following day some inappropriate highly sexual xxx pictures and most alarmingly video, of Andre's parents Rolanda and Rydeesa Correnti, the well-known Spanish aristocrats and some of their high-profile friends, had gone viral across the internet from an unknown source. The following week they were found hanged together in the basement of their historic property in Madrid and under the circumstances the police closed the case as misadventure. Some of the others shown to be there had lawyers closing down the main sites and claiming their faces had been superimposed onto these pictures to damage their reputations. Some social media sites were forced to settle out of court as nobody came forward to claim they owned the pictures. It was too late for the sad Correnties!

For such a high-profile couple this sensational story made world-wide news and pictures were splashed across the national papers. Friends contacted for comment distanced themselves due to the nature of the sex pictures. Leon had been recognised in the pictures and was now in hiding as the media wanted to get the full story and details, particularly the tabloids!

Yevana read the news with interest. First question was, who had supplied these pictures? It would not have been Andre for obvious reasons and it definitely was not Yevana who did not have any in her possession although she had witnessed Rydeesa's activities first hand. She did not call Andre; he was out of her personal life for good and luckily the Madrid project was already building up out of the ground and looking good. Staff were already being hired and the executive staff were in place. They would have an office there but would be transient as planned for all their sites.

Yevana was told that Andre was taking a sabbatical in order to be able to handle his parents' interests in Spain and take over the whole estate which was substantial. Ironically, he had reacted quickly and had moved his mother's bi-sexual boyfriend Leon into the family mansion, as it turns out they had also started an affair. How strange, she thought, how strange.

Caren viewed the news of the Correnties' deaths with disdain. 'Pathetic, just like their week useless son, pathetic.'

She had enjoyed uploading the pictures via a confidential silent partner. Andre couldn't say he hadn't been warned. He was of no further use and things had moved on in terms of being able to affect Y&T where it would hurt most, ultimately Yevana Narvik, the despicable heartless witch.

The next step

Life settled down again and business prospered. Inevitably the ongoing process of further expansion continued. They had no shortage of offers of financial support and encouragement to do so but ultimately had enough on their plate to be able to cope at this stage. The Madrid project soon nicknamed *'The Church'* opened to great fanfare and a full house for membership and bookings which continued well into its second year. At the opening Yevana dressed in the mighty yellow of the native Volta couture, a skintight set of hot pants. During the reception she spotted a wistful staring Andre but soon lost him in the crowd as he disappeared from sight.

They had made it, London was making them wealthy, shares were riding high in the business, and potential investors wanted to be part of the idea, particularly in other States in the US. The next target they had set their sights on was Los Angeles, paradise of the wannabe and playground of the mega rich and planning was progressing well with support from Chuck Bush and Ru Carter for the US team out there. The London office flew out to LA regularly having set up an office and some staff near the potential site. Drawings by Tim Robbins were already reaching an advanced stage. It looked good and their fantastic site was not far from the sea which added to the attraction. There were four hundred rooms adjoining an old ballroom: perfect. Agents, developers, estate agents, lawyers, etc were all instructed and Josh Solbar, their accountant, got the financial side prepared with local American experts. They had met Dreana a few months back in a meeting with Chuck Bush who said that her main involvement would be at board meetings, although she was to be cc'd on all business correspondence, obviously. That meeting was held in LA and to Yevana's surprise Dreana had taken the chance to grab a quick holiday with her muse, the delectable Drew Getisso. First siting was by the pool as Getisso walked past Yevana's lounger wearing only a pure white bikini bottom and huge dark shades, holding hands with Dreana who was dressed similarly but in pink. Yevena was immediately jealous! And of them both! The first meeting was cordial but very formal and no further discussions were held. Chuck was insistent that Dreana only had minimal contact with other members and acted as his trusted agent for legal reasons. 'I need assurance,' was his demanding and stern comment on being asked by Yevena of the purpose of her presence on the board.

'I just thought you would use somebody Stateside?' she remarked.

'Yevana, you just concentrate on making LA a success. I insist. Good day to you.'

While in LA they partied hard as expected in that 'Kingdom'. On completion of their business, they always headed for the social hot points where there was no shortage of attraction in any form! Toby though had started to pull back from his relationship with Summer, who took that exciting opportunity and moved on having found a very willing fledgling male movie star. Toby just knew he needed to relax more and do very little in his spare time to ensure he didn't burn out in this relentless pursuit he shared with Yevana. She had more energy than he did, so the beach and a good book was his therapy for his time in the sun and women were off limits; for now! Janice, true to form, had two young actors in tow which seemed to suit all parties. They were actors mainly to be seen on set in the San Fernando Valley area not Paramount Pictures!

During the most recent visit to LA Yurini and Yurenev turned up with a string of hangers-on. Yurini was quickly informed that Yevana was in town and had her tracked down to her room phone.

'Darling Yevana, your deal, with our current ten percent stake, sounds very good, we can't wait to take a suite there, for a couple of months even, perhaps.' Yurini was always planning her lifestyle into the years ahead which did cause Yurenev some nervousness. In this case though there was some sarcasm probably hinting at their limited activeinvolvement in this adventure in the States, although it didn't really matter to them.

'I take it you have not forgotten that you still owe me for your antics with the beautiful Mobola. What a shame, poor girl, I am still grieving,' she lied. 'I will clear this debt but you must firstly carry out a delicate task, yeez?'

'What, Yurini? I am rather busy as you suggested earlier in the conversation,' Yevana responded with a sigh of resignation of the anticipated task.

'Never too busy for your most important business partners of course, are we Yevana? Here is what you have to do and do be hasty I don't have that much time.' Yurini was now sounding a little irritated.

'There is a new starlet in Tinseltown, singing and acting to all the top hits of the moment and everybody's current favourite. Rosemary Dacone. I am sure you know of her even though you are so-o-o busy.' Yurini exaggerated the *so* to highlight the sarcasm.

'Yevana, you are to entrap this twenty-two-year-old dream of a plaything and leave her to the adults. Ciao, darling, Ciao.' And the call finished. Yevana looked at the object in her hand and carefully placed it back in its home. Bent over the bed looking out of the window towards the sea, she sighed. She did not need this but hopefully it would indeed clear this so-called debt, for good.

Yevana was supposed to be seeing a beach bum energetic boyfriend this evening where they had a lot planned, however, she put him off for the night and was quick to pull in a favour and organise an introduction to Rosemary Dacone in the VIP area at a top nightclub in the early hours of the following day and luckily they got on great and had some fun. Rosy, as she liked to be called, was a good fit into the pop star category of beautiful, fit and vibrant. Most noticeable was her preference to show off as much as possible; her midriff housed a six pack most men would be proud of! With a fair set sat above, five foot ten, and tottering on Stella heels, Yevana could see the attraction.

Her hangers-on were a pain, but Yevana soon shook off the tail and they taxied to a much more cosmopolitan adult party across in Beverly Hills, the home of an LA rapper, with spectacular views sweeping back into LA City. In fact, it was like stepping into another world as ever with Yurini and Yurenev and Yevana soon noticing bodies everywhere, that is if you looked closely enough behind doors. She had actually done very little to get this far and within moments of being at the house the girl had been whisked away. Fun loving as she was, this was probably a new kind of paradise to her, having only recently gained celebrity status.

Within a couple of hours this young lady was in an upstairs bedroom with Yurini and Yuenev having her first sample of cocaine and a male-female trifold! Yevana remained clothed and sat sprawled on a chaise longue in the shadows of the dimly lit room, staying for a while to watch for her pleasure before discretely leaving, just as Rosemary's sexual groans were slowly muffled out by Yurini! Yevana received a text the following day saying, 'we have new pet, baby, debt paid in full! Ciao xxxx.'

Yevana went to bed and slept for eight hours before being woken by Toby who had business to discuss. Shortly after that she drove to her boyfriend's basic Santa Monica one bed flat and allowed him to divulge for several hours, before she departed as she had arrived: quietly and on her own. He wanted her to leave earlier than she did as he had things planned, but with images still very much on her mind from the previous night, she wanted more which left him physically and mentally exhausted. She left her underwear as a memento! A few years older maybe, but definitely stronger she thought as she slammed the ill-fitting front door of his low rent dwelling. His current girlfriend passed Yevena on the stairs. 'Hi' was all they exchanged as they passed. Yevena noticed her from a picture laying around in the flat. She hoped he had the sense to clear the underwear and that she wasn't expecting much today!

When in town over the coming months, Rosy and Yevana attended many of the same parties and Rosy, still top of the pops as such, was seen by Yevana on more than one occasion, in the toilets sniffing cocaine off other male and female genitalia; Yurini really was a monster!

Yevana could guess quite accurately that Rosy would go the same way as their other pet Mobola. She had quickly picked up a bad habit and the Russians were in love with her! A good friend of Rosy who could see the warning signs of fame attracting unwanted so-called friends, confronted Yurini at one night club and was quite abusive,but unfortunately she was ill advised. Not long after this confrontation this friend's car left the road in bad weather and she was left in a coma. Foul play was not suspected and there were no witnesses on the outer highway on that particular night.

Los Angeles

Toby and Yevana had obviously been leading separate lives, socially speaking, for some time and were only vaguely aware of their parallel love lives. If anything, they were leading increasingly quieter lives as they were even more occupied with their business projects and the travel that it now entailed. A lot of the time was spent on their own with random sexual dalliances but nothing remotely serious and frequent. They did even consider stepping back into another relationship with each other, but they both knew it was a complication they didn't need, particularly being in each other's pocket twenty-four seven.

Within a year nothing had changed except Y&T LA to be called The Spacewalk, was born and opened to rave reviews and to capacity as had all the previous complexes. In this city and on this site it was virtually guaranteed but Yevana and Toby drove the project team to deliver an unbelievable complex. The opening night saw Andoria Rosenta, the world's favourite and most glorious and glamorous opera star, live up to that billing in the grand ballroom. Of course, aside from the bill itself, there were strings attached so far as her thirst for Yevana was concerned. Yevana and her boyfriend joined her for a post opening party in her top floor apartment joined by Rosenta's oriental PAs of course. Yevana's blonde beach bum didn't leave the complex for two days!

It was lavish as befitted the city and opulent; five-star, bordering on seven-star if there was such a thing and bettered anything being designed and built in the sheikdoms of the Middle East. On the opening night the place was buzzing and the team worked the building throughout the evening. At about three a.m. before Yevana disappeared upstairs with her boyfriend, she was sitting with Toby when they were approached by a Texan billionaire who had been introduced to them earlier. A genuine person from Texan oil – not again, thought Toby and Yevana – he had some proposals he wanted them to think over. It didn't take long as he was direct and they all parted on good terms although Toby had informed him that they were consolidating before accepting any further offers and ideas during the next two years outside of their desire to see through their current project in Salt Lake City.

Before carrying on the party into the small hours, separately, Toby caught a brief moment with Yevana sitting side by side on a seat by the outdoor pool. There was nobody else around and just a fair breeze sweeping over them in the relative quiet *city* night. He looked at her as she settled beside him. Yevana had spent the whole night in a delicate light blue Volta mini-suit and looked a million dollars. Toby, in a pale cream Vandervault suit from Savile Row, considered that they had made quite a pair. Yevana especially looked a million dollars in her trademark twelve inch mini; unbelievable pretty. Toby looked across at her at one stage and couldn't believe the beauty – he was still madly in love with her although they had not made love for over a year. Would they ever be together again?

Out

Karen concluded that she had no more use for Andre now that his parents had been outed by the release of the video images of their extreme lifestyle and their subsequent suicide. So, what to do? She thought and quickly decided, nothing. She had nothing on him now and wanted nothing; it was done. Similarly, Yevana greeted the news of the Correntis' suicides differently but ultimately with a similar result.

'Andre, darling, when I am back in London this week come over to the office Monday at nine a.m. sharp, there are things we must discuss. Oh yes, and I am desperately sorry about your parents; tragic, darling,' she said rather matter of fact really having not liked Rydeesa and thought they were both dodgy individuals who carried out their business using dubious means. Although this had undoubtedly assisted developing the Y&T Madrid project to completion it meant they would always be susceptible to outside influence and that is how it turned out. Yevana had guessed that part of the change of heart in Madrid during the early negotiations must have been with Andre's knowledge and although he would get a chance to come clean, she had made her mind up to get rid of him.

Andre came into the office in London as requested and had his normal conversations with Janice who always had a soft spot for him, before he was called in to see Yevana. They had not been together for months now but had continued to get on famously. As he walked into the office he noticed Yevana standing by her office window looking out as if in contemplation. She was dressed plainly in a dark blue maxi and heels which gave her height and authority with her mane of dark hair tied tight at the neck. She looked round at him and pointed to the soft armchair in the corner of the room.

'Hi, Andre, please take a seat,' as she welcomed him. 'How are you? You must be shattered.'

'I am fine Yevana, actually, and cannot wait to get back to work properly. Unfortunately, that will not be possible until I have sorted out my parents' estate in Madrid, which is taking some time I am afraid.' He looked into her eyes trying to gauge a reaction. He should have known better though as Yevana kept her focus like the true professional she was.

Without hesitation she came over and sat leaning against the front of her desk and asked, 'Andre, as there is no better way of saying this, I will come straight to the point. Did you have any reason to brief against us in the negotiations in Madrid?'

'Yevana, no! I didn't and I resent the question. I thought you trusted me more than that, I am very disappointed I must confess,' was his instant reaction of complete surprise which was coupled by a face that was rapidly losing its entire colour.

His mind was racing; she didn't appear to have any knowledge of his relationship and issues with Caren. He sensed also that Yevana was in a no-nonsense mode. He despised Caren for this but he would see to it that one day he would get his revenge, on his terms as it was personal and he did not want to give that opportunity to Yevana. He owed Yevana nothing and he sensed she was about to get rid of him, so he cared not that Caren might carry out her own revenge on Yevana. This he considered was a twisted game in a twisted world that Andre was determined to finish in his own way!

'Andre, as a company, you're fired, we are not renewing your contract which as you know completes at the end of the month. Have I made myself clear?' She moved away from the front of the desk and in a seamless motion walked back to the window and started staring outside once again. Andre stood up and speaking to her back responded.

'Yevana, you are the most beautiful woman in the world but when I needed you, you have hurt me and turned your back. I wish you the worst, I am a victim.' He turned and walked out of the office and out of her life.

Yevana continued to stare out of the window. She knew she was right about Andre but had no evidence and for her part that was enough; it was instinct, and she lived and depended on it.

'Janice, change the combinations and cancel Andre's account and access all areas pass.' Janice had sensed the outcome of the meeting as Andre had stormed out and acknowledged with a sad tone in her voice.

'Yes, Yevana of course, immediately.'

'Good, thank you Janice.'

'Yevana, hi, it's Ru, I'm in town, lunch?'

'My goodness Ru you are full of surprises. I have just had a bad start to the morning so that would be brilliant, yes of course I would!' As she almost shouted it out a real sense of gloom lifted in her office and an electric sensation coursed through her lower belly in anticipation.

'Okay, Yevana, darling, I'll see you at The Accoustu at twelve, Ciao,' and she called off.

Yevana loved every minute she spent with Ru, she had real class and femininity, deep beauty too.

'Hi, Dreana, it's Ru, Caren asked me to meet you to discuss your plans. I understand she is staying out of town for the foreseeable future.' Ru had been tasked to come to London to meet Dreana who had instructions for them both.

'Yes, Ru, and discretion is key but please come to SPICE, a busy cocktail bar and I will let you know what Caren expects of us. About eight p.m. tonight please. Won't take long and I have a date later so we must get on with it.' Dreana passed on the address of the bar and closed the call. Ru was still in a taxi travelling from the airport which pulled up outside her hotel as the call finished. In this classy establishment the concierge was waiting and she was escorted without booking in, directly to the VIP suite on the fortieth floor with spectacular views over the Thames. Her bags duly followed.

Ru had had plenty of time on the plane to consider if she should say no and call Caren's bluff; of course, she knew if she did that it would put her own life at risk in no-nonsense America. She knew Chuck Bush very well and had heard how he dealt with the 'opposition' without mercy! Ru didn't feel able to take that risk. She was worried that if it came to light that she was part of an ongoing plan to bring down Yevana that could have implications for him, then as a friend he might take that badly as she had not informed him when she had the opportunity. Within minutes a member of room service came to her room and hung and stowed away all her clothing. Subsequently a male and female member of staff then came and dressed her after she had taken a shower. Ru picked out a simple, short red dress, black heels and a pair of black eight denier tights. It was completed with black drop earrings and necklace. This was like preparing for a date she considered. Although it was Yevana, it always felt special when they met as they had formed a strong friendship. When in Yevana's company she felt sensations no other human had matched; ever! In fact, the night they had spent together had been so wonderful yet there was no sex just warmth, genuine warmth and comfort. The attendant went to help with panties but Ru pushed them away. Risky under the circumstances but it mattered! She adjusted in the mirror and when finished tipped the dressers, grabbed her clutch and left the room taking the escalator followed by a taxi in order to walk into the Accoustu, at midday exactly.

As she walked into a busy Accoustu she was escorted to her table where she noticed Andre sat looking at her as she approached.

'Sit down, Ru, we need to chat,' he growled. Ru looked at the waiter as if to ask for assistance but Andre spoke again.

'Sit down or the Brazil thing will quickly spread like wildfire, trust me.' She looked at the chair and the waiter assisted in seating her.

'Thank you,' she said as he walked off.

'Now Ru, don't worry, Yevana has been cancelled. I paid someone to call the Y&T offices and say you had been called to a more important meeting. You would call back later and rearrange.' The colour in Ru's face drained in both disappointment and anticipation of the consequence of what Andre might say.

'Ru, we have both been left in positions that we have become victims in Caren's game of revenge against Yevana. I have lost my parents and a priceless contract for starters if that isn't enough. I also had a great friendship with Yevana if not more and now she thinks I'm a big-time untrustworthy loser.'

'I know Andre, but I also blame myself. My previous lifestyle with my late husband would not have led me to this position,' she lamented. 'It's something I have to deal with as will you. Now while we are here let's have a glass of something nice.' Ru turned and indicated to a waiter.

'Ru, can I ask you to keep me informed about things please?' In fact, she knew he meant she was to do so!

'Yes, of course, why not?' She considered this request but wasn't worried. She knew enough to know if she needed to push a button elsewhere Andre could be dealt with.

They spoke for half an hour about their acknowledged positions and left agreeing that Ru would keep him updated on Caren's plan. They were both sick that they had got into this position and had no idea where it was leading, although they understood there were now some very high stakes being played for.

'Oh, and by the way Ru, you look beautiful, was that for Yevana?' he teased. 'Shame.' He teased again. He walked off without even so much as a glance back to her table; he didn't care. Ru sat still for a moment before ordering a double G&T. She wasn't hungry. Her world used to be so simple for so long and now it was as complicated as it was exciting. She swallowed hard.

Knowing how a court lawyer dressed it was something of a shock for Ru to meet Dreana Martel out in town in an East End cocktail bar that evening. The surprise was her clothing, very bright and what could only be described as that normally worn by a teenager, thought Ru. There was not much of it and it was scruffy! Ru was still dressed as for lunch, smart and elegant. Dreana looked even younger wearing pigtails with blue ribbons. Having texted to inform each other how they would be dressed Dreana quickly recognised Ru and thank goodness they had or Ru might have walked straight out. As they approached Ru offered her hand but Dreana was having none of it and remembering their first liaison, gave Ru a very warm embrace.

'Delighted to meet you again Ru, you always look so beautiful,' Dreana, emphasising 'again,' planted a kiss on her neck.

'Caren keeps me up to date with your arrangements. I have heard so much about you lately,' Dreana concluded with a smile.

'Thank you,' Ru replied wistfully. She had really enjoyed their first encounter, but circumstances had changed much to her own discomfort.

'Now, where are you sitting?' Ru continued looking around the busy room slightly irritated by the fact she even had to be at this meeting at all.

'Over here,' she pointed to a corner table with a soft couch type bench seat either side in an alcove. They sat down opposite each other and almost immediately Dreana asked, 'I am fascinated by your past and how you decided on a one-hundred-and-eighty-degree lifestyle change. Were you bored before your husband died or suppressed from your true yearnings?' Dreana happily ventured.

'Do you know what young lady; you are not in court now' and made the point by looking at her attire. 'Quite frankly it is none of your business, now what is it you need to brief?' Ru looked really angry and frustrated by this whole episode and didn't need this type of questioning tonight and under these circumstances. She realised she was on the back foot but wanted to get out of this bar and contact Yevana as soon as possible which she couldn't do until she knew the outcome of this meeting.

'Caren is going to ruin Y&T and all who sail in her was how she puts it, well, you and I will also assist, of course. We understand that Chuck has bought another ten percent, taking his stake to thirty percent as instructed by me. You will take the next opportunity to increase your own stake. Don't jump in but having said that don't hesitate and introduce an opportunity sooner rather than later. Is that clear?' Dreana spoke with authority.

'After which but before the next board meeting you both will have sold your share to Caren, well passed it on actually,' she continued with a slight smirk.

'No difficulties, no hassle, no litigation, easy. I will contact you at the appropriate time leading to the day of the meeting. Caren will hold the video as insurance and will decide when to destroy it. Work quickly and understand that Caren will destroy you both if you fail her. She has worked tirelessly to get to this point and will not accept failure. You have been warned Ru. Do I make myself clear?' She stopped and stared at Ru.

Ru sat staring and was not in the least surprised. 'Are you actually starting to enjoy this, Dreana? I do hope you are not in above your head.' Ru smiled and looked away as if there was nothing else to say.

'Anyway, Ru,' Dreana carried on ignoring that last remark, 'the board meeting is set for a month today, in the Los Angeles Y&T boardroom.'

'I hate this and feel disgusted to have associated myself with you people. Yevana is a lovely person,' was her overly passionate reply that didn't really explain that she knew Yevana didn't suffer fools either and dealt with her foes when she had to, fired back an unhappy Ru.

'Okay, Ru,' said Dreana as she placed a hand softly on Ru's knee, looking her straight in the eyes.

'You have the detail and I will see you in LA. You have been told. Now, I am busy and have a date. Ciao, darling.' She removed her hand and slid out of the bench and stood looking down at the much older woman.

'Outside of this I enjoyed our last taster and would love a re-show; call me.' Dreana dropped a card on the table from her bag and confidently strolled outside whilst being eyed by the majority of clientele glimpsing her rear, that was practically in view as her skirt was that short!

Ru considered that someone would be lucky tonight, but she knew it wouldn't be her! However, they were certainly going to get the good news, whoever they were.

Ru pulled her phone from her delicate clutch and pulled Yevana from the address list and pressed green.

'Hi babe, it's Ru, I am so desperately sorry, it was very important and business back in the States, please forgive me.' There was a brief silence after which Yevana said, 'I will call back in five.' It was very matter of fact and blunt.

Yevana was irritated and just needed five minutes to show Ru she did not take to being let down at the drop of a hat. Ru was devastated. She went to the loo and gave her makeup a complete refresh and pulled herself together. At least fifteen minutes later without apology Yevana rang back. They both knew!

'Ru, darling. Sorry, I had somebody in. How are you?'

Ru was shaking as fifteen minutes seemed forever. A tear ran down her right cheek, really slowly as Yevana said, 'Ru, I have really missed you.'

However emotional she felt though, Ru had to accept that she was trapped and had to live with her situation. Yevana instructed Ru to meet her in RISK underground bar once again in the East End. Travelling a short taxi ride Ru could see they were miles from the opulence of some West End establishments, then just before she approached RISK her taxi passed by Dreana who was with a beautiful blonde a little older and smarter than she was. They looked happy holding hands and Ru thought she had seen the other woman before somewhere but couldn't place it. Her taxi pulled up a few seconds later outside the bar. It might not have looked slum like but it certainly had a damp, dark and austere look and feeling about the entrance. Two massive black trench-coat wearing bouncers gave her the look, probably surprised she did not wear a coat of any sort. They waved her delicate frame inside where she would await Yevana as instructed.

'Go in get a drink at the bar and I will arrive shortly afterwards,' was the exact instruction. First thing that happened though, was a smartly dressed man in his mid-forties approached.

'Ummm, looks like you're lonely tonight and coincidentally I'm feeling lucky.' He was so pleased with himself he almost sang it! It was now eleven p.m. and this bar was only just starting to get busy as it was still early for this type of establishment. His expression changed quickly when Ru turned to look around then turned to his unwanted gaze, which was currently focused on her stockinged thighs and said, 'Darling, I am expecting my girlfriend at any moment but thank you for your concern, now if you don't mind.' Ru turned her back on him. She sensed him walk away and did not spot him again. The next two attempts she rudely ignored completely which was becoming tedious. Then, out of the corner of her eye she spotted the delicious Yevana approaching looking quite pensive but absolutely amazing, in a Volta orange one piece, heels and two black loop earrings. Wearing huge sunglasses, a tight ponytail, no bra or bag, she gave Ru a warm hug placing a gentle palm on her lower stomach. Ru let out a quiet sigh and felt her legs give way momentarily before regaining her composure.

'I have missed you Yevana.'

'Well putting me off didn't back that up but I accept your apology,' was Yevana's curt reply.

'Yevana, I have had a bad time with some business issues and it has got me down.' Ru looked forlorn and needed some reassurance.

'Well,' Yevana spoke in a whisper, 'it is unfortunate, but my beach bum American stud has flown in for a few days and will be here soon. You can stick around or I will call you tomorrow for our scheduled chat to discuss a little business, as I know you are interested in more involvement in Y&T Global; your choice, darling.'

Ru was gutted as this was not what she had planned. She didn't know what she wanted but she didn't want to go home yet. Thinking like her husband would have, she thought on her feet.

'Yevana, business now. I know you want to release some debt to move forward on the Salt Lake City project. Chuck has a twenty or is it thirty percent stake in Y&T Global and now I would like to raise my ten percent to twenty percent. You will have fifty percent controlling and the Caspinovs have ten percent at present so with Toby you will still be the largest stakeholders so this must suit you going forward, yes?' Ru was sweating a little although she didn't think Yevana noticed anything suspicious about the proposal and the sale from Yurini to Chuck hadn't been notified as yet.

'It's all so exciting and being able to participate like this without my husband is a real buzz, so exciting,' Ru repeated placing her delicate bony hand on Yevana's bicep.

'It is a take it or leave it deal Yevana from somebody you can trust to support you.'

She felt really guilty saying that and it chewed a hole in her stomach knowing that what she was doing could not be repaired! Yevana, although a little taken back by such a surprising outburst from Ru, considered it for a moment before saying, 'Yes, I agree, it is a positive offer; we accept. Come to my office in the morning and I will have briefed Toby. I know he will be happy as we have spoken about further investment opportunities and from you that will be popular, I am sure. Thank you, Ru, it's appreciated.'

As Yevana finished speaking a pair of male hands owned by a tall beach blonde bronzed young man slid onto her hips from the rear. Yevana turned slowly guessing correctly who it was and whispered something in his ear and he shuffled off without even a kiss. She grabbed Ru's hand and they left the bar and went directly to Ru's hotel suite and bed. 'Play some music, Ru. I am your prize tonight.'

Beach bum was let in as instructed by a porter at five a.m.. Yevana just watched! This was the first time she had seen Ru in such an aggressive state, like it was an outer body experience. She seemed oblivious to Yevana being there, whilst she enjoyed the fruits of his delight for the next two hours or so. Yevana had paid for his trip from the States but did not see him again until the next trip to America. He just disappeared into the London scene!

The following day Ru turned up at Yevana's office and the matter regarding the increased stake was dealt with to the satisfaction of all sides. Chuck was informed by e-mail and seemed pretty nonchalant about the whole thing.

Ru called Chuck in New York and informed him. 'It's the past now, let's just get on with it and all go our separate ways, if that witch allows us.' Chuck threw that in at the end as he knew there was very little he could do to get out of the trap he found himself in. This comment sent a shiver down

Ru's spine. She always looked on the bright side and, in this case, accepted she was now in the risk-taking business at this juncture of her life, although apart from the adrenaline, she was not sure about the overall enjoyment.

'Well, let's wait and see Chuck, darling. See you in LA.'

Ru called Dreana who in turn informed Caren.

'Good,' she replied by text, 'how is the 'news', Dreana?' Caren enquired with a hint of menace.

'I see her twice a week at present, it is going well, she really likes me. I miss you though.' Caren had heard enough; she turned the phone off. 'Stupid girl.'

Caspinov is Dead

Further afield there was some bad news from Kiev. It was all over the media.

'USA Pop Star Shot Dead in Kiev Hotel.' Yevana read on trying to wish it to be a dream. 'Young US pop star caught in gangland feud in a downtown district of Kiev known for its gangs, drugs and murder.' Reading on, it became apparent that the Caspinovs – listed as socialites and oil magnets – were at the party also which was obviously why she was there, thought Yevana. The initial summary of the circumstances was that there had been a gang related raid and an exchange of fire where several people including Yurenev and Rosy were killed also leaving Yurini seriously injured in the central state hospital. The Police stated that there were a number of deaths, weapons and ammunition seized as well as a substantial amount of class A drugs recovered from the scene.

The article and subsequent articles went on to conduct interviews of friends and enemies of which there seemed more of the latter! Yevana wasn't surprised. They commented on and substantiated the rumours surrounding the events of the previous evening and an argument. Yurini was thought to have no more than a fifty/fifty chance of survival. The media in the United States where Rosy was currently No.1 in the music charts were all describing the shock of one of their bright young stars having her life and career cut so tragically short. There were however more speculative articles behind the headlines where you could find comment from people who saw something like this happening, as she was attracting hard core elements from society who as her friends, were becoming more and more influential. Her bitter ex-boyfriend also commented about a recent split.

'I saw this coming; she got in with some very rich, deviant people; everyone has a choice,' was his bitter remark that wasn't shared by many though.

Yevana actually agreed but acknowledged her own part in the circumstances! She considered Rosy had had a weakness that Yurini had exploited but it probably would have happened in any case. In the days that followed evidence was leaked to the international press hinting at a less than blue-eyed young lady. Apparently, there were marks on Rosy's wrists and ankles consistent with rope ties and adhesive tape across her mouth. Yevena sat back at her desk and thought about what a tragic way to end the life of such a young, talented and beautiful woman; 'sad.'

Within a week Chuck's lawyers had done a deal with Yurini's lawyers to take her ten percent stake in Y&T. Yevana was contacted from Kiev and the message read, 'good luck going forward, Yevana. I will survive but it will never be the same. Ciao, darling xx.'

The facts were that she would spend the rest of her life without her beloved husband and any feeling in her lower limbs below the waist. Yevana did not try to contact Yurini as too much water had passed under that bridge. The investment change was fine for now although the shift in balance left her with some doubts but, it was fine.

As a team Y&T was financially well supported in business terms however, Yevana started to feel less at ease about how strong they were positioned with or potentially against such wealthy and experienced partners. Their stake was still controlling but not by much and she knew that if they wanted to, Ru, and importantly Chuck and Ru together, could eat them and spit them out should they choose to act aggressively. Yevana sat up in her chair dispensed with these negative thoughts and considered that they were doing a fine job of running a multi-million-pound business, and thus did not expect any such issues if they continued in this vein. The complexes continued to show full signs in all respects and other cities were keen to take similar ventures as the general idea was very attractive.

Dreana reported back to Caren that Ru and Chuck now owned a fifty percent stake as planned. They laughed about how fortuitous it had worked out and how quickly. Caren sat in bed smiling as she knew she would soon own fifty percent of Y&T Global and take control, crushing her old lover in the process by threatening to withdraw support if she didn't meet her conditions, which she wouldn't. Yevana and Toby would be history, ousted by the smarter person.

'Oh, my goodness, how clever am I and how naive is Yevana; she thinks she is so smart, sucker!' Caren was on a real high now as she was closing in on her prey.

'Dreana, darling, you have done well. I will update you shortly on my plan. Come back to me immediately when you have the date and time of the next group board meeting, which you expected to be in LA, Yes?'

'Yes, indeed I have that detail, it is in LA, I will text it to you asap.' Dreana replied anxious to finish the call before she was given any other tasking.

'How is the news anchor, still being a good little girl? I must say, seeing her and now knowing what she gets up to in her spare time, has put her in a different light so far as I am concerned. In fact, I am feeling some attraction myself.' Silence followed but before Dreana could reply Caren finished the call. 'Ghastly, why does she do that?' Dreana spoke loudly to herself as she firmly placed her phone on her kitchen tabletop. She missed Caren and it had been a while since they had been together, there was something about her which she couldn't or wouldn't shake off. But Dreana was sure that she couldn't bear it if she had to engage with any more Brad type tasks.

'Hi Chuck,' Chuck was less than impressed being called by Caren late whilst on an overnight stopover in Boston with his secretary.

'What the hell do you want, I am busy and it is late?' he snapped.

Caren smirked, 'Oops, must remember time zones, silly me. Now, sit down and listen, you pathetic creature. Not many people give you orders but get this. At the next Y&T board meeting you will inform those in attendance that you have been offered a fantastic business opportunity and sold your stake to another individual outside of the current group. At that point, as arranged, I will walk into the boardroom and you and Ru will vacate your seats and disappear; for good. I will roll from there. Ru will have sold her stake that morning also. Is that understood my Yankee friend?'

'Get one thing straight, Lords, you will never be my friend, in fact quite the reverse.' Chuck angrily jumped in.

Caren interrupted with some humour.

'I know, I don't have all the right bits do I Chuck, luv?' Caren chided with Sao Paulo in mind.

'You will have what you want. When shall we do the sale?' Chuck was in a corner and decided to cut loose, besides he had a very impatient secretary lying on the hotel room bed in front of him wearing her best lingerie waiting for some attention. His final problem was the video evidence as there was nothing to say she wouldn't use it again, so he asked, 'What of the video?'

'Don't concern yourself. It will be destroyed once I have what I want. You took an extraordinary risk and so you will have to trust me, you have no choice,' Caren reflected quickly.

'I am warning you Lords, if that goes viral I will stop at nothing to hunt you down and use all my considerable resources. Do I make myself clear?' If Caren could have seen him she would have noted his rage and small sweat droplets running down the side of his face.

'Crystal, Chuck, crystal. Dreana Martel will sort out the details later this week. Ciao, babe, be careful.' As she ended the call she remarked, 'Trouble is Chuck you have always had your own way, bully, ha.'

Chuck looked at his young secretary for a moment and slowly walked across and turned her over and tore into her backside in a frenzied sexual attack that left her shivering with fright. He fell asleep.

Caren switched calls to Dreana and tied up the remaining details to conclude the deal and what she had to do. Caren was clear she would keep the video for insurance; indefinitely! 'Poor Chuck will have to sweat for years to come.'

'Ru, hi, it's Caren, how is one? I hear you have carried out my request and have agreed a twenty percent stake in Y&T.

'Yes, that is correct Caren, I feel absolutely terrible about this, can't there be another way?' Ru was in turmoil as she loved Yevana as a friend and sexual attraction. The situation was driving her mad.

'You'll feel worse if you and your friend are seen in all your glory on the worldwide media networks, darling, Yes?'

In a very low but compliant voice Ru replied, 'Yes, Caren.'

'Right, Dreana will give you instructions to seal my deal. Basically, on my arrival at the LA board meeting Chuck will vacate his seat which I will fill as he departs the room and his part ownership in Y&T. I will then announce that I have bought your stake and ask you to leave, which you will do immediately. That is all you are required to do.'

'What of the video?' Ru tentatively asked.

'Forget it.' Caren closed the call, smirking to herself as she left Ru hanging, probably never to know of its whereabouts while she was alive.

Ru had not returned to Sao Paulo since she was made aware of the video recording although she thought Chuck still went as he was absolutely hooked; he had a problem. She started to think even his wife had her suspicions but enjoyed her lifestyle and left it at that. Her risk was her health but to a greater extent she was trapped inside a wonderful life and her husband knew it.

The finale

Ru changed her attention though. Simon was due to arrive back in New York for the weekend to attend a family birthday party. Ru decided it was ideal timing to take her mind off things for now. She would give him a few hours to attend the bash but on a very short rope; she had needs! Poor old Simon was by now fully aware of the price of his *free* uni ticket as it started to look extreme, so much so he didn't bother to call Ru on his last visit to the US. On hearing of his visit Ru immediately flew to London and the young man was summoned from Oxford for the weekend causing him to miss a rugby semi-final versus Cambridge, and he was the scrum half! He had considered staying and refusing Ru but knew he was too far into his studies to waste this fabulous opportunity he had been given. To rub salt into the wound he was told to turn up in his rugby gear. Ru answered the door dressed as a schoolgirl. She applied the Vaseline.

By the middle of the week prior to the board meeting Caren's lawyers received the documents confirming the transfer of the fifty percent stake from both Chuck and Ru would take place at ten o'clock during the next LA Board meeting. Now she felt she had prepared properly to deliver her vengeance on her ex-lover. Part of her wanted to bargain with Yevana to start another relationship of some form but she couldn't do that and sensed that was a non-starter. The previous departure had been too brutal and she could not forgive. Flight and hotels were booked and Dreana was informed of exactly what she had to do and when.

'Darling, Dreana, you now have my plan and once done I intend to move into a penthouse in No.1 Tudor Square London and you will move in with me.'

'Caren, yes your plan is clear and everything is in place as you say, but I won't be able to move in as I need my space; I have other issues.'

'Don't mess with me Dreana. I will out that News bird of yours, comprehend?'

'Yes, Caren, sorry.'

'For a smart woman you sound pathetic at times.' Caren snapped her phone shut and threw it at her sofa. There was no way she could let Dreana off her hook and they both knew it. There was trouble ahead with Drew Getisso as she was also hooked on Dreana from what she could make out. They were now seeing each other two days a week, which for a very busy married woman must be getting hard to hide. They would get caught out; it was only a matter of time was Caren's summary of the situation!

Andre was happy in Madrid now setting himself up taking over his parents' business empire that stretched far and wide. His parents' joint funeral, although taking place under a cloud, was very much a Madrid community funeral and many hundreds of mourners turned out on a damp and dreary day to pay their respects. They were well liked people who played a key role in the wider community for business and charities where they were both prominent figures. Whilst playing a part in all of the arrangements he was also planning revenge on a grand scale. He let one person in on that plan and that was Leon who had become extremely close to Rydeesa, even spending several days a week living at the family home in the months leading up to her death. Leon was good company for Andre at this time and he appreciated a friend in his hour of need which they had now taken a step further as lovers. He had become his PA also out of necessity and seemed to relish the responsibility.

Since being ejected from Y&T he had worked quickly to get the information he wanted for his plan of revenge before the new media partner changed all of the permissions. 'Book me a flight Leon. I have some business to complete and a vacation to take.'

'Toby, darling, when are you flying out for the next board meeting in LA?'

'Hi, Yevana,' he replied on the landline from his apartment. 'I was going next Monday, spending a few days talking to a bunch of potential investors interested in the Salt Lake City project then preparing the agenda for the board meeting at our LA Spacewalk Hotel Complex. I think we can get the financial deal for Salt Lake agreed at that meeting.'

Yevana thought for a minute. 'Now, can we meet tomorrow as I want to go through a few things including the agenda please, say nine a.m?'

'Not tomorrow, babe, but Thursday. I promised Summer a day in Paris tomorrow.'

'Blimey, I thought you had let that go; you never give up,' she laughed. 'Enjoy, Toby, see you Thursday.

Fay made all of Yevana's arrangements for the LA trip and prepared the meeting for Thursday, although she was not required for any minute taking on this occasion. Fay noticed Yevana was being quite secretive about some issues she wanted to discuss this week with Toby which was quite unusual as they normally liked everything recorded. All the staff had actually noticed that both Toby and Yevana had started to spend a lot less time in the offices in London. Not only that but liaison between the staff had proved more difficult over the past few months, as they spent so much time traveling as the workload increased with a burgeoning empire.

Toby still had a soft spot for Summer and she would drop her current boyfriend interest if Toby offered to take her out. Fay was in a similar position. She had strong feelings towards Yevana which felt unlike anything she had noticed or felt before in her life. She was too busy working for her boss though to let it affect her work and in any case she now had a steady boyfriend who worked in the City which helped displace some misguided emotions, as she saw it. Fay considered Yevana the most charismatic and sensual woman she had or probably would ever meet. It didn't even cross her mind that Yevana might have picked up on this and would be hugely embarrassed if that did occur, but she was sure that Yevana didn't realise what an impact she had on anyone she met. Fay's problem was she thought of Yevana when she was in bed with others. The spicy bit was that she made her boyfriend wear Yevana's favourite Volta perfume when they went to bed!

A call came in on her mobile, 'Fay, hi, can you get Yevana for me please? It's Ru Carter.'

'Sorry, Ru, she is taking no calls today as she is about to go to the Spa complex for a few hours.'

'Are you sure Fay? It is so unusual for her to have her mobile turned off. She is all right, yes?' Ru sighed.

'Absolutely sure, Ru, she is having some Yevana time; try again later or preferably tomorrow.' Fay was going out now herself and just wanted to finish the call, 'Also she has just finished a call to Toby and gave me strict instructions and no calls means, no calls I am afraid.'

'Okay, darling, I will call her later Fay.' Ru called off a little perturbed by the put-off which she wasn't used to with Yevana. Fay agreed with Ru, it was unlike Yevana to not want to take calls from Ru but she probably wanted a quiet afternoon on her own to do some thinking.

Dreana had planned a break at this time and so took a week off around the LA board meeting, in fact going a few days early with Drew Getisso on a full holiday together and in secret once again, so far as Drew's home life was concerned. Caren on the other hand hadn't decided if she was actually going to go out there at all as much of the plan was already executed and could be done on conference call if necessary. Her plan to oust Yevana and Toby from their own company didn't need her in attendance, although in the flesh might feel better! The others would do her work for her and she had sorted Carter and Bush who had been like putty in her hands. She still planned to out the Sao Paulo video after the board meeting to complete the misery for this couple. Dreana knew of Caren's plans and was very unhappy as she didn't see the need to take this final step, as it was completely unnecessary. At the same time Caren knew of Dreana's plan for the week ahead and would decide later if she was going to pay them a visit.

'Dreana' when are you travelling, darling?' Caren spoke with a feeling of authority requesting an immediate response.

'Hi, Caren, we are out tomorrow for seven days. We arrive in LA Thursday where we have booked into the Spacewalk. I can't wait, it's a great chance for a holiday.' Tentatively, she asked, 'Have you decided to come out Caren?'

'Not intending to Dreana, darling but be ready for me should I decide to change my plans, although the others do think I will be there.' Caren smiled knowing that Dreana would not be happy if she turned up under these circumstances.

'Okay,' was all she replied. Dreana was feeling more and more uneasy under Caren's influence. In time she was starting to think of a day and life without Caren.

'Just do your job and I will see you in our apartment in Y&T London. At that point you will shed your other layers.' Caren cancelled the call and Dreana slumped into her chair in chambers and a tear raced from her right eye followed closely by the left as the reality of what she had just heard dropped like a bombshell. At present there could be no life without Drew, she was so important to everything Dreana was now, albeit that was built on soft ground.

Yevana flew out to America at the weekend in time to catch some sun and a little time with her young gigolo. She needed a top up of 'manergy,' as she called it much to the hilarity of her female staff. He certainly helped do that! He was working in a bar of late to supplement his surfing activities which constituted his 'day job.'

On arriving at the Spacewalk and being whisked to her company apartment she organised a time to see him and spent the next twenty-four hours in his downtown digs and at the Santa Monica beach amongst the waifs and strays of LA society. She did a whole load of people watching in her lounger and it wasn't lost on her that she enjoyed living like this even though she had all the luxury in the world at the Y&T complexes. Although she wasn't sure it was best use of time, in the back of her mind she knew it was. Fay and the other travelling staff were already in place and dealing with the admin for the board meeting and the personal requirements. As usual it was perfect.

Toby arrived on his own on Sunday and quickly settled into his suite at the complex and was soon in dialogue with the staff over the details and other business matters. Monday was a very important meeting and he didn't want any surprises. By the evening he was ignoring jet lag and had met Fay and Summer then eventually a bronzed Yevana in the VIP lounge followed by a night on the tiles where they drank and danced the night away. Yevana spotted her boyfriend out with his girlfriend and on seeing her they departed quickly; Yevana laughed. She did have time to study the delectable Summer shaking her booty to the disco beat but quickly shook herself from that trance.

Yevana was brisk in the morning and the following day was no exception and on sitting down looked across the breakfast room to see Dreana and her friend looking like newly acquainted love birds. Their eyes met and heads nodded in recognition. They would not meet again until the board meeting. Yevana was interested to see this relationship 'on holiday' from the closet nature of their relationship in the UK. They were very relaxed and the news anchor was almost unrecognisable in so few clothes, albeit stunning too! Having eaten little, she noticed them disappear hand in hand out to the outdoor pool complex. They were no different to Yevana and her staff in that they were being treated like royalty and had complex staff offering their every need and more with Board member status.

Chuck Bush arrived on Saturday as did Ru Carter who had uni boy in tow also. Yevana noticed Chuck was looking unusually nervous at breakfast even more so when she waved him away. It was a privacy thing. Newspapers, cereal, marmalade on toast and quiet were her requirements for a perfect breakfast; in fact, she insisted on it. Thick cut marmalade was available at all the Y&T complex breakfast rooms and she hated travelling without some. Ru joined Yevana on her own in the main ante room after breakfast that morning whilst acting a little perturbed about something and didn't hang around, which was not like her. Later neither Chuck nor Ru accepted invitations to join the team for dinner instead choosing in-room dining.

Toby and Yevana had a quiet and private dinner away from the other Y&T staff in order to review and complete the agenda items and focus for Monday's meeting. At one point though and unusually Yevana's mind wandered as Ru came back into her mind. Why was she so distant and what had changed between them? She didn't need Ru Carter, that wasn't the problem. However, she knew her well enough to know she would not just withdraw like this. It would have to wait for now but she was uneasy about it. She consoled herself that much of it was down to the fact that she had her toy boy in tow and wanted lust and privacy. He made her feel young and she loved him or needed him; that was obvious. They finished their dinner and Toby gave her one of his 'I love you' pecks on the cheek and departed to the bar where he met the others for a quiet cocktail whilst Yevana headed for the main staircase and lift system.

On turning the first corner she noticed Ru and Chuck having a heated exchange in the foyer. Stopping just short and holding back from their view, she watched with interest as Chuck stuck a pointed finger into Ru's chest between her small breasts. He looked red with anger and Ru didn't look best pleased either and showered her disgust as she retaliated by punching him square in the stomach and hard enough for him to double over and start choking in agony. Her boyfriend turned up in the nick of time and quickly intervened pulling Ru away and into a lift that had conveniently opened opposite. All very strange, Yevana thought.

'Ru, hi, shame about this Y&T business but I could not afford to be scandalised, it would finish me; she has my balls!' Chuck remarked as he bumped into Ru in the foyer.

'No, Chuck, you blithering idiot. It is devastating and I wish I had never set eyes on you,' Ru responded like a wounded animal.

'You didn't say that at the time I seem to remember, my lovely,' he said smiling rude thoughts.

'Ha, lovely, you slimy git. We will destroy Yevana's dream and her empire. This woman Lords is a disease and we should have stopped her. We have been weak and looked after ourselves.'

'Well, that is life, Ru, it's business, so Monday we will do as we have been told and forget this whole business.' He poked her in the top of her rib cage between her tiny breasts and said, 'Now go and have some fun and let that little boy of yours poke Mummy,' and he laughed out loud as he said it. Ru instinctively swung her right fist into his stomach in retaliation for the bruise she would have on her chest and the humiliation she experienced as she momentarily took a step back. Being so close she felt the rush of air forced out of his mouth, not knowing where she had summoned that power that was now coursing through her veins. He doubled over in agony. Ru's muse rushed over just as Sarina Bush came around the corner from the toilets and she immediately thought he was having a heart attack and came to his aid. Albeit he shrugged her off.

Chuck started to pull himself upright and waved her off again and headed in the direction of the VIP club where he could cover his embarrassment with some scotch, doubles of course!

Ru and her 'little boy' went into the lift heading for their penthouse on the ninety-ninth floor. Feeling energised and whilst still feeling as though she was having an outer body experience of aggression, she pushed young Simon to his knees and knowing her needs he slid his hands urgently under her maxi dress and ripped her underwear down to her ankles then took his head in the opposite direction. Ru was soon breathing heavily once more whilst viewing the action in the internal mirrored lift walls. Suddenly the lift stopped and the doors opened. A man and a woman in their mid-seventies stood fixed as they surveyed the scene in front of them. Simon was being held in position by Ru's grip and didn't move. The doors shut. Nobody had moved, the lift continued its journey and the first act culminated before they arrived on the ninety-ninth floor.

The following morning there was a strange atmosphere in the late breakfast restaurant. All of the Y&T staff arrived with nighttime partners, some picked up the previous evening or morning. Yevana smiled as apart from herself it seemed Toby, who had watched a football game with a bunch of guys, was the only singleton. Yevena was soon joined by beach boy who she fed the best breakfast he would have in weeks. His treat was to take her back to his dive for the day. Whilst there his regular girlfriend arrived and started banging on his door, screaming at him, as she heard groans coming from the lounge floor. She eventually slumped to the floor sobbing as she felt a body being rammed against the door from the inside.

'She'll be back, don't worry,' he remarked.

'Don't worry, I'm not,' Yevana smirked.

Monday arrived and they all made their way to the boardroom. Also attending were a team from their US accountancy firm, their US bank manager, and a member of the Salt Lake Mayor's office who was advising them on particular items on the agenda regarding that project..

Toby knocked on Yevana's door and as she walked out past him she received a call and stopped to take it. 'Toby, you go on up, I must take a call from somebody in the business suite downstairs; I will only be a couple of minutes, I won't be late.

'Okay, babe, please don't be, some of the others have tight schedules as you know.'

By ten a.m. everybody was in the oak panelled board room reserved for Y&T board meetings and other specially authorised groups.. This room had been set up so it had spectacular views over the LA landscape and out to sea and was the pride of their business setup. Ru sat staring outside into what felt like another world waiting for all hell to break loose in this most tranquil and silenced of places. She looked about her noticing Chuck had just arrived and was sweating even in this air-conditioned room and that everything had been set out on the tables in regimental fashion by Summer and Fay. She took a long sip of the cold water from her glass and looked sideways at the accountant and bank representatives chatting away generally.

Toby walked in followed soon by Yevana who had been held up but still arrived in time to start. Ru took a long hard look at her friend who looked amazing in a light blue fitted skirt and white blouse; beautiful. Every male at the board sat mesmerised as she took her seat, many wanting to know what made this person tick and why she was single; she knew this of course! Ru knew by the end of this meeting they would not be friends, it was over, and of that there was no doubt in her mind.

'Right,' said Toby, 'let's get started, good morning everybody.'

They were soon up and running with the top item on the agenda the proposal for the Salt Lake City site which the architect described as amazing, particularly the backdrop of the Rocky Mountains and this seemed to be very agreeable to the main backer, the Rothschild Bank executive and supporting staff. Whilst business was being discussed Yevana noticed that both Ru and Chuck remained withdrawn and were definitely not engaged as she would have expected them to be.

Dreana's phone buzzed next to her on the table, she pressed accept and read the whole message from Caren.

'Just arrived darling, now, ditch that, what is she, oh yes a presenter. Yes, get Getisso out of your room, life. Don't do anything silly, as make no mistake I will get rid of it if you don't. My bags are on the way!'

The blood drained from Dreana's face. My goodness, she thought, Drew was still in bed, how on earth could she get her out when one, she didn't want to, and two, she had no time or plan to do it. It got worse as this lapse in her concentration meant she was dreaming when asked to comment on a couple of legal issues.

Yevana woke from her own trance as Dreana seemed to stumble over some basic questions which caused a break in proceedings in order that these could be addressed in smaller groups before resuming.

Caren arrived in LAX and caught a taxi directly to the Spacewalk hotel where she immediately had her bags taken to Dreana's suite. The porter gave them to penthouse room service who delivered them. 'Hi, I'm afraid you have the wrong room, we have our bags,' Drew explained to the attendant still in her dressing gown.

'No, Ms Getisso, this is definitely the room I was tasked to deliver to.' He smiled as she stooped to see the name on the address label. Drew went white. Dreana had lied to her; she had said that the relationship with Caren had run its course and it was over. Not being in a good position to know what to do next she worked quickly and said, 'Please, my mistake drop them in by the sofa, in fact, on it.' She watched him get the lift then walked straight back into the room and tore the labels from the bags. Picking the bags up, she walked across the room towards the balcony and looked below to the gardens. Clearly visible, there was nobody walking in that area. With one full swing at a time, she launched the bags with all her might into the LA skyline and watched its trajectory, praying that nobody ventured onto the ground for their mid-morning stroll. She peered down absolutely fixated as it exploded and scattered a couple of hundred meters below. Quickly, she turned and closed the balcony doors and went back to bed. Unless it was Dreana the door was not being answered.

Dreana waited for the appropriate moment and sent the text to Caren at around ten a.m. as arranged. She hesitated for a moment staring at the screen, looked up and without looking down but looking at Ru, pressed send. She wanted to say sorry at that moment as a wave of guilt came flooding around her but it was pointless, she was in too deep and helpless. She did not like herself one bit and at this point knew more than ever that Caren, somehow, had to become her ex and avoid moving in with her on their return to London.

Caren was waiting in the foyer of Spacewalk for this message and on receiving it she pressed send on her device which sent the Ru and Chuck video to several significant media outlets. The network was about to go wild.

In the boardroom it was peace and tranquillity as business progressed as normal. They stopped for coffee and some chit chat, even Ru seemed happier, thought Dreana.

Ru felt sick at the start of the meeting, one, because she didn't know how Caren was going to break the news of her shareholding takeover and two, because she couldn't trust her and expected the worst. The video was bad and would be categorised as ridicule and disgusting to her family, friends and worst of all the charities, which she had worked so well with over the years: the abuse of the vulnerable. etc. She could see the headlines now. Her friends knew she had made changes in her life since the death of her beloved husband. She thought some were acting in a very jealous manner, almost envious but she would live with it. Ru knew that there were rumours circulating about a very young man, prodigy, but nothing more sinister than that. Having acknowledged that she had been rude during this weekend in LA she sought out Yevana and pulled her out to the loo for a long meaningful hug, which they both enjoyed. Ru was the only one who spoke.

'Yevana, whatever happens I love you.' They walked out and Toby reconvened the meeting.

Caren approached the duty manager in the foyer, a smart woman with an air of efficiency about her and introduced herself.

'Good morning, I am Ms Caren Lords, I am expected at a very important meeting here.'

'Could you point me in the direction of the Y&T Board meeting please?' Caren asked expecting an immediate answer in the affirmative.

'Are you expected Ms Lords as I have strict instructions that no one else was expected to travel to that meeting room?' She knew her name having assisted in the carriage of her bags to floor ninety-nine.

'As a matter of fact, no! But I was asked to meet Mrs Carter on completion. May I wait in the board reception area? Now, it is a surprise for a dear friend and I have some flowers for her, you see.'

'Okay, Ms Lords, it's on floor 101 and the staff there will look after you while you wait for the meeting to conclude. I will call and let them know. Press floor 101 then 1664 on the decoder inside the elevator when requesting to travel up.'

'Thank you; I do appreciate your assistance on this matter,' said Caren rather relieved. It was going like clockwork.

Happy that she would be left alone to execute her plan of surprise she walked through to the central elevators. As she did so she looked at a TV screen in the foyer showing a regional news channel, where, along the bottom of the screen ran the breaking news story. 'Business magnate and philanthropist in secret foreign tryst video.'

'Brilliant,' shouted Caren just louder than she wanted to as she walked towards an elevator. She stepped into the one immediately to her front and pressed the buttons as directed and stood passively listening to the mood music as it ascended towards floor 101 and her destiny. She viewed herself in the wall-to-wall elevator mirrors and smiled in anticipation of the news she was about to impart and thinking about Ru and Chuck walking out and taking this same lift down into a different life; a storm!

Suddenly for no apparent reason the lift stopped at floor 30 and knowing the lift request for floor 101 was not programmed to be stopped en route Caren looked around as if for an answer. She turned to face the door ready to rebuke whoever stood waiting. There was a brief pause when the doors opened and a medium height man wearing casual clothes and a hooded mask burst into the escalator and with all his weight and momentum drove an eight-inch carving knife through Caren's heart and with such force it went clean through and pinned her to a wooden panel separating two mirrors opposite the doors. The assailant stared into her eyes; her mouth wide open still breathing her last breaths.

'You did this Caren, you did this. Say hello to my parents, I have a feeling you may end up in the same place!' Then, he had a thought, something spontaneous, seeing her in a smart but short skirt he dropped to his knees, slid his hands up the inside of her skirt and pulled down her panties to her ankles. He stood up and looked down at his work then up to her still staring but motionless face. It was the ultimate embarrassment, 'unlucky or was that stupid!' he spoke meaning every word. Andre turned, closed the doors then fled the scene. The escalator continued on its journey up to the boardroom reception on 101.

Janice was sat looking at her mobile phone text messages she had received from a young man she had met at four a.m. that morning. As the escalator arrived on 101 the doors automatically opened and she looked up from behind the desk, saw the doors had shut again and having not heard anybody step out, continued with her messaging. It was some time before Caren eventually arrived back at the foyer and the screaming started.

Andre had got all the information he needed and decided to follow Caren to LA. It was a hunch but he knew she would not be able to resist personally being there when Yevana was ousted from her own company; she would want to see the pain and despair in her eyes. Andre planned his move meticulously and covered his tracks to evade the well positioned CCTV on the routes into Y&T. Leon accompanied him to the States but he did not tell him the main reason for going but that it was a combination of business and pleasure. After his final act, he took the escape fire stairwell then burst through the fire doors setting off the alarm and disappearing fast out of the area. It was in a downtown back alleyway that he burned his clothes in a bin and changed into a pre-dumped set of fresh clothing.

Just shortly after Caren's murder in the escalator the board meeting broke up with business concluded and in principle they had an agreement with the bank to proceed with the detailed planning on the Salt Lake City site. The general mood was jubilant, and the board members were soon departing past Janice and the PAs moving quickly on to the rest of their busy days. Yevana noticed Ru linger for a minute or so, said a quick goodbye and watched her walk out of the room. Again, it was strange, something wasn't right however, she did not give it another thought.

Ru lingered out of ear shot to the others out in reception to get a couple of minutes with Chuck.

'She didn't show,' Ru commented in surprise. 'I take it she, Caren, has something even more dramatic up her sleeve, but good riddance, I am out of this for good.' She held her hand out, he hesitated, said nothing, looked her in the eye, took it, winked and they went their separate ways.

Chuck walked into the Spacewalk reception in the foyer and there was a media pack assembled which was being held back by staff. Ru appeared out of another elevator and her aide pulled her away to be taken to a side entrance and a waiting car. She watched in horror on the in car tv as the news anchor revealed the story on live TV across the US. Ru was trembling and her female aide in the front seat looked in the rear-view mirror and their eyes met. The aide noticed the tears forming before Ru looked away and started speaking out loud to herself.

'She did it, couldn't even turn up to face us. I'm finished.' It was a long journey back to her New York apartment but time enough to consider what this meant for the rest of her life. Simon took the brunt of her misery for the next twenty-four hours.

Chuck barged out to his car where he expected to see his wife, however, she had departed early! He was already pressing phone numbers trying damage limitation and instructing lawyers to get the video banned asap. It was too late though as the evidence was damning and already been out there too long and around the world's social networks.

'I'll get that damned woman, you see if I don't, she ain't heard the last of old Chuck Buuush.'

Somehow the lift with Caren nailed to the wall had stopped between 101 and the foyer. The lift had been recalled to reception and as the doors opened all hell broke loose and the timing was perfect. Caren stood fixed to the wall of the elevator eyes wide open looking out onto the already chaotic scene in the foyer. Immediately a guest waiting to enter one of the lifts screamed at the top of her voice and collapsed. Staff ran from all directions, placing a cordon of sorts, around the elevators and trying to give the fainting woman first aid as they could see that the figure in the elevator was dead. The duty managers and security were in a frenzy as they alerted the police at the same time trying to look after guests whilst removing the media. One female manager stood looking inside the elevator at Caren and the unreal scene of this woman with her panties pulled down. She felt a weird sensation that she couldn't explain. It came out later that evening when she had the best sex she had ever had with her lover!

Up on the boardroom table on 101, enjoying their first impromptu moment of heated sexual activity for a long time, Yevana and Toby broke off. Toby looked down on his beautiful business partner spread on the boardroom table skirt up around her waist and hair laid flat around her head with her legs hanging limp over the end of the table heels pointing sharply towards the ground. He looked up from this scene and briefly viewed the panoramic out of the windows which made him feel that he was in a concrete heaven. He did not offer her a hand up and turned away whilst they both made themselves respectful before walking out to reception. Having had the call that Yevana's boyfriend was waiting they briefly conversed with their respective PAs who had been waiting outside whilst they had their private conversation in the boardroom! They were still oblivious to the chaos on the ground floor as the police were desperately trying to bring order to the foyer before the inevitable clearing of the hotel to start their investigation. Having finished talking to Summer Toby was first to make his excuses and departed for the car park.

'See you in England, girls, I am off for a road trip, a little adventure, and a few days' holiday, Ciao.' Off he strode taking the elevator to the car parks. Summer looked on rather forlornly as she had expected an invite but said nothing. Yevana followed shortly afterwards and took the back of hotel service lift as Beach Boy had texted to say there was a problem at the front and she should avoid the foyer. She was heading for the car parks to avoid all of this. Not being able to get through to Yevana who seemed to be taking ages to descend to ground level, he called Fay.

'Fay, where is Yevana, she is taking so long? I will be moved on soon as the police are setting up some sort of cordon.' He was sounding irritated but Fay knew nothing.

'Sorry, but she has left here and will be with you shortly, bye.' Fay was packing up her things and heading out with Janice and Summer for a couple of nights downtown. Janice had sowed some seeds and more would follow!

Toby walked out and went to get his car where he had already placed his gear prior to the board meeting to ensure a quick getaway. He was soon ready having pulled back the soft top to enjoy the warm Californian climate then as he drove out of the underground car park, he received an in-car text and pulled over just outside.

'Darling, wait, we have business to complete, I will meet you at the exit!' He sat in the car which happened to be out of sight of Yevana's boyfriend when suddenly she arrived out of a side entrance and jumped over the soft top car door into the passenger seat beside him.

'What is going on out front? There are police sirens and look, helicopters everywhere.' Yevana exclaimed.

'No idea, let's get going.' Toby said with some haste.

Yevana was looking up at a helicopter as she said 'Anyway, it is done, a Texan job lot and our money telexed to our bank accounts; we are free.'

'Brilliant, now,

Gear, clothes, bags?' he asked out of curiosity, although he knew the answer.

'None,' Yevana said turning to face him, smiling.

Yevana went on, 'We may do it again one day, eh?' Toby replied, 'The thought was, perhaps we might dream of starting a normal life.' They shouted out simultaneously – 'as if!' and couldn't stop laughing out loud.

'Vegas, here we come Ms Narvik,' He pressed number one on the streaming service,' his favourite track, and applied his seat belt and looking at Yevana to do the same continued, *'Plug in Baby.'* As the first bars of the song kicked in they tore up the boulevard, out of the city, sunglasses applied, wind in their hair.

The End

Epilogue

Janice, Fay and Summer spent the next week in a round of dubious clubs and parties and having sown many seeds went back to England to find that their bosses had sold out and literally disappeared; non-contactable vanished. The new owner did not need them and sacked them with immediate effect.

To be continued...

Printed in Great Britain
by Amazon